T0158916

MAKING
OF A
GOD

Also by John Ricks

Freddy Anderson Chronicles
    Freddy Anderson's Home (Book 1)
    Protectress (Book 2)
    Colossus (Book 3)

Sword and Sorcery (Short Stories—Book 1)

MAKING
OF A GOD

EPIC ADVENTURES—BOOK 1

JOHN RICKS

MAKING OF A GOD
EPIC ADVENTURES—BOOK 1

iUniverse books may be ordered through booksellers or by contacting:

iUniverse
1663 Liberty Drive
Bloomington, IN 47403
www.iuniverse.com
1-800-Authors (1-800-288-4677)

ISBN: 978-1-5320-5808-0 (sc)
ISBN: 978-1-5320-5809-7 (e)

Library of Congress Control Number: 2018912274

Print information available on the last page.

iUniverse rev. date: 10/29/2018

PREFACE

Epic adventures are set in the days of dragons and magic, demons and undead, on a world in this galaxy in a time of great need. The age is debated by grand wizards, renowned sages, and clerics of a dozen races. It took place before the great Over God Wars but during the time of chance, and that is what we will call it—the Age of Chance.

ACKNOWLEDGMENTS

To my dungeon master, a D&D champion and specialist of more than thirty years' experience. Though we don't always see eye to eye, our love for the game gives us a common bond.

To the natural leader of our table games and the one who keeps our heads on straight, thank you for your mentoring and patience.

INTRODUCTION

Book 1 is about Charles, born a crown prince, raised the black sheep, exiled as a murderer, praised and beloved as a hero. This is his story as received from Charles himself to the ears of the great bard Singa.

PART 1

THE MAKING OF A CHAMPION

PROLOGUE

As I sit here looking out over the galaxy, anger comes to eye. Everything and everyone I have ever loved, all that I own, my princely title, my lands, and my family are gone. In one necessary brilliant stroke, I destroyed my life; I caused my father to hate me, my mother to distance herself from me, my oldest brother to draw sword against me, my oldest sister to slap me, and my youngest sister to cry and run away every time she sees me.

Still, here I am. On my own at age fourteen, exiled from my beloved country, thrown away like a bad apple, and more powerful and deadly than you could ever imagine.

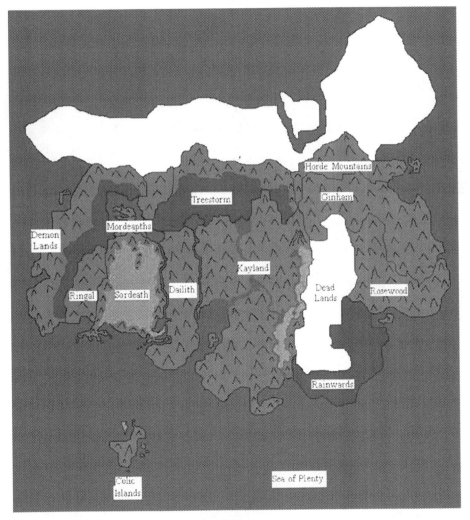

Map

CHAPTER 1

THE WIZARD ARCONAL

Dedrick Arconal, court war wizard to the king of Kayland, head of the Order of the Enchanted Eye, the most intelligent person in the castle (his view), and sworn bachelor, was sitting at his desk in the central tower trying to decipher a short essay by Prince Charles and talking to himself—his long white beard brushing the parchment, his wrinkly face frowning from the effort, his wizards' book glowing with green smoke leaking from between the pages, and his pointed hat tilting in concentration.

To his miniature flying cat, Pester, he said, "Darn it! I would have easily finished this essay an hour ago if I hadn't given the order that it was to be written in a language other than general. Why did the boy pick Draconic!"

"Do not blame the boy, Master."

"I will if I feel like it. Sure, I can speak, read, and write Draconic; it is, after all, the base language of magic. Still, apparently I cannot read or write as well as Charles. In the name of the gods, I'm having to look up half the words. There. Done."

He sat back in the old straight chair behind his big elaborately carved desk as he reread the essay. He was looking at more than just the words. He was trying to figure out more about the boy, the black sheep of the family, the son who was always in trouble. The essays from the other children were sitting on his desk. Each had its own flavor. Little Princess Amanda had written a nice essay about fire-breathing dragonflies and flowers that developed an immunity to fire. Princess Jennifer wrote about boys and how messy they are—highly expected, as she was constantly complaining about Prince Richard and Prince Droland and their inability to pick up after themselves. Prince Richard wrote about his last session in court, probably hoping that would get him out of the essay for the court. He was wrong. Prince Droland's essay was late as always. It was hard to read, messy, and left a bad taste. He wrote about the usage of undead in war and why it was needed.

Dedrick said to himself, "I will need to send Prince Droland to the court cleric, Monsignor Eric Montague, again. For such a sweet, kind, loving boy, he seems to constantly need mental readjustment. It's probably Charles! His influence is devastating to this family. Still, I see nothing to show issues in Charles's essay. He probably wrote it that way on purpose. The effort to work him hard is showing in his hand, but he is getting craftier. We are attempting to follow the king's orders by trying to keep him busy and therefore out of trouble. It's not working."

Dedrick quickly wrote a note about Droland's essay, wax sealed it, placed a spell on it so only Eric could open it without total destruction of the note, and teleported it to Eric's office in the Chapel of Solbelli there on the castle grounds. Then he penned another note to the captain of the guard, requesting triple time for Charles on the training grounds each day for a month. "Captain, I want Charles black and blue all over. He needs reminders that he cannot pull his evil little stunts anymore." This note was not sealed, and no magic was placed upon it. He left it open and gave it to a servant to carry to the captain. In this way, the information would be seen, read, and gossiped about by everyone. *Something has to be done about Prince Charles's reputation,* he thought. *For some strange reason, the servants love him. What's also strange is that the city loves him far more than any of the others. Wherever he goes, he is loved. He never gets into trouble when he is not at the castle. Perhaps sending him somewhere else would be good. Somewhere distant. A small Barony way out in Horns Sounding would be good. No, the queen would not allow it.*

A knock on the door received his attention.

"Enter."

A small immaculately dressed messenger boy opened the door, stepped in, closed the door, turned, bowed low, and said, "My lord, the queen requests your presence in her study at your earliest convenience."

"Very well. Tell her I am on my way."

"As you wish, my lord."

The boy turned, opened the door, stepped through, closed the door, and ran in the direction of the queen's apartments.

As he stood and gathered his belongings for an audience with the queen, Dedrick thought, *I will have to say something to the castle mistress. That boy's tone was not as polite as it should be, and he was not out of breath when he appeared. Therefore, he did not run fast enough. He should be punished. Why is it that children never learn until you bruise their hide? It would be so nice to simply tell them to hurry and have them do it. Since he is running, he was told to hurry. Otherwise, he would never be allowed to run in the castle. Now, why would the queen wish the boy to hurry? The best way to find out is to see the queen.*

CHAPTER 2

THE QUEEN OF KAYLAND

Queen Susan was in her chambers packing for the trip to view Duke Edward's new child, a little girl only four months old. She was dressed in a floor-length gown of royal blue and gold. Her long hair was adorned with multicolored flowers, and the jewelry she wore would make a common man wealthy enough to buy his own kingdom. She turned to Mistress Anon. "What is the child's name again?"

"Annabel, my queen."

"Annabel. That's an unusual name for a farmer's child, even if a duke's daughter. Does it not mean 'with grace'?"

Mistress Anon answered, "Yes, my queen. Still, the child belongs to the duke and duchess. I would think that they would choose a name not common in their section of land."

"If that were so, then tell me why their other three children are named Adamine, which means earth; Jorja, which means earth worker; and Millicent, which means strong worker. Are these not common there? They are common names throughout the rest of the kingdom."

"Perhaps this time, my queen, they were hoping so much for a male that they refused to think of female names until it was too late and they had to quickly think of a name for the cleric's birth blessing."

"That I could understand!" exclaimed Queen Susan. "Four girls and no heir to his dukedom. Sad that is."

"Yes, my queen. He does have three, and possibly four, very pretty young girls and one nearing marrying age. He could marry one off to the son of a rich baron, which would cause an instant heir."

"I would think that Duke Edward wants someone he trained himself. Running farming lands is not an easy task. You need to understand and love what you are doing."

In a near whisper, the queen asked, "Where is my semiformal dress? The white one with gold trim?" She looked around as if the dress should be sitting out and seeable.

"Majesty, it is in the case we just packed," answered the tired castle mistress. No less than eight servants were hurrying around helping the queen prepare for traveling to the castle at Shadow Mountain, the headquarters of Duke Edward and the Clear Water Valley and the bread-and-butter lands of all Kayland and most of the continent.

The queen reacted, as was her normal, in a quiet, reserved tone. "I would like to wear that dress when we reach the Shadow Mountain Castle. Keep it on top and unwrinkled."

Mistress Anom smiled and thought, *So, the queen is finally learning to state what she wants and not use courteousness to the servants.* "Please" and "thank you" were not needed or expected from a queen to a servant. Out loud, she answered, "My queen, it is on top, and it will be removed and brushed immediately upon arrival."

Two of the queen's personal maids looked up from packing and nodded to Mistress Anon, showing that they understood. It would not be good if the castle mistress had to repeat herself.

The door to the study opened, and Princess Jennifer quickly stepped in and quietly closed the door behind her. Jennifer was dressed in a lightweight white cotton dress with a lightweight petticoat. The dress had embroidered flowers of yellow with green leaves and stems. Her long blonde hair fell below her tiny waist and curled at the bottom. "Mother, the old man is here." Giggles erupted throughout the room.

The queen said, "Child, I have asked you not to call him that." The giggles quickly stopped. "Lord Dedrick is an old and trusted friend of the family. He has saved your father's life countless times, and I expect you to show the correct respect."

"Yes, Mother." Jennifer stood taller and formally announced, "Majesty, the great and all-powerful war wizard Lord Dedrick Arconal is awaiting your pleasure in the study."

Giggles erupted again at the exact copy of what the king secretly had the announcer prepare for the wizard's late arrival at the last spring festivity. It never paid to be later than the king.

The queen was amused but tried hard not to show it, and her frown caused the giggles to stop quickly. Jennifer quickly stepped out of her mother's way as the queen led her following into the study. The queen put out her hand in a limp-wristed way as she moved forward. "Dear Lord Dedrick, how are you this day?"

Dedrick took the queen's hand and kissed it gently while bowing. "I am doing fine, Majesty. Eric tells me the entire royal family is doing well, so I need not ask. I see you are packing; therefore, you are going on a trip. Possibly to see Duke Edward's new child? My goodness, has it been five months already? Why is he not bringing the creature to us?"

Queen Susan smiled. "Don't let the duke catch you calling his children *creatures*. I know you don't like children; however, for the safety of your head, I would watch what you say in front of him."

"Of course, Majesty."

"Yes, we are traveling to see the child. No, they cannot bring the child here. There is something wrong with the baby. It cries constantly. The clerics have not been able to determine what the cause is. They say it is not physical, but they caution about moving the poor baby. It is considered luck—and, for royalty, proper etiquette—for the queen to give the child a queen's blessing within the first six months. Fall celebrations are coming quickly, and this is the best time to go to the farmlands. I will be there for the harvest moon and the festivities. This should help quell issues with the lack of visits from the crown in the last three years. At the same time, it should strengthen relationships with the Clear Water Valley Women's Circle."

"I take it your mother is going?"

"Yes."

"May I stay here?"

"No! What is wrong between the two of you? You used to be a pair. Doing everything together, being seen everywhere together—and you used to back her up completely. What happened?"

"My queen, it is not my place to say."

"That's the same answer I received from Mother. You two are so alike."

Dedrick smiled. "What do you wish me to do for this vacation? When do we leave? Who is going with you?"

"Nice change of subject. We leave tomorrow morning, very early. Mother, Jennifer, and Charles will be going with me. Amanda is far too young, and Richard and Droland are too close to the crown as heirs to travel without a small army."

"Charles is a crown prince."

"Yes, but there are two before him. Remember when Charles saved Richard's life last year? We asked him why, especially when Richard's death would bring him closer to being king. You know what he said? 'I do not wish to be king. I do not like to run other people's lives, and I don't want the hassle associated with running courts and such. By keeping Richard alive, I stay that much further away from the pain of being king.' His father agrees that he is not the correct material for kingship and has consented to allow Charles to travel anywhere he wants. That means with escorts and between classes. Charles shows signs of great intelligence."

The old wizard said, "Near supernatural intelligence. Are these escorts or watchers? I know the king is having Charles watched night and day."

The queen said, "Your king needs to catch Charles doing something wrong. Charles always denies doing wrong, but wonderful, clever Droland always catches him and turns him in."

Dedrick frowned. "Droland needs to be careful. Charles does not like him."

"That is saying it nicely. Though Charles never shows it in public, others have heard him say Droland was responsible for most of the problems Charles gets caught causing. Though, no one believes Charles. Droland is such a sweet child."

Dedrick said, "True. How Charles could think that we would believe Droland responsible for any wrongdoing is beyond me. Charles needs to take ownership for his misbehaving."

One of the servant girls started to cry and say something but thought better of it. All the servants were looking sad. The queen took it wrong. "What is it? Oh, of course some of you are going with me. Don't worry." She turned back to Dedrick. "As for you, I am hoping you will come also. I cannot take as many as I would like, so having a powerful wizard will be a great deterrent for thieves and such."

"May I take along some apprentices? They could use the time training, and I have been ignoring them lately."

"As long as what you are teaching them is not going to cause trouble. Strange spells or spells going wrong does not make for nice traveling."

"Do not worry, my queen. I will keep it to simple spells centered on themselves."

"Good. First light tomorrow then."

"Tomorrow, my queen."

The queen turned to the castle mistress and asked, "Where is Charles? Who is getting Charles ready?" It was plain to see from the servants' looks that no one knew.

Mistress Anon ordered, "Mellissa, Joy, find Charles. He should be in the training yard at this time of day. Fetch him and prepare him for travel."

The two girls curtsied to Mistress Anon and said in unison, "As you wish, Mistress Anon." Then they turned and curtsied to the queen and held the curtsy until they were out the door. Then they walked quickly to the training yard.

CHAPTER 3

TRAINING

The large training field was empty except for Prince Charles, who stood at the ready—tall for a fourteen-year-old, lean, and well muscled. His blond hair was cut short, his blue eyes bright, and his clothes were the best light brown, studded leather armor money could buy. Staff in hand and loose as a thin hair in a strong wind, he waited. No matter what the bard's stories told of fancy staff play, a true master knew that eye contact and reflexes honed during hundreds of hours of practice were what made a staff master, not fancy twirling and behind-the-back foolery. Charles found that out the first day with three broken fingers and a knot on the side of his head. That was four years ago when he could barely carry a good staff. Today, he was matched up against two sword masters in full plate, and they were intent on adding some scars to the young prince. Of course, with Cleric Monsignor Eric Montague standing there watching the battle, the likelihood of a scar was slim.

Charles whispered to himself, "I will be healed but not before I pay with some pain for any mistakes."

Eric Montague, a short, fat, balding cleric of many years but with a vigor that made him seem far younger, looked out over the training field to Charles and nudged the staff master. "What do you think, Jonathan? I'll bet ten gold pieces that Charles gets cut twice before he hits one of the sword masters. I always say, a staff is no match for a sword."

"Eric, I'll take your ten gold just to teach you a lesson. Charles is the best student I have ever seen. If he wanted, he could claim staff master today."

"If he is that good, then why doesn't he?"

"Eric, my friend, Charles has been offered sword master, staff master, bow master, and a dozen other combat titles. He refuses to become master of anything, at least in title, until his brother Prince Richard reaches master."

"For goodness sake, how is that possible and why? I would think the little pest would love beating his brothers. Besides, how could he be that good? I have seen his brother Richard beat him several times."

"Charles is not a pest, and unless you want the entire guard down on your back, I would watch what you say about him. He is loved greatly by all but the crown. Why is he loved, you may ask? Because he is kind and good, studies hard, has respect for others and their abilities, and is innocent of most of the wrongdoings you people punish him for. He has spent so much time being punished that now it is the trainers being punished. Charles beats the tar out of them every time. As for why he refuses the title of master until Richard achieves it, Charles told me straight out. 'Staff Master, please don't give Richard any master titles until he deserves them, but I also cannot receive master until after Richard. It would look bad for Richard as the king. His little brother should never publicly beat him at anything.' Charles wants Richard to always look the best possible. He never does anything to cause Richard embarrassment."

"Oh really. Why was he sent to me for penances for sabotaging Richards's saddle at the last parade? Poor Richard spent most of his time trying to stay in a loose and sliding saddle. It made him look like he couldn't ride. How humiliating."

"Humiliating, *humiliating!* First, serves Richard right for not checking his equipment. Second, Charles came late to the parade gathering because he was with me finishing his punishment for the Jennifer issue and her missing dress. He never had time to come anywhere near Richard's horse. Third, Jenifer's dress showed up in Amanda's room, and Amanda admitted to playing dress-up, yet the punishment still stood. Two hours on the field with fresh men-at-arms constantly attacking. Charles was badly bruised head to toe, dead tired, and had at least two broken bones your acolytes did not heal until after the four-hour ride. Yet he checked his equipment and fixed the loose strap. Yes, he was sabotaged also. He sat his saddle in constant, major pain for four hours, smiling and waving at the people. I am sick of you people blaming all your woes on Charles."

"I don't—"

Jonathan whispered, "Quiet! It's about to start."

Charles stood in the center as two men in full plate professionally marched out upon the field. Charles assessed his situation. *This staff isn't even a good, solid, aged yew. It feels like green pine wood, and it has no end caps. The balance is horrible and the weight of the cheap stick has been purposefully made worse by the stupidity of someone adding a slick iron center grip three feet long and at least four inches thick, with a crack running near the center. I can't even get my hand completely around the grip. Swinging it will keep all the weight in the center, and the ends will do little to no damage against plate mail. It would be like hitting a solid wall. No damage to the wall but that crack in the grip, and the soft wood of the staff will easily break. Or worse, it will vibrate so badly it will sting and numb my hands, making it impossible to hold. The slick grip will make holding the staff impossible once I start sweating. Now I understand why I wasn't allowed gloves. This staff is useless as a staff, but it has its possibilities. Bad news for me is that both men are carrying heavy steel shields and long swords, while I have a two-inch-thick, iron-encumbered, off-balance tree limb.*

The two fighters started to circle slowly. *Uh oh. I recognize the way that one is moving his feet. Zorcor, my brother Droland's man. And if that one is Zorcor, then the other must be his inseparable twin, Tarely. Two formidable sword masters that dislike me greatly and have shown it before. Interesting. Tarely's sword slightly glows, showing it's magical. That's a foul. They are supposed to be using cheap, dull training weapons and armor, but they are using masterwork magic weapons that are probably very sharp—and I would bet magic armor and magic assistance for speed and strength. Nice work. The armor and weapons are plain looking except for that light glow, so from the master's sitting position, it will look like they are abiding by the rules. I wonder just how far Droland has ordered them to take this. Is this just another beating or an assassination? No time to waste losing my head, literally. Time to concentrate, as they are moving in.*

Charles reached out and found the point of light within his soul. He relaxed and became loose. His movements became one with his life essence, and he waited.

No word was spoken. The twins had practiced together since childhood. Their attack came without warning, without eye movement or muscle tightening. Both acted as one. Tarely's blade slashed at neck level and down, forward to back, and Zorcor's blade slashed at knee level and up, back to front, leaving no place to move forward or back and a good chance of being cut to ribbons. However, Charles did not move forward or back. He did not duck or jump. He bull-rushed Zorcor. The tactic was insane. For a child weighing less than one hundred thirty pounds to slam himself into a two-hundred-pound man wearing fifty pounds of armor during a slashing attack was suicidal. It worked. Charles was inside Zorcor's blade in an instant, and all his body weight slammed directly into Zorcor's head. Zorcor fell over onto his back, allowing Charles a chance to tumble away from the two fighters. Tarely put a hand down to help Zorcor up, but Charles ran toward Tarely, forcing him to defend himself and leaving Zorcor trying to get up on his own. In doing so, Zorcor left his guard down, and Charles smashed down with the center of the staff, jamming Zorcor's helmet guard down and nearly blinding Zorcor to attacks from the rear. Charles then lifted his staff up to defend against a two-handed power attack from Tarely. The sword landed exactly centered on the iron of the staff, cutting the staff in two and missing Charles's head by only a fraction. The blow to the staff turned the blade, and Charles took a flat smash to his shoulder, breaking the bone. Charles tumbled away in great pain but doing his best to not show it. He stood up, holding two clubs with pine handles and heavy iron heads, and ran back in. Tarely slashed out while Zorcor stabbed at Charles's feet. Charles met both blows with the clubs and ended directly behind Tarely and on the right of Zorcor. Zorcor tried to move his arm back to get a good blow, but Charles was standing on his blade, and Charles ducked Tarely's next swing while using all his might to smash down on Zorcor's blade hand. A loud crack said it all, and Charles tumbled away. Tarely followed and took several slashes at Charles, but Charles reversed his tumble and ended up directly in front of Tarely and at knee level. Both clubs slammed in, one from the left and one from the right. They sandwiched Tarely's knee and jammed the armor joint so that Tarely could not bend his knee. Zorcor was up and holding his blade in his left hand. He abandoned his shield. Charles couldn't help but think, *Bad move, Zorcor.* Zorcor came running at Charles, trying to bull him over, but Charles let him go through. Tarely had the same idea, and when Charles let Zorcor through, he also let Tarely through but did a back-smash with one club. He hit the jammed knee, causing it to bend.

Like taking a step when the step isn't there, Tarely came down hard—surprised that his leg was not where it should be. With a bent knee, Tarely was helpless; he dropped his sword and shield and tried to straighten his leg. Charles had no time to finish Tarely as he and Zorcor went head-to-head. Zorcor slashed down but curved left at the last minute, and Charles took a bad cut to his left leg. His own blood would make things slippery if he didn't finish this quickly. Charles tumbled past Zorcor and then reversed and tumbled past again on the other side. As he hoped, Zorcor followed his movement to the right and lost Charles as he went behind him. Charles dropped one club and in two hands slammed the other club into the back of Zorcor's helmet, smashing it down on Zorcor's neck and breaking Zorcor's collarbone. Zorcor dropped his sword, and Charles grabbed it and tossed it away. Legally, Zorcor was now out of the fight.

Charles turned to face Tarely. Tarely had straightened his leg and was picking up his sword and shield. Charles took advantage and ran at Tarely. His one club came down hard on Tarely's bad knee. Tarely screamed in rage and swung hard at Charles, catching him with a minor cut to the left arm. When he tried to get up, his knee gave way, and he fell. Charles did not press his apparent advantage, as he was sure that Tarely was faking the amount of damage. Charles circled Tarely, and sure enough, Tarely followed him without problem. Charles closed in but saw Zorcor heading toward his sword. Time was running out, and Master Jonathan should have seen that Zorcor was cheating. Charles ducked below a swing from Tarely and slammed the knee again. This time, he slammed it in the other direction and heard some crunching. All teachings said the game was over. Just step back and end it. Tarely was immobilized, and Zorcor had lost his sword. Still, Tarely was smiling. Charles grabbed Tarely's front and pulled him forward as he jumped sideways. Tarely was off balance and fell straight to where Charles had been. Zorcor, unable to see well with his helm jammed down, did not see the change. His killing stroke took Tarely and cleaved his helm. Tarely died instantly. Charles quickly took his club in two hands and slammed it into Zorcor's helm eye piece. Part of the metal entered Zorcor's head; screaming out in pain, he died just as Eric, Jonathan, and a dozen guards came running up.

Breathing hard, bleeding, and in extreme pain, Charles dropped the club in disgust and said, "Charge both with treason. They were trying to kill, not wound. And arrest my brother Droland for conspiracy. These were his friends."

"No, they weren't." Droland—with his dark, well-combed hair, stylish, well-fitting clothes, and magical belt and rings that lightly glowed—walked up, acting shocked. "I am so sorry. I immediately released them both this morning on your suggestion, Charles. I let them know that you said they were evil and should not be around the royal family."

Eric exclaimed, "No wonder they were out for blood! The slant on their family name for such an accusation would ruin them. Charles, I am shocked and ashamed. Two good men just died because of your foul mouth. Your father will hear of this! Hold still while I heal these cuts and the broken bone."

Master Jonathan asked, "When, this morning, did Charles tell you that these two were evil, Prince Droland?"

"Just after breakfast, Master Jonathan."

"Funny, I walked Prince Charles to combat training from breakfast and have not left his side since."

Prince Droland yelled, "Are you questioning my word, Master Jonathan?"

Charles put a hand on Jonathan's arm and shook his head just a little. Master Jonathan said, "No, Prince Droland. No."

"As well you should not." He turned in a tight twist and stomped off.

Eric watched him go and then looked at Jonathan. "Tell me truly, my friend. Is there any chance that Charles could have said anything in private to Droland?"

"Not a chance."

CHAPTER 4

CHARLES

Two young serving girls ran out onto the training field. Concern showed in their voices as they said together, "Charles, oh, Charles, my prince. Are you all right?" One saw the two dead men and started to faint. A guard caught her and propped her back up before she hit the ground. The other girl saw the dead men and kicked one, but not hard enough to hurt her toes against the plate armor.

Charles smiled through his pain while Eric was resetting his bone. "I'll be fine, lovely ladies. Thank you for your concern. Please stay away from Droland for a couple of days. He is upset that his plan to kill me failed."

Eric looked up and said to the girls, "Both of you, listen to me. You will not repeat what Charles just said. He has no proof that Droland had anything to do with this. Do you understand?"

They both curtsied and said, "Yes, Monsignor. We will do as required." Which, of course, meant everyone except the royal family would know the truth in a matter of minutes.

Master Jonathan asked, "Now, why are two lovely young ladies like you out here on the training field?"

They both giggled and started talking at the same time. Not one word was understood by any of the men. Eric yelled, "Stop!" They stopped immediately, looking like they were in trouble. "One of you at a time."

They looked at each other, and one nodded. The other turned and said, "The queen sent us to tell Charles that he is to accompany her to Shadow Mountain to view Duke Edward's new baby. We leave tomorrow morning at first light. Expect to be there for about a month, at least until the harvest festivals are over. Mistress Anon is sending maids to pack your belongings." Then they curtsied, turned around, and left.

Charles started working out the soreness in his now-repaired shoulder. "I need to go to my rooms. I am sure the maids will pack the entire set of fancy clothes Mother and Jennifer bought for me. I doubt I'll have a single decent shirt in the bunch." Charles bowed to the master and to Eric, saying, "It will be good to get away from Droland for a while. And Duke Edward has a grand library."

Charles picked up his sword belt from the lieutenant as he left the field. As Charles quickly walked away, Eric turned to Jonathan "Your opinion on this, if you please." Eric motioned to the two dead fighters.

Jonathan looked into Eric's eyes and said, "My opinion could get me killed, as it runs against everything the king believes."

"Your opinion will be kept between the two of us."

They walked together off the field of battle, talking intently.

Charles nearly ran to his rooms. When he reached them, he stopped quickly and walked slowly in. There were four young maids packing his clothes and talking.

"This shirt will look good on Charles, especially with the bright blue silk pants."

"I do love the ruffles on that one. What do you think about this yellow silk shirt with the cream pants?"

"Not unless he has something contrasting to highlight the colors. The bright green belt would be good."

"Oh, these knee-high, lace red boots will look wonderful with the bright green pants, and there's a matching red belt."

"What about hats? With feathers or without?"

"With, of course."

"That's it!" Charles walked in and said, "Out! Everyone, get out! I will pack my own clothes. We are going to see farmers! Not peacocks!"

They looked at him as if he was guilty of interrupting and then continued their conversation. "I think the light blue pants with the orange shirt would be a little too much contrast, don't you?"

"Of course not. He needs to stand out."

Suddenly, the notorious medal-on-medal sound of a sword leaving its scabbard echoed in the room. Screams were followed by four girls quickly leaving and complaining that the queen would hear of this. A door slammed shut, and one word was said, as if it were a curse, "Girls!"

Charles was in the act of unpacking everything when he heard a knock on the door.

"Enter."

In came Jennifer and two maids. The maids were staying behind Jennifer, as if counting on her protection. Charles didn't even look up. He knew who Mother would send. "Hello, Sister. How's Mother?"

"Irritated."

"Good. Tell her that I said next time she wants to pack my belongings, send men with some taste. Not girls that are color-blind."

"Charles, we bought those clothes just for this trip."

Charles held up the light blue silk pants and pulled out a long, thin knife. Jennifer took in a deep breath and started to yell, "No!" Too late.

Charles cut the pants nearly in half before tossing them aside, adding to a small pile of cut-up clothes. "Waste of gold if you ask me."

Jennifer was just about to send for Mother when Charles held up a cream shirt. He gently put that one aside. "Well, I see you're not cutting up everything."

"The cream shirt will go well with dark brown pants, brown boots, and my brown sword belt. As you can see, I did not cut up the dark green silk pants, the black silk pants, or the blue cotton pants. I will find shirts that will match these without making me look like a bouquet of flowers. The red boots are too bright but of good quality. I will have them and the matching belt blackened. The outcome should be a dark red that should look very nice." He stopped what he was doing long enough to look up at Jennifer. "I am not trying to be difficult. I am trying to look good. The maids' idea of looking good is embarrassing."

"Will you at least let them help you pack? The way you are tossing the clothes into that trunk will wrinkle them horribly."

"Of course they can. As long as they promise to pack only what I agree to. Otherwise, they get the flat of my blade as I kick them out."

Jennifer motioned for the two to start packing. They came around to the big chest and started removing clothes. Charles continued to pick out what he liked, making three piles. Jennifer asked, "What is the third pile for?"

"That is the 'I am not sure' pile. I may find something that would look good with the bright yellow shirt. The dark red pants with gold trim could be nice for a dance or something if I can find a proper shirt to go with it."

"Boys! They know nothing. Charles, that dark red is called burgundy, and that yellow is not *bright*; it's canary. May I give suggestions?"

"Please do, as long as you understand that I have the right to say no."

Just as Jennifer was picking out a belt of light brown, Amanda ran into the room.

Jennifer sternly said, "Amanda! When are you going to learn to knock?"

Amanda stopped quickly and started to tear up.

Charles came to her rescue. "Amanda has permission to enter my rooms without knocking anytime the door is left open. She knows this."

Amanda's face turned to stubborn, and she said, "That's right. And it's almost always open. Charles has nothing to hide. Not like that mean old Droland or Richard. I'm never allowed in their rooms."

Charles held out his arms, and Amanda quickly came over and hugged him. He placed her standing on the bed. She looked up into his eyes and sadly said, "You're going away, and so are Jennifer and Mommy. Grandmommy is going too. So are the two old men Daddy likes."

Jennifer said, "You need to treat the wizard and cleric with more respect, Amanda." Both maids looked up and started to giggle, but a warning glance from Jennifer stopped them. "Mother says they are very important."

Amanda said, "I will, but that old wizard smells, and you're changing the subject. Where are you going, and why can't I go?"

Charles raised an eyebrow, looked over at Jennifer, and said, "Two good questions."

Jennifer said, "We are going to Shadow Mountain to bless the duke's new baby."

Amanda jumped up and down on the bed, saying, "I want to go. I want to go."

Jennifer continued, "You are too young to travel so far."

Amanda started to become mad, and Charles could see the fight getting ready to start. He asked, "Who came to the conclusion that Amanda is too young?"

Jennifer said, "Grandmother."

Charles turned to one of the maids. "Go find out where Grandmother is, and will be, so that I can talk to her." The maid took off walking quickly toward Grandmother's rooms.

Amanda sat down and looked up at her brother. "Are you going to talk Grandmother into letting me come along?"

"I am going to find out why she does not want you to come along. We both know you are not too young. There must be a good reason. It's probably a problem with bandits, or dragons, or maybe an uprising with the dark, evil creatures. I would like to know what it is so I can protect Jennifer and Mommy. Don't count on Grandmother letting you travel with us if there may be danger."

"Dragons and evil creatures? I don't want to go. Why can't they bring the baby to see me?"

Jennifer sat down beside Charles and Amanda and said, "They will when she is better. She is sick, and that is why the old cleric is coming with us."

"Oh, I understand. Grandmommy won't want me in danger, and she won't want me near someone sick. Will they bring the baby here when she is better?" Then she saw it. The pile of bright silks, all cut up. "Ah!" She jumped down and went for the pile. "Charles, what are you going to do with these? They're wonderful. Can I have them? Oh please!"

Charles asked, "What are you going to do with all those silks?"

"I'm going to get the seamstress to help me make doll clothes."

"Boy dolls or girl dolls?"

"Girls, of course. No boy would be caught dead in these colors."

Charles smiled and said, "They are all yours. Go get one of your maids to gather them up for you."

Amanda was gone before Charles could change his mind. Charles looked at Jennifer with an, "I told you so."

Jennifer said, "You know exactly how to handle her. You'd make a great father."

"I'm a little young for fatherhood. Besides, I don't much like girls."

"That will change."

"I suppose so. Richard sure seems to go crazy when they're around."

Jennifer placed a hand over her mouth and gently laughed, "Yes, he does."

They both became quiet when they heard Grandmother outside with Amanda.

Grandmother was saying, "Well, child, where are you going in such a hurry that you have to run into your grandmother?"

"Oh, thank you, Grandmommy!" Amanda said, followed by a moment of quiet.

"Now, what did I do to deserve such a wonderful hug?" Grandmother asked.

"You're not making me go with them. Thank you! I need to go get one of my maids. I'll be right back."

Off she went, and Grandmother said, "Don't run!" Grandmother came gliding in shaking her head in wonder. "I thought I was going to have a dear of a time trying to explain to Amanda that she cannot attend the blessing. Will wonders never cease? That is a big headache removed. What happened?"

Jennifer said, "Amanda thinks that there may be dragons or evil creatures that may attack us on the way and that you want her to be safe."

Grandmother asked, "How did she find out?"

Jennifer's eyes went wide. "Was Charles correct then?"

"If Charles was the one who told her, then yes, Charles was correct. It is the exact reason the Women's Circle decided that Amanda would not attend the blessing. There have been problems with demons lately, and we do not want all the children in one place."

Jennifer said, in somewhat of a less than polite tone, "I suppose Charles and I are expendable?"

Grandmother looked at her carefully before answering. "Charles is, but if anything happens to you, there is a certain young man that would be heartbroken."

Jennifer placed her hands on her heart. "Jeffery."

Grandmother smiled. "Yes, Jeffery. He volunteered to travel with us, but his father said no. It would be a sad day if the baron lost his only child. Jeffery is looking for Charles right now so that he can ask Charles to keep a close eye on you."

"Jeffery is coming here? Oh no. I'm not ready to see him. I need to do my hair. I need a better dress. I …"

Jennifer ran out, heading to her rooms. Charles could not help but think, *Girls!*

Grandmother turned her attention to Charles. "I expect you to be on your best behavior during this trip, young man."

"Yes, Grandmother."

She sat down next to Charles. "You were attacked today. Your father is extremely upset."

"What—at losing two good men?"

"That and the fact that you were attacked in his own house."

"Yes. I suppose it would have been embarrassing for him."

She looked sad. "Yes, it was, and you're correct—he never mentioned that it would have been a loss."

"Did he mention that they were Droland's men and that Droland sent them?"

Grandmother stood up and said, "You need to stop blaming your brother for all your woes. You blame him for everything you do. Start taking responsibility for what you do, and your father may learn to like you."

"What did I do to deserve an assassination attempt?"

"You had your brother fire them with a slant on their family name. How could you do that and not expect retaliation? Now their families will be looking for retribution."

"Let them come."

"Oh, they won't be coming. Your father paid them most handsomely for their loss."

Charles looked up. "Father did that for me?"

"Yes. He used that stash you've been saving up. I'm afraid it's all gone."

Charles jumped to his feet. "What? I worked for two years to gather enough money for that magic bow. I went without when everyone else in this family had plenty, and Father just gave away my gold to appease someone whose son tried to kill me?"

"Yes. Again, take some responsibility for what you did to cause this."

"Please listen for once! I did nothing. I did not say anything about those two, and I can prove it. Ask Master Jonathan. I was with him all day. You saw me walk out with him, and I never left his side. Droland lied and used that lie to cover up the fact that it was his employees. Even if I did tell Droland such foolishness, why would Droland tell them the reason and point them to me? How did they get their hands on magic armor and weapons just perfect for fooling the others into thinking they were not magic or sharp—and in so short of time—if it was not planned in advance? Grandmother, Droland is trying to have me killed!"

Calmly, she said, "I am so glad you are going away. Perhaps the duke can turn you around and put a stop to this nonsense. I am appalled at how you treat your good brother. Just because he keeps catching you at your pranks and evildoings and turns you in, you seem to hate him. He has proof most of the time, and we have found proof in your rooms. You are a fool, Charles. Stop acting like the victim and start being part of this family." She turned and started to leave.

Charles asked, "Why is it Droland always knows where the proof is? The one with the proof in his hands can set it down anywhere he wants and say he saw me do it. Droland knows what I do before I do. Why is that, Grandmother? Do you really think I'm so stupid that I would leave evidence lying around? Think, Rebecca Steel, mother to my mother. Tell me truly. Do you believe me that stupid?"

Rebecca stopped and without looking around said, "Yes." Then she left.

The maids stood, waiting for Charles to stop crying. Sadness poured over the boy like waves at the beach. When he calmed down, he turned and started picking clothes again. Droland came by for only a second.

Snidely, he said, "Hello, Charles."

"Get out," Charles said.

"I'm leaving. I just wanted to show you the new magic bow Father bought me to make up for your lying about me."

Charles looked up and saw the bow he had worked so hard to obtain. He stood up and said in a tone that put fear in the maids and Droland, "Get out! Now!"

Droland quickly left. The maids busied themselves packing, and Charles numbly continued to hand them items to pack.

Jeffery came by and stood in the opening of the door, watching. "I just found out that Jennifer is going to Shadow Mountain and you are going with her. Is this true?"

Charles looked at him.

Amanda ran in with three maids and grabbed the pile. Then she looked at Charles and said, "I heard what you said about Droland. Shame on you." Then she left.

That hurt Charles more than everything else. This time he wasn't crying. He was angry.

Jeffery saw the look of anger and backed out, saying, "Use some of that anger to protect Jennifer, will you?" Then he was gone.

Charles sat at the table. He penned a message, sealed it, and handed it to the maid. The maids finished packing and left riding clothes out for the next day. Then they took the bags and trunk downstairs. Charles closed and locked the bedroom door. He climbed into bed, but sleep did not come easily; he was so angry he couldn't stop shaking.

CHAPTER 5

TRAVEL BEGINNINGS

I thought, *I am too tired and worried to sleep. Sometimes it really is a pain to be the youngest boy and a prince.* I got up early and walked down to the stables to check the preparations for the trip.

Monsignor Eric Montague was already there. "Good morning, Prince Charles."

"Good morning, Monsignor. It's nice to see you up already."

"Our God understands the need to leave early. He does not mind my prayers if I need to call on him a little early now and then."

"Your God, not mine. Though I believe in him and love him, I do not see the same returned."

"Solbelli loves you dearly, Charles."

"He has a poor way of showing it. Please watch me closely so that no one can blame me for anything."

"Agreed."

Everything was packed and in wagons or on horseback. My stallion stood ready and nervous in anticipation of travel, and I had to calm the big gray several times. I removed the tack and saddle and checked them over. Just as I thought, there was a cut along the cross strap. I ordered all tack and saddles checked.

Several cuts were found in other equipment and changed before Mother and Sister arrived.

As soon as they entered the grounds, Eric moved to the queen to report.

"Good morning, my queen."

"Good morning, Eric."

"I am sad to report, my queen, that Charles found tampering with his equipment and ordered a check of the other equipment, where other evidence of tampering was found."

The queen said angrily through her teeth, "Yes. Charles probably did it last night and let us find it today to try to look good. I sometimes wish I never had the boy."

Eric answered, "But, my queen, as you requested, we watched him all night. He could not have. It would have been impossible."

"Very well."

The queen started to mount when Grandmother came out with the wizard Dedrick. They talked for a while and then mounted.

Captain Shane said, "Move out in fours."

I admired the way the captain set up the party. Columns of four lancers, ten deep, started the procession. Mother and Grandmother moved out just behind the first column. Next came another column of four lancers, ten deep, and then Jennifer and me. After Jennifer and me, there were twenty knights in plate armor riding heavy warhorses. Wagons and over one hundred foot soldiers were last. The king must have been expecting something. Normally Mother rated only half that many.

We marched down through the city too early for most to be up and about. The march was easy, and I did not mount my gray. Everyone else was mounted. I stayed on the right side of the horse, walking. I did not want to be where Jennifer could strike up a conversation. I did not feel like conversation; I had far too much on my mind.

When the last soldier left the city and started on the long road to Shadow Mountain, four priests from the temple of Commeatus appeared in the middle of the road, blocking the way. I quickly mounted the gray, rode up to the four priests, and dismounted. Eric was starting to argue with them, and the captain was about to order their removal.

I yelled over the shouts, "Captain!"

Everything went quiet. "Yes, Prince Charles."

"I asked for these clerics, as the people watching me should know. Last night, I sent a maid with a note to the temple, asking for clerics who can check for curses, poisons, and evil and can give us a blessing for our travel. Have Monsignor Montague watch them if you want, but they are going to go over every inch of this group, looking for issues, before we move another step."

The queen pulled up on her mare. "Charles, call it off this instant. I will not have the procession held up for your pranks."

"Mother, go back to your place. As queen, you are in charge in the city and castle, but in the field, by law, the ranking male is in charge. I am a prince of the realm." I looked around and laid my hand on my sword. "Anyone want to argue the point that I outrank them in the field?"

No one said a word. I looked at Mother and asked loudly, "What harm will it do to have our people and supplies checked by known, good clerics?" Louder and looking at the men, I asked, "Where is the prank in wanting to ensure the safety of the queen by having our supplies checked for poison?"

The men all mumbled in agreement. The queen reluctantly turned around and went back into line.

I turned to the clerics. "Thank you for coming. Please check the knights first. If they pass, then take them with you to check the rest of the men and women. Check everyone for poison, evil, and curses. If found, let the knights handle it. Then we check the supplies."

The four ran down to the knights and checked for all three issues. None were found. Then they started at the front and checked toward the back as the knights fanned out to ensure there were no escapes if someone tried to run. About midway back, a man driving one of the first wagons tried to duck into the wagon and stash something. He was spotted and stopped. He had a small vial in his hand that he tried desperately to hide. The knights held him and the vial until the clerics reached them. One cleric went up to him and said, "This man is evil." The knights held him tighter.

Another cleric, magically checking for poison, pointed to the vial and said, "Wash your hands well before eating anything." The knight looked sick at the thought.

All others were fine. Then they started at the front while all the wagons and horses were unpacked. They found an evil-aligned assassin's dagger in the man's belongings, and half the food was poisoned, as well as some of the queen's belongings—garments she would wear close to her skin.

Eric dispelled the poison, but the queen asked for everything that was poisoned to be destroyed and replaced at the first town, including the three garments. Meanwhile, the wizard Dedrick Arconal was preparing to interrogate the assassin using magic, but before he could, the man died. Somehow, he just died.

Servants repacked everything that was still intact. The four clerics of Commeatus gave blessings and insisted on accompanying the queen. She was about to refuse when the captain said quietly, "If what just happened is any sign, then I think we may need them, Majesty."

I rode my gray back up to the front. "Captain, please take charge."

"As you wish, my prince."

The queen said, "Are you not going to gloat, Charles. You were correct."

My eyes were roaming, looking for signs of us being watched. For a second, I turned and looked directly into my mother's eyes. "I take my duty to protect the queen seriously—no matter what you think, Majesty." I turned my gray and headed back to my place in line.

I heard them whispering as Rebecca asked her daughter, "Do you think Charles was responsible for the man and the poison?"

The queen answered, "Mother, he could not be. He only found out about the trip last night. I have had him under constant magical watch, and his father has also. He did nothing and told no one except the clerics, and that note was examined, and the clerics were watched very closely."

"Who then?"

"I have no idea, Mother, but I'm beginning to have suspicions."

"So am I, child."

The trip went along well for the rest of the day. Dusk came quickly, and camp was set. Guards were stationed and alert. The four clerics of Commeatus stationed themselves by my tent with a watch on the queen's tent at all times. Protection spells were spoken, and I could see them floating there. I could also see the gaps, and I mentioned so to Eric. He checked it out and then plugged the holes. Then he looked at me strangely. He walked over to the wizard and talked quietly to him.

The wizard looked at me. Then he did a spell and pointed a finger directly at me. I felt it wash over me, and I stood up, walked over to them, and asked, "Why did you place a spell on me? It did not stick."

Dedrick answered, "That spell was not meant to stay. It was a quick check of your alignment. I am happy to say you are of goodly alignment, my prince. Still, the check only takes the best average."

"Why did you feel it necessary to check?"

Eric said, "Answer me this, Prince Charles. Can you see magic?"

I looked around at the magical lines and their strengths and answered, "Yes, why?"

"Because it means you are of natural magical talent."

I was in shock. "Magical talent! Please explain."

Dedrick answered, "It runs in your father's blood, though it is rare that it shows. Your great-great-great-grandfather was a gold dragon after all."

I had been told of the gold dragon. It was known history that my ancestry was part dragon, and I was allowed to study all the history I wanted. One of the statues in the great hall was of a dragon said to be my grandfather several times removed. However, it was never mentioned that having dragon ancestry could cause me to have magical abilities.

I smiled. And then I smiled even bigger.

Dedrick's look turned to confusion. "Having magical abilities as royalty is not good, my prince."

I looked at Dedrick and laughed with joy. I turned around several times with my arms held out and thanked, out loud, every good god I had ever read about. This brought major attention to me. Jennifer, Mother, and Grandmother came over to find out what was going on. Most of the guard and the captain gathered around.

Eric asked, "What do you find so funny about this deplorable situation?"

"Deplorable? Deplorable! This is wonderful!"

Mother asked with mirth, "What is so wonderfully deplorable?"

Eric said, "Prince Charles has just proven that he has natural magical talent."

Mother, Grandmother, Jennifer, and most the servants placed their hands over their mouths and sucked in air as if they were stunned to silence. Mother started to say something, but nothing came out.

I turned to Dedrick and asked joyfully, "Can you send a message to Father, Richard, Duke Edward, and the legal counsel, letting them all know?"

Mother was nearly in shock as she said, "No! What are you doing? We need to keep this quiet. We must hide your abilities. We cannot let your father know. He will be furious."

I calmed down and asked, "Why would Father be upset?"

Grandmother whispered, "Because, child, if you have magical talent, you can no longer be a prince. You know the laws."

I smiled. "You are incorrect, Grandmother. I can no longer be a crown prince. The laws of Kayland state, and I quote, 'No creature with magical power can hold a position of power within the government.' The laws go into long explanations, illuminating why this is the law, but to make it short, they state that power corrupts, and absolute power corrupts absolutely. Therefore, no creature can have both the power of magic and the power of position. Now, what that comes down to is this: I cannot become king, duke, or baron. I cannot hold any elected position of power. Nor am I eligible for any blood position of power over more than five hundred people. Nice little legal statement that protects royal blood from being kicked out with nothing. I am still, and can remain, a prince. However, I no longer have the right to hold great responsibilities for long periods of time. I can be placed in charge of small groups like this one to protect the queen. It's a great responsibility but no real power. Eighty years ago, there was Prince Halbert, my grand-uncle. He learned magic, as you well know. They found out when he made his sister glow brightly green. He was still a prince, but instead of becoming king, his younger brother became king, and Halbert became the head of the Protection of Travel Agency—no real power but plenty to do."

Grandmother asked, "Then why do you seem so happy? You can no longer be king or hold a great position of power within Kayland. That is very limiting."

I smiled. "How many times have I told you that I don't want to be king? I don't like telling people what to do with their daily lives, and I don't like sitting in court making decisions, when I never know if I made the right one or not. I will say it again. I am not interested in power!"

Mother said, "I thought you were just trying to make us believe that so we would not watch you for deception so closely."

I turned to the group surrounding us and said, "I would never say anything bad about the queen. The queen is the wisest and smartest person in the country, but my mother is mental when it comes to her youngest son." I turned to Dedrick. "Please pass the word. Charles is magical. Ensure that my brothers know so that they realize I am no longer a threat. I never was, but they seemed to think so. Now, I have a big decision."

Grandmother asked, "Decision?"

I smiled at her. "What style of magic will I learn? There are all kinds, you know." I turned and headed back to my tent, knowing I would receive individual visits from Eric and Dedrick, trying to talk me into their type of magic.

Grandmother watched me go and then turned to Dedrick. "Send those messages. I want everyone to know how proud I am that my grandson is going into the magical trades." Mother echoed her statement with tears, and they left for their tent.

★★★

Jennifer watched everything in confusion. Thoughts were flowing through her intelligent head like a raging river. *If Charles is telling the truth about not wanting power, and it seems that he is, then many of the pranks Droland claimed he did would not make sense. There would be no reason to humiliate Richard unless Charles was evil and Dedrick checked. He is of goodly nature. This does not add up. Something is wrong with this. Charles saved our lives earlier. Mother told Grandmother that he could not have set up the poisoning, as he was being magically watched. Then the question is, Who and why? It has to be someone close to the family. Surely not Richard. He would have nothing to gain. He is next in line for the crown. Droland? I cannot see it. He is such a sweet boy. Something is wrong, and Grandmother is beginning to understand what. Stick close to Grandmother.* She turned and headed to the women's tent.

★★★

In Mother's tent, the conversation was heated, strong, and loud enough for me and most everyone else to hear.

The queen was pacing and talking to herself. "Charles is pulling something. Maybe he has found some loophole in the laws."

Grandmother was just as upset. "I don't think so. They plugged all the potential loopholes, shortened the law, and made it just as plain as possible."

"If you were as intelligent as Charles, could you not find something?"

"I think Charles is playing it straight for a change. I think he truly does not want power. He never grabbed it when given the chance. You know this."

"That little brat is up to something, and it's big," Mother said. "I don't know what, but I think we are all in trouble."

There were no maids and no servants in the tent. When the yelling started, they all left. Only the three were there for more than four hours now. I walked in with hand on sword and a look of distaste. In very quiet, punctuated words that screamed major irritation, I said, "If you two do not shut up so the rest of us can get some sleep, I am going to have you tied and gagged. You may be able to sleep in your saddles tomorrow, but the rest of us need to be alert. Now, go to sleep or I'll order Dedrick to spell you to sleep. And stop talking about how much you hate me in front of the troops!" I stormed out.

Mother said, "I think we should go to bed."

Jennifer said, "I think we should apologize."

Grandmother said, "Not while he is in that mood. Did you notice he had a hand full of rope behind his back? Good night." She quickly went to her bed. The others did the same.

CHAPTER 6

THE VILLAGE

The next day, little was said to anyone in the family. I rode and walked with all the others, spending time talking to the troops, trying to reassure them and lift their spirits after last night's issues emanating from the ladies' tent. I received many backslaps and apologies from the knights and older troops. The younger men had no idea what to say. I tried my best to raise their spirits by joking about my magical abilities and all the fantastical, strange things I would do—silly things like tying my boots without having to bend down and having a bird wake me in the morning. We talked long on making magical weapons and armor. This was something they could understand, as it was part of their everyday life. Making magical armor that would not rub or chafe would be great. Making a sword that would change into an ax when you needed to chop wood was a favorite. Making a bow that could bend the shot around obstacles was thought of as well. The most popular was spelling women to shut up. Every man there would have liked to have that spell. Soon spirits were high again except with Mother and Grandmother. I had no idea what Jennifer was thinking. She watched me closely but seemed to be listening to Mother. The look on her face was one of tossing out some of the things Mother was saying. I thought, *It would be great if my sister started thinking for herself.*

The captain must have read my mind. He said, "All girls get to that point eventually. It is better if they do it later in life, as their mothers generally have good advice. In this case, I would have to say that it's good timing."

I looked at the captain and said, "Captain Shane, my good friend. It would depend on what she is disagreeing with. Still, after hearing that argument last night, I would have to agree with you. At this time, it's probably much better if she comes to her own conclusions."

The captain said, "I want to thank you for spending the day talking with my men. They were feeling a bit discouraged this morning. They seem to be of much higher morale this afternoon."

"My pleasure, Captain. When do we rest for the night? People are looking ragged after staying up half the night due to Mother and Grandmother."

"We come upon the meadow town of Wells Sounding in about an hour. We will spend the night there and leave early in the morning."

"Wells Sounding is small, but there is an inn. Is Mother staying in the inn? I would not suggest it, Captain."

The captain smiled. "That's why I came back to talk to you. The queen is insisting that she stay in the inn, and so is your grandmother. I don't think it wise, given the recent issues. I would prefer to keep her within the circle of troops and not in a place that could quickly become a fire trap in battle. She will ask you to persuade me."

"She will find that impossible, but dress up a maid and have her go to the inn with guards and Dedrick's best apprentices. Make it look as if she were the queen. Once in her rooms, have the wizards magically shift everyone back to the camp and keep a watch on that inn. I don't want the owners harmed, but I want to know if the problems were just with home or if they extend out here."

"Good idea, my prince. I shall have it done." The captain hesitated. "My prince, I think we have another problem. I would not have thought of it, but one of the maids told me some things about Droland that make me worry."

"Go ahead, Captain."

"At the last minute, the king ordered me to take the mountain road, as the forest road is too dangerous at this time. The reports suggest the forest has demon problems."

I thought for a moment. "Captain, this group is not designed for mountain road battle. Lancers will not have a chance to get up to speed for a charge. The knights will be near useless, and the men you brought are for forest fighting, not open-ground combat."

"I know this, and I was shocked when I saw the orders for the makeup of the troops, but who am I to question the king?"

"My father ordered this complement? That's not like him."

"I thought it came from him, as it bore his seal. But one of the maids saw Droland use the seal for something only minutes before I received the orders."

"Interesting. It would be just like my brother to pay no attention to the presence of servants. He feels that they are so far below him that they make no difference. How foolish. Servants are the heart of the castle. They have the true pulse on what is going on."

"I agree, my prince."

"Captain, we have to follow my father's orders. If you received orders to take the mountain road, then we take the mountain road. How long before the turnoff?"

"We should reach the northern mountain road in three days, Highness."

"Did the orders require haste?"

"No, Highness."

"Is there an easily guarded safe place between here and there?"

"Two days from now, we will reach the edge of Matins Rainbow. The valley is small. Hard to get into and out. I could defend that spot from an army with minimal troops for months."

"How long would it take to train these troops into other positions? Say, mounted long sword, foot lancers with short sword, and light, mounted spears?"

Proudly, he said, "I picked these men myself. I could have them well trained in three days, four at the most. They know most of the differences now, so it's just a matter of tactics and types of orders."

"Good. Start now but keep it quiet. We'll finish the training when we reach Matins Rainbow. Purchase what you need in town or make it from the woods. If at all possible, you will have your four days, Captain."

The captain bowed in his saddle. "Thank you, Highness."

I saluted smartly. "For the queen's protection."

He smiled and saluted back. "The queen's protection."

We camped that night. Over dinner, Mother and Grandmother both mentioned that the inn would be a welcome rest. I pretended irritation at the captain and ordered him that under no circumstances were the queen and the head of the Women's Circle to leave this camp.

The captain pretended chastisement and said, "As you wish, Highness."

My mood kept Mother and Grandmother from asking for anything else. Later, when most were going to bed, I watched as several women, escorted by a handful of men, were taken to the inn. The captain had waited until the ladies were in their tent before making the move.

A little after midnight, the inn caught fire and started to burn. The four assassins were quickly caught, and three were killed in the fight. We lost no one, and the fire was put out by the clerics and Dedrick. All occupants were removed in time.

All the noise, shouting, and the additional guard suddenly surrounding their tent woke Mother and Grandmother, as was reported to me later. They tried to come out, but the guard stopped then. "Sorry, Majesty. Orders from Prince Charles."

"Then at least tell us what's happening."

"Prince Charles, the captain, and the wizard set it up so that it looked like you were staying at the inn. Someone set the inn on fire. There is fighting going on up there. At the same time, the occupants are being saved by the clerics that Prince Charles brought. His Highness said it may be a decoy and ordered your safety and continued stay in your tent. His Highness made it very clear, Majesty. If you leave the tent for any reason, I had better be dead trying to stop you. He does not want you seen."

"Very well. Carry out your orders."

"Yes, Majesty."

Mother went back inside.

When the fire was out, as prince, I personally compensated the innkeeper for his trouble and the repairs to the inn. I did not have to, but little niceties from the crown are always good for public relations. He thanked me greatly for saving his inn and said that I did not have to compensate him, but he held onto the bag of gold like his life depended on it.

We took the assassin a little ways away. I ordered, "Hold him tight."

"Yes, my prince."

I looked at the assassin and asked, "What is your name?"

He spit at me—a prince. I was shocked, and so were the men. Several moved in, and swords were pulled. I motioned for them to stay back. I said, "Fool of a pig. You see this man on your right? That is a war wizard. The cleric next to him is using a spell called Circle of Knowing, so we will know if you lie, and if you don't tell us everything you know, including where you're from and who hired you to kill the queen, I am going to order the wizard to rip it out of your mind." I let that set in for a second.

He asked, "If I tell you what I know, will you set me free?"

I thought for a second. "No, but I will give you your weapon. You spit at me. I think I have the right to teach you manners."

He smiled a wicked little mousy smile. "Done. I am Ted Noris. A guy calling himself Fred Cleaves gave me and my boys ten gold each to burn down the inn. As the innkeeper tossed me out last week and has refused me service since, I agreed."

I looked at Eric. "He's telling the truth, my prince."

"Know where this Fred Cleaves is or what he looks like?"

"He's a short dark man with a strange accent, smooth skin like a baby's, and no hair that I could see. He wore a hood on his cloak, so it'd be difficult to see. Smelled of something burnt. Said nothing of where he came from."

I looked at Eric. "Demon?"

Eric answered, "Demon."

I turned to the assassin. "Did you know the queen was staying at the inn tonight?"

"I knew."

"Sergeant, give the man his dagger and form a circle of blades."

I stepped away. The circle was formed, and his dagger was returned. It was a wicked-looking curvy dagger but not magical, or even masterwork, and not poisoned. "Someone, lend me a dagger. Mine is magical, and using it would not be fair."

A standard-issue dagger was pulled and tossed into the tree next to me. "Thank you."

The one who threw the dagger said, "I would be more than happy to do this for you, my prince." Rounds of the same brave talk echoed through the circle.

"Thank you. However, he tried to kill my mother. He is mine."

I pulled the blade from the tree and entered the circle. The fight did not last long. He was not trained as I was. I made it quick but very painful. As my blade slowly entered his stomach and his eyes widened with surprise, I said, "Spit on me if you must, but never threaten my queen!" I twisted the dagger and pulled it out. When he collapsed, I cleaned the blade on his shirt and handed it back to the soldier. I walked off with several guards and Dedrick flanking me. Cheers erupted from the circle as I walked back to camp.

At camp, Mother was still in her tent. I went over, and the guard announced me. Mother said, "Come in, Charles."

I entered. "I am surprised you are still awake, Mother. Hello, Grandmother, Jennifer."

Jennifer said, "Hello, Charles, and thank you for saving our lives again," looking at Mother as if to remind her.

"My duty and my pleasure."

Mother asked, "Well?"

I took a seat, even though it was not offered. "I thought about your request to stay in the inn, and the captain and I agreed that if I was not here, you probably would stay at the inn. Therefore, we set it up to look like you were staying there. Did you receive your dress back?"

"Yes. My maid returned it just after the fighting started."

"Not much of a fight. They were just local tuffs hired by another. They are dead now, and no one else was harmed. I used some of our traveling gold to recompense the innkeeper for his trouble. Everything is quieting down. I had planned to stay up the night, waiting to see if anything happened, but it did, and that's that. Bed is looking very good. I am sorry, but I must insist that you stay in your tent the night. If there is another hired assassin that we missed, your life may be in danger. Is there anything you need before I retire?"

"No."

I looked long at her before getting up and leaving. As I left, I heard Jennifer say. "A thank you or a hug would have been nice, Mother." Then she noisily turned over as if anything Mother could say now would not be listened to.

CHAPTER 7

FOREST WALL

The next day was long and hot, but it came and went without issues. The captain was deep into training his men, and they were all for learning. I took charge of leading, which put me up front with the first lancers. On the second day, I sent out five scouts to ensure no ambushes, and they reported back often. One did not report back on time, so I stopped the troops for a rest and sent four to find him. They reported back.

"Bandits, Your Highness. Just inside the forest edge. We saw the body of our man being dragged away and covered up. The horse was led off."

"Any idea how many?"

"No, Highness. There are at least twenty-three by count, but we had to move off when they sent out watchers."

"Were you seen?"

"No, Highness. We left long before the watchers could mount the hill."

"Good, and well done. Tell Captain Shane I need to see him and pass the word on the way back."

"Yes, my prince."

They rode off, one on each side of the column saying, "Bandits up ahead. Bandits up ahead."

It wasn't long before the captain came riding up. "Bandits?"

"Yes, Captain, and they killed a scout in Royal Guard uniform."

"How many?"

"There are at least twenty-three in front of us."

"Are you expecting more in the back?"

"I don't know, but I would like to know."

The captain took the hint and sent out eight scouts in pairs to find out if others were around. The rest of the front scouts returned and reported nothing; therefore, someone waiting on the side to pull in behind us was not the plan. Something tickled my spine, and I realized that magic was being used up ahead. I motioned for Dedrick and Eric to come forward.

"Bandits, Your Highness?"

"Yes. Why is it I can feel magic being used somewhere in front of us? You never told me that was possible without doing a spell—and then the range is highly limited."

Eric answered, "When one first finds that he can learn magic, it is normally because he can do something others cannot. Your ancestor could make things glow, but that faded with time, and he had to learn the cantrip called Illumination. My sister made me invisible, and for years she could make anything invisible at will. That also faded. In time, your ability to see and feel magic will fade. The interesting thing is you should not be able to detect it without line of sight and to a maximum of thirty feet in front of you. You say it feels some distance away?"

"About where the bandits should be."

"Do you feel anything about the magic? Is it hostile or beneficial?"

"It is nether. It is something wrong—as if someone was creating something wrong."

"Evil?"

"Not that type of wrong. More ... incorrect or misleading."

"Illusion. They are creating an illusion."

Dedrick said, "Hiding some of their fighters so they can flank us. Or hiding the archers so they can surprise us and reload without being attacked. Want to have some fun, Your Highness?"

"Depends. What's your idea?"

"I do a Superior Invisibility spell on a bear and teleport him into their ranks."

"Where are we going to get a bear?"

"Ah, good point."

I could not help but smile. "No bears around, but how about that bee tree we saw back around the last corner? Can you manage something with that and not get us all stung?"

Dedrick thought for a second. "Hm. Yes. I think I can manage that. I could put a force around it. Someone would have to detach it from the bottom. I could float it in the air until we are close and then remove the force and drop it into their ranks."

Smiling, I said, "Dedrick, go prepare your tree then. Eric, please gather the clerics. We need to talk."

Dedrick left to gather his apprentices and some men with axes, and Eric left to gather the clerics.

Mother rode up. "Charles, what are you planning to do? We cannot sit here all day."

I rolled my eyes at the captain and turned to Mother. "If I deem to sit here all day, then we sit here all day, Mother. If I decide to sit here for a week, then we sit here for a week, and if I deem to have you tied into your saddle and led around by your daughter for falling out of rank when we have bandit problems, then I will have you led around like the child you are exhibiting! If you want to do something, prepare to tend the wounded as we bring them back."

Her eyes went wide. "Wounded?"

The captain quickly took her reins and led her back into rank, saying. "Please, Majesty, he is making plans for your protection, and we don't know the size of the group. They are hostile to royalty and may outnumber us. They are using high-level magic and could possibly have demons with them. Don't push Charles right now. We are trying our best to come up with a good solution to this issue. Unless you want Charles to do something you will regret, then stay in ranks and follow orders!" He turned around and returned to me.

"Thank you, Captain."

The captain whispered in an exasperated tone, "If you order her spanked publicly, I will do it myself, my prince. Even though it will be my head when the king finds out."

I had to smile at that. Mother would have a fit, and so would Father. Or would he? Interesting thought. "Captain, send out some soldiers and let the enemy know that we know they are there. Don't let my men get in harm's way yet."

"Highness?"

"Trust me, Captain. I have an idea."

Eric was returning with the clerics as the captain gave orders for a column of archers to go take a peek and be seen looking and seeing. "Kill any watchers you can find but don't give chase or come close to the forest. There are magical traps waiting for bold men. Take a look and return."

Eight archers left, riding quickly straight up the road and off toward the hilltop where they would have a view and possibly take out a few watchers.

Eric said, "Your orders, Highness?"

"If demons are involved, what can we expect?"

"Almost anything, Highness. Magic that is possibly high level and evil, traps that are deadly or maiming, as they like to hear the screams, and life draining to make you weak. They will fight dirty and run if they think they are losing, but they will return at night or when they have an advantage."

"If I were a good tactician, I would use my enemy's knowledge against him," I said.

"How so, my prince?"

"I would fight with a small group and run away at the correct time, knowing my enemy would give chase. My main force, or a trap, would be waiting for the one giving chase. How long will the illusion magic last before they have to recreate the spells?"

"Highness, the spells last depending on the caster. If you felt it all the way over here, then the caster is very high level, and the spells could be permanent."

"What do we have that can see through illusions?"

"I could do a Correct Vision spell."

"Not spells, Monsignor. I want items that can see through illusion."

"I do not know, my prince."

"Please find out. Check the two rogues we brought and ask Dedrick. I want to use as few spells as possible."

"What will you gain by this, Highness?"

"Cleric of Solbelli, why do you question me?" He did not move but continued to wait for an answer. "Very well. Both sides are limited in the number of spells they can do per day, correct?"

"Of course."

"If we can see their spells and see them redo some of them, then we can find out what or who is casting the spells. If we know what or who is casting the spells, we may be able to find a way to deplete their resources simply by waiting or dispelling. At the minimum, we will know who to target first. We may even find out what traps they have set, though I would not count on them all being magical. Now, would you be so kind as to follow my orders before I have to have you punished?"

"Of course, my prince."

Eric and the other clerics took off, looking to see if anyone had any Lens of Correct Vision—not a common item, but history told us to always know what our resources are. Many battles had been lost by men who had no idea someone in their own ranks had exactly what they needed to win.

The scouts we sent to the rear and sides returned. There was no one behind or to our sides.

"Captain!"

The captain turned in his saddle and looked over his shoulder at me. Then he turned his horse, and he and his lieutenants trotted up. "Yes, my prince."

"I know that we received reports that there are no enemies behind us, but set watchers just the same."

"It will be done, Highness." He motioned to a lieutenant, and the lieutenant took off down the column. The captain smiled. "The tree is ready, my prince, and the bees are angry."

"Excellent. Have the archers take the hill overlooking the forest. Move the tree into position on the hill and wait for orders. Then move the lancers into battle formation but warn them that, on command, lances are to be dropped and swords drawn. On that same command, they are to move in line through both sides of the forest road and surround the enemy. They need to take them out quickly and return to the queen. Do not allow them to chase anything or anyone. Move in, strike hard, and move back. Have the foot soldiers move in behind the lancers and pick up the lances. Then have them return immediately to the line and ready the lances for the return of the lancers. I will need the lancers ready if we receive a frontal attack. Have the archers ready to fire into the enemy, if they see any, and then return to the line immediately. And, Captain."

"Yes, my prince."

"No prisoners."

"Highness!"

"No, Captain. We cannot afford to carry prisoners with us, nor can we afford soldiers to escort them back to the king. We have no choice, as I will not allow them loose in our lands and on my people."

"Understood. This is a strike and fall back maneuver. You are attempting to find out their strength. When will we know to move?"

"When the tree hits the forest ground, count slowly to twenty-five and move fast. The bees will not chase a quickly moving target when there are so many slow, easy targets afoot."

"I am sure the lancers will move quickly, my prince."

I had to smile. "They had better. I don't want to waste healing on bee stings."

The captain and his lieutenants hurried down the line, and soldiers started to move. Bowmen and several foot soldiers headed on the run to the hill, and I saw two enemy watchers quickly stand up to run. My archers took them both out. They made the hill with no issue, and Dedrick, levitating the tree, started the move to the hill. The lancers and foot soldiers moved into place just this side of the hill and out of sight of the forest. With the lancers leaving, I ordered the knights to protect the queen, and they positioned themselves and the rest of the foot soldiers into three circles, two facing out, the center circle facing in. Three knights dismounted and flanked the queen.

I rode to near the top of the hill and belly-crawled to the top to get a good view. Eric came up behind me.

"One of the rogues did have a Lens of Correct Vision, Highness. He is with us now."

I looked back and motioned him forward. He was very good at not being seen, and in that twenty-foot movement I lost sight of him twice. I was looking down the left side trying to find him, but he whispered in my right ear.

"I'm here, Highness."

I turned my body. By the smile, I would say he knew he startled me.

"Do you have the lens?"

He pulled something out of his pocket. It was a small pink stone. Opposite sides were cut flat and polished. "Highness, you look through this side and please close one eye before looking. If there are illusions, then the conflict will dizzy your mind if both eyes are open. It's not the best lens."

I took the tiny stone and looked. I saw no difference. I handed it back, "You take a look and tell me if you see any differences."

He took the small stone, but before using it, he carefully looked over the terrain and the forest. When he was satisfied that he knew what was there, he put the stone to his eye. "Highness, see the outcroppings of rock on the left about two hundred feet into the forest?"

"Yes, I see them."

"Note that there is smooth ground on both sides."

"Yes. Good rallying point."

"They are not rocks, and the smooth areas are not there. That is a trench with spikes. It's hard to see from here, but it is not rocks."

"Anything else?"

"Yes, there is a knot of movement to the right side of the forest road about one hundred and eighty feet in. There is a small stone giant tied up there and about fifty men waiting on horseback."

"Nasty. If we hang around long enough for them to reach us, then those men could be used to push us into the trench they forced the stone giant to make. Anything else?"

"That is all I see, except the two sorcerers standing behind the men that are waiting. One has a tail. The hundred or so archers in the forest are in plain sight, so I would guess you know about them."

"Yes. They are the bait." I wrote what we saw on a piece of parchment and gave it to an archer. "Send this to the captain." He rolled it up and tied it near the arrowhead. The arrow flew straight and low to the knight's formation where an archer was waiting. He picked up the arrow and sent it to the captain. An arrow in flight is a signal for the enemy. No sense telling them anything. This way, the arrow stayed low and out of sight.

I gave time for the captain to read and warn the lancers and foot soldiers. Then I gave the order for the tree to be smashed down on the road between their archers. Dedrick touched the tree, and it disappeared. I quickly looked out to the forest road. The tree was falling from about one hundred feet up. The old rotten tree shattered when it hit the ground, and thousands of bees flew out in a rage. Dedrick wiggled up next to me on the top of the hill. All the enemy archers on both sides of the road were standing up swatting at bees. Very shortly, the lancers shot out from around the hill and rode into the forest on both sides. They dropped their lances just before the forest and drew their swords just as they were entering. They surrounded the enemy and smashed them. No man alive can fire a bow accurately when his body is being attacked by hundreds of angry bees.

The rogue said, "My prince, the men on horseback and the two sorcerers are moving toward the lancers."

"Anyone left with the poor stone giant?"

"No, Highness."

"Think you can sneak down there and release him without being killed?"

He smiled, took out a potion, and disappeared. The lens was pressed into my hand, and I heard him run in the direction of the giant.

I stood up and ran down to my horse, giving orders to prepare to fire and retreat. "Take out the magic users first. All bolts and arrows at the magic users."

Dedrick and Eric were following close on my heels, hoping that the archers realized I was talking about the enemy magic users and not them. When I reached the knights, the foot soldiers were already arriving with the lances and standing them up so the lancers could grab them without dismounting. I quickly changed orders. The enemy would not expect lancers, as we just used them and they dropped their lances.

"Knights, mount and take up lances. Foot soldiers, hand lances to the knights and then protect the queen. Knights, prepare to follow me. We are charging the enemy." I pulled out a soldier and ordered, "Run and tell the captain to join the fight on the hill."

All the knights mounted. Dedrick and Eric moved to the back after boosting my abilities with increased strength and constitution. I led the knights on a charge up the hill. As we moved, the archers fired and then ran down the hill. They saw us charging up and moved out of the way. As we reached the top, I saw that the enemy horsemen were charging up to attack my archers. We had the high ground. My heavy cavalry (knights) slammed into the enemy and ran them down. Fireballs and lightning bolts slammed into the only magic user in the enemy ranks, and I found myself face-to-face with a demon wielding a long sword made of some dark red metal. My horse clashed with his demon mount, and my trained heavy warhorse started attacking his evil creature. I parried his blade several times, trying unsuccessfully to find an opening. This demon was good. The demon was wearing me down and would win if this kept up. I had already sustained several cuts, and they burned like fire. Something was wrong. He seemed to know my moves before I executed them. Then it hit me, and I concentrated on making a strong left strike and did a right instead. My dwarven forged blade went right through and removed his unprotected head. He had been reading my thoughts.

I looked around me, and the battle was over. The lancers had joined with the knights and finished off the ones trying to escape. Clerics were healing our wounded, and knights were killing the wounded enemy. I hated taking no prisoners, but my hands were tied. I would have to beg the gods for forgiveness later. Right then, I had too much to do.

I checked my mount, and he was in fine shape, just a few bites that would be healed easily. I walked the big gray to the top of the hill to check on Mother. She was doing as asked, helping tend to the wounded. All three of the women were working on men, and several maids were tending to horses. There is one thing good about the women of Kayland. They may be pests at times—well, most of the time—but when it comes to work, they are not afraid to get their hands dirty, royalty included.

Having four clerics from Commeatus helped tremendously with healing, including myself, and they were invaluable during the battle. I was beginning to appreciate Commeatus far more than the other gods. We lost eight men total: one knight, six lancers, and one of Dedrick's apprentices. Dedrick teleported home that night and reported to the king. When he returned, he was with six more war wizards and a dozen clerics. He had a note for me from Father.

Charles:

I am saddened and shocked to hear of this attack and the other attempts on your mother's life. You did well at command. Over one hundred and fifty enemy dead and only eight of ours. And you did this with minimal support. Your bravery in battle in taking out the lead demon yourself does not miss our attention, nor does your zealousness at protecting your mother and our queen. Our highest award is awaiting you upon your return, and all your men will be rewarded. I know you took charge by rank, but now you have the king's blessings. I am sending you a few more magic users to round out the troops.

My sadness is great to hear you are no longer a crown prince. My blessings on whatever type of magic you chose to study. We can always use another war wizard. I know how you love to read; a good sage could be helpful to the kingdom. Remember, you are needed and wanted. I can think of a hundred places where I could use your talents. Both your brothers are sad at your loss.

King David

I looked up after reading the letter. Dedrick was right there talking with another wizard. "Dedrick?"

"Yes, Highness."

"What were my father and my brothers' moods when Father penned this message?"

"Your father was acting sad that you are no longer a crown prince. He questioned me about this several times. I have been around him long enough to know he was relieved, not sad. Richard was sad and very worried. For some reason, Droland was furious. Though he pretended sadness, you could plainly see he was mad about something. Your father noticed this and told Droland, 'Do not be jealous. It is beneath you. We know you are a better man than Charles. You will have a chance someday to prove yourself in battle. I have every confidence in you.' Then your father started giving orders for magical reinforcements."

"Great. I want all the reinforcements up front now." I turned to one of the clerics from Commeatus and whispered, "Can you do a Circle of Knowing?"

"Yes, Highness." He cast silently.

Six war wizards and twelve clerics came forward from around the camp. I looked them over. I recognized all of them. One stood out from the rest as a friend of Droland. They were seen together often. In addition, one of the clerics was a friend to Droland's wizard. I pointed them out and said, "You two, front and forward." They complied. "Go home and do not let me see you again on this trip."

The wizard made the mistake of saying, "We were sent by the king."

The cleric of Commeatus said, "That was a lie. He was not sent by the king."

I asked, "Oh, and who were you sent by?"

The cleric said, "The great Prince Droland sent us to ensure you are not trying to harm the queen."

The cleric of Commeatus said, "Droland sent them but not to protect the queen."

Droland's wizard said, "A Circle of Knowing is not evidence, as it can be easily fooled." He added a belated and snide "Prince Charles."

Swords came out of their sheaths, and men started forward. I held up a hand to stop them. "Were you under orders to lie to me?"

The cleric answered, "No."

"Good then. Execute both."

Mother yelled, "Wait!"

I turned to Mother, and my irritation was easy to see, "My queen?"

"I will not have you killing the crown's servants."

I looked at her long and hard, and then I turned to the wizard. "Do your orders, from anyone, have anything to do with harming the queen?"

"No."

The cleric of Commeatus yelled, "That is a lie, Highness."

"Did your orders to harm the queen come directly from Droland?"

"I will not answer any more of these illegal questions." He placed his face in the air as if to say, "You are beneath me."

Eight arrows and four swords hit him almost instantly. He died.

I turned to the cleric. "Did your orders to harm the queen come directly from Droland?"

"No. They were relayed by one of Droland's flunkies. I believe his name is Latoff."

"How were you to kill the queen?"

"We were to kill her in her sleep and blame it on you."

Eric asked, "Why would you do something like this? A cleric of Solbelli."

Droland's cleric nearly hissed, "I haven't been a cleric of Solbelli for decades, you old fool." Then he attempted to complete a spell—but it was hard to do with an arrow in his mouth and a dozen swords hacking him to pieces.

I stepped back.

The captain ordered, "Clean up this mess. And if anyone else joins this party, I want to know instantly."

I questioned the intentions and faiths of the other magic users, and they were all fine. One wizard was sent by Richard to investigate and report. "To spend my life, if necessary, to save the queen and the prince."

"Ah, my only good brother. Well, you may certainly stay if you will give me a God oath that you will inform me the moment those orders change and ten minutes before you execute them."

"My prince, you have my God oath."

"Thank you, and I am sorry for the necessity."

"I think it is understandable under the circumstances."

I smiled and turned to the cleric. "Thank you for the Circle of Knowing."

"My pleasure and my God's pleasure, Highness."

I turned to the captain and said, "That spanking you promised?"

"As you wish, my prince."

Captain Shane grabbed the queen's arm and marched her to one of the wagons. Grandmother went with them and shooed off any witnesses. Others were telling the newcomers why. I won't go into detail about what the captain yelled at her or Mother's screams. Let's just say Mother walked the next day instead of riding and was very quiet. The murmuring around the troops was approval, and the servants told me later that Grandmother approved also, though Jennifer was shocked. Dedrick sent a message to the king in detail over what happened. The message back was, "I wish I was there to do the deed myself. Sounds like it was definitely needed! If it were a man, I would expect his head or the skin flogged off his back, but a good spanking is enough for a woman, as they are all beloved. On another note, I do not believe those two magic users were working for Droland. Someone is trying to frame my good son."

CHAPTER 8

MATINS RAINBOW

We reached the Valley of Matins Rainbow late the next day. Scouts had already checked out the little valley in advance, and two wizards did a recheck with two rogues and half a dozen fighters. There was a small hunting lodge in the valley but no occupants at that time. I thought, *Droland never goes hunting, and this is not on the map. We may be safe here, but the longer we stay, the more time Droland's allies have to set up an ambush.* I wished greatly that Mother or Grandmother would see the truth. If Father could only see past the smiles and compliments, he would know and put a stop to the issue. Fat chance of that happening. It seemed like Richard might be coming around. Doing his own investigation was a good start. Jennifer was lost. She couldn't get over the fact that I had Mother spanked.

Mother stayed away from me for the first two days in the valley. On the third day, she approached. "Charles."

I looked up from going over plans with the captain and other key leaders. "Yes, Mother?"

"May we talk?"

I moved out from the makeshift table and started walking down a path that no one seemed to be using at the moment. She stepped in beside me.

"Charles, why are we sitting here in this nice place? We are supposed to be heading to Shadow Mountain."

Well, that was a change of tone. She was actually being nice. I answered, "Father ordered us to use this complement of men, and then orders came down with the king's seal for the captain to take the mountain road to Shadow Mountain."

"I'm sorry. I do not understand what that has to do with us staying here."

"Father would never have sent those orders."

"Why?"

"Father knows battle and expected us to run into trouble. For mountain road battle, this is the worst possible complement of men. The roads wind far too much to use lancers, and heavy cavalry is useless for anything except blocking up and holding position in the forest, and less useful in the mountains. We will be massacred unless we retrain them before we continue."

"May the gods preserve us. Do we know who sent the false order?"

"Talk to your maids about who they saw using Father's seal. You won't believe it coming from me. Anything else?"

"Charles, I know you think I hate you. Please understand. You have been the black sheep for so long that it is hard to feel otherwise."

I turned to walk back. I was sad, and I would guess it sounded so in my quiet voice. "Mother, I have been painted black by someone with a silver tongue."

I kept her in my peripheral vision. Mother did not follow. She stood there watching me head back to the table to continue planning. Then she lifted her dress enough to move through the grass and nearly ran to the lodge.

The captain watched her go. "You finally told her why we are here, my prince?"

"Yes. Just before she confirmed that she hates me."

"She will see the truth someday, Highness."

"I know, my friend, but I am afraid it will be too late."

One of the lieutenants boldly asked, "How many times do you have to save someone's hide in your family before they start believing in you?"

Most everyone looked shocked. I smiled. "About eight I think. I'm not really sure." I winked at the captain. Everyone laughed, and we continued planning.

★ ★ ★

As soon as the queen made it back to the lodge, she ordered all maids and servants to the main room. Grandmother and Jennifer entered and sat down.

Mother said, "The two of you will follow my orders in this. Is that understood?"

Mother was hot, and Grandmother and Jennifer were not about to argue. "Yes, Mother, I understand."

"Of course, child, as long as it does not undermine the planning to save your life."

Mother calmed a little. "So, you also are starting to believe in Charles?"

Grandmother said, "How many times does he need to save my life before I start believing he wants me alive and someone else wants me dead?" She didn't tell Mother that she had one of the wizards magically watching Charles.

Mother turned to the servants and maids. "Listen closely, as this will be your only chance. For the next three hours, or for as long as it takes to finish this talk, you are immune to punishment for anything you say. You can say the king is a fool or I am a fool, and no one will do or say anything about it, and no one will hold it against you afterward. What is said in this room will stay in this room." She looked at the old woman who cleaned her clothing. "Martha. I know you have opinions that you share with other maids about me and mine. I want you to tell me your opinions about my sons, Charles and Droland."

In fear, she said, "Majesty?"

"You are a good woman, Martha, and I trust you. I know you have children that you have raised to be good men. Two of your boys are in the Royal Guard. I need the truth about my sons. I need—no, the country needs the truth about my sons."

"My queen, the country knows the truth about your sons. It's your family that is blind."

Shock echoed around the room until the queen said, "Please help me see."

"Very well, my queen. Fact, Dorland is evil, and Charles is good. This was verified by the paladin Joshua just before he suddenly died of poisoning. The king was told, but he did not believe. Fact, Charles was in punishment or study with witnesses for most of the things Droland blamed him for. Fact, Droland was seen at the place of crime and then either entering or leaving Charles's apartments. Twice he was seen with the item of proof in hand while entering Charles's rooms. While entering, my queen! Fact, Droland has secret meetings with people who are known enemies to the crown. We have seen him talking to a person known to be an agent for the demons. Fact, the only two servants bold enough to tell on Droland died in their sleep that same night. Fact, we believe you are blind to the good of Charles because of the silver tongue of Droland. Fact, Droland used the king's seal and then had orders sent to Captain Shane to take the mountain road and to not take any more magic users than absolutely necessary."

The queen look shocked. "These are facts and not just rumors?"

"We saw it happen ourselves. These are witnessed too, my queen. They are not exaggerations or rumors."

The talk went on for several hours. It took time, but the queen managed to get all of them to open up and tell all they knew. When the meeting was over, the queen broke down and cried. Grandmother did not. She gave a written message to her wizard with orders to sneak it to the king without him knowing where it came from. The message stated, "King David, your kingdom is at stake. Droland is conversing with spies from the demon realms. He is planning a takeover. Tell no one. Do your own investigation. Talk to the servants. They know, and they have seen more than you could imagine. Be careful. I warn you in secret, as I wish to continue living. It seems that anyone who tells on Droland dies."

Back at the castle, the message was delivered, and the king read it. He showed it to Richard and Droland. "Someone is trying to undermine this family. Find out who it is and arrest them."

Droland took the message and said, "I will do this for you, Father. Do not worry. I will find them."

The king smiled down on his favorite son. "Find them and bring them to me."

"I will try, Father. I know that, of all people, you can command the truth from them. But they may put up a fight. I will try to bring them to you alive."

"I know you will, son, I know you will."

Droland left. Richard watched him go and said. "Father, what if the message was true?"

"Nonsense. Droland is not evil and would never do anything to jeopardize this kingdom. You should take example from him. He would make a better king than you."

Richard knew that was the end of the subject with his father. He walked back to his apartments. On the way, he stopped off at the general's office. "General."

"Yes, Highness?"

"No one, especially Droland, is to enter my apartments. Find guards loyal to Charles and me that have nothing to do with Droland. Separate them and make them my protectors. Double my guard, including inside my rooms, and have a cleric with a wand to detect poison at all meals. Keep my food separate and Droland's flunkies away from it. Have Mental Watch placed on me and the king without the king knowing. I want to know, and I want you to know, if we have a change in our mental abilities or if we become dominated. I am going to have one of my cleric's place Mental Watch on you."

The general growled, "I can think of a dozen other precautions that need to be taken."

Richard said, "Do them."

"It's about time you came to your senses." The old general got up and walked down the hall to give the orders.

Richard said to himself, "I wonder how many people know. Could it be true? My wizard seems to think I am in danger also. That business with Droland's wizard and cleric was nasty, but I'm beginning to see why Charles is taking such precautions. Maybe, just maybe, Charles is right. I wish I knew who that message came from. I'd warn them."

★★★

Back at camp, I was preparing for sleep when a message came from the castle. "Highness, a sealed message has arrived. It's for your eyes only."

"Who is it from?"

"It has the king's seal, my prince."

"That means little. Very well, set it down outside on the rock by the fire and have Wizard Dedrick and Monsignor Eric Montague come to my tent."

"As you wish, Highness."

Dedrick was over talking to the queen, and Eric was talking to the clerics from the castle. They both came as quickly as they could. Mother and Grandmother came also.

I walked out of my tent and surveyed the assemblage. Apparently, a group of clerics followed Eric, and several wizards followed Dedrick. When the captain saw all these people running to my tent, he ran to me also. Of course, his lieutenants followed, and so did many of the men. At least fifty people were standing outside my tent. "Gentlemen and ladies, I am sorry for the confusion, but I only needed one wizard and one cleric. I received a message from the crown, and I need them to check it for issues." I pointed to the rock with the rolled-up scroll on it. Within seconds, everyone had cleared away from the rock, but no one left.

Dedrick said, "I will check for evil and powerful magic. Eric, please check for poison and curses." They did, and it was poisoned, cursed, evil, and full of powerful magic. Only the gods knew what else.

Still, I was a bit curious. "Anyway to read it without getting burnt?"

Eric just stared at me as if I was losing my mind, but Dedrick said, "Yes."

I smiled. "Never know unless you ask. How?"

Dedrick smiled. I can turn someone ethereal, and they can move their head through the message, reading as they go. It is difficult to read that way, as the words are very close to the eyes. But if you close one eye and focus with the other, you can do it. I have done it several times with old, crumbly scripts. None of the evil on it will affect the ethereal, so the reader should be safe."

"Good, then turn me ethereal."

Dedrick turned white. "Not you, my prince. One of my apprentices will read the letter while another takes notes. You have not been taught how to read magic and, as you are magically inclined, may inadvertently trigger something."

"Very well. Please continue."

Dedrick called forward two men and gave one a quill pen, ink, and parchment. On the other, he placed a spell that made him invisible. The cleric next to me was using some spells and could hear him as he moved to the letter and bent down. I could barely hear the words even in the surrounding silence. Not a heartbeat or a tiny breath from fifty people disturbed that reading.

So, little brother, you sent a message to Father telling him all about me. Father does not believe your paddle. He does not know who sent the note, but he foolishly gave it to me to investigate. My wizard traced the message to someone near you, wherever you are hiding. Only you would be so brash. Coward! Why did you not sign it? That would have made Father hunt you down. Now I am forced to take matters into my own hands. If you are reading this, then the matter will shortly be ended, and all with you will be silenced. I will give a great performance showing my sadness over your timely death.

Droland

The head came out of the scroll and turned to Dedrick. "My lord, the magic is a Find Object spell. They know where we are or at least where this message ended.

I yelled, "To arms! To arms!" Men started to scramble. "Dedrick, Eric, protect the women. Captain, we planned this out. You and your men know what to do. Move it! Lieutenant, help me with my armor."

We were ready for the attack. We were very lucky, as twenty high-level magic-using demons teleported right into our trap. All twenty demons died before they could spell their way out. After the forest battle, we knew what we were fighting against, and we had prepared well.

We started packing and were on the move before daybreak. Mother, Grandmother, and Jennifer were in wagons—covered up, silent, and nervous. Maids were riding their horses and wearing their clothes. We reached the beginning of the mountain road by midday. We did not stop. There were no lancers now. My cavalry was all light and mixed with sword and bow. Runners were out ensuring our safety ahead, and clerics had Mental Watch on each runner so we would know if any issues came up the instant they manifested.

CHAPTER 9

THE LONG ROAD

The mountain road was easily twice as long as the forest route. The road was narrow at points, but ambushes were not possible if one was diligent and had men to check the way. Small caravans sometimes took the mountain road to avoid bandits. Large or heavy caravans could not make the trip because the road became quite steep. Going up was never a problem for a wagonload of goods—just add more horses or men to push or pull. Going down was near impossible, as most downward slopes ended in a quick turn or a cliff, and the horses had a difficult time going down slowly. Additionally, areas sometimes collapsed, and avalanches sometimes blocked the road.

Father sends troops down this road several times a year to ensure safe travel. Duke Edward does the same from his end but only a short way into the mountains. That was the surprise. Duke Edward and his men showed up on the fourth day. They were ragged, and many needed healing, including the duke. Thanks to Richard, they had heard of our problems, and the duke decided to come to our rescue. After checking him to ensure he was not a demon in disguise or being mind controlled, we welcomed him with open arms. Having ten clerics with us helped a lot. The duke's men were extremely beat-up.

Once we tended to the wounded, I asked Duke Edward, "What happened, sir?"

He looked up after watching the wound in his arm close and the hairs grow back. "Demons, Highness. That's what happened. Prince Richard sent message that the queen was in trouble. We put together this group to come help with the travel, and we had to fight our way here. The enemy was not prepared for someone coming from our direction. They were waiting for you. Knew where you were and everything about you. Beat that knowledge out of one of the enemy survivors. Seems they think you're using lancers and heavy cavalry. I see you're not that stupid, boy. Your scouts saw us hours ago. Thank you for speeding up. I lost many men. Saving these is appreciated."

"You're welcome, sir. Thank you for the rescue."

"We're not out of this yet, boy."

Duke Edward was probably the only person, besides Father, who could get away with calling me "boy." If I had a choice, he'd be my father, but I had no choice in the matter.

Adding nearly eighty trained mountain fighting men and the duke, a seasoned general who had just temporarily cleared the way, was a boost to morale and gave us a chance to make up time. I addressed the duke. "Sir, did you leave any demons or magic users alive?"

"Not that I am aware of, boy. You know me better than that."

I should have known, as he taught me most of my tactics. "Good." I turned to the captain. "Have everyone mount up. We are going to be moving as fast as possible for the next two days. The way is temporarily clear. I'm going to take a chance that it will take the enemy time to transfer a good size force to these mountains. Get them together, Captain, and move them out. And, Captain."

"Yes, my prince."

"Warn the troops. We won't be stopping for the night."

"Highness, we could try to push straight through. It's only four more days if the road is clear."

"No, Captain. The road will not be clear that long. Droland cannot afford for us to reach safety. We rest tomorrow night and prepare for a long fight to Shadow Mountain."

The duke looked up. "Droland?"

I looked at him sadly. "We have proof that Droland is behind the demon attacks, sir."

"Figures. I never liked that boy. Always smiling and saying nice thing to everyone. Never down to earth with the truth. My daughters don't like him either. They say he's always using the same lines on all of them. Droland thinks they are stupid because they come from the farmlands. Fool! Farmland women may not know big-city ways, but they know an evil, lying sewer rat when they see one."

For some reason, I hugged the duke. It just came out. I must have turned red, but the duke hugged back and then held me at arm's length. "That bad?"

"Yes, sir." I turned and mounted. We headed off as fast as the wagons could go. We used rope and heavy warhorses to speed them up and slow them down. We made good time until late in the second day. One of our scouts died. The cleric who was mentally watching him reported it instantly—where, when, and almost how.

"Highness, he was traveling point about half a league ahead. He was surprised, then afraid, then in immense pain, and then dead."

"Thank you." I turned to the captain. "One of your men?"

"Yes, Highness. If something made him afraid, then it was not an avalanche or falling."

The cleric added, "He did not move before death. If he fell over the cliff or was hit by an avalanche, he would move at least a little downward, if nothing else. It seems he died in the saddle."

"You can tell that with that spell?"

"Yes, Highness."

"I need to learn that one." I turned to the captain again. "We knew our luck would not last forever. We have something up in front of us that kills very quickly."

Duke Edward said, "I have been thinking about all you've said. They failed with subtlety at the start, they failed with an ambush at the forest, and they failed with surprise in the valley. I would use brute force next. Darn that mountain. It keeps us from teleporting to my castle or anywhere close."

I said, "If I could be sure of a safe place, we would have already teleported the queen there. I do agree with your thinking; blocking up our passage with deadly brute strength would be their next tactic. Hold us long enough for reinforcements to catch us in the rear. Pin us between them and then smash us. Captain, send out two rogues. Give them any spells they want. Find out what's waiting for us."

Two rogues came up. They received several spells, including Flying, Invisibility, and Lesser Silence. Silence was placed on objects and then handed to them to take. They flew away, and we started making plans.

Soon the rogues returned. I felt the spells first. "Gentlemen, something using spells is coming. I can feel the spells." The duke gave me a funny look.

A cleric said, "The rogues are returning, Highness."

"Good. Maybe we'll find out if our planning is on the right track."

Two rogues, no longer invisible, came around the bend and landed near us. The clerics immediately started healing. Both rogues were bleeding and badly burned, and they smelled like Dedrick's lab.

One rogue said, "The road is clear, Highness."

I looked at them, astonished, and asked, "How would that be if this was an information-gathering assignment?"

They looked at each other, a little ashamed. "Two rogues, Highness. You can't expect two rogues to not mess with the enemy if they see the chance. We saw a perfect setup for two rogues to cause major damage to the enemy and took it."

I was both elated and upset. "Explain."

"Yes, my prince. We took off over the mountain and behind the rocks until we were well past the designated area. Then we flew down to the road and worked our way up until we found the enemy. They were watching their back but neither heard nor saw us coming. There were about ten demons. One had a leash with a small black dragon on it. The dragon did not look happy and fought the magical leash but could not get away and had to do his master's bidding. One demon was clearly in charge and using magic. I went to backstab the magic user. Del went to play with the dragon."

"Play with the dragon?" My eyes must have shown their surprise.

Del took up the conversation. "While Fred stabbed the mage, I stole the leash and ordered the dragon to attack the demons. You should have seen the surprise when the one trying to control the dragon could not talk. The dragon ate him first. Soon it was just the dragon and us."

The captain asked, "How did you plan this if you were silenced?"

Fred said indignantly, "We weren't silenced. Two brass pieces were silenced. I tugged on the string holding Del and me together and took him a ways away. We put down the brass pieces and moved where we could talk."

I had to ask. "Two things. First, why did the mage not use magic on you? I did not sense that kind of spell. And second, what happened to the dragon?" Several of the men looked around the sky apprehensively.

Del answered, "Oh, that's simple. I snuck my copper in the belt pouch of the leash holder, and Fred placed his down the shirt of the mage. Lesser Silence only takes up a five-foot area. Hard to use spells or control a dragon if you cannot be heard. Oh, and the dragon promised to return home to its mother if we let it go. It flew off north. It was a bad fight. The moment we attacked, we became visible."

I smiled. "I should give both of you the highest award possible, but you disobeyed orders and took the chance of leaving us in a position of not knowing what's out there. We'll call it even. You have your bragging rights, and the captain won't have you flogged."

The captain said, "Dismissed, both of you, and don't ever disobey orders again. The prince is in a good mood or your hides would be mine." The captain patted them on the back and smiled proudly.

I said, "Captain, that group was meant to hold, not destroy. I think we have company coming up behind us fast. We need to get moving and find a good ambush place."

The duke said, "I know just the spot if we can make it. It's about half a day away. We'll have to travel all night again."

"I don't like that. We are already tired from two days' travel and no rest."

The duke said, "This place will give us a good chance of holding off an army without even trying. Most of us can rest when we get there. We can take turns holding the line."

I trusted the duke. If he said that was our best hope, then we needed to get there—and fast. "Captain, move us out and make haste." The captain nearly ran to give the news. The line started moving quickly.

Early the next morning, we reached the summit. The duke and I were both trying to help a wagon uphill. I looked around. "Duke, this is a bad place to be caught with our armor off."

"Boy, save your strength and push!"

I went back to pushing, thinking how I love the straightforward way they speak in the farmlands. I realized I love farming also. Every time I visit the duke, I end up talking with the farmers. I find them easier to understand and far more straightforward. No politically correct jibber jabber, no skirting around the issue. A farmer tells you just how it is, but you have to ask first. He expects you to know. In addition, I love seeing what I planted blossom and grow, and it doesn't hurt that the duke has three lovely daughters who are actually nice to talk to. Not like the ones at court.

Captain Shane came back to us. "The road becomes very narrow just before the top of this rise. I'm changing the men to single file. Movement will be slow. We hold the high ground already."

A little while later, the last wagon reached the top and took off on its own. The duke looked over at me with a smile. "You always like getting your hands dirty, boy, but you should be in the front directing the troops."

"The troops are in good hands, and the men like seeing their prince with the same blisters they have."

We both smiled, as those were his words to me the last time I visited. We climbed into our saddles and headed for the front. The knights were bringing up the rear on foot—a solid steel wall to gain us time if necessary, though I truly would have hated to sacrifice them. There was no need to worry. We reached the ambush point in plenty of time. Runners reported seeing a large contingent of creatures only a few leagues back and coming fast. We donned our armor.

Duke Edward said, "This is it."

I looked around and asked, "What?"

"Look closer, boy, and think of tactics."

From where I stood, I could see almost a quarter league of the road we were just on. There would be no surprises from that direction. The road switched back and forth up to my position at a steep climb. It had been extremely difficult getting the wagons up that rise. To my right was a long, even section of road overlooking the entire hill. A good bowman could easily pick off a target anywhere on that climb. *A good bowman.* I was in charge of over one hundred great bowmen. However, my bowmen would be in plain sight, and the front section of the enemy could pick them off. Still, a cross bolt would lose a lot of power shooting nearly straight up like that, and it would be difficult for the enemy to hit a target shooting up a hill at that angle. I watched the knights and their tower shields reach the ridge. At the tightest place, they had to go no more than three abreast. They could stop the enemy there as my bowmen picked the enemy off. The other knights could supply cover with those tower shields.

I smiled at the duke and said, "Thanks, my friend," and patted him on the shoulder. "Captain!"

"Yes, Highness."

"Bring everything and everyone to the top of the summit and set up camp way back. Prepare for wounded. Set up a barricade at that narrow junction down where the road reaches this turn. I want to trap the enemy along that long, narrow upslope. This section flattens out, and there is a great view of the entire road. Set bowmen all along this flat. Have them hide behind the knights. The knights are to use their tower shields as cover for our bowmen."

The captain looked at the areas I was pointing out and smiled. "Good setup, my prince. As long as they don't have very many magic users, we could hold this area and take out a large force. But they can backtrack and hide behind the hill. There they can wait for reinforcements, and we will have to stay and hold."

"Order the bowmen and shield knights to stay out of sight until the enemy is all the way to the barricade. Once they are bunched up, have the wizards remove the section of road behind the enemy. They'll have no place to run, and we can pick them off. Ensure the archers understand that magic users and flying creatures die first. Have a group watching the barricade. I don't want the enemy teleporting behind the barricade to attack the knights from the back. Have fighters spread out and watch all around for creatures trying to flank us. Captain, keep it quiet. I want them to think we left a small contingent for delaying tactics and the rest of us are running for our lives. Make the group at the barricade look ragged and wounded."

The captain took off, quietly giving orders to his lieutenants.

"Duke Edward."

"Yes, Highness?"

"Please protect my mother. Take two magic users and as many fighters as you need."

He saluted with fist on breastplate. "With my life, my prince."

I put a hand on his arm, "Father has not visited because Droland has been poisoning Father against you. Father is confused and doesn't know who to trust anymore. I trust you more than any man alive. I'd trust you with my life."

"Something needs to be done about Droland, my boy, and soon."

"I know. Believe me, I know."

Everyone was pulling back, and one of the drivers yelled, "Make way." I had to move or get run over. Camp was pushed back until the lieutenant that was placed in charge was sure they would not be seen or heard. Men were following the duke toward Mother. It appeared to be all his men except a magic user and one of the Commeatus clerics. I thought to myself, *The duke does not trust our troops any more than Father trusts him. Good man. I worry about which men belong to Droland every second of every day.*

A long line of knights with bowmen were standing at the ready only fifty paces behind the flat. Each man had filled his quiver and stuffed arrows into his belt. One, with big ears, had an arrow stuck behind one ear and an extra bow string hanging from the other. They were so tired. I could see it in their faces. We had to make this quick and then get some rest.

Dedrick and Eric came to me. I asked, "You two know what your part is?"

Dedrick answered, "Yes, boy!"

I looked up at him in anger but saw the smile on his and Eric's faces and burst out laughing. The troops looked at us and smiled. Laughter can do wonders for bringing up spirits.

Dedrick said, "If the enemy takes the bait, then I will be in position to collapse that rock above the turn down there when the last of the enemy is within range of our bowmen. That will effectively cut off a retreat. Eric is to be ready to heal bowmen and knights on the bowline. This plan is contingent on the enemy trying to remove that barricade without slowing down. I do not see why they would be that foolish. What are you going to do?"

"I will be the bait."

I pulled my bow and headed down to the barricade while Eric and Dedrick were yelling, "No, my prince! No!"

I reached the barricade as the first of the enemy came into sight around the turn. I held my bow in one hand raised high above my head and yelled, "We hold them here! We hold them for the queen and Kayland." Cheers from the barricade rang out all around me.

The enemy saw me and charged up the hill, yelling, "Kill the prince. Kill the prince."

A magic user of some type started to fly up to check ahead, but when he saw me, he yelled, "The fool stayed behind to protect his mother. Kill him. Kill him now, and our path to the queen will be wide open. Look at their tiny numbers. The dragon did his job well. They are all wounded. Kill them quickly and eat that fool prince."

The magic user flew directly at me. I nocked my bow and waited. He flew erratically, trying to dodge, but lost his concentration and smoothed out while drawing a rod. I fired and took him in the breast. It did not even slow him down. I nocked and fired three more times before he reached me and died at my feet from over twenty arrows that hit him from the little knot of men assigned to protect our flank. I stepped on the rod and then kicked him over the side of the cliff. I picked up the magical rod and put it in my belt. At about that time, the enemy hit the barricade with such force the knights lost three feet of ground. But then the enemy could not back up for another slam. They blocked each other's way, and they kept coming in, pushing hard to get at the barricade. They crawled over each other, and our archers took the ones on top out. I literally stood on the backs of two of our knights, fighting with both swords to stem the tide. Then bang! The rock at the turn crumbled, and within seconds, arrows were clouding the sky, destroying the enemy. They tried to back up, but there was no place to go. It rained arrows down on them, and bolts returned fire toward our men. The bolts lost so much energy they bounced off the shields. Our arrows gained in energy and pierced their armor. Magic users flew out from their group, trying to escape, only to be concentrated on and killed instantly. The smart ones used Magical Shift to get around the block, and Dedrick was waiting for them with six other wizards. Only the ones who could teleport got away. Very few of those made it, as magic users were first, and many died before they realized what was happening. They were so surprised not one spell came toward the barricade. I was cut in a dozen different places, but a potion or two took care of that. This part of the battle was over. We needed rest.

I ordered the captain, "Ensure there are no others to attack us. Set up guards and search the enemy for magic. Recover any arrows and bolts you can find intact. Before this is over, we may need everything we can obtain to fight with. When you are done, dump the bodies into the gorge. We rest and sleep today and tonight. We push on tomorrow, and we may not stop."

"Understood, Highness. That was a very large force, my prince."

"Yes. This is more than just an attempt on our lives. I am afraid that you, the duke, and I may not gain much rest, my friend."

He smiled a wicked smile. "At least I can say I fought in a battle where we killed two thousand demons, and no one died."

I looked at him in astonishment, as I had been about to ask what our losses were. "None?"

"None, my prince." He bowed lower than I had ever seen, and cheers rang out. I did not even realize that others were watching. The captain turned and started barking orders. Men scrambled, revitalized and ready for another battle.

I thought back on my lessons. "Don't allow energy renewed to fool you. It lasts only a short time and weakens your enemy greatly. If you notice that the enemy has a second wind, then stand back and protect yourself. Let the renewed energy flow through your enemy. Then take him when it is over and he is weak and helpless." Now would be a bad time for another battle. My men were quickly becoming weak and helpless. I went to check on Mother.

Mother, Grandmother, and Jennifer were near her tent helping a knight who required his arm to be regrown. The women and clerics were saying to hold him, and he was about to scream his furry. One of the clerics tried to tell him, "Losing an arm hurts. Growing one back is worse. We need to hold you."

The knight's lieutenant was running toward the clerics. I walked over before the lieutenant could reach them. "Let him go!" Everyone let go of him quickly.

The knight sharply sat up and saluted across his chest with a stump. "My prince."

I looked sternly at the others as the knight's lieutenant came up. I said loudly enough for all in the area to hear, "A knight does not require someone to hold him." I looked at the knight and said, "Give me your knife." He used his other hand to remove his knife and handed it to me. It had a good, hard wood handle, wrapped in strong leather. "Place this handle in your mouth so we won't have to replace teeth and lie back down." The knight smiled, placed the knife handle in his mouth, and lay down. "Now hold still, *my knight*, while the cleric grows you an arm to defend the queen with."

The knight did not move as I looked him in the eyes. "Go ahead and start, Cleric. Something all of you should know. A knight never needs someone to hold his hand!"

The knight bit deeply into his dagger handle as the cleric started the process. The knight bit the leather in half and nearly the handle in half before the cleric finished. I never took my eyes off his, and he never took his eyes off mine. There was a smile of determination on his face, and when the cleric finished, the knight opened his mouth and said in a weak voice but in a tone that bespoke of pride, "See, my prince, I still have all my teeth."

I unclipped my dagger and sheath from my belt. It was a good blade, magical, with perfect balance. "Yes, but you ruined your dagger." I placed mine on his chest and said, "Have this one, my knight."

I walked away as the knight held up my dagger and yelled, "The prince!"

All knights in the area echoed, "The prince!"

I smiled as I walked off to check the rest of my troops. The knight's lieutenant fell in behind me with six other knights. I whispered to the lieutenant just loud enough for the others to hear, but no one except the knights, "If any of you are thinking of cutting off your arm or leg to get another one of my daggers, don't! That was my only one."

One said, "Darn."

The others clapped him on the shoulder. Soon I was surrounded by knights, and they blocked my way. The lieutenant stepped forward and said, "We know what you did back there on the road. You put your life on the line with the rest of us to give us a chance to make the trap work. Being a prince, you are a knight by birthright. I claim you a knight by blood and deed. Blood spilt fighting side by side with other knights, placing the queen before yourself and your life, and having the courage to face the enemy and bring them to you when all odds were against us surviving." He raised his voice. "I claim you knight in battle and spirit."

Cheers roared through the troops. I must have turned red, as the lieutenant said, "And he has the humility of a knight. He blushes well." The cheers turned to laughter, and many gauntleted hands slapped my shoulders. I took it all with a smile but had the first cleric I could find heal my bruised shoulders and arms.

CHAPTER 10

THE BLESSING

The troops rested that day and night. The duke, Captain Shane, Dedrick, Eric, and I spent most of our time in conference. The duke said, "Charles, you cannot be correct. Even Droland isn't that bold."

I turned to him and said, "Duke Edward, the evidence points to a major war with the demons. That last group was far too big to be a raiding party, and they reached us way too fast. They had to be in the mountains already. Besides, they knew their target was the queen."

The duke shook his head. "Agreed, but making a pact with demons and killing off his family just to be king! I can't believe it. I won't believe it."

Dedrick added, "I know he is after you, and for some reason your mother, but making pacts with demons? Droland is not stupid. He may be power hungry, but he cannot believe that demons will actually allow him any control if they take over our lands."

I thought for a second. "Agreed, he is not stupid. There has to be some underlying reason for this. Droland must have been promised something that he wants very badly."

Eric asked, "Badly enough to betray his family and kingdom?"

I answered, "Yes. Perhaps he does not plan to live here after the battle starts, and perhaps he does—I do not know. I plan to find out if he is behind this war. As soon as my charge to get Mother to safety and watch the blessing of your child is completed, I am going to investigate our forces along the borders to the demon realms. I will not have us overrun by demons without a good fight. We will plan this out more, and in secret, once we reach your castle. Until then, we concentrate on getting the queen to safety. Agreed?"

Everyone agreed. As they left my tent, I stopped Dedrick and waited for the others to leave. When everyone was gone, I turned to the wise old wizard. "Dedrick, Father is in trouble, and so is Richard."

Dedrick said, "I've had word from one of my spies in the castle that Richard has ordered precautions. He has gathered all his and your loyal men and stays in his apartments unless well accompanied. Clerics are checking for poison at every meal and on everything constantly. People coming and going are searched. Your father is being closely watched, and the watchers are loyal to Richard."

"This is good news, and thank the gods Richard is starting to see the light."

"Yes, my prince."

"Dedrick, when we reach the castle, you and I will be making a teleportation trip out and back each night. I am going to find out what's going on. Be ready."

"My prince, we will have a hard ride two hours' south of the castle to get away from the interference that Shadow Mountain creates for magical travel."

I said, "Then we'll have a cleric ready for mending saddle sores."

Dedrick smiled and left.

It was a quiet uneventful night, and I slept well. The next morning, we broke camp early and headed out. Morale was high, and we made fast, easy progress. The worst of the road was behind us. Two days later, we reached the duke's castle. The Castle of Shadow's Shadow.

Shadow's Shadow was built at the foot of the Shadow Mountains and is protected from all sides by two hundred feet of cliff wall. Water comes down from the mountains in a great waterfall. The river runs from the base of the waterfall through a wide cliff and off the south end into the valley below. The castle was built on the cliff, with the river running through it. It is probably one of the most beautiful sights in the kingdom. A large city sits busy at the bottom of the cliff, its center about a league out from where the waterfall reaches the bottom. At one time, the river ran around the city, until the city outgrew the large island. Now there are bridges crossing the river, allowing access to both sides of the valley and the island city, and houses reach nearly up to the castle cliff.

We rode into the castle to cheers and cries of anguish as people saw the queen but did not see their husbands with the duke's men. Still, there were many who returned, and as the men dismounted, there were hugs of joy.

Mother and I had not talked for days. I decided to end the silence. As I rode by, I said, "We're at the castle, so you're back in charge. Your orders, Majesty?"

She looked at me kindly and said, "Thank you for saving our lives. My orders are simple. Keep command. You're better at it than your father."

I was shocked, and my face had to have shown it. The duke reached out and pushed my jaw shut. Mother rode ahead and dismounted with the rest of the women, a smile on her face as she greeted the duchess and her daughters. The duke said, "Boy, you need to learn, or my daughters are going to rip you apart. Never try to get the best on a woman. They always win. Now you're stuck with command, and she knows you hate taking command more than anything else. Queen's orders. You have charge while she's here."

"You have any caves nearby?"

"Yes. Why?"

I turned to him and said, "I'm thinking of becoming a hermit."

The duke laughed. "Won't work. She'll have you dragged back. Besides, she's right. You are better than your father."

"Right now, that's not hard to be. Let's talk about what you're going to do to ensure my mother's safety while in your care."

"My care?"

"Yes. She passed it to me, and I am passing it to you. I am magical and cannot legally take that big of a command. Besides, I have the blessing and other issues to attend, as you well know. I will probably be sleeping during the day most of the time, as I will be awake most of the night."

"Understood, my prince. This is my plan." We headed into the castle with his captain talking to our captain and orders for the watch already flowing smoothly. The watch was tripled. All of the royal family were constantly watched and protected. The way the duke set it up, even I could not see a way in without being instantly detected.

The duke and I did have an argument over the number of escorts that would accompany my nightly missions. He won.

I was not allowed to see the baby until the wizard and cleric determined that she was not ill and not possessed. However, I could hear her now and then. It was a weak cry, lowering in volume as she tired and gaining strength after a short sleep.

I knew what was wrong. I didn't know how I knew or what I could do, but I knew. I tried to get to her side to help, but I was not allowed in.

Mother and Grandmother did everything they could to comfort the child. Jennifer almost never put her down. Still, she continued to cry. It was time for the blessing, and the child was still crying. The blessing could not continue.

There had to be total quiet for a queen's blessing. Everyone was gathered. Thousands were in the courtyard. Finally, it was my turn to take my place beside Mother. I walked in, passed Mother, and walked up to Jennifer and the child. I took her from Jennifer, placed a finger on her lips, and said, "Do not fear, little Annabel. I am here. I will protect you." Instantly, she stopped crying. She looked directly at me and cuddled closer. She closed her little eyes and fell asleep in my arms. A very tired baby girl.

I handed her off to her mother. The duchess looked at me as if I were a savior. I smiled and shrugged. With sadness in my voice, I said, "The gods have given her a gift. She knows that a great catastrophe is coming to this land, and she is afraid." A look of great determination crossed my face as I said, "Now she knows I will protect her no matter the cost." I bent over and kissed her cheek. I turned and walked back to my position.

The room was silent until Grandmother whispered, "That boy is full of surprises."

Now that the child was quiet, the blessing could come. Mother held the child in her arms and placed a hand in the anointing oil and then on Annabel's head. She said the longest and most beautiful blessing I think I have ever heard. She let the gods flow through her, allowing inspiration beyond that of normal mortal men or women. Even Monsignor Eric Montague was impressed to tears of joy.

The crowd went wild with celebration once the child was blessed. When they quieted down, the queen held up a hand, and everyone went silent as the queen addressed them.

In a most humble and sincere voice, Mother did something I would have never expected. She addressed all saying, "I am sorry, and I apologize." The crowd was so silent I could hear the sound of butterfly wings near the bush to my left. Mother continued, "I am sorry for not coming sooner, for ignoring people who are most dear to my heart, and for not visiting my close friend, the duchess. I have no excuses, and therefore I am also apologizing for my family and the king. I also wish to thank the duke and the wonderful men of Shadow Mountain for coming to our rescue. Without them, we may not have made it this far. Evil times are about to come upon our lands. Prepare. Be ready. Though I will spread this word to all I know, of all my subjects, you will understand and take heed. Today, we feast for the blessing of the child." Here is where her voice changed to determination and anger. "Tomorrow, we watch, wait, and prepare for battle. My son," she motioned toward me, "is going to do all he can to prevent this demon war, but should he fail, we will end it for him, for the king, and for our children!" She stepped down. There was no quieting them now. Cheers and bold talk rang throughout the day. I am told it continued throughout the night. I wouldn't know. I was not there.

CHAPTER 11

WAR

Dedrick, Eric, Duke Edward, and eighty good men accompanied me as we rode south from the Castle of Shadow's Shadow. Due to the mountain's unique ability to mess with extra-planner travel, spells like Teleportation and Shift and all planer travel were forbidden. Often, those trying to use extra-planner travel ended up lost forever or in parts spread throughout the mountain range. The interference lasted until one was about five leagues from the castle, but seven leagues was safer.

After three hours, we reached the place that Eric normally used for his travels to and from this area, the Shrine of Commeatus at Mist Crossing. The shrine was a typical shrine to the god of travel, but it also had an artifact stone called the Stone of Travel. Using this stone, one could teleport up to eight people anywhere within the kingdom, except around Shadow Mountain or places that were protected against that type of travel.

We approached with caution, but there was no one there. The men fanned out to keep watch while the duke, Eric, Dedrick, one apprentice, two Commeatus clerics, a knight, and I mounted the stone. There were only two ways through the mountains from the demon realms, the Higger Pass and Crooked Pass. We were going to see both tonight. One of the clerics prayed, and we were no longer standing on the stone. We were on a granite road and almost run over. An entire regiment of three hundred men were riding past the Shrine of Commeatus only a league southeast of the fort at Crooked Pass. When eight men showed up, swords were drawn and bows pulled. Someone recognized me and yelled out, "The prince!"

The column came to a halt as the word was passed up line. The captain came riding back with three knights. He dismounted and went to one knee.

"Rise, Captain."

"Thank you, Prince Charles. Highness, what is going on?"

"I will answer your questions after you tell me why three hundred men and their captain are not at their posts."

The captain reached into his saddlebags and pulled out a scroll. He handed it to me. It read:

Captain Drins:

We cannot supply you with the reinforcements requested. We are having a problem on the western border with the Undead King. You are to take all your men, leaving a minimal crew, to the fort at Dragonback Pass.

I checked the seal, and it was from the king. I handed it back and looked at the captain. "Captain, do you trust me?

"With my life, Highness."

"Then we will talk when you are back in the fort and ensuring that the demons have not already taken over. Do you have horses for the eight of us?"

The captain raised his hand, and quickly eight horses were provided. He turned to the men that were now on foot and ordered, "Catch up as quickly as you can." Then he yelled, "Turn this column around and head with all speed back to the fort. Move it!"

The column did a quick about-face and shot out north toward the fort. We were there in little time, and some very worried men let us in. Three dead demons were in the center of the fort, and men needed healing.

The captain said, "Report!" as clerics tended to the wounded.

"They were testing us, Captain, checking our strength. We killed these three, but one got away to report."

The captain turned to me and waited.

I shook my head and turned to the duke. "Believe me now?" I did not give him time to answer. "Get me ink and a pen. Captain, Droland has sided with the demons. He is using the great seal of the king to divert our troops from the demon front. Hold this fort at all costs. We are going to Fort Simons to send reinforcements. You hold this fort with your lives. I will be back after I warn the Higger Pass, if I don't die in the attempt." I took the pen while Dedrick held the ink bottle. On the back of the king's message I wrote, "Droland is using the king's seal to destroy Kayland. Pay no attention to any messages from the crown. Pay no attention to anything coming from anyone. If Droland shows up, arrest the trader. Only if Prince Richard or the king show up in person, and you authenticate that they are not demons in disguise, will these orders change. On penalty of death. Prince Charles." I handed the order to the captain.

He read it and said, "We will not let the demons pass this point! You hurry up with those reinforcements."

"Dedrick, Fort Simons please."

He capped the ink and put it and the pen away. He looked over at his apprentice. "You know that area?"

"Yes, my lord. I was born near there."

"I am placing us one hundred feet in front of the fort main gate. Can you match?"

"Yes, my lord."

"Duke, Charles, Eric, and two others are mine. You have the rest. Grab hold, gentlemen." We reached out and took his arm as he said, "Aegretudo Eo Ire Itum," and we were at Fort Simons.

I stepped out and yelled, "Hail, the fort! Is General Parndom there?"

A voice from the fort yelled back. "It's the middle of the night. Who are you and why do you want the general?"

"I am Prince Charles, and Kayland is under attack. We are coming in."

We started forward. The gate stayed closed. As we approached, an old mage looked over the top. "Yes, that is Prince Charles, and no, it is not another horrific demon. Open the gate, fool."

The gate swung open. As soon as I made it inside, I could see that the general had already been told there was some issue. Now a runner was entering his cabin to tell him it was the prince. "Dedrick, parchment, pen, and ink please." I wrote out the same orders and added major reinforcements to the fort at Crooked Pass. As soon as the general reached my position, I handed him the orders. He read them over with eyes narrowing.

He turned to me and said, "So, this is why the demons have been testing us. Tried to pretend they were Prince Droland. We killed that one almost before we checked. I'll have two thousand men, supplies, and all kinds of magic up there in eight hours. You coming, Highness?"

"I need to warn Higger Pass, but I'll be there before you."

"That a challenge, my prince?"

"Yes, it is."

"I'll take that challenge." He turned and started yelling orders.

Dedrick looked over at his apprentice.

"Same as before, my lord. I know that pass a little less, but I should make it."

"Same as before. All touch me."

We were instantly in front of the fort at Higger Pass. The others did not make it. Suddenly, they showed. The apprentice apologized, "Sorry, my lord. I missed the intended target."

Dedrick said, "Darn, you had to use your last teleport."

"Yes, my lord."

"Not your fault. I am asking a lot of you." Dedrick turned to me. "Highness, when we leave here, we are on our own."

I looked at him. "Understood." Then I turned to the apprentice mage. "Thank you for getting them this far."

"Your welcome, Highness."

I stepped forward. "Hail, the fort!"

An arrow shot out and landed between my legs. I am quite sure the archer would have hit me if he wanted to. Whoever it was yelled, "Who are you and what do you want?"

"I am Prince Charles, and I want to talk to the one in charge."

"If you're Prince Charles, then you would know who's in charge."

"Captain Kroko had better still be in charge and manning his post."

"It is the prince. Open the gate. Highness, hurry up and enter."

We ran to the fort and in through the gate. We were surrounded by men with swords out and pointed directly at our hearts. A knight captain said, "Check them. If even one is a demon, kill them all."

Some boy held a gem to his eye. "Father, they are not demons."

Everyone went down on one knee. I smiled. "Rise, good men of Kayland. Rise."

They all stood. I turned to the knight captain. "Did you not receive orders?"

"I received orders all right. The most absurd orders I have ever received. Then I received a visit from Prince Droland backing up those orders. He left only an hour ago."

"What did your orders say, Knight Captain? What did my demon-loving brother tell you?"

His eyes widened when he heard "demon-loving brother." He said, "Your brother told us to follow your father's orders and help with the battle going on with Duke Edward's people. Seems that Duke Edward's people are uprising." He looked over at Duke Edward and smiled. "Hello, Cousin." Then he turned to me. "Your brother seems to forget who is and isn't related. I not only ignored the order. I sent word to my friend at Shanloade. Reinforcements will be here in two days."

"Good job, Knight Captain, but two days is a long time off. I am expecting you to be attacked in just hours by half the demon army."

He smiled. "So am I. That is why there are hundreds of traps in the woods and everyone is sleeping fully armed and in light armor. My prince, I have been preparing for war for three years. We will hold them. I have enough arrows here to stop an entire army. You cannot breach the wall once I drop the rock." He pointed to the north wall. "That magically protected wall stands three hundred feet above the pass, and yes, siege engines could destroy the doors if you could get the siege engines up to the doors. Once the rock drops, the entire climb will crumble, leaving a rock mess that will take days to clear, and the ones doing the clearing will be under constant bow shot the entire time. I have changed my complement to almost all archers. We have some mages and clerics but mostly archers, and they are the best in Kayland."

I looked at him hard and said, "Drop the rock."

He looked stunned. "Highness, are you sure? If I drop the rock, then the pass will be closed for a long time."

I said, "If I were going to try to bring an army through here, the first thing I would do is stop the rock from dropping. I would bring a mage or two who could place magic on it so that it can't drop."

"They would have to get close to the rock and use magic that we would detect."

"When Droland was here, did his mages inspect the rock?"

The knight captain looked like he had just sniffed out something bad and said, "Yes, they did, and they insisted on reinforcing the dropping mechanism."

"Knight Captain, if that rock cannot drop, will you have time while being attacked to find out why?"

"No, Highness."

I ordered, "Drop that rock now!"

The captain turned to his men. "Drop the rock!" Wheels turned, ropes broke, and the rock was still in place.

I looked at Dedrick.

Dedrick smiled. "I'm on it, Highness." Dedrick and Eric ran up the battlements and dispelled all spells. The rock stayed in place. Then Dedrick said a spell and flew around the rock. When he reached the other side, where we could never have seen, he yelled another spell, and the rock instantly dropped. I watched as the rock took out every last bridge and most of the road heading up the pass. It also rolled down into the pass, crushing hundreds of demons that were cleverly hidden beneath ground-colored hides. The war was on.

Dedrick flew over to us and said, "Stone Merge. They used Stone Merge to meld the stone into the natural rock of the wall. I disintegrated the part in between. Now, Highness, now I believe."

Duke Edward sadly said, "As do I. As do I."

I turned to the knight captain. "Can you handle this?"

"Now that the rock is down, it's just a matter of handling what they teleport to the south. It will take days for them to get enough to build anything to breech our walls, and reinforcements are on the way. Yes, we have it handled."

I looked in his eyes and placed a hand on his arm. "If at all possible, I will be back."

The knight captain clasped my arm. "I know you will. You know what must be done. Get to it." He turned and said, "No mercy. Kill as many as possible. I want the south walls fully manned, and I want it yesterday! You're late!" Men started running.

I turned to Dedrick. "I need to go to StarHillm-Merge. Somewhere safe and as close to the palace as possible. The King's Knights Inn would be best."

Duke Edward said, "I know what you are going to do. Let me, my prince."

"Father would have you killed, and Kayland would be thrown into turmoil. No. I must do this. If Father has me killed, then so be it. I will not stand by and watch my brother destroy my family and my kingdom. I need the knights to get me to Droland, and I will accept Dedrick's and Eric's help, as they are following orders. You will stay here, out of the capital city and away from Father. I will not have you implicated. Tomorrow, Dedrick's apprentice can teleport you back to your lands. Tell Mother, Jenifer, and Grandmother I love them dearly. Tell little Annabel not to worry. I am protecting her." I hugged him. "Goodbye, my friend."

He hugged me hard. "Goodbye, my prince."

I turned to Dedrick. He touched my arm, and we were gone.

We landed in the stable of the King's Knights Inn. The stable boy was frightened, but Dedrick calmed him. "Look, boy, I need to know who is in the inn and what they are saying."

In a shaky voice, he answered, "My lord, they are the knights loyal to the king. They are talking about how Prince Droland ordered them out of the castle for the night so that they could look for hidden traders. They are worried and upset. They should be at the king's side."

I stomped out and headed toward the back door. Dedrick and Eric were on my heels. I walked straight through the kitchen and out into the assemblage. There were nearly fifty knights assembled, all saying, "This is an outrage."

"Knight Captain, let us back in. I don't trust those orders. The king would have never given them."

"The orders came from the king. You recognized the seal."

I walked to the center. "That seal was done by Droland to get you away from the king so he could kill him."

Many went to knee. The knight captain said, "Do you have proof?"

Eric stepped up and said, "On my oath to my God, I tell you, Droland has made some kind of pact with the demons. We are under attack at two fronts and now here in the castle. I have seen orders with the seal for our men to abandon the fort at Higger Pass and Crooked Pass. Droland showed up himself to ensure the orders were followed. And they sabotaged the rock."

One of the knights said, "Then the demons have entrance to our lands without hindrance."

Dedrick said, "No! They don't! Prince Charles has worked all night to ensure that the passes are protected, but Prince Droland could change everything again if he is not stopped."

I stepped up again. "I need to get into the castle and to my brother Droland. I want half of you to clear my way to his room and the other half to protect the king. Are you with me?"

Cheers rang out, and they poured out of the inn. The gate to the castle was just a city block away, and they went right in and gathered forces as they went. Nearly three hundred men ran toward the throne room. The rest cut right through my brother's men and mages. Droland's people died very quickly, and I was nearly carried to my brother's door by the throng. One of the knights kicked the door open, and they poured in. Droland was talking to two demons. The knights were enraged. The demons teleported away before we could kill them. Droland did not make it, as I cut off the demon's arm that tried to grab him before teleporting. The knights stood around in a circle.

Droland pulled his blade. "Well, little brother. You are a hard one to kill. I have tried to save you this dishonor. You were caught trying to kill Mother, the king, and your brother Richard. At least that was the plan. Now I will have to kill you myself. It's a shame. Killing you personally will get me exiled. However, I will be back."

His attack was slow and foolish. I cut him to shreds before he could realize that all those times in practice, I let him win so that he would look better as a crown prince. I had no time for idle chatter. Others would be dying. "Dedrick, disintegrate that body." I pointed to my brother.

Eric exclaimed, "My prince! He is dead. Why in the gods' name despoil the body?"

"Because Father loves his favorite son so much he will have him resurrected. No body means he will require a full resurrection. This will make it more costly and difficult. The gods will pay close attention to a full resurrection. If you asked Solbelli to fully resurrect someone evil that had been making pacts with demons to destroy many of Solbelli's believers, would he allow it or slap you down for asking?"

"I would never ask it of my God."

"Father will find someone, but if the only way to bring him back is to use an evil god, maybe, just maybe, Father will start to see the light. Dedrick?"

Dedrick stepped forward, and while moving his hands in a strange way that nearly blurred, he said, "Annihilate!" My brother turned to green dust. Then he conjured an air elemental to take the dust and dispose of it.

I turned to the knights. The knight captain was right behind me. "Knight Captain."

"Yes, Highness."

"I am going to Crooked Pass to help with the fight. Tell Richard what I did and what is happening. Then tell the king. I will return after the demons are forced to retreat. I will face my father and take my punishment. All others were following orders and had no act in my brother Droland's death. Go. Dedrick?"

"I know, my prince. Crooked Pass." He reached out a hand to me, and Eric touched his arm. We materialized a hundred feet south of the gate right in the midst of demons. My swords were still out, and I immediately started cutting them down. Spell after spell exploded throughout the demons. Eric ran out of good killing spells and drew his Morningstar. We fought back to back.

Someone from the fort saw our plight and yelled, "The prince!"

Someone else yelled, "If it's Droland, kill him!"

"It's Prince Charles!"

"Protect the prince!" was screamed out a hundred times.

Arrows started slicing through demons, and they had to back off. We ran to the fort and were let in quickly as the gate slammed shut again. Fighting was going on all around us. Nothing to do but fight. I ran to a part of the wall that demons had won and cut the demon mage nearly in half. After that, everything was a blur. I fought until my arms felt like they were going to fall off, and then I fought more. I was at the top of the south battlements facing three huge demons and about to die when a hundred arrows slammed into them. I looked over the side.

The general from Fort Simons was sitting on his horse, which looked exhausted. "You going to let us in, Highness?"

"As soon as I check that you're who you appear to be."

I ran down the tower and told Eric. He had saved a spell just for this and climbed the rampart. He yelled back down, "It's the general, Highness."

I ran down to the gate. "Open. Our reinforcements are here."

One of the older soldiers grumbled, "Bout time."

We opened the gate, and two thousand soldiers entered and cleared the place of demons. They mounted the walls, and arrows started flying again. I had not even realized that we had run out of arrows. The general took over, and the battle ran long and hard, but no walls were breached again. The demons turned on the next day when twenty war wizards showed up to arrest me and joined the battle instead.

CHAPTER 12

TRIAL BY FATHER

As soon as the battle ended and the general announced, "Stand down," the war wizards surrounded me.

One old and grisly wizard I knew as Lord Gellar spoke up. "Prince Charles, we arrest you in the name of the king of Kayland for the foul murder of Prince Droland and many loyal men and wizards in Prince Droland's care. Furthermore, we arrest you for starting a war between the demon realms and Kayland. You are to accompany us to the castle of Starl Iillm-Merge where you will await your father's displeasure."

I said, "I will come quietly, but only one need take me. The rest are to go to Higger Pass to reinforce that fort."

Dedrick, Eric, and I were teleported directly back to the capital city's main gate, where we marched the long road to the castle. To the dismay of the one wizard and the added guard, we were accompanied by cheers and shouts of joy for our brave deeds. I talked to Dedrick and Eric the entire way.

"Now remember. No matter what you say to my father, he will never believe that Droland had any part in this war or anything to do with demons. The evidence could pile up until it filled a room, and Father would still believe that I was the perpetrator. In addition, I killed Droland. No one else had any part of the conflict between Droland and me. They followed orders in getting me to him, and that's it."

Dedrick said, "But, Highness, you will be prosecuted for high treason and beheaded."

"I wish. I truly do wish Father would just kill me. No. There is too much evidence to support my claims. He will do something worse. Much worse."

Eric knew, but he still asked just so the wizard and surrounding guard would know. "What could be worse than execution, my prince? Your mother would never allow you to languish in the dungeons."

As painful as it was to verbalize, I answered, "Father cannot afford for me to be kept in the dungeons. I would be there for all to know. He would fear rescue attempts and Mother talking him into letting me out. No, Father will take away everything he knows I love—my family, my friends, and my country. I will be sent into exile." Tears were pouring down my face. Being cut to pieces in that battle was no pain compared to my heartbreak. "What waits to be heard is the depth of the exile. If I am sent into exile, to protect Kayland from my being used, I will need to take my own life."

Dedrick exclaimed, "Highness, that will not be necessary! Injudicious politics! I never understood this 'depth of the law' thing."

I smiled at the old wizard, knowing full well he did understand, as he was the one who taught me. "Father could simply tell me that I am not allowed in Kayland ever again. A simple exile with only one condition. Or, he could go much further. It matters not what he decides. Exile is exile, and I cannot allow all I have worked for to perish in wars between brothers."

When we reached the castle, my brother Richard was standing at the gate waiting. When he saw that I still had my swords, he drew his and ordered me to remove all my weapons. There was raw determination in his face. This was hard for him, but he would do as Father ordered. We removed our weapons, and Richard led the way to the throne room.

Mother, Grandmother, and Jennifer were at the entrance to the throne room. The wizards had been sent to recall them home. Grandmother and Mother turned their faces from me as if I were diseased. Jennifer came up to me with tears in her eyes, saying, "I'm sorry, but I must. Father must see, or we all ..." She slapped me hard, and I went to my knees. They walked off. I slowly got up and continued, my pain increasing with every step.

Annabel ran away from me crying, "How could you!" My heart sank, and I started to tear. When Father saw this, he smiled a pained smile. He did not even talk to me. I was taken to the dungeon and placed in irons waiting my father's displeasure. He had to have time to pull together all the evidence.

"Hello."

I looked around for the voice. It was hard to see in the darkness. I answered, "Hello. Who are you? I am Prince Charles."

"Prince Charles, Prince Charles, I do not remember a Prince Charles. I am Drinlen. I am a druid."

"Good day, Drinlen the druid. I am Prince Charles of Kayland, son to King Truss and soon to be exiled."

"Exiled? Why?"

I explained everything that happened and everything leading up to that point, including my finding out that I am magical. "So, as you can see, the king will have no choice but to place me in exile."

"Ah, I see. Thank you. First good news I have had in years. Have you picked a magical direction yet?"

"Good news? No. I haven't had much time."

"Good. Very good. We have something in common. We both hate Prince Droland. You see, I came to this land as the last of the northern druids. The demons attacked and wiped us out to the person. I was saved, as I was hiding where they could not go. I am the Opener of Ways. I doubt you understand what that means at this time, but you will. Droland found out that I was coming and had me imprisoned out of spite, for my race and what I represent. I have been here for five years waiting for you. Can you reach the cell bars nearest me?"

"Waiting for me?" I reached out and felt his touch on my hand and a shock.

He said, "There, it is done. Now I can die in peace." In a very tired voice, he added, "I have opened one way to you. Good luck, little druid."

I called to him several times. He did not answer. I wanted him to explain. Now he left me with a riddle and no one to answer. The guards came. "What is it, Prince Charles? You can't be hungry yet. You've only been in here for an hour."

"Guards, I think the man in the next cell has died."

"It's about time. We haven't fed him in three years. Prince Droland's orders, you understand."

They took the light to that cell and checked. His clothes were there on the bench, full of dust, as if he had turned to dust and died after touching me. "Well, that's strange. Druid, you know. Never understood druids. Three years no food and sits here as if waiting for something. Never pleaded, never asked to see the king, nothing. Just waited. Then he up and turns to dust. Strange."

I had to agree. "Yes, very strange."

The guard turned to me. "Say, you need anything?"

"No. Not yet."

"I'll bring you some fresh water anyway. You need to wash off that blood."

He left and returned with a large bucket of fresh water. I had forgotten that I just finished a major battle and was nearly covered in blood. He took off the chains and watched me wash up and clean my clothes.

"You'll need to put them back on, as I have to chain you back up. Sorry, my prince."

"I understand. You need to do your job." I put the wet clothes back on, and he attached the chains. Not tight but tight enough. I wasn't trying to run anyway.

I thought much on the old man and his riddle. It was three days before I was summoned before the king. I was given a bath and fresh clothes first. Then I was brought before the king and made to wait while my crime was read.

"Number one: high treason—killing a crown prince."

The list was short, only one item. I was expecting much more—all the things Droland had done and blamed on me, setting them up so that Father would believe I had done them. After all, he had placed in writing that he saw me using the great seal and consorting with demons. He had made it look like he was investigating the issue to protect Father. Apparently, Droland's plans worked only until the evidence was brought forth and Father learned more about his second son in three days than he had in sixteen years.

The king sat defeated on his big throne. He was looking down with distaste at the task the law said he must do. Richard was standing at his side. Father said, "Charles, you could have spared him. We could have worked this out. Now you leave me little choice. How do you plead, Prince Charles?"

Sadly, I said, "I plead guilty to killing my brother, Majesty. I would kill any man who committed the treasons he committed. I did it and no other. All others were following my orders and are innocent of any crimes."

Father said, "What Droland did is unforgivable, but what you did is also unforgivable. The treason of killing a crown prince is death for all but royalty. For you, it is punishable by exile. You will be escorted to your rooms. You are to gather only what you can carry, nothing more. You are to leave this land as quickly as possible. A wizard will teleport you to the border of your choice. You are to never return to Kayland on penalty of death. Do you understand fully your sentence?"

With sadness in my voice, I said, "I understand, King Truss." For the first time in my life, I did not think of him as Father. "I understand that you were blinded by Droland's smooth talk. You should have seen through his false face and dealt with him yourself. Instead, you forced your youngest son to take matters into his own hands. Now you lose two sons. You seem to take no pleasure in my punishment but please understand it was an act made in desperation due to the inability of a father to see the truth. Richard is far more a son to you than Droland ever was. Yet, because your grand sword was stolen while under Richard's watch, and because Droland flattered you at every opportunity, he and only he was your beloved. Open your eyes wide, King Truss. The best son stands by your side. Open your eyes before someone opens them for you."

Father's face changed quickly to anger. "You blame me and now threaten me?"

"No, King Truss. It is not a threat. I have tried for years to open your eyes, and you have kept them closed tight. I am not man enough to make you see the truth. I knew I would be exiled. I knew I would lose all that I love, but sometimes you have to give up what you love in order to protect it."

The king was mad. "Go—get this fool child out of my sight and out of my kingdom."

I was led by several wizards to my rooms. I did not need much. I did not plan on living long. Still, I packed a magical backpack called Natura's Deep Pocket Haversack. I had received it as a present from Richard the year before. It weighed only one pound when empty and only three pounds when stuffed full with a hundred pounds of provisions. I filled it with a tent, bedroll, extra blankets, all kinds of supplies, food, water, gold, gems, everything except weapons. I strapped a new magical dagger to my right leg and another to my belt. My swords had been returned to excellent condition by the knights while I was in prison, and I set them on my back. I loaded a Natura's Deep Pocket Quiver with two bows, sixty arrows, and five replacement strings, none magical. Dedrick came in and set a magical bow down on my bed and then left. It was not the one that Droland had, but it was nice. I packed it and would have thanked him if I could have. I packed in total silence. Eric came in and set down a ring with a note and then left.

"To whom it may concern: This is a ring of Elemental Comfort. You will still feel cold and heat, but it will not bother you very much. I know you have been wearing the Ring of Essentia I gave you over two weeks ago. Keep it on. You will need it. It will take care of all your food and water needs. Eat and drink once in a while to keep your system working properly."

I sat down after placing the ring on my right hand. Annabel walked by, but when she saw me, she screamed and ran away. Someday she will understand.

Richard came in and waited. He said nothing, just waited. I had the feeling he had been sent to ensure I received no more presents. I picked up the quiver and set it below my haversack at my lower back, still reachable. I put on a cloak that covered everything and hooded my head from the weather, and then I walked out. I went to the teleport stone in the castle by the shortest route possible. A wizard was waiting for me, and so was Father.

The king said only one word, "Where?"

I knew exactly where I needed to go. "The border of the Eleven Kingdom, to Treestorm Forest."

Father's mouth dropped open. "We are not on good terms with the elves. They will kill you on sight."

I looked up into his face, and he knew from my expression. I was purposefully going to my death. I said, "Good."

The old wizard walked me up onto the stone, and we departed. I was exactly on the northern border between Kayland and Treestorm. The wizard vanished, leaving me on my own. I crossed the border marker and sat down on a hard, cold rock to have a good, long cry. My life to this point had been difficult, painful, and exasperating, if not downright hateful, and now I had lost everything, and to save what I loved, I had to die. You have no idea how hard that is on a fourteen-year-old. You'd cry too.

CHAPTER 13

THE TRAP

I must have fallen asleep, as a bird landed near me and woke me up. It was early morning, and dew covered everything. I was high in the mountains overlooking Treestorm, a vast ancient forest that used to be split between the northern druids and the forest elves. Fourteen years ago, a surprise attack from the demon realms destroyed the druids. The elves gathered forces and forced the demons back over the Dragon Head Mountains. I could just make out those mountains in the distance as the sun hit their snow-covered tops. Father tried to claim a portion of the forest through some old treaty agreement, but the elves would not hear of it, and I don't blame them. We had already devastated our forests with overcutting and fires to make way for ranches and more grassland. Their representatives left Kayland, and now the elves protected the border jealously. That was just before my birth.

I had always wanted to see a full elf, so I gathered myself together and headed boldly down the mountain pass, hopeful to see one before they kill me.

It was deep into the day when I heard a bird call. There are plenty of birds in the mountains, and I had been hearing bird calls all along, but this one was different. It was just the end of summer, the beginning of fall, and this bird should have flown north for the summer and not returned for another three months. I looked around but did not see any snow geese. They are easy to spot in the air and only land in or near icy water.

I said, "I don't recall the map showing any lakes up this high, and it's a little early for blue-tail snow geese, don't you think?"

An elf stepped out from his hiding place down the path. He had a bow that was mocked and wore clothing that blended so well with the surroundings that I had a hard time keeping focus on the man. We watched each other for a long while. I walked over to a small bolder and sat down. He sat down in the middle of the path. In my best Elvin, I said, "Nice day. Think it will be cold tonight?"

He smiled. "Your tongue is difficult to understand, but if I heard you correctly, then yes, it will be cold. I am surprised you slept all night on that hard rock. It was very cold at the top of the pass."

So, he's been watching me for some time. I wonder who he called to. I answered, "I was very tired."

"Why, young human. Why would a wizard of the court of Kayland drop you off on our border and leave without a word but with a look of great sadness? Why would that child cry himself to sleep? I have much curiosity."

I had to smile. "He dropped me here because I asked him to. I cried myself to sleep because of my loss."

"Why would you ask him to send you here?"

"So that I could see a full elf before I die."

"I am flattered that you wish to see a true elf, but what is your loss? Do you believe you are dying? Is it some curse or some sickness that you bring us?"

"No, my friend. I expect to die when I continue down this pass. Is it not your intention to stop me?"

"It depends. You may die here or you may die below. It is up to you."

I laughed. "If I choose to die below, may I then have the time to learn a little something about the Elvin people before I die. I have many questions, and you are a rare sight." I truly was curious about the elves, but I did want to die. "This does not mean that we are friends and that you should let me live. I hope and expect you to keep your word and kill me."

It was his turn to laugh. "If you go past the place you are now, you will die before the sun rises again. You have my word."

I stood up and walked in his direction. His look changed to one of great sadness for only a tiny second, and then it returned to impassive. In Elvin, I said, "Hello, my name is Charles."

"Hello, Charles. I am Elequel. I did not realize you actually wish to die, or I would not have given my word so quickly. Why do you wish to die so badly?"

I took off my quiver, my haversack, my swords, and my knives and handed them to him. He made a quick hand signal, and five other Elvin archers stepped out. Two took my weapons, and one shouldered my haversack. "I wish to die because all I have ever loved is lost to me. I am in exile for killing my brother, Prince Droland."

"Then you are Prince Charles. My apologies, but I see no loss in the death of your brother Droland. Our spies have seen him several times with the demons. You have just fought a great war destroying thousands of demons. We expect that Droland was party to that."

"True, he was the instigator. Still, I took his life, and that requires, by law, that I leave Kayland and never return."

"Sad that is, to do such a great thing for your country only to be condemned. But that is no reason for death. You are young. It is not time for you to die. There must be reasons for you to live."

"There are a few."

We walked down the pass for some time before he asked. "And they are?"

I said, "I have recently found that I am magical, though I have yet to learn a spell. I can see spells on things. You have two on you now and had four when we started."

He looked at me with a smile. "That is a good reason to live. Are you not willing to learn magic?"

"I love to study, and if I could, I would spend the rest of my life in study. It is the reason I have chosen your lands to die. I wanted to learn about elves."

"Do you have another reason to live? You mentioned you had a few."

"I suppose there is a small chance I can get this exile removed. Though it is a very small chance and will take me most of my life. In addition, recently I met an old man. He gave me something. A riddle of sorts. I would like to solve it."

Elequel said, "These are all good reasons for a human to live."

I laughed. "Are you trying to get out of your promise?"

The elf said sadly, and now he wasn't trying to hide his feelings, "I will comply with my word unless I can talk you into relieving me of it."

"I see. The chances of that are slim. I have good reasons to die. While I am alive, my father and brother have to worry about me. Others could try to use me to undermine them, and I could be used to gather forces against them. I will not let my kingdom fall apart just because I live."

The elf looked long and hard at me as we walked toward the forest. The other elves said nothing. They knew I was going to my death and their friend had to kill me, willing or not.

We reached the forest at midnight and walked straight in. There were wonderful trees all around us, and it seemed impassible, but the elves knew the way and found paths I could not see. We walked through the center of a gigantic tree with roots that twisted and twined around the trunk, making areas to jump over and climb under. I saw a tree that looked like the roots started at the top and dropped down to the ground in wide trunks that looked like a waterfall. At first it appeared to be many trees, but Elequel pointed out that it had no trunk—just roots that grew up instead of down. My favorite was a tree so big you could build a small town in its branches and use the limbs as byways to drive wagons. It took an hour just to pass that one tree. Flowers and ferns were in abundance. Around one turn we saw a white stag. Everyone stopped. Elequel said, "Charles, this is a good sign. The white stag indicates something great is about to either happen or start."

We walked until near dawn. I turned to Elequel. "The sun will rise soon."

"We are almost there."

We continued to walk deep into the forest until we reached an old portion with trees that stood taller than I could see while looking up without falling backward. There was a small opening, and we entered a meadow completely enclosed by these giant trees. It was like standing in a fort with impossibly high walls. In the center was a magical portal. The magic was so powerful I nearly fainted and had to fight hard to remain standing. It looked solid from the front, but it was so thin I could not see it from the side. Elequel stopped me in front of the portal. The other elves gave my equipment back, and as I put it on, they helped me adjust everything so I would be comfortable.

Elequel said sadly, "Charles, my new friend. This is the druid Trap of Time. If you step into it, you will instantly die. No one has entered the druid realm for fourteen years. Those who have tried are stopped in time until they die of old age and turn to dust. Then they are blown out to fertilize these trees. It takes only a blink of an eye. If you are serious, step in and you will be dead."

He stepped away, leaving me in front of the druid trap. I said, "Thank you." With shaky legs and immense effort, I walked into the trap and right through to the other realm. I was still alive! I could see and hear the elves yelling on the other side, and I tried to walk back through. I bounced off an invisible wall. "Elequel. You promised!"

"Charles, you should be dead!"

"Why am I not dead?"

"I do not know. Can you go further into the trap?"

I turned around and walked off about twenty paces and returned. "Yes."

"You're ... you are not supposed to be able to do that!"

"I do not care. I am supposed to be dead. Now I have to do it myself!"

I took off my equipment and walked to the nearest tree.

"Charles, don't! Don't do this. This is wonderful. You do not understand!"

I paid no attention. I climbed up as high as I could and jumped headfirst. When I hit the ground, I felt my neck break and my head split before I died and was walking through the portal into the druid trap again. I turned, and the elves were standing there looking and yelling just like they did when I first entered. "Elequel!"

"Charles, you should be dead!"

The astonishment must have shown in my eyes.

"Charles, are you all right?"

"No, Elequel, I am not all right. Do me a favor. I want to try something. Walk back against the trees and stay there."

They turned and walked back to the trees. I pulled my knife and stabbed myself in the heart. And do not for a second think that was not one of the most difficult things I have ever done, but I was determined not to allow others to use me against my family and country. It had been done in the past many times and often against the wishes of the one who was exiled. I died and was walking into the trap again. The elves were yelling and saying exactly what they said before, standing exactly where they were the last two times, and my knife was in my belt sheath.

"Great. Just great!"

"Charles, you should be dead!"

"Elequel, I killed myself twice and keep returning to this exact point where I am just walking into this trap. Not only did you not keep your promise, you led me into a place where I cannot die. Is this some strange idea of an Elvin joke? I assure you, it's in very bad taste."

"Charles, my friend, this is no joke. You just entered a place where the elves have been trying to get into for years. When we found this gate five years ago, we knew we found the Northern Druid Suppository for Magic and Knowledge. They have been collecting magic and knowledge for tens of thousands of years." He turned to one of the other elves and said, "Quick, tell Farsite. Go!" He turned back to me. "Charles. Stay here. Don't go. Don't go anywhere."

"Very well. Perhaps this Farsite can help get me out of here. You have a promise to keep."

He smiled. "I will live with failure. The sun is already up."

I said, "Darn." I sat down and waited. The elves started making camp, so I guessed that it would take time before this Farsite arrived. I unpacked and set up my tent. Then I went looking for wood for a fire. I found plenty of wood and started a small fire, cooked some food, and talked to Elequel about the history of the elves. I found out a lot of things, and he was good at telling stories. He should have been. I thought he was a little older than I; he was 218 years old. He told me to respect Farsite.

"Charles, Farsite is almost three thousand years old. Even for an elf, that is old."

I was shocked. "Three thousand?"

"Yes."

"I have a question for him then."

"What?"

"Doesn't it get boring?"

Someone on the side said, "Yes, it does."

Elequel stood and bowed low. "Great one."

An old, white-haired elf with an irritated look came into view. He was flanked by two impressive elves, one male and one female. They looked like Mother and Father at their most formal. I stood and bowed to Farsite and then to the other two.

The man smiled. "He is thinking that we are possibly the king and queen."

Farsite sat down. There was nothing to sit on, but he sat down about two feet off the ground and did not fall. I'd never seen Dedrick use that trick.

Farsite said, "Well, Prince Charles, the predicaments you humans get yourselves into. It is amazing. Yes, we are often bored. At such times, we transform into trees so that time will pass well for us. I was a tree for several years until a few minutes ago when I was awoken."

"I am sorry for the disturbance, um … Great One."

He smiled. "You may call me sir or Farsite. Great One is a little much."

"Yes, sir."

"It is times like these that make life worth living. Now, open your mind so we can see your plight. Then maybe we can determine a course of action. Believe me. I do not want you in there any more than you want to be."

"Don't want a human in here?"

"You see much, young one. Yes, we do not want a human with the knowledge that is in that place. It would be devastating if the wrong type were to have it."

"My mind is open."

The most beautiful lady I have ever seen said, "He is already wide open. He has not developed the ability to shield his mind." She turned to me and said, "Thank you."

"For?"

"Thinking I am beautiful. Now be quiet while I look."

It was several minutes, and I watched as my life flew past in segments. All the good parts and all the bad parts. Some areas they watched two or three times—when I became aware of being magical and joked about it, my thoughts and dislike for power, the druid in the cell, killing Droland, my father's anger, and my pain at my little sister's fear of me.

Farsite opened his eyes and said, "Your brother deserved to die. You are not a murderer. You are a hero. Your father will see the light someday, and so will your sister."

"Thank you."

Farsite continued, "I know why you are in there and cannot leave. Remember the druid in the cell next to yours and his riddle?"

"Yes. He put a spell on me that faded." I held up my hand and looked. "I can no longer see it."

The male said, "You cannot see it because you used it. It is gone."

The woman added, "That druid was the Keeper of the Ways of this place. The last of his kind. Not even the southern druids can enter into this place without the keeper. The northern druid keeper saw something in you, something beyond our understanding, and searched you out. He knew he would die soon, and so he granted you a one-way trip. He told you, 'I have opened one way to you,' and he gave your open mind an unvoiced command. 'You want to see the full elves.' He gave you the command so that you would choose this direction for your exile, and he opened a way in so that the knowledge of the northern druids does not die. He did not give you a way out. The trap is still working. Once a week, you will find yourself stepping into the trap. Everything will be exactly as it was when you first stepped in. The fire wood will be back where you found it and not burnt. We will not be here. The other elves will, and they will be exactly the same each time. They will send for us, and we will come unless you tell them they already did that. You are stuck in a seven-day time trap, and each restart will be our first. We will not remember, but you will. That is why you remembered killing yourself twice. The only way out is to learn enough knowledge to know how to make the trap and disable it. As this trap is the pinnacle of all knowledge the northern druids gathered, it is going to take you a very long time. No, you cannot die. You cannot age. Your body is part of the trap. Your mind is the only thing free."

"Can't the gods help?"

"The gods will be very interested in talking to you as soon as you can exit the trap. No earthly god known has the power to enter that realm. That is why so many magical items were stored or hidden there. Many are evil and cursed and will possess you if they can. Don't touch anything until you can read and understand magic and identify the item's alignment and whether or not it is cursed. Do not let good aligned items fool you. They will take over your mind also."

"Why?"

"To advance their agenda of course. Good has an agenda as much, if not more, than evil. Always remember: everything and everyone has an agenda."

"And yours?"

"Ours was to get you out of there and kill you so you would never go back in."

"Thank you for being honest."

"We normally are. We are not human." Before I could say anything, he added, "You are tired. Camp here until morning but then find the Temple of Knowledge. You will know it when you see it. Learn to speak Druid first. That should help you figure out a lot of the other books. Then learn incantations. Spells like Study Magic and Understand Language will help you in this task."

"Will you be here?"

"If you need. At the beginning of the week, simply ask for me. Elequel will be here. After all, to us, it will be the first time you entered and the first time we've meet. You will have to explain things. Goodbye for now. I will stay this week in case I can help in some small way." He stood up and left to join the trees.

I watched as he grew and turned into one of the giant trees. Then I listened to the trees talk, or what sounded like talk. Before going to sleep, I relieved Elequel from his promise.

CHAPTER 14

THE TEMPLE OF KNOWLEDGE

I camped that night, but at first I could not sleep. There was far too much to think about. After a while, I realized that everything came down to three facts: (1) I could not kill myself; (2) I was stuck in time and therefore could not affect the outside world; and (3) the only way out was to do what I loved the most, study and research.

Maybe I had died. Maybe this was the place where good people went. A perfect place where you could study all you wanted and there was no one around to tell you what to do. You had no responsibilities except to do whatever you wanted. And! Whatever you did, it did not matter, because everything went back to exactly the way it was each week. I was very happy. I crawled inside my tent and fell into a good night's sleep for the first time in years.

When I awoke the next morning, to the calls of a bird I had never heard before, it took a moment to realize where I was. I climbed out of the tent and packed my belongings. Choices, choices, which way to go? I was in a nice druid grove with several fruit trees and many of the impressively tall redwoods. There were well-marked paths leading in all eight compass points, but I could not read the language. I took out pen, ink, and parchment and started to make a map, and then I realized that in one week, the map would be gone, the parchment back in my haversack, and the ink back in the bottle. So, memorization was going to be important.

I thought to myself, *If I was a northern druid, in which direction would I place the Temple of Knowledge? North, of course.*

Duke Edward once told me, "Boy, if you ever find yourself in an unknown place and you have no idea where to go, check out all directions for a little each way. It's the best way to make a good decision, and you have the added advantage of knowing what's behind you and to your sides." So, I headed south.

It wasn't long before I came across farmlands. The crops were divided into thousands of small plots. Many were not edible. Most were trees, plants, and other things you find in a forest. It was as if the druids had samples of every type of plant needed to grow or to restart a forest. There were invisible entities tending the plants. I could walk right through them and did. That's how I found them. They were very cold. After that, I looked for the magic they were made of and saw hundreds of these creatures. The one closest to me was transplanting a small fern into a bigger container. I tried to talk to it and affect it in some way, but I could not. I walked on, and the forest grew until it was a full-size young forest with birds, bugs, and animals, and then it ended. The next section was swamplands.

I walked through the swamp area rather quickly. There were interesting things to see, like the trees that grew above water with the roots holding them up and land forming around the roots, thereby creating more land, and the lily pads that looked like small forts with sides, towers, doors, and everything. I did not stop to look closer, as there were a lot of bugs, and some were real pests. The next area was something out of a nightmare.

I slowed down in this area, as it seemed to be alive. There were no birds, no bugs, and no animals. The plants ate them the moment they entered the area. I stayed in the center of the path in the hope that they would leave me alone. Wrong! As soon as I entered, they attacked. I hacked my way along for several paces, and then all of them backed away and returned to their places in the small plots. In front of me was one of the invisible tenders of the plants. It was looking me over. I tried to walk around it, but it continued to block my way. I tried to walk through it, but it was solid. Soon there was another invisible tender, and another and another, until I was surrounded by the creatures. I tried everything to get around them. I tried to walk through them but could not. I tried to go back toward the swamp. No good. They had me trapped. I sat down and waited to see if they would eventually go away. They did not. I attacked one, and I was walking into the druid trap. They had destroyed me so quickly I didn't even see how they did it.

"Charles, you should be dead!"

I turned around to see Elequel standing there with the same astonished look on his face.

"Elequel, you do not realize this, but we have been through this before. I am stuck in a time trap, and we act out this same thing over and over. Don't send for Farsite. I have no need for his knowledge at this time. I am off to check another direction. Bye."

"Charles! Charles, wait. I don't understand."

I was already checking out the west direction and paid no attention to him. I figured I would see him and hear his voice a few thousand more times. Right now, I had to remember what I had just seen. Farmlands of a sort, to the south. Now to see what was west.

I walked for a good long time before I came upon the first opening in the grove. I stood there staring at nothing but starlight. I was about to fall off the edge of the earth. I backed up and ran back to the center of the grove. Who knows what would happen to someone who fell off. I did not want to find out. Dying was one thing, but that was not my idea of dying. Then it hit me. I didn't want to die anymore. I had a reason to live. Study My reason to live was to study. I could study all I wanted, and it would not affect my brother or the kingdom because it happened all in one week. I never had to leave. I could simply stay until I ran out of things to learn. Since I had to memorize everything, I could be there forever.

I checked out the east and found the other end of the earth. This time I stood there boldly and studied the stars. They were not the stars of my kingdom. *My kingdom.* Kayland was no longer my kingdom; however, this place was. I studied the stars of my kingdom and rejoiced in the freedom of not having anyone to tell me what to do or any responsibility for another.

Then sadness hit me. *I am responsible for another. I saved Annabel from Droland's reign of demon terror, but is she safe? I gave her my word I would protect her. Was there another issue? Did I miss something?* There was a nagging feeling that Droland was not the issue she was afraid of. Something worse, something devastating, something deadly was waiting to happen. I knew it as sure as I was still alive, but I did not know what. Suddenly, there was a need to hurry. I ran back to the center of the druid grove and took the northern path. I still had four other paths to check, but I could do that another time.

I walked only a few hundred feet before the grove cleared, and there stood the largest building I have ever seen. Bigger than my father's castle by far. Almost as big as the capital city. The building was still a long way off, so I increased my pace. At one point, I passed a stream where I stopped long enough to freshen up. The temple was towering over me, and I was still a long way off. When I finally reached the foot of the stairs leading to the temple, I stopped. The stairs were thousands of steps and steep. There would not be any place to stay the night.

I set up camp on the bottom platform of the stairs to the Temple of Knowledge. Food was cold, as I saw nothing to burn in this area. I climbed into my tent just after dark and went to sleep. I awoke in the middle of the night to the sound of people talking.

I quietly reached for my swords and peeked out. There were two druids standing about five feet above the ground, talking in a language I did not understand, as if I did not exist. I crawled out and stood up. They did not seem to notice me. I walked over and said, "Hello." They did not seem to hear me. I tried to grab a foot, but my hand went right through. Ghosts!

The ghosts talked for a few more minutes and then walked on. I looked around. There were thousands of ghosts all going about their business as if they were alive. I tried to talk to some but could not. Only a few were talking a language I understood, and it was evident from those few that these were the spirits of the most prominent of all the druids. The long-gone heroes of times past. I listened to as many as I could until daybreak when they disappeared. The unspoken spell of reverence and wonder vanished like a cool breeze that could not be caught. I realized that I had been staring, opened mouthed and childlike, listening to all the great stories.

I packed my belongings and started up the steps. The first step I placed my weight on started speaking to me in a language I did not understand. I stopped and listened, but the words ended. I took the next step, and again I heard an unknown language. I stopped and waited until it stopped. The next step, the language was in Standard, the universal language throughout the planes.

It was a simple message. "Good morning, young human. You are on the Steps of Creation leading to the Temple of Knowledge. If you are in the wrong place, please turn back and see the keeper at the bottom of the steps. If you are looking for knowledge and have a specific request, please see the keeper at the top of the steps. Have a nice day." Three more steps, and the same message was in Elvin. One hundred and thirty six steps later, the message repeated in Draconic. I lost track after that. I was in good shape, but going nearly straight up steep stairs that had no banister, nothing to hold on to, and no way to stop myself from falling was difficult and time-consuming. I reached the top shortly after dark. Looking back down, I could see that clouds had moved in, and I could not see the bottom. I was a long way up, and this was just the start of this building. I could not pitch tent for the night, as there was no place to pound in the stakes to hold the tent sides out. I pulled out several blankets and fell asleep on the hard stone.

The ghosts returned that night. I listened to the ones at this level and then went back to my blankets. In the morning, I packed my belongings and headed for the temple. The doors were closed, and so I tried to open them. They did not move. I looked for a place to enter, like an open window or something. Nothing. I went back to the doors and knocked. Nothing. I said everything I could to get the doors to open. I pleaded, I prayed, and I tried prying. Nothing worked. That night, I listened to see how others gained entrance. The ghosts said something in their language and entered. I waited for someone speaking a language I understood to enter. Never happened. Finally, near morning, I decided to try to memorize the most common statement I heard. It was almost daylight before I had it down. I walked up to the door and repeated the statement, "Ego abeo hic comperio. Ego voluntas nullus vulnero," and the door opened. (It was Druid for "I am here to learn. I will not harm.") I quickly entered.

It was dark, and I had to wait for my eyes to adjust. The place was packed with writings. There was no keeper at the top. I was on my own, and it could take me years just to find something important I could read. Something in a language I understood. Hopefully, a book with directions around the place. I placed my equipment down and started rummaging through the piles. Several hours later, I found a book on different wedding ceremonies across the planes that was written in Elvin. Just before dark, I found a parchment on King Helmond, the wise king of Cathestine. I knew of Cathestine. It was the name of the country of Kayland several thousand years ago. Our stories, passed down from generation to generation, went wrong someplace. The great and wonderful King Helmond, who we had nothing but hero stories about, was a drunk and highly corrupt king according to this manuscript.

The day was nearly over. It was becoming dark, and there were no lights. At least nothing to light except books, and I did not wish to disrespect the temple by burning books. I put the book and parchment into a pile and then pulled out my bedroll and fell asleep on a long bench. Bad mistake. It becomes unbearably cold, even with an Elemental Comfort ring, when a ghost sits in your space. I let that happen several times before I found a corner I thought no one would be in.

The next day, the search continued, and the next day, and the next. My pile continued to grow. On the seventh night, I went to sleep and woke up walking into the druid trap.

"Charles, you should be dead!"

All my gear was on my back just as I started, but I remembered my pile of books and scrolls and parchments and everything I had read. I did not even acknowledge the elf's statement. I ran back to the temple, entered, and my pile was gone. Darn. I don't know why I thought it might still be there, but it was not. I started over, and this time I began on the right side and worked my way around. I kept track of the days and mentally marked the last area I searched. I continued this routine for years before I found it. Oh, there were times when I gave up and felt sorry for myself, but the thought of baby Annabel being harmed always brought back the need to continue. Finally I had what I needed. I mentally marked where I found it, and I studied the Standard to Druid translation of an entire book on travel cooking for the next eight weeks.

I had barely finished room two, and now I had to go back through every book I had gone over from the start. There had to be something that directed people where to go. It could not have been in the memory of the keepers. There was just too much for anyone to keep track of.

I went back to the first room. Now that I understood Druid a little, I noticed the little writing along each shelf. They were letters and numbers in ascending order. I went in the other direction and found the first section, A1. At the beginning of the A1 section, there was a little metal plaque that read "Directory: Aaisen." In a fit of glee, I nearly ran around the room reading all the plaques until I found "Directory: Draconic." Ah, the language of magic. If I could learn some simple spells, like Speak with Ghosts, I might be able to talk to a keeper. I traversed the shelves under the directory of Draconic and found a reference to a room with spell books. Room 78143D. I thought, *78143D, 78143D, don't forget that number, 78143D*. I took off to explore the temple for the first time. There were room numbers. I started in room 101. The room that I found the translation in was room 102A. I checked most of the rooms on that level, and they were all between 101 and 999. I found many stairs going up and down. I went down, and the numbers were (-)1001 through (-)1999. I went up, and the numbers were 1001 through 1999. I went up again, and they were

2001. I went up twenty sets of stairs, and I was at 22001. Oh yes, they made this easy. I shook my head and started walking up the steps while checking on the level number every twenty or so flights. I was on the seventy-first floor when I found myself walking through the druid trap and heard, "Charles, you should be dead!" Figured.

My mind said my legs were wobbly, but my body said I had just finished an easy walk down a mountain and into a forest. I ran back to the temple and started the climb. I reached the seventy-eighth floor of the massive temple and found the room I was looking for, 78143. I entered and found 78143D. I started reading the covers of all kinds of books on magic. Some of the books were highly magical. Those were in separate closed cabinets. I stayed away from them. I found a group of books titled The Beginner Mage Series by Golden Main, and I started on book 1, *The Origins of Magic*.

It was three weeks before I reached the place where the set of books actually taught you a spell. The first six very thick books talked about where magic came from and the thirteen major warnings. Other books had warnings upon warnings about the use and abuse of magic. I memorized those warnings, as I did not wish to "Tare a Rip in the Essence of Life" or "Start the End of Time." No thank you. The most understood of all the warnings, and currently the most concern, was more a law than a warning, "Action and Reaction. Whatever you do (your action) starts other things in action (reaction to your action). This is called The Principle of Action and Reaction, or Cause and Effect. Some actions cause reactions, which cause reactions, which cause reactions and so on. This is called the Ripple Effect. A beginning mage is fairly safe if he can remember that the higher level the spell he casts, the more destructive the reaction may be. A good example of this is the Dead Lands. This use to be a paradise until a foolish, short-lived elf"—leave it to dragons to think elves short-lived—"tried to cast a spell using the Staff of Nature to turn back time. The ripple effect destroyed all life in the entire region, including the elf. That area cannot hold life to this date."

I'd seen that area. I didn't know how long ago that book had been written, but the area still could not hold life. Dragons wouldn't even fly over it. It couldn't be crossed or lived in. Foolish people had tried and died. It was rumored, however, that a very high-level mage made a tower out there in the middle someplace. I guessed it was the safest tower ever.

The first spell, or as the book called it "cantrip," was Illuminate. The book said, "Now this spell is one of the simplest spells that anyone can cast. It is nether divine nor arcane. All spell casters can cast it. It requires a paw with one claw and a voice. Hold one paw up and close to your body so that one claw is pointed up and the others are curled down. Your gripping claw should be gently touching a curved claw. It would be a loose fist, except one claw is pointed up. Now, slowly move your paw directly away from you while saying 'Lumen' when you touch something. Try it. Don't worry if it does not work the first time. Keep practicing."

I held my hand in the position and said, "Lumen," as I moved my hand away from me. I touched the book, and nothing happened. I tried again. Nothing. I could see the spell attempting to work, but it dissipated before I touched the book. I did it again, but this time I did not finish the word *lumen* until I touched the book and the book glowed. Not brightly, about as much as a good candle. However, the book did glow. I had cast a spell. Until that point, I was not sure I could. Now that I knew I could, I practiced making light for hours. The spell didn't last long, only minutes. Still, I could light up the room with several lights if needed.

I sat back down and turned the page. "Illuminate was a good cantrip to start with. You can see the outcome, and that makes things fun. Another simple spell, or cantrip, is Study Magic. This spell requires a paw with two claws and a voice. Place your right paw across your face so that it is on the left side of your snout. Make a fist, except two claws that are next to each other and pointed toward you. Without touching your face, bring the two claws across your eyes. *Do not claw your eyes out!* As your claws are crossing above your snout, say the following: 'Legere Veneficus.' If you did this correctly, then you should be able to read the magic writing on the next page."

I turned the page. There was nothing there. It was blank.

I did as stated and felt the spell go on my eyes. I looked back down at the page. The writing said, "Good for you. You just did a Study Magic spell. Please continue to the next page."

This book had been written for someone very young, but who was I to complain. I had just learned two spells. I was so happy I did not even care that I was just walking into the druid trap. I practiced the two spells all the way up to the seventy-eighth floor, pulled out the book that magically replaced itself in the bookcase, and sat down to read some more.

"Another good cantrip to learn is Find Magic. This is almost like Study Magic except you need to concentrate or the spell goes away. This spell requires a paw with two claws and a voice. Place your paw in front and above your snout. Make a fist. Use two claws that are next to each other to point directly at your eyes (be careful). Move your paw away from your snout, directly out from you and down a little. As you are moving your paw, you need to open your paw so that it is open and flat. As your paw is moving, say the following: 'Deprehensio Veneficus.' If you did this correctly, then you should be able to see magic on this book."

There was magic there, but I could see magic naturally, so I did not know if the spell worked.

I continued to read the set of books until I had every cantrip memorized and practiced hundreds of times. The end of the set of books said, "For those of you who are ready to continue to a higher level, see my book *First Circle*." I checked the bookshelf, and there were many more books written by this author. *First Circle* through *Fourteenth Circle* were there. I pulled *First Circle* down from the shelf and started reading.

I lost track of time. I read, memorized, and practiced for years until I made it to *Fifth Circle*. Nothing was working for me there. Fourth circle was intermittent. Third circle I could do several, and then I had to rest. I realized I needed to practice until I was dead tired every day to increase my abilities. So, I started using my spells every day until all were used up. Soon, I could do a few more, and then fourth circle became easy and worked every time. Luckily, it was a time trap because I did a lot of damage with Fireball and Lightning Strike before I realized I could go to the edge and shoot spells at the stars. Not like I was actually going to hit one. Spells have limited range, and stars are way out there. I wondered if there was anything that explained the stars. A book or something. I would check in between practice and study. I could use all my spells quickly at the beginning of the day, and as I needed to stretch my abilities before I could learn another spell, I had weeks and sometimes months with nothing to do. So, I read. I read everything in the Draconic area that was not strong magic, and then I branched out to Elvin. By the time I could do most of the eight circle spells, I was hitting another stop. Something was keeping me from going further. What to do? What to do?

An idea hit me at one point. *What if I am not pronouncing the Draconic correctly?* I could read and understand, but was I pronouncing it correctly? I tried using Understand Language, a simple beginner's spell, and found out I was way off on several pronunciation issues. Once I had them down, I attempted ninth circle again, and it worked. I finished ninth and tenth circle in only six hundred years.

Now what? I still did not know how to get out of this trap. *Druid trap so learn druid spells.* I found the section on druid spells and started studying. Things went much quicker, and I had the first circle down pat in only days. The second through sixth were just as quick. Seventh circle started giving me problems, so I used Understand Language again and found some issues. I made it through ninth circle in only two hundred years.

Druids have some wonderful abilities. It was fun changing myself into different animals, but I had to have seen the animal first. I used summoning to call to me different animals and then learned to become those creatures. I eventually learned to become monsters, other humans, and creature of all kinds. I could become a gigantic dragon of any color. I had summoned one of each color just to learn them. I summoned Caelums, demons, devils, every type of creature to learn firsthand their languages. I checked out the magic items and found thousands and thousands of items, all fully charged and ready to be used. The old elf was correct. Some were cursed, and many were sentient. These I stayed away from. I finally found out how to talk to ghosts.

I waited until late when the ghosts appeared, and then I became a ghost myself. Simple spell. They saw me, and many asked what I was doing there. I told them in Druid, and we talked about how I was to leave and enter. None knew. These were not the Way Keepers, Gate Keepers, or Guardians of the Law. All three could help me, but there were none there. Believe me, I searched and searched. I did learn a lot of things from the druids that were there. I thought I was good with weapons, but they showed me ways and movements that made me look like a child beginner. They showed me ways to use spells in conjunction with other spells and fighting. They also showed me an area where I could safely practice without taking a chance of harming anything.

We practiced at night, trying to destroy each other. They continued to change tactics, forcing me to continuously do so as well. I died a lot, but I learned a lot from that type of practice. I now knew what spells stacked and what did not, what harmed movement and what did not. I found it difficult to cast spells in full plate armor but easier if wearing nothing that hampered movement. I learned skills from the druids like how to cast silently or without movement, how to increase damage, take up more area, and make a spell last longer. I learned to do a spell very quickly, but to do this, I had to prepare the spell earlier. That took away some of the flexibility of not having to prepare spells, but if I knew what I would need ahead of time, I could prepare and do twice the number of spells in a given time. They were surprised about that, as they said, "Sorcerers cannot do fast spells."

One said, "This one is part wizard, druid, and bard. As long as he prepares, he should have no problem."

I learned the limitations of spells and my body. I learned to appraise gems, jewelry, and art. I learned to sculpture, paint, play music, and sing. I was filled with knowledge from the ages. I learned to hide, sneak, disguise myself, and concentrate in battle. I could now fire four arrows at the same time and hit four different moving targets while riding a horse backward. I was so used to my weapons they were like extensions of my arms, and I could hit hard with each and destroy an enemy quickly. I could draw my sword, run in, strike, run out, and hide in one quick move. I knew the anatomy of every creature and could do a sneak attack that would do major damage. I could open locks of any sort, find, disable, and make traps of all sorts. However, I could not find a way out of the druid trap.

Purely out of boredom, I started learning divine spells. Clerical spells come from the gods. A cleric prays for his spells each day and is given, by his god, the number of spells he can handle. Once in a while, the god will know something the cleric does not and will grant him a different spell instead of the one he asked for. All in all, I thought you needed a god to do divine spells. I talked to some summoned Caelums about this, and they let me know that if you have the ability, anyone can do divine spells. It is really just a matter of learning them. A few clerics, not many, never pick a god. What this means is they don't get special abilities given to them by a god. Blessings or aid, after requested, might not come at all, or it could come from a god they don't want to associate with.

I learned divine spells, and I could do all spells up to and including miracles. Though, where the miracle was coming from, I had no idea, since gods could not reach into this plane of existence.

I talked to a Caelum about this, and he said, "Gods can enter and affect this plane of existence; however, not the normal worldly gods. There are gods that govern our gods. They can see into and allow the miracle if they have a reason."

"Who are these gods?"

"Please bring me back tomorrow, and I will tell you what my goddess allows me to."

I brought him back the next day. "Good morning."

"Good morning, Charles. The goddess Natura says she will allow you this information on one condition."

"She does know I can always go to another god to find out?"

"She knows. She wishes that you will contact her upon leaving this place."

"I see no harm in that. If I can ever leave, I will contact her."

"Charles, this is not through prayer. She wishes you to go to Caelum and see her in person."

"Ouch. If I do that, I could be made hers. She has that ability. Is there a neutral place that I could meet her where I would be assured that I will not be destroyed on sight or dominated?"

The Caelum smiled. "She said you would not trust her in this. In truth, you would be a fool to do so. There is a plane called Sanctuarium where creatures in complete safety trade and sell from all the planes. It is a major way-fare for travel on the planer border. In this place, the great god Commeatus has a temple that he protects as a place where anyone can come make deals and not fear treachery. Gods use it to make deals with other gods. Seldom is it used for mortals to speak with gods, but I think he will allow it, as he is just as interested in speaking with you."

I said, "I like Commeatus, and that sounds like a place I would like to see."

The celestial said, "The plan you have discussed with me is of great interest to many of the gods. Especially the laws and the way you wish to run this place. They need you for this, as they cannot personally interfere in the affairs of man. It is the issue with good and evil. If good shows up, then evil can also, and they cancel each other out. The first to interfere always loses, as the second can undue everything and force his, or her, own plan to take effect. However, you can interfere, as you are not a god, and this will help many gods. They are willing, especially since you have not aligned yourself. You are what we call a champion. The problem is not being aligned means we don't know who you are going to end up being a champion for."

"That's easy. I am not going to be a champion for anyone. I will do what I think is morally correct in my own views. If that includes doing things that make the gods happy, then so be it. If it makes someone upset, then so be it."

"Charles, you have no idea how a god can force you to see things their way. If a god wants you to do something, they will make it affect you in such a way that you will decide, on your own, to take action."

"Then they better not let me find out they did that."

He smiled. "Charles, do not threaten the gods. You cannot harm them, but they can harm you greatly."

"Gods are easy to harm."

"Oh. You think so."

I smiled. "You destroy all their temples and make sure people fear for their lives if they even think that god's name. No followers, no god. Gods gain power from the number of followers they have. What happens when a god loses all that power?"

"That would not be a good thing."

I frowned. "It's cut throat up there and down there. Just as at home. Politics can destroy a god. In the hidden hells, a devil told me, it's a matter of killing the boss. Afterward, if no one challenges you, you are now the boss. If there are challenges, you need to fight for what you want. If you become weak, someone is going to displace you. I would imagine it is the same up top, only in a nicer way."

"Charles, do not let the gods know you know this. You will be dust before you take two steps out of this place."

"If one god turns me to dust, would not another bring me back just so I could take revenge? Just tell them this, and it is the truth. I am normally very good with a little neutral for needed times and a tiny bit of evil to spice things up."

The Caelum smiled. "This they would understand, and all would agree that you will make them a good champion. One will win you over in time. They have infinite time."

"Sadly, so do I now."

"You have found the truth of aging?"

"Yes."

"I will let her know."

I said, "Tell her that I will talk with a Caelum from Commeatus. If it is agreed, I will meet her there when I am out. I have one thing to do first, and then I will call her from this building you mentioned. I will receive directions from Commeatus."

"Thank you. I will let her and Commeatus know."

"Please make it quick. I have to summon the Caelum today, as tomorrow I go back to the beginning of the week."

"I will tell them immediately. Give me one hour and then do your summoning."

He disappeared. I waited an hour and summoned another Caelum while thinking of Commeatus. He showed up immediately and handed me directions, saying, "Memorize this, and yes, you will be protected. Commeatus likes your plan."

I memorized the directions, and the next day as I was walking into the druid trap, I turned around and sat down.

"Charles, you should be dead!"

I smiled and kindly said, "I know, my friend. You have told me that every week for over three thousand years. Please ask Farsite to come talk with me. You may tell the great wizards and all the trees surrounding this vale that I will be coming out of the trap in a few moments. I do not wish to harm anyone, so please tell them not to attack."

He motioned for the same elf he always sent to go get Farsite. It was nice to know that some things never changed. "Charles, you just stepped in."

"I know. It is a time trap, and to you, I just stepped in. To me, I have stepped into this trap more times than I can keep track of. I know it has been over three thousand years, but how much over I do not know. I could not write it down and keep track, as each week the writing disappeared. Each week, everything starts back at day one, except my memory."

"Then how can you leave now?"

"I studied until I knew the secret."

"You can actually walk out? Then why don't you?"

"Because the trees, as you can see, are becoming the wizards set to protect this grove. They do not protect against something coming in, as you may have thought. They protect against something coming out."

"That is correct." Farsite came around the corner.

"You were much faster this time, my old friend. I must thank you for all the help you gave me at the beginning of this quest."

"You are welcome, though I do not remember, as it did not happen yet."

"Now it never will. I am ready to leave this place." The trees were down, and in their place stood fifty of the greatest Elvin wizards.

Farsite said sadly, "I am sorry. You cannot leave this place. It cannot be allowed."

I stood up, walked out, paralyzed all of them with a simple spell, collapsed the gate, picked it up, and placed it in my belt pouch. I turned to the wizards and bowed in respect, and then, as I disappeared, I removed the paralysis.

CHAPTER 15

THE DEAD LANDS TOWER

During my studies, I found out that there truly was a very powerful mage that built a tower in the Dead Lands. His research was very dangerous, and he did not wish to take a chance on harming others. He had an item I needed for my plans, an artifact of great power. I found a description of his tower and the main room, and when I left the Treestorm Forest, I used a Superior Teleport spell to take me there.

I truly doubted that the Elvin people would follow me there, even if they could discern my location. Just in case, I placed spells around the tower that ensured no one would find it. If they could travel across the Dead Lands, they could walk right past and not see it, and scrying would never succeed on the tower or me—not with the protections I put in place. There were protections left over from the old druid mage that built this place, but I reinforced them, as I was now better than he. I found his body, or what was left of it, on the first day.

The book he had been using was still open, and the creature he had summoned, that tore him to bits, was long gone. I used spells to check the book. The thing was evil and waiting for me to use it. To its disappointment, I left it alone.

While studying for three thousand years, I developed a plan to make myself better. I was intelligent and wise due to all the studying, practice, and druid guidance. I was strong, fast, and could sustain a bit of damage. However, I was not so good that I could not be dominated by good or evil. There are many ways to "take someone down," and I wanted to decrease the chances of it happening to me. For what I was planning to do, I was going to need some serious protection and not magical. I needed to be greatly enhanced. Therefore, I needed to talk to more than just two gods.

I spent the next three days checking out the tower. It was very large and had many secrets. I found several nice magical devices and a lot of very rare ingredients for making potions. There was a forge to make weapons and armor, and everything needed to make scrolls, wands, rods, and staffs. Apparently, this mage had several hobbies. There were many items only half-built. I wondered why until I found his journals. The last entry read:

"In my endeavors to make a better staff, I have run across a minor issue. All my attempts to make items that do not lose their power and never need recharging have failed. I am going to use the *Book of Calling* to summon a genie to help enlighten me. I will try for someone powerful this time. The others have had little knowledge."

Very well then. The fool summoned a major genie and expected to live through it. Even I was not that crazy. I may have summoned major genies while in the druid trap, but that was with the knowledge that I could not die. Good thing too. I died at least twenty times before I convinced one great genie to talk with me. The only reason he did was out of curiosity. After that, he allowed me to summon him many times. Still, each time I had to tell him something we had agreed on beforehand, or he would kill me instantly. Especially since he would not remember me after the week ended. I was powerful but not *that* powerful.

Go ahead; summon a minor god. Not me. I did that as well, and it displeased him. There wasn't much left in the trap; he destroyed everything. He said, "Now you will never escape. You will go mad being here alone." Luckily, the northern druids were good with traps. At the end of the week, I was walking back into the trap, and everything was perfect. I never summoned a full god. The druids were good, but they may not have been that good.

After setting everything up the way I wanted, I took the druid trap out and opened it up. I walked in. Home sweet home. I went to the Temple of Knowledge and looked up the *Book of Calling*. I found the article I needed on the (-)23567th floor.

"The *Great Book of Calling* was created by Spittle Blackbottom of the Blackbottom Devils in the fourth level of hell. He created it as a joke to pester some of his most hated friends. The book is evil, and when touched, it will take over the creature and make him learn enough magic to summon one of Spittle's fiendish friends. The friend would then kill the creature that summoned it. The book made it into the hands of the demigod devil Smokeheart. He changed it so that he was not in it anymore and then added pages so that others he disliked were. Over the centuries, the book has had hundreds of creatures added to it, and eventually it became intelligent. Now, being an artifact, it drew power from Smokeheart, who allowed this in order to have a little fun. Whoever starts to use the book is watched by Smokeheart. He always knows where the book is. Warning: If you find this book, do not touch it. Without preparation, it will possess you. You can safely handle the book if you maintain a Safeguard from Evil spell."

I then looked up the plane I was to go to for this meeting. If they traded things there, then the Leaches might have a store there. I needed to use the Leaches to cause the gods to react. I had read about the Leaches in an old book called *God Fears*.

"Leaches are strange humanoid creatures that feed off magical power. They love artifacts, as they are a renewable magical power source. It is said that their cities run off this artifact power. The more powerful the artifact, the better. They pay well for artifacts. The gods hate these Leaches, as it is their power that the Leaches use. Every artifact is powered by a god. Every time an artifact is sold to the Leaches that God loses power, as the artifact is drained, repowered, and drained over and over. The God who aligns himself with an artifact or creates an artifact has no choice except to power that artifact. Though the gods try to slow the recharge down as much as possible, the recharge unavoidability takes place, causing the god to drain his power trying to keep these artifacts powered up. Several minor gods died before they realized the issue. They made many artifacts, and each one found its way into the Leaches' hands. The Leaches are scrupulously honest and never steal an artifact, as it is widely known that for many artifacts, you have to obtain it honestly or you cannot command it. It takes years for the Leaches to drain an artifact and decades for the artifact to recharge."

That was enough information for me. I had a good plan that would either get me killed or highly protected. I found the information I was looking for, and yes, the Leaches had a store there. It was their main store. While still in the druid trap, I went to the buildings that held the magical artifacts. There were thousands of them. I found magical sacks and displaced chests and loaded up about one thousand minor artifacts. Little things I would never need. I made sure there was a lot of evil in the choices. In fact, most of the artifacts were evil. I walked out of the

Druid Suppository for Knowledge and Magic and back into my tower. I did the required Safeguard spell and grabbed the book, placing it into one of the magic sacks. I was loaded down with a dozen sacks and keys for the chests. Any one weighed very little, but all together, they weighed a lot, even with the sacks being artifact level. I had them fully loaded and needed to get going.

CHAPTER 16

THE PLANE OF TRADE

I plane shifted to Sanctuarium. The guard at the entrance was nice. He was a Halbruzie demon standing about fifteen feet tall with bright violet eyes and four arms, two with pinchers, and two holding a huge halberd that glowed and sputtered with electricity.

In a booming voice, he said, "State your business."

"I am here to trade."

"Very well. Have you ever been here before?"

"No."

"The rules are simple. We do not care what your alignment is or what your prejudices are. Here, everyone is the same. You could be a god for all we care. Harm someone, and we will come after you. Stop someone from doing his legal business and die permanently. Make a deal and not follow through, and you will answer to the queen. She hates when someone tries to wiggle out of a deal. Watch the wording of any deals. What you say could mean something else to another. Don't start a fight, as we will finish it. Don't get into a fight, as we will finish it. If you have a problem or need help, then every corner has guards. Call out, and you will receive help. Need a legal interpreter? Just ask. One will come to you instantly. They cost, so make sure you know what it is going to cost you before you hire someone's services, or they will jack up the price something horribly. It's completely legal to charge for anything, and if you are dumb enough to not agree on a price ahead of time, then you lose everything you have on you. That does not include your soul, unless that was in the bargaining, or servitude. We have no slaves, indentured or otherwise. It's too easy to enslave those not used to this place. Be careful. Anywhere you need directions to?"

"Depends on how much the directions will cost me."

"Very good, tiny human. That's thinking. I normally charge fools that don't ask a hundred gold. It's free to those intelligent enough to ask."

"I am going to see the Leaches."

"Ah, have an artifact to sell, do you? I bet you want to get rid of that as quickly as possible. Well, don't spread it around. Gods will try to stop you from seeing them if they find out. If they try to stop you, just yell out if you still can." He pointed. "See that door marked High-Level Trades?"

"Yes, sir."

He smiled at the "sir."

"You walk through that door and trot on down the main street. Their offices are on the left side about a league into the trade district. Good luck."

"Thank you, sir."

I walked to the door and walked through. I was at the beginning of a long road filled with shops. A league was about three miles, so this was a very big place. There were eating establishments all over. Inns that advertised food and private rooms for haggling, and everything you could possibly want for sale. The streets were clean, and there were guards everywhere. Creatures of all kinds flew, crawled, shifted, and walked lazily up and down the street, looking like they knew what they were doing. Some walked into and out of the stores. One human, who stood without clothes and looking very pained, was complaining to one of the guards. The guard asked him, "Did you agree on a price before the transaction?"

The man answered, "I forgot."

The guard said, "See the city magistrate for work until you can gather enough money to get home."

The man nearly cried as he called, "Magistrate!"

An official-looking man instantly showed up. "Not another one. You would think they would learn and either pay for their return before they start the transaction or be able to planer travel. Come with me." They disappeared.

I continued down the street until a large creature that smelled something awful stepped in front of me.

"Hello, little human."

I looked up and said, "Hello, Demigod Smokeheart, sir. My name is Charles."

"I know who you are, Prince Charles. Funny that you know who I am."

"Just a guess. I happen to be carrying something that you are tied to."

"Yes, someplace in one of those magical sacks, you have my book."

"Pardon, Demigod Smokeheart sir, it is my book. It is aligned to you, but I won it fair."

"I will not stand here and argue over my book, fool human. You will give it to me now."

"What are you willing to pay me for it?"

He let out a great roar and raised an enormous fist, easily twice the size of my head. Twenty guards instantly showed up along with an official. "Need arbitration?"

I paid no attention to Smokeheart's ranting as I asked, "The cost?"

The little man answered, "As it was this creature that raised his fist to strike you, the cost of arbitration is to him. Though you can ask for it."

I smiled and said, "How interesting. Start a fight, and you can end up paying for it in many ways."

The arbitrator smiled back. I wish he hadn't, as his smile indicated that he was looking at a pawn about to be eaten. "New at this, are you?"

"First time here. That information will cost you one hundred gold."

He looked at me, shocked, and the guards all looked at him. "Officials of the plane do not pay. We are exempt."

"How much to make me exempt for the duration of this arbitration?"

Smokeheart was listening to the conversation but dared not move with twenty of these guards around him.

"You set the price. One hundred gold, and all things said and learned are free."

I paid the gold and then explained the circumstances to the arbitrator.

He turned to Smokeheart and asked, "Do you agree with the statements or would you like to amend things? You do know, of course, if the item in question was gained legally by the human, then it is his to do with as he wishes." He turned to me. "I suppose that you are going to sell the item to the Leaches?" He pointed to the store across the street.

I smirked. "Actually, no."

Smokeheart's eyes widened. "You were headed there."

"I am headed there but not to sell, to trade."

The arbitrator frowned. "Trade? With the Leaches? Good luck."

"Thank you. I will need it."

Smokeheart asked, "How much for the book?"

I answered, "What artifacts do you have to trade with?" Now, in all honesty, I found in my studies that Smokeheart had a very good aligned ring that did multiple things. First, it took no ring space. Normally you could have only two magical rings— one ring on each hand or they interfered with each other and were either useless or blew your hand off. In the case of this ring, it could be worn next to another magic ring without any such issues. You have to love artifacts. The ring granted the wearer immunity to mental control of any kind and allowed you to know when someone tried it and who and where that someone was. It was made for a paladin of Commeatus to fight vampires. But it would be great for me when I went to see the gods.

Smokeheart thought long on this. "I have an artifact." He reached out his hand, and in it was a rod. With my ability to see magic, I knew that this was a lesser artifact. One of the weakest I had ever seen.

"No. I am not trading down. This book is a major artifact. That is a minor artifact and a lesser one at that."

Smokeheart said, "Very well." He sent it back and pulled out another, but this one he did not touch. It just floated there.

I looked carefully. It was a major artifact. I asked, "Before touching it, may I check this item using spells?"

The arbitrator said, "Yes, of course."

I did some quick spells, and the ring was good aligned. So good that it had intelligence and wanted me to be good and worship his god. It was not the ring I was looking for. It was a ring of Good Alignment.

"That is definitely a major artifact." I looked up at Smokeheart. "Do you really wish me to instantly be good aligned?"

He thought for a second, and the ring disappeared. "Not really." Another ring instantly showed up, and he held this one even though it burnt him a little. "This is a disappointing little ring. It is my only other artifact. It is good aligned but does not care what alignment you are. It burns evil to handle it."

I did the correct spells, and this was the ring I wanted. "Yes, I will trade for that ring. If nothing else, I can trade it to the Leaches and receive what I would receive for the book."

"Done."

I did the Safeguard spell and took the book out. I handed it to him, and he gave me the ring. I took out a scroll and did a full categorizing on the ring. It was the one I wanted. I put it on and felt its power working to protect my mind. "Nice ring, Smokeheart sir. Now the gods cannot mess with my mind."

"True. I am surprised you know that, as that little spell will not identify that ability with an artifact."

"Oh, I knew you had it and found your book just so I could trade for the ring."

"Think you're smart, do you?"

"I know I am not. That is another reason I need the ring. I have something else you may like."

"What?"

I pulled out three minor artifacts that belonged to him and then looked at the Leaches' store. Some were standing outside. They could feel the power and wanted in on the trade; however, during arbitration, they could not interfere. "Are these yours?"

Smokeheart looked back over his shoulder at the Leaches. "Yes, they are mine. What do you want for them?"

"Two things. I want the other artifact ring, and I want you to grant me three wishes and swear you will never remove them. I know you can. I will wish for my strength to be increased three times."

"Done!"

I felt my strength increase and watched him set the ring at my feet. He took the artifacts and left. I did a Safeguard from Good spell and picked up the ring. Then I placed it in my sack and said to the arbitrator, "Thank you for your help."

"You are welcome. The demigod left without paying, so there are a few of us going to his place to collect." The arbitrator turned and disappeared along with the guard.

I walked over to the Leaches. "Want to trade?"

In a singing tone that had rolling Rs and stretched Ss, they answered, "To maintain confidence and keep the gods from interfering, let us move into the shop."

I said, "First, I want it understood that anything said is just thinking until it is agreed to by both parties. Second, any costs in transactions, information, or any other hidden cost must be talked about first and agreed upon, or the cost is free. I do not want to be blindsided with costs I am not aware of. Any such costs instantly nullify all transactions, and we walk away owing nothing."

"You are a wise human. Very rare. We will enjoy a straightforward trade for a change. There will be no costs. Only trade that must be agreed upon by both you and us."

I walked into the Leaches' shop.

CHAPTER 17

THE TRADE

As I walked in, I took time to look around. A simple straightforward shop for one thing only—trade. There were no lounging areas for long-term haggling and no refreshments. Just a simple bar like you would find in any shop with a shopkeeper.

The shopkeeper asked, "How may we help you?"

I knew this was deceptive and a good way to make it look like they were doing me a favor. I said, "I am not sure if I will be helped as much as I will be helping you. I have one thousand minor artifacts with me." Eyes that were nearly closed opened wide for a second and then quickly returned. "As a mage, I have learned as much as I could about your race, and I find it interesting that all artifacts eventually make their way into your hands. Is this true?"

"Yes. I am flattered that you would study my race. May I ask why?"

I could see the spells in the room, and I was very glad I was wearing the mind protection ring. But there was also a very high-level truth spell in place, so I said, "I have a need to learn. I love learning. However, I studied all creatures so that I would know how to defeat them if attacked."

"I see. A war mage that wants to be a sage."

"Trying to figure me out? I am a divine sorcerer."

"A divine sorcerer. That is a new one to me."

"Divine sorcerers practice both divine and arcane spells. I can do both equally and do so instantly without preparation or godly influence."

"How nice. Does that not limit you in your abilities?"

"It did for the first thousand years, but after that, I found it much easier."

This threw them way off track, as I was telling the truth, and yet I was human and had a very short life. They instantly thought, *Powerful and dangerous.*

The small talk stopped at this realization. "May we see and appraise the merchandise?"

"Of course." I started taking out the artifacts. I filled the room and still had many more to take out. They opened a side door, and I nearly filled that room also. The look on what they call a face said it all. They were overjoyed. A quick discussion took place in their language. Problem for them was I could talk their language also.

"He has enough power here to run several cities. We need this badly. Many of our coveted artifacts are out of power, and they take forever to recharge. Our cities are running out. We need this."

"I know, but we do not have enough to pay for even half of this. What will we trade him?"

I smiled and said in their language, "You can trade me other artifacts."

They looked astonished. "You know our language. I do not detect any spells on you, and that ring does not grant that power."

"As I said, I studied your race."

"We have no artifacts we would part with."

"Yes you do. I am willing to trade for used artifacts. Items that are drained and require time for recharge. They are nearly worthless to you, but I am willing to deal if you trade for the entire amount. Say, one fully powered minor artifact for one drained but chargeable artifact one level higher. Therefore, one minor for one medium, two minors for one major, and four minors for one grand."

"That is a good price, old human. We loathe parting with something that can be recharged, even if the charging takes many years."

"Why? You will get it back. All artifacts eventually come to your hands."

They started arguing, and one said, "Please stay here. We need to talk in private." His head turned sideways, and he added, "Thank you for being honest enough to let us know you understand our language."

"You are welcome. I wish to bring many more minor artifacts and my medium-level artifacts in for trade. Therefore, I want good relationships with you. I will be here for a while. Do not take too long. Others can feel their artifacts open in this place."

"We will return very shortly."

I waited for a few minutes, and they returned with another. This one looked like he was in far more power than the other two. He turned into a human and put out a hand. "Hello, I am what you would call a king. My name is King Colless."

I bowed and then took his hand. "Nice to meet you, Majesty. I am Prince Charles, exile of Kayland on Duewir, in the Milky Way Galaxy second hub, in the Prime Material Plane."

They looked disappointed. Most humans would be nervous around royalty and might make quick and bad decisions. I had seen it many times in my father's court. I would not be so inclined, and they now knew it.

"Prince Charles, we agree to the exchange. The required artifacts are being brought to this place as we speak."

"Stop. There are other stipulations to this exchange."

He looked at his two storekeepers with a look of displeasure. One said, "Sire, this trade was above our ability to approve. We could not continue."

The king shook his head. "Understood, Prince Charles. What other stipulations?"

"First. Whatever I exchange for, it cannot have the power to harm me. Second, I must be able to pack up everything and leave with it—so no huge items unless you provide the transportation, and my sacks and chests do not count in the trade, and neither does anything I am wearing."

"Is that all?"

"That is all that I can think of."

"The first is simple. They are drained, and with that ring, none can take you over. You cannot be harmed by them. However, they will charge much quicker once the gods realize they are not in our hands or our agents' hands. Some will charge instantly. We will ensure that they will not harm you unless you activate them. Is that fair?"

"Yes."

"The second is also easy. The items we are bringing take up space but only three times what these do. We will provide safe transportation to anyplace on this plane or the Prime Material Plane. It is understood that your personal possessions and transportation items will not count. Is that fair?"

"That is fair, Majesty."

"Very well." He motioned with a wave of his hand. "Take all this away." Many Leaches came in and gently took every item stated. Slowly the rooms started to fill with other artifacts. My sacks and chests were filled, the two rooms were filled, and they started on a third room. At one point, a chime rang, and the rest returned to their home. They were very happy with their charged new artifacts. The king came to me. "I am told you have more."

"I have many more. This was all I could carry."

"We look forward to your return, Prince Charles. Where would you like these delivered?"

"To the Temple of Commeatus in this city."

"Would you like to go with us?"

"That would make it easier if it does not cost too much."

He smiled. "It is free." He waved a hand, and we were on the steps of the temple. The Leaches could not come in, but one hundred acolytes of Commeatus were waiting for me and took all the artifacts into the temple very quickly. I shook hands with the king, and he departed.

I stopped the first acolyte and asked, "How much will this service cost me?"

Frowning, he said, "We do not play the trade games. This costs nothing, and using the rooms to meet the goddess will cost nothing. If there is a charge for anything, we will inform you first."

"Thank you. It is nice to be in an area where I do not have to be overly careful."

"Commeatus knows you like him. You turned to his priests when you needed help and trusted them, and he filled them with extra spells. You thanked him in your actions toward them and your praise for the spells they used to help you. Though that was thousands of years ago for you, it was three weeks ago for us. He is pleased with you. Though you did just sell two minor artifacts of his to the Leaches, you gained from them many of his more powerful artifacts, and he believes you are going to do more."

"He is correct. I plan on releasing many of the higher-level artifacts."

"What you will do with them is in great discussion between the gods. You have their curiosity."

"Good. I will identify the ones I wish to keep and either sell the rest back to the Leaches"—thunder and clouds started gathering inside the temple—"or trade them back to the gods that they belong to for enhancements or things they may realize I will need." The clouds quickly dissipated.

The acolyte said, "The gods do not like those that trade with the Leaches, but you are different. You trade to help the gods reclaim their property instead of trying to make a profit. They are impressed and pleased."

"Good. Maybe they won't strike me down just for the fun of it."

He smiled. "You have no worry of that here. Come. We have refreshments and a place for you to tidy up. You want to look your best when you meet the goddess."

I said, "I need to drop off these and then return for more. I would love to have the bath after I am done." I followed him deep into the temple. I dropped off the sacks and chests in the immense room where they had set down the other artifacts. I emptied out the sacks and chests and left to exchange some more. It took eighty-one trips and six days to exchange everything I wanted removed from inventory. Most of it was junk, evil, cursed, or far too dangerous for me to use, but the Leaches did not care. God-given magical power was all they cared about. Size, properties, curses, and alignment meant nothing to them. I traded one grand, evil, cursed item that would destroy me if I touched it for five grand artifacts that I might have been able to actually use. And I knew that evil artifact would never show up on the Prime Material Plane again. When I removed the last item I wanted gone, I collapsed the druid trap and placed it in my belt pouch.

When I made the last trade, I returned to the Temple of Commeatus. I now had over twenty thousand artifacts that were useless until they charged, but some were already starting to charge quickly. That should get some attention. The acolytes took my sacks and chests to deposit in the artifact room. They took me to another room supposedly connected to the one that had all my artifacts. Hard to tell when there were no doors, no openings, no way to decide where to go.

I had a bath with oils, and they stripped me and took my clothes. When I finished my bath, or I should say when the acolytes finished washing me, I dressed in my old but freshly mended, cleaned, and pressed clothes. The tub disappeared, and a table with one place setting of food and drink appeared. I thought it wrong to check for poisons and such, so I sat down and enjoyed some truly heavenly food and nectar. Much better than the spell Protection Banquet, and I thought that was the best possible. When I was done enjoying myself, I said to the air, "Thank you for the bath and sustenance. I am not sure if I am blessed to have sampled such fare, or cursed that no other food will ever taste good to me now that I have sampled the best."

CHAPTER 18

GODS, GODS, AND MORE GODS

An old man walked in with a smile. He looked like he was ready to go someplace and just returned at the same time. He was small but straight. He had a walking staff that radiated such power I nearly fainted. He radiated so much power I did faint and was held up by an invisible force. He was lovely and had such charisma that I nearly fell to my knees to worship him then and there. I gathered myself and went to one knee. "Commeatus the Traveler."

His smile turned to a frown. "Rise, Prince Charles. I am surprised and disappointed that you did not prostrate yourself before me."

I wanted to go to my belly and try to dig myself as low as I possibly could to prostrate myself and show proper respect to this wonderful god. In a shaky voice, I said, "Great God Commeatus, it is most difficult not to prostrate myself before you. It is taking all my abilities not to. But I dare not. If I prostrate myself to you, then I would need to do it for all the other gods to show impartiality. I would not be able to achieve my goal, as I would be spending far too much time lying face down on the floor."

He smiled. "Still thinking you are impartial. How freshly naive. I have a hard time believing that you would not worship Solbelli. He is your father's god, and you used to pray to him constantly. I can assure you that he claims you."

"Great God, I do not see how he can claim someone whose prayers he never answered."

"Foolish child, he was busy elsewhere and paid no attention to a babe that became bitter."

Now I was becoming defensive and stopped using titles and honorifics. "I became bitter because of what was happening and the lack of an answer. Please don't tell me he could not interfere. He could have, at minimum, sent a priest to let me know there was a reason. But there wasn't a reason, was there?"

"Solbelli is a busy god and does not have time for answering all prayers. No god does. At that time, you were not very important."

"You probably mean that I was not very important to his plans."

"True."

"Great Commeatus, for a long time now, I have understood just that. I cannot count on the gods for help or advice unless I am part of their plans. Sad that is. I would gladly listen to advice when given, but I will always remember that they have their own agendas, their agendas may not match mine, and they may be busy. I will rely on my own abilities."

"Foolish, foolish child. You have no choice in anything we do not give you a choice in. Speaking of abilities, you told my acolyte that you would trade my artifacts for increased abilities. Enhancements you called them."

"If I have a choice. Once I identify the artifacts and keep the ones I need for my plans, I will gladly trade for making me a better human. I don't want wealth or power. I would like to be better myself. I feel the gods know what would make me a better human and someday a good champion."

"Then you would be our champion. How nice. We normally pick our own. However, right now there are many gods that are both mad with you for trading their artifacts to the Leaches and happy you returned a great number of artifacts that were draining some dry. In addition, they wonder if you know where some certain missing artifacts are. We think the druids took them." He started walking me toward the artifact room. "I want you to see what you have created, little one."

We walked into a room full of gods and demigods. Over two hundred of them. I did not faint, but I would have been rightly justified in doing so. Each god's acolytes were sorting artifacts and placing them onto tables near the god they belonged to. Some had finished and were standing by a table as if guarding or talking to another god with little to no care. Commeatus placed a hand on me, and my ability to see magic went away. He said, "Such a minor ability would have faded anyway."

I looked directly at him for the first time since I fainted. "Thank you, Commeatus. That was very kind. I was expecting some godly interest, but I was not expecting this many."

"I was expecting more. The Leaches gave you a good representation of all the gods' artifacts. These gods want their artifacts back, and so do I. However, this is a trade and therefore meets the requirements of this tiny plane. I do not wish to lose my temple here, so I am complying with the trade rules."

Solbelli appeared out of nowhere and said, "Most of us believe you should donate them to our churches. Your father would give mine back without asking for anything in return. You are not your father, are you?"

I had not known he was there, but when I heard his voice, I cried. Here was the god that had forsaken me into exile, the god that refused to listen to my prayers, the god that ignored me in my times of need, the god that ignored my country and allowed my brother to make a pact with demons and almost get away with it. He heard my prayers, he knew what was going on, and he did nothing. I took a minute to calm myself. I did not acknowledge his statement or question. I turned to Commeatus and said, "Great God Commeatus, for your help with this, I will look at your artifacts first."

He walked me past many gods and to several tables. "These are my artifacts, or the artifacts of the demigods that are aligned to me." Several extraordinarily beautiful ladies and men were standing at the tables. One touched me, and I instantly knew what each artifact did. I bowed to them and picked up the first item I thought I would like to have. The Staff of Travel, a grand artifact and very powerful. With it, I could travel anywhere in any plane of existence except the druid plane and a few others protected by Over Gods. I could even travel around Shadow Mountain or teleport directly into my father's castle throne room. I told them, "This I would love to have and use. And it will help with my plans. The rest is yours for raising my abilities one level each and a promise you will never take the ability raise back. After all, my agenda may not match yours all the time. Though I will try not to displease you."

His smile was radiant. He raised a hand, and I felt everything increase. He said to one demigod, "Take these to a safe place."

A small childlike goddess walked up and asked, as if I had no right to not answer, "Your plan to correct an old issue on your world? I see it in you but not details. Your mind is blank for some reason." She looked at my hand and then asked, "How long will it take?"

I bowed low and answered, "Great Goddess, it depends on which plan. The first one I expect planting in three years and completion in five, given free will to correct things the way I wish."

She looked up at what appeared to be her mother and said, "That will work. We will agree to that time frame."

Commeatus said, "Then there are only two holdouts."

I had no idea what they were doing. It sounded like voting on my plan. However, I had not told anyone my plans since my escape from the trap. Somebody had been reading my mind before I received the ring. Darn.

I moved to the next set of tables and instantly knew what was there and what each artifact did. I selected two items from that table and said, "You may have the rest for the raise of all my abilities and the same promise." I felt my abilities go up, and it felt good, very good. The demigod that the items belonged to nearly beamed with pride while looking at a glowing, beautiful goddess I did not recognize. I looked over to Commeatus questioningly.

"Charles, this is the goddess of blue light. She has no followers on your planet, but sometimes it affects her followers. She is pure good. All the gods and demigods will be most happy to have you use their artifacts. It uses their power but in a way that allows them to grow. The Leaches use the power in a way that destroys them. Besides, they can keep better track of you if you are using their artifact. The gods can find you anyway, but artifacts make it much easier. The demigods would have a difficult time finding you without them. Oh, and yes. The moment you escaped, a dozen gods read your mind."

"Commeatus, why is it you can read my mind while I am wearing this ring?"

"It's my artifact. I can bypass it at any time."

I turned to the goddess of blue light and went to one knee, saying, "Thank you, Great Goddess. I am most honored."

She smiled bigger and said, "I like your manners, Charles."

Something was wrong. They were being too nice. Not treating me like a child or fool for bringing them together. I said, "Thank you, Great One." I turned to Commeatus. "As far as the 'finding me' is concerned, oh well. I suppose being findable can't be helped."

He laughed long and hard. "You see. You do need the gods—or at least their toys."

I smiled at him. "Everyone needs the gods. I know I do. I have a burning need to believe in someone. However, I need to find a god I can trust and who will pay attention when needed. In return, I will do my best to make that god greater." Several gods laughed as if I had no idea.

Solbelli said with amusement, "That is a bold and improper statement, child, since you belong to me."

I said most humbly as I turned and went to one knee, "I beg your pardon, Great Solbelli, but at this time, I belong to no god. Your agenda and mine do not match, Great God Solbelli. In addition, your inattention when I was a child and needed you gives me the right to choose another, one that I can trust."

Solbelli turned angry, and his hand rose. I remained kneeling, waiting for him to strike me down.

Commeatus yelled, "Stop! This is the Temple of Commeatus, and you have no right to strike a guest of mine. Charles, you may stand. No one will harm you here." I stood up. Commeatus turned toward Solbelli and said, "Do not threaten a guest of mine again." Then he turned away and led me to another table. Amused, he asked, "What are your thoughts on alignment, child? Yours seems wavy and difficult to lock down."

I would have laughed at the question, as I knew he already knew the answer, but I was still waiting for Solbelli to strike me down. His anger was evident. "Great Commeatus, I may be mistaken. You would know better than I, but I believe I am mostly good. I try to be good all the time, but sometimes I tend to be more noncommitted. I can't help it. It just turns out that way. Once in a while, especially if someone attacks me or threatens me, I become evil. That seldom happens, but it can and does. Spices things up a little." I winked at a particularly beautiful devil girl who looked to be about my age and said, "I sometimes have some very evil thoughts."

Silvestris, the god of nature, said while looking at the devil, "Nothing evil about those thoughts, boy. Have them myself, I do. The evil retribution thoughts need work though."

Another god, one of pure evil, said, "They do not. When someone attacks you without warning you, then kill them. Kill them and take as long as you can about it. Leave no enemy behind is what I always say." On the side, he said, "I'll loan her to you anytime you want, boy. She can teach you ways to handle a woman that no woman knows."

I looked at Commeatus and said, "See? That's why I can never be perfectly good. I happen to agree with that god's opinion of enemies. Except I try to make it quick and painless most of the time. In addition, being a virgin at that specific time in life where women are beginning to become interesting, well, that was a nice offer in my mind."

Commeatus shook his head laughing and said, "She'll rip you to shreds while you sleep. I feel the good in you, and it is great good, but I also feel the evil in you. You could never be my follower, nor could you be Solbelli's." He turned to Solbelli. "He is not always your alignment, my old friend. He is a bit chaotic."

Solbelli was calmer and said, "I will ignore the alignment issue. He is needed."

Commeatus said, "I understand. But what about after he is no longer needed for your current plans? Would the alignment issue be prevalent then? I would say it would. No, he needs someone that is slightly good and very forgiving."

Another god yelled out, "Or one that couldn't care less if he drifts one way or the other."

The discussion went on for hours while I continued to walk around the room, pick out the items I wanted, and receive blessings. At one point, a demigod said to his goddess, "I cannot raise him higher. He is already higher than I am."

"Then I will raise him for you." Again, all my abilities went up, and I said my thanks. This got the attention of several gods that were close. I picked out what I wanted and then tried to make the same deal with them.

"Little Charles, we very much want to raise your abilities higher, as we want our artifacts. However, you are becoming demigod level. You are far from ready for such a turn. Your strength is near mine, and no god will raise you higher than their own abilities. You have twice the strength of a gargantuan death serpent, are much faster than an elder spirit runner, your constitution is double that of a black dragon, your intelligence is so high you may find demigods coming to you for information, your wisdom is beyond mine and near Proba, and you are so beautiful and have such charisma that even the gods are looking at you with love and lust. You will find your mental ability to withstand command or domination attacks, even without that ring, greater than most demigods. With your speed, I would be surprised if you could be caught in a fireball or lightning strike even if a god used it on you."

"Then what would you suggest? What ability could you grant that would make me better without raising my base abilities?"

A very lovely goddess dressed in white with eyes of ice said, "I will make him immune to cold. That way he can visit me all he wants."

"Good idea. Charles, will you agree to be immune to fire?"

"Of course."

"So be it."

I felt something wash over me, and a devil came over and placed her hand on my arm. She flared up into flame for only a second, and though I felt some heat, it was not uncomfortable. She said, "Well, that worked. He should have turned to ash."

Commeatus looked at her sternly, and she said defensively. "What? You could have raised him."

Again, I thought to myself, *Something is wrong. This is way too easy.*

The next goddess made me immune to cold. Then a god made me immune to electricity, and this went on until I was immune to things I had no idea existed. Now fire, cold, lightning, sound, acid, poison, a lot of death spells, and twenty other things would never harm me. I could breathe water and move normally under water. I thought that was good until a greater god made it so I never had to breathe. One god gave me "Great Regeneration." Demigods were giving me supernatural abilities like perfect flight extraordinarily fast at will all day every day, and planer travel at will without the need for spell components. By the time I was finished with most the gods, I did not need half the artifacts I had collected, including the Staff of Travel. I gave some of them back. When the gods saw this, they waited to see what I would pick from their piles and then gave me that ability. Understand Language was a spell I didn't need anymore because I knew all languages. They were being so free with their gifts I became extremely suspicious. What I did not know at first was they were playing a fun little game with me and all of them were in on it. Power him up but control him completely. Though it was designed so that only one god had the key, and I had no idea who that god would be.

Now that I was watching for something, I caught one goddess adding control into her blessing and watched for it in the next three. I checked for it in myself and dispelled it before they could make it permanent. I secretly nullified each control spell. As they said them, I said one also. A counterspell to their control spell. I did it silently and without movement. My spell was hidden inside theirs so no one could notice. I erased all the control. It was difficult, as they were far better than I. Still, they had no idea because of the ring, and Commeatus was busy talking to another god. They did not hide what they were doing as well as they could have. They could not see that part of their spell was not taking effect, and when the last god was done and tried to close the control permanently, I stopped it. I stood there powered up to a maximum.

Solbelli came to me with a smile. "Was that fun, child? You are now the most powerful human I have ever seen that is not demigod or god level. You could do almost anything you want anywhere you want. Who's going to stop you?"

I smiled back at him. "No one except myself, Great God Solbelli."

"Only yourself? And why would you stop yourself?"

"Great God Solbelli, you are a god. Do you not know why I do what I do before I do it?"

"Humor us, child."

I now knew. They allowed this for fun. They could have taken their artifacts. They allowed this out of boredom. I remained very serious even though I wanted to laugh. I answered, "I did not do this for power. I did this so that I may fix several problems that the gods cannot interfere with. You could fix the problems in an instant, but it will take me many years of hard work. When I have completed these issues and I am ready to move on, I am sure other worlds, solar systems, galaxies, and planes (universes) need the same services. Is this not true?"

Solbelli answered, "How interesting. You are offering to supply us with a service we could easily do ourselves but won't because it gives our opposites power. It is true. Many places have or will be destroyed by creatures that think they know what they are doing. They don't, as you didn't."

"I didn't?"

Solbelli shook his head. "Charles, Charles, Charles. You think the gods would allow you all these benefits without placing some control on the way they are used? How typically naive. We have chosen a god for you. You will obey him in everything. You have no choice."

"My dear and Great God Solbelli, I am surprised that any god would want me. I am a handful."

"Yes, and now that you are immortal, you are a threat to many of us with all those powers."

"I am no threat to any god or demigod that does not attack me. I do not wish to have followers. I do not wish to tell others what to do or try to guide them in their lives. If a god has an issue with what I am doing, then please talk to me. We can work things out. You do understand that to place me under one god gives that god a champion that he or she could use against others?"

Solbelli said, "Oh, child, of course we know. We argued about that exact issue. We have a god that is purely noncommittal. A god that is beholding to none and has sworn to us that he will not use you against us or ours."

"And does this god agree that this control is needed?"

Solbelli said, "Surprisingly, no. He thinks that you will do what is right. He trusts that you can work on your own and therefore it won't be any skin off his back to have control. But if you start doing something he disagrees with, he will stop you and put you in your place."

"I like that. What is this god's name?"

Silvestris walked up. "I am that God. You are to worship me, and I will use you in any way I wish."

Several of the gods and goddesses looked shocked. One said, "That is not what you told us. It is not what we agreed on."

Silvestris said, "Oh well."

I turned to Solbelli. "Bad mistake, Great One. Silvestris wants a war with the humans so that nature can take its rightful place instead of hiding in holes. I am partially in agreement that nature has been dumped on and way past the point of war. It is a shame, as many of you will lose great numbers of your followers during this war. I could be ordered to wipe out all humanoids on the Prime Material Plane."

Many were looking at Silvestris. Proba asked, "Is this true, Silvestris?"

"You know how I dislike the humanoids. What would you expect? When you asked what I would do with him, I told you. I will have him correct the issue. You did not ask what the issue is." He turned to me. "Now, boy! Bow down before your god."

I smiled and said, "No." Everyone was in shock. Either by Silvestris's treachery or the fact that he apparently could not control me. I walked over to that female devil demigod, put an arm around her, and kissed her with passion. Then I let her go and returned to my place. "I don't take orders unless I want to. I don't give orders unless necessary. And I have my own agenda." I knew I was about to be dust—or worse. Several gods were looking very distressed at me and at Silvestris. I needed to align myself quickly. I looked around until I saw Natura, the good goddess of nature. The most beautiful goddess I have ever seen. To the extreme surprise of all, I walked over to her and prostrated myself.

She smiled down at me. I could feel it deep within me, and it felt wonderful. "Rise, Charles."

I stood up. "Do you mind if I pray to you and Silvestris once in a while? I am a good friend of nature and may need your opinions sometimes."

"Will you listen to what I have to say?"

"I will always listen to both of you. I will decide what is correct myself, but I will listen."

"I take you as a shared follower with Silvestris, if he agrees."

I went to one knee and said, "Thank you. I will do my best not to disappoint." I got up and went over to Silvestris and looked him right in the face. "I need you. Even with your pranks. I am trusting the goddess Natura to help me see through them. Still, I need your input to my plans, and I need you to keep my mind straight so that I am not looking at only one view." I looked at Natura for a second. "She is a most lovely view, and it may be difficult for me not to zealously follow everything she says."

Silvestris laughed. "She is that, boy. I have never denied she is a good thing to look at. However, you would do better worshiping that devil demigoddess. At least with her you'd get a little something now and then. Natura is cold as ice and after thousands of years probably still a virgin."

I could feel the look she was giving him, and it said, "You will pay."

Silvestris continued a little nervously, "I will protect you from her wiles and point out when she is being prejudiced again and again. You do know that woman and I don't get along very well?"

"Yes, I do know. I love her and always have. I did not know that until I met her. She is the good I need in my life. She will keep me on the correct path. You are the straightforward, pull-no-punches, tell-me-as-it-is mentor. I need that just as much."

"Good. I like a follower that I can look right in the eyes and talk straight to, without having to soften my words. I will share your worship."

I went down on one knee. "I will trust and love you until you prove it is no longer wise to do so."

"Get up, boy. You want to talk to me—let's do it face-to-face."

I stood. "As you wish. I will erect temples to the two of you in all the places I repair. The people I allow into these places will be gently encouraged to follow you through example. I will not force or tell someone whom they should worship. But the greatness I will do for them they will know comes from the two of you."

They both smiled at that. Solbelli whispered, "Darn."

Silvestris looked at me with one eye raised, one nearly shut, and a small twist of his head. A look that said I pulled one over on him. "How is it you do not have to obey me, boy?"

"My dear god, I recognized that more than blessings were being used. I just spent over three thousand years studying magic. Did you think I would not recognize and neutralize a control spell?"

Proba said, "That spell is considered, by humans, as somewhat evil. We were thinking you may not have studied evil spells."

"I studied everything."

Natura asked, "Everything? Do you know what other artifacts are hidden away within the Druid Suppository of Magic and Knowledge?"

"I do, and yes, the Great Sun Rod is there. I will be using it."

Proba said, "That makes you very dangerous to us."

"Good thing Natura and Silvestris have control over me, then."

"They, by your own words, only give opinions."

"True. However, I will listen and normally obey. They will guide me. I will not be a threat unless of course they think I need to be."

Something appeared in the midst of the gods, and the gods went to one knee. I did not get a chance to see it, as Commeatus grabbed me and pulled me down with him. Anything the gods respected was probably something I did not want to upset. I didn't even look up. My eyes were shut, and I kept them that way. I felt something lift my head by the hair, and then something slammed into my forehead.

Instantly I was in a pain so intense that I cannot describe it. Telling you a thousand icy-hot knives were slammed into my brain and the blades crawled throughout my body would be making light of the pain. Yet I did not pass out. I could not. All those buffs to my abilities made it so I would not. I opened my eyes and looked at the thing in front of me holding my hair. It was pure energy of some kind. It took no real shape. In my head, as if the ring were nothing, it said, "You like artifacts so much. This one will ensure you do not go beyond our agenda!" The creature disappeared.

Gods started standing up and looking around. Natura came to me and held me in her arms, rocking me back and forth as a mother would a child, saying, "It will be over soon, my little one. It will be over soon."

As soon as they saw the way was clear, most gods and demigods departed by the quickest means possible.

Solbelli looked down at me and said, "This is the first time I have seen them attack a human child."

Pravus said, "It is the first time I have ever felt sorry for one."

Silvestris said, "Cursed. They cursed him. That artifact is an abomination."

Olkey said, "No human can learn to control that artifact. What were they thinking! He can never have contact with anyone. We should kill him now."

Natura said, "It will not do any good. This Star Fire is attached to his spirit. He will always have it, and no one can remove it. His soul cannot be trapped or harmed with this in him. I do not have that kind of power. This will set our—and his—plans back a little."

Commeatus placed a hand over the artifact and intoned something I was in too much pain to hear what it was. He said, "Together, all the gods that were here tonight could not remove this. It is a grand artifact even to an Over God."

Solbelli and Pravus said, "I'm out of here." They quickly left. All the others, upon hearing that it was an Over God grand artifact, ran nearly screaming from the room.

Commeatus looked at Silvestris and Natura. "Will you also abandon him?"

Natura said, "No. The artifact is starting to activate, and when it does, our lives are in danger. Still, I will not leave him until he is able to control his body again. Then I am afraid I must. I will explain it to him first."

Silvestris said, "He needs someone he can trust. I will stay also. Though it may mean my death."

Natura said, "You will not die if you do not talk. Both of you keep quiet. I will take the chance."

Both said nothing. I do not know how long she held me. When the fire and ice storms, the acid wash, and everything stopped, I looked up at her shakily and lovingly. She smiled, placed a finger on my lips, and said, "Do not talk. Say nothing. Can you understand me?"

I nodded.

"This is what just happened. When a large number of gods gather together, it attracts the attention of the Over Gods. They were watching us to ensure we did nothing that would harm their plans."

I nodded.

"You know that everyone has their own agenda. So do the Over Gods. They see something in you that they like and can use. If they thought you were a hindrance to them, you would be dead. They saw that you slipped our control. That is a bad thing to them, so they put in a control of their own. You now have a Star Fire. You know what that is? I think all know the story of the last famous creature that had a minor little Star Fire placed in him. He made a great king until he became old and lost his memory. He died from the Star Fire's curse. Do you know that story?"

I nodded.

She continued, "That minor Star Fire made it so that no one could lie to the king without experiencing great pain until they told the truth. You have a Star Fire reserved for only great gods. You know the level of artifacts. If you placed this artifact up to the Staff of Nature, another Over God grand artifact, the Staff of Nature would not even seem masterwork in comparison. You now have one of the greatest artifacts in the known galaxy, and it will kill many if you cannot control it. You see, yours is so powerful that I am having a difficult time looking at you. Even to a greater god, you are overwhelming to look at. This Star Fire's curse is that you can never lie or tell half truths. You will not die. You simply cannot lie verbally, whether knowingly or unknowingly. Illusion spells may be possible. Deception may also be possible. I do not know. Also, and this will hurt, no one can lie to you. Even if they do not know they are lying or telling a half truth in any way. If they do, they will feel pain that will quickly increase until their body dies and then their spirit dies or they tell you the truth. I cannot take this from you. Its attachment is beyond a normal god to remove. Death will not relieve you of this curse. Do you understand?"

I nodded.

With tears in her eyes, Natura said, "You must go someplace where no one is or will be. You must stay there. Unless you can find a way to control this curse, you must stay alone for all eternity."

I stood up, went to one knee, and kissed the hem of her dress to show my obedience. I stood back up and turned to Silvestris and saluted. I then turned to Commeatus and saluted. I picked up my magic sacks and magic chests, and I walked over to the corner and pulled out the druid trap. I opened it and walked in. I went far enough away to ensure I could not hear them, and I lay down. After a day like that, anyone would need some rest. Besides, I needed time to go through what just happened.

Outside, Natura said, "You know how long it has been since someone loved me like that? Someone strong enough to kiss the hem of my dress. Someone who dared to have a little lust in his heart. Over a thousand years."

Silvestris wondered out loud, "He walked into the druid trap a near demigod and extraordinarily powerful. What will he walk out as if he learns to control that thing?"

Commeatus said, "That thing has powers you cannot comprehend. Not even a god can lie or deceive him. I do not think the Over Gods could lie to him without penalties."

Natura said, "If he does not come out within one week, then he is never coming out. To him, each week starts over, and it will be a long time before he learns control, at least a few thousand years. And in that time, he will develop, become greater, stronger, more intelligent. To us, he could walk out at any second. Why is he not going in further? Why is he looking at us like that?"

POST LOG

I was just walking into the druid trap. I turned around and watched them for a few minutes, knowing that they would stay there waiting for me for the entire week. Commeatus and Silvestris would leave for short periods of time, but Natura waited for me. I walked out looking toward the floor.

With an astonished look, Natura said pleadingly, "Charles, you must go back in. You are too dangerous."

I slowly raised my head. My unnaturally bright blue eyes looked through her and deep into her soul. Her entire life lay bare before me. I walked up to her, took her in my arms, and kissed her passionately. I whispered, "I have learned control, and you are correct. I am very dangerous."

2
PART

THE PLAN

PROLOGUE

Charles stood on the top of Dragon Mount Peak and looked out over the expanse of barren land, a land dead and unlivable. A land drenched in sunlight so intense that in most areas the soil cracked and crumbled, creating an impassible and ever-changing land of crags and crevasses so large they could not easily be crossed. During the rainy season, the land flooded and was covered twenty feet deep with fresh water for half the year. This created a lake so big that many called it an inland sea. Yearly, the rain muddied and mixed the topsoil, filling in the cracks, smoothing out the land until the entire region was a flat expanse of mud. Then the dry season would crack it again and completely change the landscape. No roads, no paths, nothing except topsoil for as far as the eye could see. Every few years, dragon bones could be found deep in the crevices of the dried-out land. Once every hundred years, large sections were uncovered where thousands of dragon bones lay like a graveyard of strangely shaped ivory trees. Those years went unnoticed by living creatures, as no one crossed this barren land except the undead. Hundreds of leagues of impassible, waterless, hot land for six months, or a sea of deep mud for the other six months.

This was the Arid Realm of Sordeath, the undead lands, a paradise lost, destroyed during the Dragon Pepper War and the realm of the undead king. This was the land Charles promised the gods he would make a paradise again. The plan many gods called him fool for. A task even the greatest gods did not want to undertake. A task that evil and good both wanted completed. It had to be done soon or hundreds of thousands would die of starvation, and it had to be done politically correctly or hundreds of thousands would die in the wars it would create.

CHAPTER 1

PHASE ONE—THE
UNDEAD WAR

I thought about the layout of the continent. The Arid Realm of Sordeath sat in the Dragonback Mountains just west of Ringal (King Tyler's Land) and east of Dailith (Queen Alluvia's Lands). My father's land of Kayland sat on the east of Ringal. The Elvin lands of Treestorm Forest spanned the north of Kayland and Ringal with just a few leagues touching the northern border of Sordeath's Dragonback Mountains. The Mordepths (Dwarven King Golden Fist) were in the head of the Dragonback Mountains at the center northern edge of the Sordeath. The rest of the northern border was taken up by the Demon Lands, which also spanned the north and west of Dailith. To the south were the Sea of Plenty and the Colic Islands (pirate lands). Above the Demon Lands were the Ice Lands (unclaimed). To the east of Kayland were the Dead Lands (unclaimable). To the east of the Dead Lands was the Rosewood (Witch Queen Cursegranter). To the north of the Dead Lands and Rosewood with just a little touching Kayland was the Ginham (King Odoray). North of Ginham but south of the Ice Lands was the High Horde Planes (orc and goblin territory). South of the Dead Lands and Rosewood were the Rainwards (shared forest lands of the southern druids and the Aroan elves).

I stood and looked around while continuing my thoughts. Most of the realms depended on Kayland for food, and Kayland's food source was Shadow Mountain, the headquarters of Duke Edward and the Clear Water Valley. Several realms had outgrown their respective lands and what their lands could produce. The druids and elves refused to cut back the forests, thank the gods, and therefore needed food from Kayland to help with their population growth. Rosewood could have cared less. Very few people crossed into the witch queen's lands, and few returned alive. The dwarven lands were starting to depend on Kayland for fruits and vegetables to help wash down the rocks. Ringal had always been dependent on Kayland, and that was the only reason they did not attack. Dailith was protected from Ringal by the Sordeath, but Queen Alluvia had the Demon Lands bordering her on the north and west, and little to eat in her mountainous country besides mountain goats and sting weeds. She got her food from Kayland by ship. The Colic Island pirates stole anything they could to survive. Ginham was hostile to Kayland but needed the food and therefore did not attack anymore. The last time they attacked, everyone else was very upset, because their food had to go to Kayland war preparations. Five nations put Ginham in its place. King Odoray said at the time, "Happened once. Lesson learned. Won't happen again."

I remembered reading about a drunken party after the war with Ginham. King Golden Fist, King Tyler, King Farsite, Queen Alluvia, and my father sat around the big table making grand declarations. One of their drunken boasts was "If any man, or woman, defeats the undead king and his army, I will declare him king of the Sordeath and the Dragonback Mountains." All agreed, and it was written up and made law. "Fool kings and queens, remind me not to drink."

I sat down contemplating the first part and probably the easiest part of my plan. How do I defeat the ancient undead, demonic, vampire letch king of Sordeath and his extremely powerful undead generals, captains, and ten thousand undead soldiers? When the law was made, the letch king only had two thousand undead soldiers. It seemed the undead king was building up forces for some grand plan of his own. There were ways to destroy undead, but to put to rest ten thousand tortured and angry souls was not going to be easy.

I sat there thinking to myself, *I could tease them out into the open and have the earth swallow them up, but many are ghosts, and this would not affect them. They would just swarm up through the ground, and the rest would dig their way back up and attack me. I could take on twenty or even a hundred ghosts and live, but a thousand or more? Not going to happen. I could attack the castle and challenge the king to a dual. No, he is evil. Why should he play on my terms? He would send his entire army to wipe me out. No, I need to destroy his army to get to him.* Then a thought crossed my mind. *Oh, that's an interesting idea. It could work. No harm in trying.*

That night, I sat watching the Black Castle of Greater Darkness. Every four hours, a patrol would leave to travel toward the three passes and return. Difficult for humans to do, but flying or floating undead paid little attention to terrain. The group that headed toward Sweetwater Pass consisted of about five hundred creatures, mostly human zombies given the ability to fly. There were a few ghosts and one captain, a large Demconie. Demconie were rare demon apes with six arms protruding from their spine that were long enough for the Demconie to use for climbing or walking like a spider. Normally they used them for ripping their food apart. Giant in size and stronger than a dragon, the Demconie were deadly and extremely quick, but this one was not undead. I hid in the mountains, and as they flew by, I said a simple spell called Insanity. I turned the captain insane. Then I did a shift to the rear of his troops. The moment he went insane, he stopped, and one of his troops bumped into him. He took it as an attack and smashed that troop. The fight was on. I sat back and enjoyed. All I had to do was destroy any undead trying to escape and report. Only two tried, and I took them out easily. The captain was last standing, but he was so beat up I destroyed him with the first spell. I then used fire to destroy the remains while saying prayers and blessings for all of them. No sense leaving the letch king replacement materials. A letch king can always put the parts back together. Step one complete.

I teleported back to the spot overlooking the castle and waited. Sure enough, five hundred more left in exactly four hours. They even had the same complement of creatures, except the captain was a Blue Scraper, another nasty creature, but again not undead. This was the biggest Blue Scraper I had ever heard of. It had to be at least twenty feet tall even hunched over like it was. I did the same thing, and it worked again. I was wondering if this would work a third time, so I teleported back.

I waited, but no third group. The other two directions kept coming and going, but I could not attack them yet, as that would ruin my plan. The next night, I showed up just after sunset and watched as the largest dragon I have ever seen flew overhead. It was a gargantuan red undead dragon. As soon as he passed, five hundred troops left for Sweetwater Pass.

"So, they have a watcher." I had seen where it came from. Directly above the castle was a great dark opening. I thought it was for rain drainage during the winter. I was wrong, and it nearly got me killed. This was the lair of something almost as difficult to destroy as the letch king. I flew up into its lair, and it stunk. I was expecting undead everywhere, but the dragon lived alone. I found its treasure. This dragon had been collecting for a very long time. I took it all. It took me almost four hours, using every spell I could to move the treasure to my location in the Dead Lands. My tower was nearly full, and it was a big tower. Then I went back, grabbed a zombie, used it to wipe the ground and erase my smell, and then left it to walk around acting lost.

When the dragon returned, the roar was enough to make one want to curl up into a fetal position and whisper, "Mommy." He was furious and with good reason. He flew out of the cave and started looking. I teleported away before he could find me, mostly because I was not sure the zombie trick had worked. I made my way back to my hiding place in the mountains. The five hundred were just returning, so I turned the captain insane. This time, I had to levitate a ghoul and toss him into the captain. The battle was on again. Several took off to report. I had a difficult time trying to keep them contained. I did, and I finished off the captain and destroyed all the remains.

The next night, I showed up at the castle, and all the many hells had broken loose. The undead dragon was now dead, and the castle was all torn up. It hadn't looked good before, but now it looked about to fall apart. Undead were burnt up in the fires that the dragon's breath created. The letch king was out on the battlements looking for something. He was probably looking for me. I was not sure, but I would bet those two holdouts at the god artifact party told on me. "Snitches!" The letch king was missing three captains, one thousand five hundred undead, and now several thousand more undead were sent to rest due to the efforts of the dragon. He was down to just over half his troops. He did not look happy. I went away for one week. Gave him time to think something was going on but no information as to what.

I returned, and things looked back to normal. I knew better, but that was what he probably wanted me to think. Little things had changed. For example, the troops leaving to go to the passes. Before, he was sending out unintelligent, incapable, undead, easy prey. Now his easy prey included vampires and creatures capable of sending mental thought back to him, teleporting away, or curing insanity. Ghosts were prevalent, and some stayed underground. This was going to be a little more difficult.

I went home and into the druid trap, grabbed the artifact called the Sun Rod, and then returned. I waited for them to obtain some distance from the castle but not so far that they could not ask for help. Once they were in place, I did an enlarged Mass Enrage spell, taking in as many of the intelligent nonvampires as possible. Then I went invisible and teleported into their ranks. Once I found someone enraged, I pushed another into him, and then I teleported out and back to my vantage point. The fight was on. I used the artifact Sun Rod to create sunshine just above their heads, and the vampires all turned to dust. I did not wait this time. I teleported to the next group and did the same thing, and then I teleported to the third and repeated the performance.

All three groups had creatures return to the castle ragged and warn. Some were still enraged and attacked the nearest creature they could find. I added to the riot by teleporting into the castle and causing insanity on the last three captains and two generals. Normally insanity, bewilderment, or enrage does not work on undead, but a greater insanity works on any single creature, and at my level, bewilderment and enrage work on any creature that can think. I also did a Greater Travel Lock on the balcony the letch king liked to watch from and then teleported out. I watched from my hidden vantage point and saw creatures pour out of the castle as the three captains and generals fought everything and each other.

At one point, the letch king came out to see what was going on. I teleported down and did a solid Force Confinement around him. I had seen him come out during the day, so I knew that daylight was not affecting the ancient vampire letch king, which meant that he had his demonic soul hidden away in another part of the castle. Oh, he was mad. He tried everything to get out and then glared at me. I was totally invisible, hiding, and silent, and he knew exactly where I was. He was looking right in my eyes and becoming upset that his domination was not working.

I took off to find out where his soul was hiding. If you are powerful enough to pull out your soul and hide it, then you can hide it almost anywhere. The problem with doing this is you need to spend time with your soul every few days or so. If not, the body starts to die, and you become a ghost. I did not want this powerful being becoming a ghost on top of everything else. I needed to destroy that soul and quickly. I had no idea how long he had been out of it, and I did not want to take a chance that he was coming due for a visit.

I did a simple spell that looked for spirits without bodies. That did not work, due to the vast number of ghosts in the Black Castle of Greater Darkness. I tried looking for his casket, but I found twelve of them in different places. This could take forever. It was a big castle, and I had to fight my way through almost every room. Besides, I would run out of resources eventually. At one point, I nearly died due to an ambush of several dread wraiths. The only thing that saved me was the fear factor. They liked to frighten their prey first, and I had a contingency spell on me that "If surprised, teleport one hundred feet away." After that, I prepared for them and disrupted all of them as they came after me.

Three days later, I found a room full of covered vases. Hundreds of them all in neat little rows on shelves. The entire room, fifty feet by fifty feet and twenty feet tall, was filled floor to ceiling with small vases, and they all looked alike. There were invisible creatures dusting and cleaning. There was no clue which one held the letch king's soul. I tried detecting undead, and they all had undead in them. Each vase held a nasty ghost or wraith. What's a sorcerer going to do? I did a quickened, widened, maximized Smash spell destroying every vase and then teleported out of there.

One thing good about spirits, they do try to return to the body if released. I waited one hundred feet out from the balcony. The letch king was sitting there smirking at me. I smiled back and continued to wait. Every ghost and wraith in that room came flying out trying to kill me. I called upon Natura, and using the power of a god, my high charisma, my clerical level, and with an artifact parapet of turning undead, I destroyed them all in one move. All except the one that stayed down by the force confinement. The one trying desperately to get into the space and back with its body. I quickly moved within range and destroyed that soul. The undead letch king was now dead, but I needed him destroyed or he could come back. I dispelled the force confinement and teleported the body high into the air, up where the sun was just coming over the eastern mountains. The body turned to dust and dispersed.

Once the letch king was dead, every vampire in the castle died. That was a surprise. A major vampire can choose to have his vampire offspring attached to him in such a way for control. However, most would not care. Apparently, this letch king had decided to protect himself from his children by ensuring that if he died, they died.

The captains were still fighting the generals. The generals were winning. I waited until the fight was over and walked up to the last standing general. He was an undead devil of great power. His god was flowing through him, and he was still powered up fully. He glared at me.

I said, "How interesting. Your god is directly interfering with my plan."

He talked in nice, even tones. "You have made a mistake, human child. You have just interfered with Pravus's agenda. He is not happy." He attacked me, but I was not there.

He screamed his rage and looked all over for me. I wasn't paying attention, as I was laying down traps all along his path. I took my time setting up ten deadly traps, all good aligned. Then I went to the opposite end of the path and pulled my swords. He heard the adamantine leave the golden sheaths and turned. His smile could not have been bigger. He pulled his massive two-handed claymore and started forward at a run. He ran right through every trap, and they all went off and did nothing to him. My best traps did nothing. I realized that, as long as his god was helping him, I had no chance. So I left. He followed. So this time I went someplace he could not go. The Dead Lands. Right in the middle. My tower. He showed up outside my protections, and I watched as he slowly started dying. Even his god could not protect him from the Dead Lands. He teleported away, so I teleported to the Black Castle of Greater Darkness. He was there and not in very good shape. I pulled my swords, and he turned. His god had finally left him. A god can only help so much before other gods start taking grand advantage. He pulled his claymore and ran at me, right back through my ten traps. Magical traps tend to reset. He set three off before he was drained of all his strength. I walked up to him and destroyed him easily. Then I collected my traps and went home.

When I traveled home last time, I had noticed a difference. That dragon treasure that filled up my tower was gone. My tower was not filled up anymore. Someone had come into my home and taken all my treasure. Not that I needed it; after all, I had plenty in the druid trap. But the idea that someone had stolen my treasure before I could go through it and pick out what I wanted irked me to no end. My evil side peeked out.

CHAPTER 2

THE ABYSS

I looked around, and sure enough, in the thief's hurry to take everything, he took some items that had belonged to me from the start. Bad move. The treasure, which I was not close to, I could not trace. However, my personal belongings, like the bow Dedrick gave me, I had great fondness for and knew very well. I could track that bow anywhere. I went into the summoning room and started my spells. It took eight days, but I located it. It was sitting on the 523rd Plane of the Abyss. Interesting—that was where my father's sword was traced to by Dedrick.

I gathered the items I needed and plane shifted to the 523rd Plane of the Abyss. I was immediately noticed. When you are a light-tan-skinned little blond blue-eyed human standing in the middle of a city full of huge dark-red-skinned fire demons, you tend to stand out. They quickly surrounded me.

One big demon standing at least fifteen feet tall said, "Look here, dinner."

Another said, "More like snack."

A third asked, "What's it doing here? It must know we will eat it."

The first one said, "I no care. Food." He attacked and died almost instantly. This made the others think. They attacked as one. No spells, I needed no spells, just my two grand artifact swords. I killed eighty-seven before they backed away.

One asked, upset, "What you want? Why you here?"

I answered, "I am here because someone on this plane is a thief. What I want are my items back."

One pointed. "That way, nine days. You not live long going that way."

I repeated the act every place I teleported to. Finally, one intelligent demon asked, "Why are you killing my minions?"

I looked up, way up into his eyes, and said, "Someone on this plane has taken something precious to me. I want it back."

He smiled. "You are looking for Goresomemor. He is an outstanding thief who has been stealing from the Prime Material Plane, as well as others, for hundreds of years. He would be the one that took your item. He lives in a castle exactly 349 leagues in that direction, little human. You are good with those swords, but you will not pass his guards. No demon on this plane or any other will attack him. He is well protected."

I said, "He is dead!" I disappeared and showed up exactly 348 leagues in the direction indicated. About one league away was a castle that could rival the old castles made by giants in the Age of Disaster. It was immense. Something big lived there. I did not see a lot of rooms or windows, but the few buildings I could see made dragon caves look small.

The wall surrounding the castle had to be a thousand feet tall. The one and only gate was big enough for eighty men to walk through without touching each other. The size was daunting at first until I realized, "I can fly. Who cares about how tall the wall is?" I waited that night to be fully charged. I sat there making plans. *These are demons. Spell casters are abundant. They fight to* make rank or get trodden on. *Their entire life is a struggle. They take advantage of anyone weak to gain rank.* That was the in. That was the way to fight these creatures.

I went invisible and teleported to the castle wall in the back. I slowly flew up the wall until I could just peek over. There was a captain, or some such important demon, giving orders. I snuck up on him and cut his hamstrings. He dropped, and I flew away.

The other demons took advantage and killed him. Then they fought amongst themselves until another demon in charge showed up. He stopped them and looked closely at the body. He roared at them for killing one of the captains and killed them all. Then he called some others and claimed victory over that captain and his minions. He was very happy, and some of the other captains congratulated him on his victory.

I tried to teleport away to think, but I couldn't. Bad news, as I could easily be detected. I sat there hiding and trying to figure it out. I spent a few hours walking around invisible to find out how they were magically moving within the castle walls. I watched several come and go and found out they had a password they added to the spells. I waited two days and did the same hamstringing thing to another captain. Everything played out the same. I did this eight times, and finally someone decided that this had to stop, and the big guy came out.

Goresomemor was black as night. He moved like a shadow and used shadows to move from spot to spot. He was at least fifty feet tall, yet it was hard to keep an eye on him. He quickly put the few remaining captains in their place and looked at my latest victim. He knew. He looked around, did some spells, and looked around again.

Glad I did not stick around. I hid without magic, as I knew he would be looking for invisibility. He roared at his captains, saying, "Fools! This is the work of a thief. Something is trying to steal from me. *From me!* Go guard or die. If it gets in and takes any of my hard-won treasure, *you will all pay!"*

I thought, *Great.* I teleported in, took the most seeable treasure available, and disappeared. I placed the picture under a bed, set a trap in the throne room, and teleported out. In no time at all, I heard his roar again.

He came out of the castle and started beating up on the captains, so I teleported down and waited. The captains fought back and did very well. Goresomemor was nearly out of spells and cut up fairly badly before he destroyed the last captain. He walked back into the main room, triggering my trap when he sat down on his throne. You have to give me credit here. Putting a trap inside a throne made of demon skulls was yucky. I'd heard some bad things in the books I'd read, but reality was far worse.

As soon as he sat down, sunlight flared in six directions, leaving no shadows, and I attacked. I did a quick Travel Lock on him and then placed a Force Barrier around both of us. I was in with him and he with me, but he had no special weapons, and there were no shadows to hide or move around in.

He looked down at me and snarled, saying, "Little thief, you did well taking one of my paintings. I thought you gone. Your greed in coming back for more will be your death."

I said, "Hello, thief. You took my treasure and one of my personal items. I am here to kill you, not to steal."

His foot kicked out and nearly hit me, but I was ready. I ducked and then changed into a gigantic white dragon. Now we were eye to eye. I was fresh, and he was severely wounded but healing at a fast rate. I attacked, claw, claw, bite, wing, wing, foot claw, foot claw, and tail. None hit. This demon was very well protected.

He fought back, claw, claw, bite, wing, wing. None hit. I was protected as well.

I concentrated and dispelled magic on him and watched as he showed signs of losing some color. I did a fast Dismiss Magic, and more signs that his power-ups for the previous battle were dispelled.

His claw, claw, bite hit with one claw, and it hurt. I healed almost instantly, which shocked him.

With his power-ups off, I did a full round attack on him. I hit with every swipe and did a rend. He turned and tried to beat his way out of the force confinement. I tore him to pieces, and then he regenerated. In my anger, every time he became aware again, I chewed up on his body. It took a while for me to be able to calm down enough to drop the body and disintegrate it. "No more regeneration for you." I took his artifact Ring of Rejuvenation and put it in my belt pouch. Then I dismissed the force confinement. I spent the next two days clearing out that castle of all treasure, including my father's sword. Someone sent me a message during the cleaning.

> Charles, there is an artifact in that mess that was stolen from one of my demons. He needs it to run his realm, and since you just killed his only rival, my demon could bring grand chaos to this plane if he had that artifact. He is outside with his minions waiting for you to come out so he can attack you and take his artifact from your dead body. However, I know you will kill him and his minions. I prefer that not to happen, so I am making you this deal. Trade with him. He has a grand artifact he cannot use that you need for your plan. Trade him the Morningstar of Devastation for the Great Staff of Nature, and I will forgive you the death of my letch king.
>
> Pravus

I searched the stuff I confiscated and found the Morningstar in question. I did research on its powers and decided I could afford to let it go. It was too evil for me, even in my revenge anger. I went back to the demon castle and caused a lot of fighting sounds and flashes. Illusions are wonderful. I walked out doing several protection spells and holding the Morningstar in one hand. I opened the main gate by hitting it with the Morningstar. The massive iron gate crashed outward as it shattered into thousands of pieces. I looked out on what had to be hundreds of demons with demon bows all pointed at me.

A big demon in the center walked forward, held out a hand, and said, "My Morningstar."

I did a silent, nonsomatic spell of Projectile Turning and then looked directly at him. I took the Morningstar and flipped it so that every one of the nine destroying heads slammed into my other hand. My hand and body should have been completely destroyed, and without my protections, it would have been. His eyes went wide.

He said in a voice not so confident, "You are used up. You were fighting hard and used up your spells. Your clothes are torn, and you are wounded. We saw the battle going on. We could try to kill you where you stand, but we are allowing you to go. You did us a favor by destroying that shadow demon. But before you go, I will have my Morningstar." His arms and wings opened up, and he flared into fire.

In a tiny voice, I yawned and asked, "What was a shadow demon doing in a fire demon's realm?"

He looked at me, realizing that his fire did not touch me or cause me alarm. "He came long ago and took over. He was powerful and took our greatest weapons, including my Morningstar."

I smiled. "Then by right of combat, I took this little toy artifact back. It belongs to me unless you have something to trade."

He was confused. The artifact in question was the greatest artifact he knew about, and I was calling it a toy. His shaman did a spell and fainted. He turned to look and then turned back to me in anger. "Why did you attack my shaman?"

"I did not. He did a Find Magic spell. Wake him and ask what he saw."

They woke him, and he whispered to the demon, "Lord, he is an artifact so great I cannot look at him when detecting magic. It is in him, part of his soul, it is him."

Now the look on the demon's face was tinged with fear. "What would you trade for that weapon?"

"What do you have?" I turned the Star Fire up a little.

He whispered to another demon to go get the goody stick. The demon looked pained, but he left. "I have an artifact equal to that one." Pain shot through him like ice putting out flame. He went to his knees. Arrows shot toward me and magically turned toward their senders and hit hard, killing several. No other attacks came.

I said, "Quickly, tell the truth, and the pain will stop."

"It is not as good as that one." The pain continued.

"Tell the truth, and the pain will stop."

He had no idea what he needed to say, but he was not dumb. The only choice was "It is greater than the Morningstar." The pain stopped.

I looked at him apologetically and said, "The artifact I am part of, that is part of me, is a Star Fire."

"You are cursed by the gods, then."

I noticed that he wasn't in pain on that statement. "Yes, I am cursed."

The demon returned with the goody stick and handed it to me. I looked at it and felt the power of many Over Gods. I knew I had just found a treasure worth, if not equal, to the Star Fire embedded in my head. "Okay, this is a good start. What else do you have to trade?" I was not lying either. This was a great start, but the chances that I would be allowed to keep it were slim.

The demon complained, "The Star Fire showed us. It is worth more than the Morningstar."

I said, "No. The Star Fire showed us it is a greater artifact than the Morningstar. It did not show what it is worth to me."

"What would you have?"

"Simple. I would also have your god oath that you will never use this Morningstar to invade my world, my plane. I do not want to have to take it away from you or anyone else that may be using it. If I do, it will disappear forever."

"You have my god oath as long as my god does not order otherwise."

"Good enough."

I handed the Morningstar to the demon, and he raised it over his head. Cheers erupted from the other demons. I shifted away and then planer traveled to home. I took the staff and all the treasure I had gathered inside the druid trap for safety. When I stepped out, there was a Caelum waiting for me.

I said, "Hello."

She looked at me and around me. "You have it, don't you?"

"Have what?"

She looked irritated and said, "The Great Over God Staff of Nature. You know what I meant."

"I don't have it with me at this time. Besides, don't the gods have their own Staff of Nature?"

"Yes, but it is not nearly as powerful or as dangerous." She looked at the druid trap and started forward.

I stopped her. "Where do you think you are going?"

She looked at me sadly. "Let me go. I was commanded to retrieve the staff or die trying."

I looked harder, and sure enough, there was a command spell of some sort on her. I dispelled it, and she stood back a little. I asked, "Now, why would someone, god level, command you to take the staff from me?"

"First, thank you."

"You are welcome."

She smiled a brilliant smile. "I was sent here by someone that wants the staff badly. Bad enough that he will try to take it at every opportunity. You will never be safe as long as you have it."

I thought, *Clue number one, she said he.* I turned down the Star Fire so she could lie a little but I would still know. I said to her, "Please continue."

In a secretive tone, she said, "The only way to be safe is to give it to a god that can protect it."

I nearly choked but did not show it. That last was a little lie. I really should let the Star Fire loose on this female; I turned it up a little. "What God would want the hassle? I suppose Pravus wouldn't mind."

She nearly fainted. "Few gods have the power to …" She started to pain up, so she changed the sentence. "Protect it from the other gods." There was a proud look on her face as if she had just pulled something over on me. I turned up the power of the Star Fire so that she would start thinking a little better about trying to fool me.

"Really, what gods would those be?"

"There is really only one"—pain drove her to her knees— "that I would give it to." The pain continued and became worse, and she started to panic. She choked out, "There are many gods that can protect it." The pain stopped.

I asked, "What God are you representing?"

"I don't …" Pain shot through her again. "Solbelli!" It was more of a prayer, a call out for her god, than an answer, but the Star Fire only cared that she told the truth. The pain stopped.

I walked around her, thinking, and said, "I am not keeping you from leaving. I have not harmed you. Your own actions are what cause you pain. Either stop trying to fool me or leave."

She finally found it in her to stand back up, but tears were in her eyes. "I should be dead. Why am I not?"

"I control the intensity of the Star Fire. I cannot turn it off or lie myself, but I can control how much it affects others." I smiled. "I turned it up just a tiny little bit."

She looked about to flee and then thought better of it. "Do you really think you can use that staff without repercussions?"

"I know I can."

She waited to see if I would be in pain. "That staff was here from the creation of this galaxy. It has been around since before the creation of this world. No one other than a god has ever used it without doing great harm. What makes you think you are better than them?"

I did not smile at this question. It was a good and honest question. It was evident that Solbelli, the grand god of war, did not want me causing more destruction than I was trying to repair. Heck, I did not want me causing more destruction "Please tell the great and powerful Solbelli that I will study what the gods have used it for, what harm has been done with it, why, and what good. I will consult with my two gods before I use it. I will not use it without both of them agreeing. In addition, if both of my gods wish it, I will give it up in a way that I feel proper."

She looked like I had just told a lie. "How can we trust you on this? That staff is the most dangerous thing on thi—" Pain shot through her. "It's not the most dangerous thing on this planet." The breaths she took were deep and long, and she stood back up with tears pouring down her cheek. "Now what did I do?"

"The Star Fire knows the truth even if you do not."

"What is more dangerous than the staff?"

I looked at her sadly.

She stuttered, "You. You are." It was not a question but a statement of fact. She disappeared with a look of great fear.

I slowly shook my head. *Not my fault I have the darn thing stuck in my head and attached to my spirit!* I turned it down as far as it would go, took a bath, changed clothes, studied the staff, and then plane traveled to Caelums.

CHAPTER 3

CAELUMS

I learned a long, long time ago that when you do something major and it could affect the family, then go see Mother and Father in person. If it was good, they could use it to their advantage. If it was bad, they could mitigate it and make it go away, with punishments of course. I was hoping that this was something good. Unexpected but good. I did not need punishments. Natura and Silvestris were now my family. I plane traveled to the universe of Caelums.

I was wearing my best and felt way underdressed. I was also drawing a lot of attention. I looked like a bum compared to these creatures. Everyone looked like shining white angels—beautiful, kind, and motherly or fatherly. I disliked this place immediately. That plane in the abyss was better and more suited to my current temperament.

A tall male stopped, looked down at me, and said, "I see you are lost, child. May I give directions?"

I smiled. "What is the cost?"

His smile diminished just a little. "There is no cost for helping another."

I smiled brighter. "I like that. I am truly sorry, but some other planes are so hard on me."

Now his smile increased greatly and proudly. He said, "Here, you are welcome. We will not be hard on you."

I touched my forehead where the Star Fire was embedded under the skin. It flared up a brilliant blue to match my unnatural eyes. The veins of the Star Fire shot blue throughout my body. I said, "I cannot tell a lie. This is a beautiful place."

He looked sad and ready to flee but maintained his smile. "Those directions, accursed child?"

"I am looking for ether the Temple of Natura or the Temple of Silvestris." I added proudly, "My gods."

As soon as I said their names, a Caelum appeared from both. The tall man said, "These will help you." He quickly left.

I looked at them and said, "Hello."

A Caelum from Natura took my left arm, and a Caelum from Silvestris took my right arm. Both started to pull in different directions. The Caelum from Natura said, "He mentioned Natura first."

The one from Silvestris said, "He called for directions to our temple. I will show him in person."

I pulled my arms out of their grasp and said, "You may be at odds with each other, but I am not. I will see Natura first, as she is so beautiful, and my eyes would love to see her again. I am in great need of her wise advice. I will see Silvestris second because I trust his opinion greatly. Besides, he has used my new staff more than anyone in history that I can find."

Both said, "New staff?"

"What? Weren't you watching? I have the Over God Staff of Nature."

I found myself in a temple, and it wasn't Natura's or Silvestris's.

Before me was a god talking to several other gods. They were treating him with great respect, so I did also. The Star Fire whispered to me, "Solbelli. The rest is illusion." I smiled and waited. It was a long time before he called me forth. He had been waiting for me to lose patience. After over nine thousand years in the druid trap, I had enough patience for the two of us.

He spoke in a booming voice created to intimidate, "Where is the staff?"

I looked down at my feet and said, "I'm sorry. I don't like someone trying to fool or intimidate me." I turned the Star Fire up to half full power.

In an angry voice, he yelled, "You." He fell off his throne in great pain. His eyes showed great surprise. I touched my forehead, and the Star Fire flared. He stuttered out, "You do have the right to not answer." The pain stopped.

I said, "Great God Solbelli, I am most disappointed, and I am hurt, that I caused you such trouble."

Natura and Silvestris walked in as if this place meant nothing to them. Natura asked, "Finished playing with my champion, Solbelli?"

Silvestris said, "With that embedded in his head, did you really think my champion would not see through your farce?" He turned to me. "You can control it, can't you?"

I turned it way down and bowed to both. My eyes stayed a little longer on Natura and what she was wearing. It made her perfect figure stand out nicely.

Silvestris smiled and said, "Boy, you keep looking at her like that, and she is going to slap you."

I realized he was telling the truth and averted my eyes while saying, "It may be worth it." I turned to Silvestris. "Why is it, my gods, that Solbelli has tried twice to steal the staff from me and you seem to have no idea?"

Natura answered, "Solbelli has created some issues that have kept us very busy, so we did not know. Isn't that true, Solbelli?"

Solbelli looked at my head and said, "Yes, it's true."

Several other gods came in and stood around. Natura said, "Come, Charles, we need to leave."

Silvestris said, "Too late."

An Over God showed up. Thanks to the Star Fire, I could see it for what it truly was. I prostrated myself instantly. It spoke. "Charles, you have done well. You have learned control. The staff is yours. I will put a stop to this childish god play." He held out a hand, and the Staff of Nature, which was hidden in the druid trap and protected in every way I could think of, was in his hand. He floated toward me and touched the staff to my forehead where the Star Fire was embedded. They glowed together, and he stepped back. "Now, the Great Staff and the Great Star Fire are together again. They cannot be parted." He left, but the staff floated over to me, and I took it gently as if I had owned it for all eternity.

More gods were showing up. Soon the entire temple was full except a little circle around the three of us. Solbelli came down to me and touched the staff. His fingers came quickly away as they started to crack and fall off. I said a quick healing spell through the staff, and his hand healed. I don't know why I knew to do it that way, but the Star Fire probably had something to do with it.

He looked disappointed. "The Great Staff of Nature. It belongs to the Star Fire. The Star Fire is you, and therefore the staff belongs to you. How insane is that? You are not even a god. A demigod, yes, but not a god. Yet you have been chosen. Why?"

I looked sadly at him. "I do not know. All I wanted to do was fix two little problems and get back with my family. I doubt I can ever go back for more than a brief visit now. My family is now Natura and Silvestris. I will obey them, mostly. But my life is nothing as I envisioned it. And just when I think I have things worked out, something else changes everything. A demigod?"

Silvestris answered my question. "Yes, Charles. By learning to control that thing, you have passed beginner demigod and progressed to major demigod, and you did it without followers. Few even know you exist. You could become a god with enough followers."

I looked at him with distaste. "That's the last thing I want. The two of you can have them."

Natura nearly laughed. "We will gladly take them and treat them well. You deserve a reward for finding the staff. What would you like?"

I looked her up and down, and she was about to slap me, so I said, "If you are serious, I do have a request."

Silvestris asked, "What would you like?"

"When I finish my paradise, I will need help informing others that I am ready for creatures to populate the forests and other areas, and I would like unicorns."

Natura placed both hands over her heart and took in a breath.

Silvestris said, "You just made someone very happy. Natura loves unicorns. There are only a few left in all the planes. They have been hunted to near extinction."

I said, "They will be protected in my lands."

Silvestris turned a little angry. His moods were easy to see. "What about others of nature's creatures? There are many that are becoming extinct."

I looked at him and did not have to force tears. "I know. All creatures that are not evil and will do no harm will be welcome and protected in my lands."

Solbelli said, "Why not evil? It is a part of you. I watched as you ate that shadow demon over and over."

I blushed. "I told you. I become a little evil when I am attacked. I can't help it. Someone that becomes a little evil in times of need is not basically evil. I'm talking full-time evil. Why not evil? Because the demon realms are on my northern border, and I will need to set up alarms. I cannot do that if the creatures I allow to live there set the alarms off constantly. I will not allow the demons into my lands because they would eat the ones I am trying to protect, including unicorns." Silvestris was starting to spin up a little, so I added, "And all my protection laws will apply to all, especially humans. I do not see them as anything unique."

Silvestris looked surprised, and then he looked at my Star Fire. "You cannot lie. You really meant that, kid?"

"With all my heart."

Silvestris put an arm around me and said, "Let's go to my temple and talk about how to use the staff." He looked at Natura's angry face and changed his plan. "Better idea, let's go to Natura's place. She always puts on a great feast. Best food you'll ever eat. All three of us can talk about your plans and the staff. Did you know that staff was used to make the first unicorns?"

We disappeared and were walking into a temple of simple pleasures. Life was all around, and there were plants and birds of all kinds. It was like being back in the druid trap, only this was smaller. Still, it was an amazing temple. Everywhere I went, the temple continued on.

Silvestris saw my wonder and said, "Nice trick, isn't it? From the outside, you see a wonderful but smallish temple. From the inside, there seems to be a lot more space."

"No trick. The space is there."

"What?" Silvestris looked shocked.

I said in wonderment, "I can see through all illusions, remember. This is not a trick. There is exactly one thousand times more space inside than the outside allows for."

Silvestris looked at Natura and cringed at her smile. Natura said to no one in particular, "A feast for our guests." Instantly a feast was presented for her inspection. She walked around the table and pronounced it a proper curse.

Silvestris exclaimed, "Curse!"

I placed a hand on his shoulder and said, "That was for me. When we were in Commeatus's temple, he fed me a meal that I pronounced a curse. I told him, 'I am not sure if I am blessed to have sampled such fare or cursed that no other food will ever taste good to me now that I have sampled the best.'"

Silvestris said, "Boy, you have a lot to learn. Commeatus does not know good food. Wait until you taste Natura's. It's made from all natural ingredients picked at their perfection and prepared by Caelums that have spent their entire lives learning the best recipes."

I grinned. "I thought the two of you did not get along well together?"

Silvestris leaned in and whispered, "We may not see eye to eye on some things, but no one puts on a spread like Natura. You make a good excuse for me to come over and eat more often. Please make it a habit to visit all you want. The only thing she can't do is wine. The best wine in the entire plane is made by the northern Treestorm elves on your own planet. Tens of thousands of years of practice, you know. Natura has great nectar though. You'll love it."

I raised my voice to normal, even though I knew Natura heard every word when we whispered. Her smile told me she found Silvestris amusing sometimes. "Dearest Natura, goddess of nature and joy to my eyes."

Natura said, "I appreciate your admiration, Charles, but 'joy to my eyes'? Come now." She said that as if to say, "You had better not take it back."

"Do you like wine?"

She smiled fondly and said, "Yes I do but only in small quantities."

"I don't drink, but I have some wine you may like." I put out a hand, and a dusty bottle was in it. You have to love magic. "Silvestris told me it's a very good wine." I did a light magical cleansing on the outside of the bottle and handed it to her.

It floated in the air until she saw the markings and smiled; she reached out a hand and took it. "Nice, very nice. I will keep this northern Treestorm wine for an important occasion. You do know it is over two thousand years old and just aged correctly."

Silvestris was looking back and forth between us and nearly drooling. "You have Treestorm wine? Where did you get northern Treestorm wine?" That has not been around for many hundreds of years." He turned to Natura and said, "Hide that, girl, or the rest of the gods will be visiting very soon."

Natura's right eyebrow shot up for only a second. The wine disappeared, and she said, "Please sit. I think Silvestris has some unanswered questions that I would like to know the answer to myself. You are full of surprises, Charles. You make time pass nicely."

The compliment touched my heart like no other, and it must have showed. Silvestris cleared his throat loudly.

I said, "Oh, sorry. I am not used to being around goddesses, and I think I am far too naive to be around for long. I will be leaving soon. To answer your questions, I destroyed a shadow demon that had been stealing things from us for many centuries. He had a nice wine cellar, and I took that also. In addition, he had three grape vines in a glass box in status. I took everything."

Natura looked on with interest. "This shadow demon, was he on the 523rd Plane of the Abyss?"

"Yes, my goddess."

"And you took everything?"

"Yes, except I had to trade the Morningstar of Destruction for the Staff of Nature."

She waved that away. "The Morningstar is nothing. Did you find any necklaces?"

"Hundreds." She was looking a little irritated, so I added, "There is one with tiny unicorn charms on it." I held out a hand, and it appeared. "I was going to keep this, as it reminds me of you, but the delicate little bracelet is made for a female, so I am not likely going to wear it."

Natura asked, "May I borrow it? One of my followers is in need of it."

Silvestris looked closely at it. "That artifact is dangerous to men. It grants the wearer beauty, not charisma, but great feminine beauty."

I sat the bracelet down and did a supernatural ability. I disguised myself. I was now a very beautiful little blue-eyed blonde-haired girl just coming into her sexuality. I was dressed in a long gown that showed nothing and everything. I said in a seductive voice, "I learned a lot from that devil demigoddess." I reversed the disguise, and I was me again. "As you can see, I do not need this artifact." I picked it up and handed it to Natura. She stared at me, so I asked, "Are you all right?"

She smiled and took the bracelet. "That was a great disguise. I watched you do it, and even at goddess level, it was difficult believing it was you. Two questions. How did you learn to do that, and what will this bracelet cost me?"

Silvestris said, "You need to tone down that little girl or you will find yourself in great trouble. She was wonderful."

I laughed. "When I was trying to learn control of the Star Fire, I took advantage of Malificus's offer and summoned that devil demigoddess over and over. She didn't mind, and I am no longer a virgin. The bracelet is free. Any artifact I have, that I do not need, which belongs to either of you is yours. A benefit of being my gods. I plan on being a benefit to you as much as I can." With a little smile of mischievousness, I added, "I have to do something to make up for the issues I create."

Silvestris laughed, but Natura went serious and said, "I am disappointed with your behavior concerning the shadow demon. You need to watch that temper. If you use the Staff of Nature when you are angry, you could unravel the entire plane. It is that powerful."

Silvestris became serious also. "Charles, my boy, she is correct on this. It is a concern that you have the staff when we know you turn evil at times. Even the evil gods will be concerned. Getting angry and starting to destroy the hidden layers of hell or Caelums would get you destroyed instantly. The gods will put up with much but not mass destruction of their followers. Some gods want you dead now."

Natura added, "However, there are too many of us that want you to finish your plan. We will have to explain what you are planning to use the staff for or there will be more wanting you dead."

We talked through dinner and made small changes to my plan. Places where I should use that staff and where it would not be proper. I was surprised at some of the suggestions for use but agreed with doing so. They wanted me busy working the plan for the next few years so that others would have time to become comfortable with the issues. During the feast, and when I was nearly stuffed, some other gods came in demanding to know what I was going to do. They had heard about the shadow demon and were starting to worry.

I instantly went into an attitude of great respect. Not hard to do, as I did respect those two, and showing willingness to do as told was easy. You've seen the look on children who truly love their parents, at least for the moment.

Natura answered the other gods, "Charles will be leaving us to return to his place in the Undead Lands. He will be there for years trying to correct the issues. After the issues are corrected, we have hundreds of other issues for him to correct. He will be far too busy for many years to help you with any other issues or to do anything else, so please don't ask. We have given him instructions on the use of the staff and forbidden him other uses. He will comply. There is no question about that."

The gods looked unbelieving.

I touched my forehead to flare the Star Fire. That got their attention, and I said, "I will do as planned. It is much and will be very difficult. I will be very tired, but I will do as my gods require."

Silvestris said, "The plan to fix the Sordeath calls for him to be nearly wasted in energy every night. He will be near helpless. We will need to protect him. First, so that he can complete this work, and second, so that no others attack him and cause him to become unstable."

Every god there agreed to watch and help protect. Some offered their champions to come to the Sordeath to help guard me. Natura said, "No, he does not have time to ensure your champions are out of the way when he uses the staff. Please keep all creatures out of the Dragonback Mountains and the Sordeath until we say it is clear."

Silvestris said, "Charles will be placing protections throughout his lands to keep everything and everyone out. Not even birds or insects will enter when he is working."

I said, "I do need the help of some stone giants. I know where they are hiding. I will go to them and ask for their help."

An old god, tiny and bent, said, "I am their god. They are cornered in a small place in the northern shadow of Shadow

Mountain. I will let them know you are coming. They do not trust humans. They will attack you if I do not tell them otherwise. They know the mountain will come alive soon. They need a new place to hide."

I looked at the old god and said, "If they help me, there will be a place for them in my lands, and they will not need to hide. I have thousands of leagues of rock mountains that they may roam. Eventually, there will be others sharing the mountains, but all will follow my laws and live in peace."

The god looked deep within my soul and at my Star Fire. "Even humans?" He nearly spat out the question.

I looked back with the same intensity. "Especially humans. There will be no difference between one species and another. If a pixie leads a human to his death, the pixie will answer to me. If a human kills a pixie, the human will answer to me. I will know the truth of any conflict, and I will correct the issue with a hard hand and without prejudice. I am not planning on building jails and prisons. Punishment will be swift and final."

The old god smiled. "Fool child, you are a demigod. You will not be able to stay there and run the place. You have much work to do. Who will run it for you and with such passion?"

I smiled back. "The one who put the passion in me. Though he does not know it."

After much continued discussion, the other gods left. Silvestris also left. I was just about to leave when Natura touched my arm. There was lust in her eyes. She said, "Let's find out what that demon demigoddess taught you. I may need to do some corrections."

CHAPTER 4

PHASE TWO—
GIANTS AND ELVES

It had been about two weeks since I went to Caelums. I was just cleaning up the last of the undead. Many undead fled the earlier fighting, and I had a lot of hunting and destroying to do. Sorry to say, some skipped the border, and I had to chase them down and kill them in several other lands. I went in disguise, but luckily everyone cheers those who put the undead to rest, especially since undead tend to kill the living when loose.

Once all the undead were taken care of, I started phase two. The first part of the phase was doing blessings and consecrations on the castle and lands and dedicating the lands to Silvestris and Natura. Silvestris and Natura—every time I see the gods, I come away with more to do and more responsibility. They are so far above me I cannot even see when they are talking me into something. From now on, the plan includes staying away from them as much as possible. Besides, I didn't tell the gods all my plans or what my agenda was, which was making Natura a little suspicious. Natura. I thought the demon demigoddess was great. Gods, was I wrong. Way wrong. A man could get lost forever just thinking about Natura … I shook my head hard, trying to clear my thoughts. I was doing it again. I could not get Natura out of my head. I said as loud as I could toward the heavens, "I have work to do!" I continued blessings, consecrations, and dedications until I had the entire land covered permanently. It took another three weeks. In with the blessings were triggers to warn me if evil entered my land or if someone tried to dispel the blessings. I found three more ghosts that way. My land was finally clear of evil.

A Caelum of Proba and one of Commeatus showed up at my Death Land Tower one morning. They actually knocked. I answered the door and welcomed them in. "To what do I owe this pleasure? How are two of my favorite gods?"

Commeatus's Caelum said, "They are concerned. You have taken a very large amount of land and made it impossible for any temples or shrines to be erected other than to your gods. Have not Commeatus and Proba helped you at times?"

"Yes, they have. Have a seat." I called forth three glasses and some northern Treestorm wine and poured for them. I filled my own with fruit juice. They stared at the wine bottle and quickly sipped the wine. Their eyes went wide.

One asked, "Why do you not drink? This is the greatest wine in all the planes."

I shrugged. "I don't drink anything that makes me not me. Would you want me to get drunk, knowing my power and instabilities?"

They both said, "No!"

"Good. Now, to answer your issue. I am thinking back on my first meeting with my gods. I told them I would erect temples to the two of them in all the places I repaired. That the people I allowed into these lands would be gently encouraged to follow them through my example. But I would not force or tell someone who they should worship."

Proba's Caelum said, "True. I was there, and I remember."

I added, "I don't recall ever saying I would not allow others to build shrines or temples, and I did say I would not force others to worship only my gods. Having no shrines or temples would not force others to worship my gods, but it would limit them. I suppose that's not really fair."

Commeatus's Caelum agreed, "No, it is not fair."

I smiled. "Yet there are many lands where the worship of nature and the gods of nature were outlawed after the war with nature. Silvestris and Natura are locked out of several lands where Proba and Commeatus are encouraged."

They looked at each other and back to me. I added, "I think this evens things out until these other lands change their laws and start allowing the worship of my gods. Don't you?"

What could they say? They said it sadly, "Yes."

I tried my hardest not to smile. "Still, Proba and Commeatus did help me several times."

"True, true, they did." I could hear the hope in their voices.

I took a swallow and put my glass down. "I will allow several small temples and shrines to your gods when I am ready and your priests come to me to ask and point out where. Is that good enough? I do like your gods and would like to please them without causing mine alarm. And, with Commeatus, a god I respect greatly and who has been a great help to me, I will allow my roads and byways to receive his blessings."

They were ecstatic. Both raised their glasses and toasted the decision. "To Charles, his open mind, and his love of the gods."

I raised my glass for a second toast. "To helpful gods, may they live forever in our hearts and memories."

Both said, "Forever."

They were eyeing the bottle of wine, so I put it away. One said, "Don't let Oprepo know you have that."

I smiled. "You tell Oprepo that I share my wine with friends. Besides, I have a lot more."

Their eyes went wide again, and they disappeared.

I laughed and laughed. *Now the seed has been planted. Let's see how it grows. Which gods will want to help and therefore have temples in my land?* My gods and I had talked about this very thing, and they were the ones who told me to leave room for other gods. I agreed with them but only to a limited extent.

I finished preparing for travel, and when I was ready, I teleported to the northern edge of Shadow Mountain and found the caves of the stone giants. The caves were on the Ginham side of the mountains. They were gone and had taken everything with them. I looked all around and called out in Giant, but they were very gone. I did find a note. "Our god told us. We are on our way." That was all it said. However, a hundred giants could not travel through several lands and not be seen.

Let's see. If I were a stone giant, how would I travel across country? I'd take the mountain route of course. I may have to go down into the lower lands when the mountains become too steep. Still, the mountains run all the way to Sordeath. It would be the safest route, even with short periods of travel through the foothills. The mountains split Kayland and Treestorm and then Ringal and Treestorm. Humans normally do not get along with giants. Humans' fault, not the giants'. So, I would make my low travels on the Elvin side. I don't know how elves look on giants, but it can't be worse than humans. Time to see my old friend Elequel.

I teleported to the mountain pass between Kayland and Treestorm on the Treestorm side and started down the path. It was not long before I found a section where a lot of something big had walked through.

An elf came out. "Hunting giants, human?" He spit out the word *human*.

I thought, *An elf with a bad attitude. This could be fun.*

I looked at him and touched my forehead to flare the curse. "I would be careful how you address me, child." Then I ignored him as I studied the tracks. It looked like more than a hundred giants, but it could have been more. The elf was taken aback by many things—the curse, the lack of interest in his presence, and my calling him child. He had to be a young elf, less than a hundred years by my guess.

He became a little bolder. "If you come further into our land, we will have to kill you."

I looked up from tracking the giants. "You are not the first to make that statement, child. I seem to recall an elf named Elequel who promised me my death at his hands before dawn, and another called Farsite who told me not to leave the druid trap or they would have to kill me. Cannot elves think of another line?"

Elequel stepped out. "Charles?"

"Hello, my friend."

"Charles, it is you." He came forward with a smile and took my offered embrace. He motioned for the others to stand down. "I thought to never see you again, and here you are, only a moon since we met. You have changed greatly and in so short of time. Many are upset that you took the Druid Suppository of Magic and Knowledge with you. They are looking for you. How did you get cursed?"

I smiled. He did not seem so old and wise to me anymore. "It is a long story, my good friend. I will tell it to you as we go to see the trees in the grove. I have something to make up for the loss. I think they will like my gift."

Elequel said, "You are very powerful. Are you here to do harm?"

I knew his worry. "I will not harm. If attacked, I will simply leave. It would be a shame to not except my gift, but I will understand. So, the northern elves are upset that their attempt to kill me backfired and they lost something they could never use anyway. How interesting."

Elequel warned, "Charles, there are southern druids here. They have come for the trap. They think they know how to enter. They are extremely upset that you have it, and they blame us for using it as a death trap. It was not intended to be used that way."

I shrugged this off. "I do not care what they think or want. There are reasons that they are not to have it. Still, my being here may be difficult for you. I can come back another time. Right now, I am looking for my giants."

Several elves quickly said, "No!"

One continued with, "Do not leave. Farsite would have our hides."

It was an exaggeration, the Star Fire told me, but I would guess not by much. "Let's head on down then."

We talked for hours as we traveled down the same path I took so many centuries ago and yet only a little over one moon. Elequel was astonished with the things I told him. I had learned a lot from the druids, and some druids were bards who taught me how to tell a good story. I could make a stubbed toe look like an adventure taking years and never tell a lie. This Star Fire, now that I had control, was not that bad. But I was not going to tell them that. Let them come to their own conclusions. I made the adventure sound more astounding with every turn of the path.

We reached the grove, and someone had already run ahead and told that I was coming. They set protections and traps that should have caught me and froze me solid. I waved my hand, and all the protections and traps dispelled. They didn't even slow me down. I walked up to Farsite and said, "Nice way to say hello again."

Farsite said, "Hello again."

A druid started to come forward, but bows were quickly drawn, and he stopped.

I asked, "Having trouble?"

He smiled. "Not really. Not with them." He touched my forehead, and the Star Fire flared. "So, it is true. The gods have placed a curse on you."

"They wanted control, my old friend."

He looked skeptical. "Did they achieve their goal?"

"Good question. It is difficult to say. Just a second please. Star Fire?" The Star Fire flared to light and stayed there bright as a noonday sun, a blue light that nearly blinded the others. I waited until they were ready to hear what I asked. "Star Fire, did the world gods achieve their goal of controlling me? Ah, I did not think so. Did the Over Gods achieve their goal? Not yet? Thank you." The Star Fire went down to barely glowing. I turned to Farsite. "It seems that both are still trying."

Farsite looked sick. "The, the Over Gods have touched you?"

"This is their curse."

Everyone backed up except Farsite. He hugged me and said, "I am sorry, my old friend. I did not know that our use of the trap would cause so much trouble for you. If you want, I will kill you and put you out of your misery."

I laughed. "My friend, that is a very kind offer, but I am not in misery. I have a lot of work to do for the gods. Having them keep me busy makes them feel much easier about me being around. But I am enjoying myself. I am sorry if I caused you worry."

Farsite became a little more worried. "Which gods are you friends with?"

"I am trying to be friends with all the gods, but my heart belongs to Silvestris and Natura."

He loosened up greatly. "Those are good gods to be loved by and to love. I worship Proba."

I smiled. "I was just visited by one of his Caelums this morning and one from Commeatus. We had a conversation about my new lands and allowing others to worship Proba and Commeatus there. However, they were most interested in my wine."

He smiled and said proudly, "The gods like a good wine, but none has ever compared to northern Treestorm wines."

I held out a hand, and the bottle I used that morning appeared. "You mean this? It's what they were drinking. They went off to tell their gods and I think Oprepo." The bottle disappeared from my hand, and a scroll appeared. It startled me, and I dropped it. I looked around for the thief and then picked up the scroll.

Farsite said, "If you want your wine, do not hold it up and say Oprepo's name. Especially if it is northern Treestorm wine. He will always react." Then somewhat upset, he asked, "How did you obtain a bottle of northern Treestorm wine?"

I opened the scroll and checked out the writing. It was a Full Resurrection scroll. "Nice, thank you, Oprepo. A Full Resurrection scroll. Very nice. You do know I can do my own full resurrections? Next time, let's haggle. I could learn a few things from the master."

Laughter filled the glade and was gone.

Everyone was looking at me. Farsite asked, "You can do your own Full Resurrections?"

I answered, "Yes, but I am limited. This scroll may help in a time of great need." I sent the scroll into the druid trap. "To answer your other question, I killed the demon thief that took your wines. I now own his wine cellar. I own a lot of your great wines, and I don't even drink."

Elves were getting upset, and I knew why. The wine had been stolen many years ago. The shadow demon I destroyed took it all and then destroyed the vineyards. The fires destroyed every vine there. Before that, the wine was never allowed out of Treestorm and never sold to humans. What the elves did not know was the shadow demon took one of each type of grape vine and placed them in a status box, preserving them for all time. Another trophy.

I decided that letting them hang was not polite, and I brought forth the box. I sat it down in the center of the grove. I said, "Something else the thief took."

Farsite looked it over and started to cry. I'd never seen an elf cry, but to him, this was a miracle that even the gods could not pull off. Farsite said, as the other elves looked closely into the box, "These are the three original vines. The fathers of all our grapes. From these came the northern Treestorm wines." He looked up and said, "Charles, what will you do with these? By right, they are yours."

I kept my pomp and circumstance look and said, "This is a gift from me to you for causing you so many problems when I visited last time. True, they are mine legally, but they are yours morally."

I will not go into detail about the love and hugs I received for that gift. Let's just say ... creatures and their alcohol. I will never understand what they see in becoming silly, mad, tired, or, in general, out of their minds. In my opinion, fools all.

When things calmed down, I said, "I see you have friends with you." I looked at the southern druids. Farsite reluctantly introduced me. He did not want trouble, and the druids were not happy, and it was easy to tell.

One said, "You took our—"

He fell to the ground in pain, and it was getting worse. I leaned down and said, "The curse."

He quickly croaked out, "The northern druids' knowledge!" The pain subsided.

I looked at him and said, "Please don't lie near me. The Star Fire cannot stand people that lie, and I am trying to be nice."

He looked pained still but said, "I am wondering how you came to walk away with the druid trap, as the elves call it."

"That is an easy question to answer. I was trapped in the trap by an old druid that gave me a one-way trip in, though the elves did their part. I had to become a grand druid to work out how to leave. In doing so, I learned how to pick it up and take it with me. As the old druid gave me the ability, he thereby gave me the keys and the ownership to the suppository. As the elves were inappropriately using it, I took it with me when I left."

The southern druid looked upset. "We feel that the southern druids have the right to have that suppository."

"Tell me. When the northern druids were going to be attacked by the demons, they sent out a request for help from their southern friends. Why did you not answer that request?"

They mumbled amongst themselves for a moment, and then he turned to me. "We had our reasons."

I could play this game as long as they could. I was not in a hurry. But I did not like foolish politics. "Good. What were they?"

"Our reasons are for us. They are not for humans to understand."

"I am a great druid as well as a human. Humor me. I may understand more than you realize."

"I suppose it is possible that we could not help in time."

The Star Fire let me know he was avoiding and not telling. Everything is possible, and therefore that was the truth.

I was upset. "You know as well as I that everything is possible and therefore what you said is possible. However, it is not necessarily the reason. I will tell you this. The northern druids did not think you worthy to have their suppository, and neither do I." I turned to Farsite, ignoring the rants and raves of the southern druids. "Farsite, I am looking for some giants. Seen any?"

He looked at the druids and smiled and then turned back to me. "Yes, about a hundred stone giants went through our lands only eight days ago. They were packed as if they were going away permanently. We wondered over this greatly and asked them where they were off to. They said, 'Paradise.' Can you explain this?"

I told him what I was attempting to do for the gods. He was amazed and asked, "You destroyed the letch king and ten thousand undead in less than two weeks?"

The southern druids became quiet and stopped verbally threatening me.

"Yes."

"Then I pronounce you King Charles of the Dragonback Mountains and the Sordeath." He patted me on the back and said, "Amazing. If you do nothing else, that was worth your learning the druid knowledge."

I laughed and said, "King Fargen Farsite. You know as well as I that being a king is not that much fun. Still, I am worried about the giants. How do the Elvin people feel about them crossing their lands? I must confess, I would be more concerned if they were crossing the human lands. Humans are far less forgiving."

King Farsite said, "Do not worry, my friend, as they are welcome here. We have told them that they can stay in our mountains, but the mountains have too much iron and granite. They need pumice and limestone to eat, and they know that your mountains are full of pumice, limestone, tufa, marble, and other soft stones. What do you need with the giants?"

"They will help me build the dams to stop the flooding. I will pay them well in land and wealth for trade with others. If they are willing, I have a hundred things I need built out of rock, but the dams come first."

"They are most pleased to have their god bring them such great news. But how will the humans take giants living in their lands?"

"My lands, my friend, and that is a big difference. I am friendly with all nature's children. All sentient beings are equal in my eyes. I will not allow prejudice to enter my beliefs. I know this is hard to believe after all that humans have done. I cannot stay in my lands, as the gods will send me other places, but you know another human who has been fair to all, do you not?"

"Yes, your mentor."

I smiled and vanished. Another seed planted.

I teleported to the mountaintop and looked around for movement. None—so I teleported to the next mountaintop. The giants were below me and just a little ahead. They were making good pace. Right then, they had stopped to eat. They found a small outcropping of steatite and sat down to munch and dig enough to carry with them. I teleported near them and watched. It took a few minutes but a child, only twenty feet tall, noticed me.

She pointed. "Daddy, Daddy, a tiny creature. Can I have it? Can I?"

With a grunt, Daddy stood up and looked where she was pointing. In a voice as deep as the ocean and crumbly rough as though he talked very little, he said, "No, my little pebble. That is human. You stay away from them. They do not like our kind."

He picked up a very large stone club and turned toward me. In rough Standard, he slowly asked, "Why you here? Go away. We not harm anything."

I spoke in Stone Giant, slowly and as low as I could. "I King Charles. You headed my lands, my mountains. You left me message." I held up the message.

He came closer, and I stood my ground. Giants don't like it when you show fear. They mistake it for loathing and become angry. He took the message in a hand big enough for me to sleep stretched out in. He smelled it, and it nearly disappeared up his nostril. "It smells like my message. It looks like my message. You one our god say have home us. Do work you?"

"I have work so big all for thousands of years will marvel at how grand stone giants are."

He smiled. "Big work we do. What we get for work?"

Now all the giants were standing around and waiting for this answer. "I will give you four things. A safe mountain range to live out in the open and not hiding. You will share it with others of nature, but the entire Dragonback Mountains will be yours to roam."

Many heads were nodding, which nearly caused a strong wind. "For your work, I will pay you a good fair wage so that you will have plenty to trade with." More nods and some looks of distrust. I was beginning to hate using the curse, but everyone recognized it and knew what it meant. I touched my forehead, and the Star Fire flared. "As you can see, I tell you the truth." Now all heads were nodding, and one female giant, only fifty or so feet tall, petted my head in sorrow for my curse. It tipped me off the rock I was standing on, and the leader caught me before I hit the ground and placed me back on my feet. Almost all were laughing. The little girl was looking at her mommy, upset. She reminded me of Amanda when Richard nearly broke one of her dolls. This is why humans and giants don't get along. Giants have a different sense of humor from that of humans, especially when the humor is at the human's expense. I laughed with them and flew up onto the shoulder of the woman. I said, "Thank you for your show of kindness."

She smiled and said, "Welcome, tiny person."

I flew back to the rock and turned to the others. "I will set laws in my lands that all creatures are equal. Giants are the same as all others, including humans. No one will be better than someone else." This got a round of stone clubs beating on chests and nearly caused an avalanche with the noise.

"Last, I will ensure that all know you built the fantastic things we are going to build so that they all have respect for what stone giants can do that they cannot."

I was scooped up and carried around for several minutes, until someone asked, "How long will this last?"

I was placed back on my rock and looked at with expectation. "Which part?"

"All."

"Dragonback Mountains will be yours to roam forever. I am expecting other creatures that love mountains to wish to share the land with you. The pay will last as long as the work lasts, and that will last for a very long time and possibly forever. The laws will be in place and protected forever. And I will set your work with your sign and names in Laststoneite."

Everyone was cheering until I said Laststoneite. It became very quiet. The leader said, "No can create Laststoneite. That lost form of changing."

I flew up an inch and touched the rock below me, and the entire boulder turned white as a mountain flower. He reached for me and lifted me up while his club came down and shattered on the boulder. Several others did the same, and their weapons shattered. They mumbled in awe, "Laststoneite."

It took a few minutes before they stopped staring at the white boulder. The leader said, "What you make into Laststoneite you make forever. What is this job?"

We talked well into the night and part of the next day. They were now clear on what needed doing. Good thing too, as the rainy season was just about on us, and they needed to be in place to see where dams were needed. Stone giants are the greatest builders the world has ever seen. It is sad that only one hundred are left. I will allow that number to increase greatly. They also make grand troops.

I teleported back to the Dead Land Tower and rested that day and night, and then it was back to the Sordeath. I had a lot of work to do and only five years to do it in. Soon my land would be flooded and hard to map, so I had to work fast. I took a flat circle of rock and started magically creating maps of the entire land, Dragonback Mountains and all, by slowly flying up and down, back and forth over the land until my eyes had seen every inch of it.

There is an eighth circle spell called Map that would give me a general map of any given area, but it would be crude. The tenth circle Greater Map is far better and would provide some good details. The Staff of Maps is an artifact belonging to Commeatus that I happen to have and he does not know it yet. The Staff of Maps gives me details to the fraction of an inch and updated to the present. It can even give me maps of the past, but not the future. I have used it to watch where armies are and where they are moving to. I have also used this map to watch my father's throne room and look for reactions that showed he knew the letch king was dead. So far, no reaction.

Yes, the map even goes inside buildings, and I could watch Duke Edward's daughters dress and undress, but why would I? Lovely as they are they could never meet the standards that the devil demigoddess and my goddess have set in me. I have been highly spoiled.

However good the magic is I needed a map I could mark on so that I could make plans and share them with the giants. You cannot write on map spells and hand it off to another. However, the grand mystics' spell called "Seen" can recreate anything you've seen in grand detail onto a flat surface. When I finished the map in detail and with annotations I spelled a very large copy. Then I spelled up twenty more large copies. The original I put away. You can only spell up copies from the original, and I did not want it messed up. I turned one very large copy into an even bigger map by using the spell "Expand Object." I made that permanent and then changed the stone to Laststoneite so it would never break. It was totally white. Laststoneite always is. No writing would stick to it, but stone giants knew how to add color and details that did stick—a trick I didn't know, and I wasn't going to break taboo and ask. I guessed it had something to do with their spit. I was not sure.

Laststoneite is an interesting substance. It is impossible to break, bend, or change. Even gods cannot change it. Almost all the old temples in Caelums are made of Laststoneite and for good reasons. A temple made of Laststoneite is nearly impregnable, resists magic, and will never wear. Nothing sticks to it, and it does not get dirty.

There is a bridge that crosses over the River Loren in Kayland. It is said to date before the Age of Magic, and that predates many gods. The bridge is plain, simple, and thin and still looks new. The marks where the stone cutters chipped the bridge from original rock are still there even after thousands of years of wagons and steel-shod horses crossing that bridge. During some wars, wizards tried to destroy the bridge to slow down the approaching enemy but failed. Spells do not affect Laststoneite. My mother has, as a prize possession, a comb made of Laststoneite. It is nearly priceless and still has all its teeth. Everything ever made of Laststoneite still exists. Very few things were made, and that makes it worth a king's ransom.

Every time some extremely high-level wizard changes something into Laststoneite, he pays for it with headaches and stomach cramps that make him want to scream. It matters not the size, the comb or the bridge; the payment is the same, and each time the payment becomes worse. That is why there is very little Laststoneite in the planes. Ancient wizards were brave but not stupid. Pain can kill. The gods were braver and made temples, but even they stopped. The spell was lost to mortals due to lack of use.

I am different from most. The fight with the Star Fire caused me pain you could never begin to imagine. It took thousands of years to tame it, and the pain was long and difficult. The pain of creating Laststoneite barely phases me and does not increase like it should. I don't know why. It is painful but tolerable, and I can change its shape. Shush, don't tell.

With the map completed, I teleported to the giants' leader called Hard Stone Crunching Early in the Morning. What a name. "Hello, Hard Stone Crunching." Three giants turned. It's a popular male name. Almost as popular as his daughter's name, Pillar of Lime with Streaks of Granite during Thunderstorm. Giants name their children after what they are doing at birth for males and what the baby reminds them of for females. For stone giants, there is always a "when" after the name, as it sets them apart.

Hard Stone Crunching said, "We are mapping the areas that flood. Soon it will rain and we will watch. I do not like being all spread out."

"We talked about this, Hard Stone Crunching. All they have to do is call my name, and you and I will be there to help, except your daughter. She called me eight times so she could play. I am a busy person."

"I know. I was sent to her also. Your spell need not be on children. Please, not more on children. They think it funny."

"I know."

"But we not trust you fully yet. How you help us. You so tiny."

I reached out and lifted him up. My strength being what it was, I could beat a stone giant in an arm wrestling match. "I will earn your trust." I flipped him around several times, and the children started laughing. I put him down. He sat down laughing too.

"You strong for human."

"Potentis, your god, helped to make me strong. Funny god. He likes to be seen as a feeble old man sometimes."

"No wonder you strong! Potentis tell me trust you. He watches you closely. Say you have his best artifact."

I put out my hand, and the artifact was in it. Iceimer, the Rod of Shaping. With it, one could shape stone into very refined and elegant structures. I handed it to him. "You may borrow this. I want it back when I need it. Do you know how to use it?"

He bowed to me. "I know. Potentis tell. I take. Guard with life. Use help you. So will whole tribe. Potentis say you not stay forever. Say another I already trust take you place."

I smiled, "Yes, but he doesn't know it yet. It's a secret."

He smiled, and his teeth were clean and white. Chomping on stone will do that for a giant. Mine would be all broken. He said, "I keep secret. No worry."

I put a hand out to touch him. "Thank you, my friend. This is a map of my lands you can use."

He gently took it but saw what it was made of and stopped being gentle.

He said, "Good. Rock carving break too easy. This much better. We show you dam needs on this. Take time find all in all mountains."

I said, "Just find the big ones for now. We will start building them during the dry season, and we can look for the others during next year's rains."

"That good plan. See you if call or when rain end."

I left thinking, *I am not sure what he is worried about. It takes an army to bring down a stone giant.* There must have been a few dire bears in the mountains they crossed, as his little girl was playing with them as if they were dolls. I laughed to myself. She was having a heck of a time trying to put a dress on one of the bears.

CHAPTER 5

CASTLES AND DAMS

I went to the Black Castle of Greater Darkness and started to clean it up. There was a lot to do, and I wanted to make the castle the light of my land. I also needed to find new names for my land and castle. Black Castle of Greater Darkness and Sordeath were not places my sisters would want to visit.

Black Castle received part of its name because it was made out of calcite, a common black stone that is easy to cut and shape. The problem is it is also easy to destroy and knock down. Not a single tower was still standing, and most walls had gaping holes. Worst of all was the entire castle was leaning on the ledge. After removing anything worth a copper, I changed into a great dragon, gold of course, and tipped it over. Time to start from new.

Making a castle from scratch is easy but takes a lot of planning. First, you need to have an understanding of castles. I spent most of the winter going to every keep, castle, and large building used to house officials outside of Kayland that I could find. I talked to the servants first. I even went as myself. I told them I was going to build a new home and needed information. After all, I could not lie. I also told them I was thinking about writing a book on the subject. I was able to get into almost any place and find out information on anything I wanted. Several queens took me on special tours, told me of secrets, and gave me information few ever knew. They showed me the changes they made and would make if they could. They wanted so badly to have their name immortalized in writing. The best information came from castle mistresses. They heard all the complaints. Kings told me of royal needs and the reasons for more than one throne room. "A massive room for entertaining and general court, a normal room for private parties, and a small room for things held in confidence. Don't forget to add a map/war room for planning with plenty of room for a buffet." I learned so much about castles that winter that I actually wrote that book, magically of course, and had prints made for all who had helped. The Star Fire insisted, as it was too close to giving my word. I refused at first, but the pain eventually changed my mind. I even put my true name on it: *Great Places of Royalty* by Charles Truss. It was fully illustrated with fantastically accurate paintings and portraits, one of the boredom-enticed hobbies I picked up in the druid trap. Using the staff, I watched as Mother received the copy I had sent to her through a third party. She could not believe it. She cared little about the book, as now she knew I was still alive. Jennifer was interested in her room, especially when she noticed that the room was exactly how she had just recently changed it, and she was portrayed standing at the full-length mirror in a new dress she had just had made.

Dedrick and Eric had magically searched and could not find me, and now they tried again. I stayed hidden. Eric was so frustrated it was almost comical. Father was furious. "How! How did that boy obtain exact paintings of nearly every room in this castle! Before and after paintings about the changes his mother and grandmother made and up-to-date depictions of every member of this family and staff. How is this possible!" I nearly fell off my stool I was laughing so hard. I put the Staff of Maps away. I had work to do building my own castle, and my face hurt with all the laughing.

Now that it was summer, I helped the giants build dams. We finished eighteen that summer, and that was quite a feat, as the first dam spanned a section nearly a league across and two thousand feet high, with end towers going up another three hundred feet. I wasn't planning on towers or stairs from the bottom of the dam all the way up to the top of the towers, but the giants insisted. These towers were big enough to hold several grown giants, and the stairs were giant size with human-size stairs as a railing for the giants and a small rail outside the human stairs so people would not be blown off the steps. In winter, it got windy up near the top. Using Iceimer, the Rod of Stone Shaping, the giants adorned each with symbols and fantastic rock carvings that depicted nature, my gods, their god, and giants and myself working as one. When we completed the big dam, the giants added gigantic statues of the gods at the bottom where the holes came out to allow water to escape at a formulated pace, and statues at the top of the gods of nature and Potentis in their various forms. After we checked to ensure we had the forms correct, I turned each one into Laststoneite along with the eighteen dams. When I finished the main dam with all the statues, we had visitors.

Three Caelums came down, one in giant form and two in human form representing Potentis, Silvestris, and Natura. They flew around the dam checking all the carvings and statues and looking at the base and sides. The giants were all bowing and praising Potentis. I stood there and waited. I could not help but smile. The giants were wonderful artists and did a loving job of representing each god perfectly, with statements at the bottom of each statue and carvings so all would know and understand.

I had seen the gods in person, so I changed their perspectives considerably, but they understood and took my suggestions with humor and reverence. I had to visit Potentis twice to get his other aspects down perfectly, but he did not mind.

The Caelums returned to us with tears of joy. One said blessings to all of us for such wonderful proof of our love for our gods. Another whispered to me just before they left, "Solbelli is going to be so jealous."

Winter hit shortly after that, so I went back to planning and building my castle, and the giants went to find new places to control the waters.

Soon the castle planning was completed. All I needed to do was build to the plan. I needed the depths of the castle built first, so over the next month, and using Annihilate spells, I opened a solid rock section in the top of the cliff two hundred feet deep, two thousand passes long, and three thousand passes wide. I included small drainage holes that drained to the waterfall, or where the waterfall would be when I finished. Then, with the help of several giants and teleporting marble from the sea bed near my southern coast to my castle, we started filling in the floor print until we had the bottom dungeon floor completed. I even included several secret rooms. Each wall was only as thick as two fingers, and several busted until I made supporting sections that were much thicker. I used the spell Greater Stone Contour to make each piece seamless with the rest of the castle and the rock outer walls while the giants held the pieces in place. We added the stairs and then protection spells on every foot of the structure. When we were finished, no one would be able to magically enter my castle without permission, and no evil would ever be able to enter without major pain and alarms all over. Anyone planning to do harm would find themselves unable to cross the threshold, even if invited. We added the ceiling and more protection spells. Then we started on the next level. When we were finished with the dungeon section, we had eight levels that had twenty-foot ceilings and plenty of room for storage and one of the most protected treasure rooms possible. All of this took up the entire lower section except twenty feet deep. I needed the twenty feet for soil for a garden on the first level. I capped this off with a slight slant so that water could run down through the section without hindrance or having standing water, which would be bad for tree roots. Then I added four raised stairwells leading down into the lower section that were protected from all sides so water could not enter my dungeon as it soaked into the garden soil.

Now it was time to see how good I was. I walked down through the entire dungeon checking out all sections. The doors were not placed yet, so walking through was easy. Everything seemed great. I needed to check for leaks, so I took a bottle of Forever-Flowing Water and set it to fill up the top part. If we did everything correctly, there should be no leaks into the lower sections. We spent the next two weeks under water plugging holes. Thank the gods for spells like Drown Man's Breath and Movement Independence. I could move under water without issue, but the giants could not. Once we had everything correct, I asked some friends, Air Elementals, to help me dry the whole thing out. Afterward, I filled the top with water again, and everything held. After emptying the water, I used Shape Rock spells to add holes in the correct spots to cause some airflow through the bottom sections. That had been the main complaint about dungeons—damp, dark, and no air, making it difficult to breathe. I added sewers that fed into the waterfall. They would be virtually invisible and impossible to reach, and the water flow would suck air from the top down through the bottom and out the sewage holes, causing fresh air throughout the castle. It would also cause it to be cold during winter, so I added holes in the center of the walls from bottom to the top for the air to come through. That way, we could close the doors, and the air would continue to flow to the bottom but not so much through the living spaces. In addition, the sewers automatically cleaned themselves so there would be no blockages.

It took all winter to complete this section of the castle, and soon it was spring, so we started on more dams. This pace continued for the rest of the year until I had over sixty dams and a fairy-tale castle with towers, spires, a defendable wall with cover and spikes to keep dragon attacks to a minimum, a garden area, barracks, two temples, and a gate that was impossible to break. When we were done and all the statues, carvings, special details that I had seen and liked at other castles, and special details that I thought about when I saw what others had done and knew I could do better were complete, and all the protections were in place, we furnished the entire place with doors and windows and hangings and everything a castle needs to make it a home. We fixed up the kitchens and put in shelves until we could think of no more. All the brackets were made of stone. Everything was smooth and shiny, except the floors, which were roughed up and adorned with fantastic carvings and some smaller statues, with larger statues in the temples. Then we removed everything we wanted movable, or not turned into Laststoneite. We triple-checked that everything was in place we wanted turned and everything else was out and far away, especially the hinges for the doors and windows. It would be bad if we kept both parts of the hinges together. You cannot make a chain out of Laststoneite because if one link touches another during the turning spell, they become one. I did not need the doors to my stone ovens to be closed permanently, so everything not tied down was removed from the cliff. I turned the cliff and my castle into Laststoneite.

My castle stood on a pillar of pure Laststoneite, eight hundred feet in the air, with a long Laststoneite bridge attaching it to the rest of the mountain. The winding mountain road went to the flat plan below and was under constant view and bowshot from the castle walls. With the protections built into the Laststoneite and the way the entire castle was built, I could not see a way that anyone, without major help from the gods, could ever take the castle over. This place was as safe as I could make it, and that was very safe. Phase two was completed—time for phase three.

CHAPTER 6

PHASE THREE—
RIVERS, STREAMS,
AND IRRIGATION

My entire country, except the surrounding Dragonback Mountains, was still flooded because all my dams purposely leaked controlled amounts of water out of holes at the bottom. Now it was flooded all year long, only not as deep. I needed to control the flow and force it into rivers and streams for irrigation. I talked to the giants and gods, and we worked out how many and where the rivers and streams were needed and a very interesting way to have uncontrolled leaks of water in the forests and control the irrigation at the farms.

We started by building an aqueduct across the eastern mountains so that the water flowed from a very large lake into hundreds of lakes across my eastern range and then from those lakes down into the valleys through carved out streams and rivers that flowed into a big carved-out river along the eastern edge of the valley. Aqueduct building did not go unnoticed by Ringal and King Tyler's people. Neither did my changing the channel at the southeastern end by cutting out marble and granite. Still, they were not about to enter into Sordeath and the land of the undead king.

King Tyler's people spent many hours watching my mountains and building an army to protect their lands. They also sent several sets of spies to check out what was happening. One shot at a stone giant that was doing his job. I destroyed that human in front of the giants and sent the remains to King Tyler with a note: "Dear King Tyler: One of your spies tried to harm one of my stone giants. I am sending his body back to you for resurrection or proper disposal. Please stop sending spies into my land, as it is not appreciated at this time. I have defeated the letch king, and I am working on making my lands livable. I am using stone giants to help build dams and aqueducts to control the water, and I do not want visitors at this time. May the gods bless you and yours, King Charles."

He sent a message back that I allowed through. "Dear King Charles, or whoever you are: I am not fool enough to believe a single word in your letter. I will be watching and prepared to defend my lands. However, my priests say that I should stay away at this time. King Tyler."

I never did get along with King Tyler. He took his land from a good king by force and killed the old king's entire family. He was a usurper and a thief and would likely attack me at some point. I set extra protections along my sea side where he might try to attack. Then I set a wall at the eastern pass where he could not see. The wall was made of Laststoneite and was one thousand feet tall and fifty feet thick, with two large doors at the bottom. Both doors were removed and turned into Laststoneite separately and then hung. I added five crossbars of Laststoneite and made the ground Laststoneite for a hundred feet down so he could not dig his way around my wall. The wall was built smoothly on their side and had stairs and towers on our side.

There were six signs on their side, spelling out my laws, also set in Laststoneite. The first sign was about the laws, and the next five gave the top overriding laws.

King Tyler was a fool, but I'd always gotten along well with Queen Alluvia, on my western side, when she visited Father. She was a good queen in a hard-to-control land. Right now, she had no idea about me, and I was hoping to keep it that way for a while longer.

We finished the eastern aqueduct and started the western aqueduct and dams for another hundred small lakes. Then we carved out streams and rivers down into the valley, creating a river running my entire western edge. Then we did the same starting from the northern mountains, creating two carved-out rivers crossing back and forth like a chain down the center of my land and running wide enough to nearly touch the eastern and western rivers. Each place the rivers touched, we created large lakes with many streams, then went out and watered the land the exact right amount. Many ended in fountains that flowed high and beautiful. All of my rivers ended flowing south through hundreds of lakes and finally into the sea. All the stone was turned into Laststoneite. Now my land was perfect for planting. No unauthorized wet areas and no areas too dry. Most of all, all those lakes plugged nearly every way through the mountains except one pass on each side that I left open with a towering wall and doors I could shut—and did.

Bridges and roads came next. With over five hundred lakes, four main rivers, hundreds of other rivers, and thousands of streams, I needed bridges. The giants were wonderful at using the rod to make bridges that were beautiful to look at and made everyone crossing think of our gods. I did keep them down to one Potentis statue for every ten each of my two gods. They were not happy about that, but I explained my promise, and they agreed that I had to keep it. It was their fountains that astounded me the most. How someone so big could make such tiny details was nearly unbelievable. Some of the biggest bridges were long enough to add all the aspects of the three gods, so I allowed that but added Commeatus, the god of travel. They built them, and I turned them into Laststoneite after ensuring that there was a plaque with their names and the date when they made it. All in all, with the help of some fantastic artifacts, that took only a year. Time for phase four.

CHAPTER 7

PHASE FOUR— PLANTING

Now that the structure was completed, I needed plants, food, and creatures. The creatures were Silvestris's and Natura's part. I had to create food, living space, forests, and orchards, and I was pulling my hair out trying to figure out where to start. Then it hit me—the Treestorm Forest had creatures that wanted increased space. They could help plant.

One morning, tree fay were all of a sudden in my lands, and I didn't even ask for them. Proba told the elves, and the elves told the tree fay, and they came to see me at my new castle along with twinkle dogs, centaurs, southern druids, dryads, gnomes, a *lammasu*, two nymphs, *grigs*, nixies, pixies, fairies, and many other creatures.

After greetings and refreshments, we sat down in my empty garden. The tree fay dug in their roots and smiled. One said, "All your land is rich with good soil. It will make a wonderful forest. It will grow quickly and strong."

Another tree fay said, "The soil goes deep and stays unspoiled. I will have a difficult time pulling out my roots from this place. It is very tasty."

I said, "Thank you, my friends. This soil has been running off the mountains for thousands of years. It has not been used since before the Dragon Wars. Enjoy all you want, but there is much work to do." I brought out a parchment map of my lands with drawings of where I needed what and placed it before them.

They studied the drawings and made comments. One elf said, "Much of this land will be forest. I estimate nearly one-third. That includes the area for what you call recyclable trees. I am amazed that you would allow such."

A tree fay said, "Yes, the biggest part is forest, and we have many trees that are not sentient. We could plant these at the recyclable areas and expect them to be cut, trimmed, and replanted. There would be no problem with this, as long as the humans do not cut into the forest proper. I do not wish to plant my brothers and sisters and then have the humans, orcs, and goblins decide they need more space."

I looked at him with sadness. "I worship Silvestris and Natura, the gods of nature. Do you really think I would allow anyone to harm my forests? No, my friends. I have a great reason for a large forest, and I will explain this reason to the humans and any others that wish to live on my land. I learned this reason in my studies. Few knew except the northern druids, and they did not say anything, which was foolish in my opinion."

A dryad said, "I want so much to believe, but even with the curse on you, I find it difficult. What did you learn that makes the forest necessary in your eyes?"

"First, there will be no goblins and orcs unless they can behave. I will throw them out if they start cutting into my forests. I will do the same for the humans that cannot hold to the laws. However, I do not think they will break the laws. The humans are having trouble with births, children are having trouble breathing, and more are dying each season before they reach their first year. The deaths are fewer in places where there is a lot of vegetation, especially trees."

A tree fay said, "I do not understand. Why would humans do better around trees?"

I said, "Not only trees but all green leafy vegetation."

A small pixie said, "When we moved out of the low lands and into the rocky mountains to escape the human hunters, we found that we were having the same problems. What causes this? How can we stop this?"

I sadly said, "I am sorry for your birthing troubles. The cause is twofold. First, the Dead Lands and the Undead Lands used to be full of trees and vegetation. They have been void of life for too long. Second, the humans cut back their forests and combined all farms into one area, and that includes the other continents. The issue is trees and all leafy vegetation absorb in what we breathe out. They need the impurities of the air to survive. They purify that air and let it out as pure air. All other creatures breathe in what tress and leafy vegetation let out. We need the pure air to live. With the two Dead Lands and the cutback in vegetation in all the human lands, we have created an imbalance. The creatures are breathing out more than the vegetation can purify. This will kill off all creatures, and that will kill off all vegetation. We need to rebalance and purify the air to keep this from happening. The only way to do this is to rebalance the vegetation with the creatures that breathe. My land will be mostly vegetation. My lands will include forests, orchards, grasslands, and farms where the numbers of creatures are low and the amount of vegetation is high. Then I plan to give this land to a good and trusted friend and start repairs in the Dead Lands. He will build cities for trading, places where an army can reside, towns, and villages. He will provide protection for all."

There was complete silence for some time. Finally a tree fay said, "I always knew we needed the little creatures for fertilizer. They create so much of it. But I did not know we need them to breathe."

I added, "One human needs ten trees. Ten trees need one human or creatures of equal size. They do not need to be together; still, having them all in one place is fine. The winds are ordered by the gods to keep the air mixed up so that all get the correct amounts. The oceans have the same problem. Fish and other breathing creatures need the plants that grow in the sea, and the plants need the breathing creatures. The tides and storms mix and spread the air in the water, allowing for an even allotment."

An elf said, "Amazing. I had no idea. We, of course, love the forest and have not had this problem. That others are dying due to the lack of clean air was not known to us. Would this not balance out at some point?"

"It would have if the Undead Lands and the Dead Lands were not created. The world used to balance itself constantly until it was thrown out of balance by the Dragon Wars, which were caused by a god curse for Dragon Pepper and an elf druid that thought he could use the Staff of Nature to turn back time. Fools would have killed us all if it wasn't for a northern druid, my good friend King Farsite of the northern elves, and some very loving and understanding gods. Because of them, I can fix these two problems and give the world a chance to balance itself again, thought it will be a long and difficult battle. That you are all here to help will make this easier and much faster. I am running out of time for this project. I need the planting completed in three years, and then I need everyone out of each section and off my lands."

There was general outrage. One fairy yelled, "Human! Why do we have to leave after we would work so hard to plant for you?" It turned deadly quiet.

I smiled and talked gently to calm them all down. "I am sorry, little fairy. I did not state that exactly how I should have. What I said was true but apparently taken wrong. I will be using the Staff of Nature to ensure all planting goes well. Doing this is not dangerous to life. Then I will use it to grow everything quickly. In only moments, I will change three years' worth of planting into twenty years of growth. This is very dangerous, and if you stay, you too will age twenty years or turn to dust. When I have completed that task, then you can move back in and will be very welcome. I was simply telling you that I do not want you harmed."

They all looked embarrassed. Farsite leaned over and said, "Next time, be careful what you say. I nearly had heart failure. Who do you think talked most of them into coming here?"

I leaned back and whispered, "You nearly went from saint to enemy number one."

"Yes, and I have to live with these as my neighbors." He raised his voice and asked, "After the final growing, would you entertain an Elvin city?"

I said, "As long as you are doing good for the land and get along with everyone else. Anyone can come here under the following circumstances." I thought, *Here it comes, the kicker that may stop this entire group.* I was addressing the king of the northern elves, the king of the dryads, the queen of the fairies, the top tree fay, and leaders of a dozen races. *Well, here goes.* "I am the king, and I will be turning this over to another human, and you must follow him." All hell broke loose. I raised a hand, and it became quiet. "This land is important, and I will not have wars between you. Many of you barely get along. This human is a known good and honest man that I trust to run this land fairly for all. He is doing the same for his part of Kayland as we speak."

Someone asked, "How are you going to get Duke Edward to give up his post? He is a great human, and I trust him. There are few humans I trust, but I do trust him. We have lived on his lands, and he has always treated us fairly. However, he is sworn to Kayland and your father. Your father will not help you. He used to hate you. Though he does not anymore, he cannot help an exile."

That was the first time I heard that Father did not hate me any longer, and I paused in shock for a moment before I answered. "That is my problem. If I cannot obtain Duke Edward, I will be very surprised, as eight gods have hinted to me that he would make a great replacement, and they seem willing to help make it so. However, I need it to remain a secret from the humans. If they knew, they would blame me for all their disasters."

Some laughed, but most were nodding their heads. They could live with Duke Edward's rule, and I needed them to know it was coming so the duke would have fewer problems moving in. "In addition, I need the duke in charge and you to help him. There are wars coming, and we need to protect this land for all our sakes." More nodding of heads. Good. "Personally, I will not be holding court or telling you what to do. You are now and shall remain, for all I care, in charge of your people. I am not going to have the time to play king. If we are attacked, I will need you all to help protect this land, but other than that, you're on your own after the planting and growing. The laws of this land are the same as Kayland except for five laws that override all others. If you cannot comply with the laws as such, then do not stay here."

A tree fay asked in concern, "The laws of Kayland are fair if someone enforces them equally. I have heard of Duke Edward and believe it will be so, but what are these overriding laws?"

"I'm glad you asked. One: anyone harms one of my unicorns, even on accident, they are guilty of a horrible crime against my god, and the punishment will be final!"

Heads nodding and murmurs of "That's fair" were prevalent.

"Two: all sentient creatures are equal in the eyes of the law and will be treated equally. They can hold positions of authority throughout the lands as long as they do not abuse that authority. A pixie that harms a human will be tried the same as a human that harms a pixie." Great cheers rang out and continued for some time.

A pixie asked with concern, "What do you consider sentient? Humans don't consider us as more than animals."

"Any creatures that can dream, speak, read, and write are sentient. Now, not all of a species learn to read or write, but if their race can, then they have the ability and are considered sentient."

"That would include pixies; we can read and write. Some of us can."

I smiled, knowing that pixies had been picked on for as long as time had kept record. I bent down to her and said, "You will not be hunted on my land." She flew up and hugged me with tears in her eyes. I let her, and then I stood up.

"Three: evil is not allowed in my lands, ever, for any reason." No cheers to that.

An elf asked, "I don't understand that one."

"It is simple, my friend. The northwestern section of this land borders the demon realms. I need to know when demons enter so that I, or the duke, can stop them before they cause harm to others. Therefore, I set up alarms all over my lands. If evil resides here, it will constantly set off my alarms. I would never be able to protect my people from demons, or worse, evil humans. Humans have many evil people, as they don't believe in outlawing evil in general. I do not wish to change their ways. I just don't want the problems they create." Now cheers went up.

"Four: there will be no wasting on my lands. If you cut down a tree, you had better use every bit of it and then replant.

If you go hunting, it had better be for food, and you had better use the meat, hide, and bones. If you used something that can be replanted, you must replant. No hunting lodges with humans that kill for fun. Not on my lands!" All stood up and cheered and clapped and cheered some more.

"Five: no army will enter my land to cross to another. All lands bordering my lands are protected from attacks from other lands. I expect the same from the other lands bordering mine. I have a little mental problem. I become very angry when someone attacks me or my lands. If that happens, I will be using their lands to increase my own. I don't give back what I take. Attack me, and you had better win, or you lose everything. I become very mean when it comes to protecting myself and my people." Cheers rose high, but some were looking worried and deciding not to try to change my plans. I was reading some minds, and they were either with me or planning to take over when I was done. Now they were thinking that trying to take over would be a bad idea, especially if I was backed by the gods.

The talks went on for eight days. We discussed everything from where we would obtain the seeds and what insects we would need to what was in it for each one and why plant this here and that there. Generally, it came down to everyone would supply their best seeds, and I would provide seeds form Kayland and the druid trap. Elves and a dozen other groups would plant the tilled soil with help from several creatures I had never seen that could actually till the soil. Dryads and fairies, with other groups, would plant meadows and the grasslands. Tree fay and many forest creatures would plant the forests and orchards. Almost everyone was happily volunteering for work to make it a great place to live.

The southern druids were still mad at me and volunteered for nothing. They sat there listening and kept quiet. Their thoughts were, *It will not be difficult to talk our Aroan Elvin friends into attacking and taking over this land. Most important is getting our hands on the suppository.* They asked, "King Charles, where is the northern druid suppository going to be placed?"

The answer was not simple. All that knowledge should not go to waste. I could bring it all out, or most of it, but who was I to decide who got to read what? My answer did not please them greatly, but it gave them some hope. "At this time, the Suppository for Knowledge and Magic will reside where I reside. It will move where I move. I am most concerned that the knowledge residing in the suppository does not become lost to the world, but at the same time, I know that there is knowledge of a hundred ways to destroy this plane of existence. I would not willingly make that knowledge, or other war-type knowledge, available to anyone. Someday soon, I hope, I will be looking for people who wish to or need to learn. I may entertain having creatures that I can trust take over running the suppository. At this time, I am too busy to entertain finding those trustable creatures. I will talk to the gods about this and obtain their opinion."

Their thoughts were, *We cannot upset him. At least not until we have the suppository or can get our hands on it. We know how to enter, but we need to find it.*

I stood up, walked over to the middle of the garden, and opened my arms wide. The suppository came and stood tall before me. I anchored it down and said, "If you wish to try, I will not stop you, but I will tell you this; it is suicide. I know how it works, and it is not some simple spell or password. If the key is not given to you, then you cannot pass into the suppository."

I did not need to watch. Two tried, and two died. The five that were left looked very sad. One asked, "Will you entertain allowing someone to enter to obtain knowledge?"

"When I know I can trust the person. Even then, I am limited. I can only allow someone in for one week. After a week, they will be spit out as if they never entered. They will not be able to depart with anything, or remove anything, or teleport or summon in someone who can remove items. It is simply not possible. We enter, stay one week, and exit as if we just entered. Time will not have passed for us, but we will be there one week. You will be able to keep the knowledge you gain but nothing else."

The oldest druid said, "This would be significantly helpful at times."

I was watching his mind and knew he wanted a certain spell, one I could easily give him, but he wanted to research it and test it. "I will do this once to show you what I mean." He walked up to me, and I walked him in. I guided him to the correct spot and helped him learn the spell he needed. It was an earth healing spell. We learned a lot that week about each other, and now I trusted him far less. We walked out exactly when we walked in.

He went to the others and said, "I have the knowledge, brothers. I have the knowledge."

They departed, never once volunteering to do anything, and now I knew why. Their lands were dying. Overpopulation had caused massive cuts into the forests, and they were having birthing problems as well. They were returning to try to stop the deforestation of their lands, even if it meant war with the elves. They did promise to help with the planting of the Dead Lands. "If you ever make it possible to live there."

Creatures were leaving, and I had work to do. I needed to break the law, and I had to be very careful in doing so.

CHAPTER 8

BUYING SEEDS

There is only one place that I know of that has all the types of seeds I need and that is Clear Water Valley in Kayland. The central hub for trading is Diadem Lake. Problem is, I am in exile and it's the death penalty if I enter Kayland. I thought to myself, *"I believe it's time for a very good disguise. Now who would farmers appreciate, respect, and sell to, at a good price, their best seeds. Not the stuff they export but the good seeds. Someone from Clear Water Valley—that is important to them. Someone they can haggle with and win against but still respect. A lord? Possibly, but not so high in rank that haggling is out and not so low they have little or no respect. A lord of Kayland originally from Clear Water Valley. Who would they not know? Someone from the south border along the sea. There are a lot of lords down there. Where would he be going with the seed and why? Someplace far away and not likely to be checked on. Sinaguard! No one has been living in Sinaguard for over a century. It is never visited, and it would be just like Father to station some unknown lord to the place. The farmers may even take pity on him and give him strong, healthy seed so that it has a chance of growing something. A lord newly stationed to Sinaguard in the northwestern range bordering Ringal and the Treestorm. Dangerous land and never visited, but several rock-hard,* large valleys that could be planted if soil could be brought in. Just the type of project Father would try to push off on someone not important. I would need a lot of seed, and I would pay good prices; after all, it's the king's money. Being a king, I don't have to tell them which king I am talking about.

No, won't work due to transportation. A lord would have it sent by wagon. That won't work unless I raid my own wagon trains and send the seed to Sordeath by magic. By magic? Hm. Why not be a wizard who has been tasked with trying to plant in the Sinaguard area? Father would send a wizard to do this if he was mad at the wizard. Rotten job for a magic user. Mean thing for the king to do as punishment for some wizard using his powers inappropriately. No, can't be punished for that. The farmers would not trust him. Let's see ... how about for stealing a kiss from some baron's daughter? That's it! The farmer boys have a game they play when trying to get attention from a young lady. They steal a kiss. However, it is highly frowned upon in the cities and especially with lords and above. Several farmers' sons have gotten into major trouble for doing the same. They may even think I was sent way out to Sinaguard to keep me away from a baron sworn to kill me if he saw me around his daughter again. Perfect!

Due to the Star Fire, I was going to have to actually plant some of the Sinaguard. I moved some soil there and set up two small valleys for planting.

I changed my look but not much. Being seventeen and almost eighteen years old, I looked the part of a young man who would steal a kiss. All the hard work I had done building the castle and dams had built muscles and study lines. In addition, I looked like a wizard. I didn't have the wide-eyed innocent look or that lack-of-experience look of a young wizard. At least, I didn't think I did. I had little hair on my body, but I needed a haircut, as it was getting long. Easy spell and quickly done. I turned my hair a typical boy's red, including eyebrows and eyelashes, then widened my nose and shortened my ears. I changed my eyes to brown and added a fresh, tiny scar to my chin. I made the changes permanent and nonmagical so they could not be detected but I could easily change them back. Then I dressed in clothes that a farmer's boy would have if in his temple best. Strong cotton, natural colors, with just a hint of wear. I added a worn cloak and boots that could handle the mud. The entire look said, "Farmer's boy no matter how he is trying to hide it." Possibly some money but not overly wealthy, some experience but not much, and lots of hard work. The type of clothing that a farmer would buy for his son if he could afford it and his son was becoming a wizard. I packed some simple belongings, changes of clothing, toiletries, and some gold in a Natura's Deep Pocket Haversack. I also picked out a good nonmagical staff made of Clear Water Valley hard wood with iron shod ends. I used a spell to mask the magic on my two rings and the Star Fire and teleported to Diadem Lake.

I purposely landed right in the center of the road that would be used the heaviest and then ducked and ran to get out of the way while farmers and others were yelling at me and nearly busting a gut laughing at the young wizard that foolishly teleported himself right into traffic that could kill him. Someone grabbed my arm and pulled me out of the way.

"Boy! You need to be more careful!" He nearly pulled me down the street to a point just out of town and off to the side. "Study this area for at least an hour so you know a good place to teleport without getting yourself killed." Then he stomped off.

I knew the man. He was an old adventurer, turned farmer, turned sheriff. I studied the spot carefully for an hour or more and then looked up. People were staying their distance but were smiling. In their eyes, I was an inexperienced young man, something they saw every day, and one that did what he was told and was willing to learn, something they saw every day, wearing clothes that did not put him above them, something they saw every day, and generally looking apologetic, something they would expect of a proper young man. If I had come in looking arrogant, with money and throwing my power around, I would have gotten all the seed I wanted—none of the good seed, but they would have claimed it was the best. *Speaking of claiming, I'm going to be haggling, so I better turn the Star Fire all the way down. Don't need them to know I am cursed. Farmers are superstitious, you know.* At that point, they saw a boy just like their sons, and that was comfortable for them. For farmers, comfort and familiarity are important. I went over to where the sheriff was sitting and rocking.

"Excuse me, sir."

He pointed to the badge and said, "I'm the sheriff, boy, and don't you forget it."

"Yes, sir." I paused as if trying to think of what to say. "Sheriff sir?"

With a smile, he said, "Yes."

"Thank you for showing me a good place to teleport. Could you please direct me to a place to spend a few nights, sir?"

There were many others milling about. This was a small farming and trading town on the southern shore of a perfectly round lake called Diadem Lake. They all wanted to know what was going on. They were mostly smiling, as they were comfortable; otherwise, their looks would be disapproving. He stood up and looked long and hard at me. "Depends on what your business is, boy."

About this time, most visitors would be saying their name and demanding that the sheriff use it. They would be disappointed, as the sheriff would never use the name for someone my age; a farmer's son was a "boy" until he planted and harvested his first crop, and then he earned the right to be called a man. Many of the people were waiting for me to explode. "Sheriff sir, I need to do a lot of planting and need some exceptional seed. I believe that this town would be a good place to find the best seed."

"Well now. Why would you, a wizard-wannabe, need to do planting?"

I purposefully blushed, and his eyes squinted. "Something wrong, boy?"

I looked at him somewhat shamefully, "Sheriff sir, I love gardening and planting. I used to work on the farm when I could. Right now, I am tasked with a big project, and I will need a lot of seed."

"Big project?"

This was the difficult part. I had to say it so that the sheriff and others would think it punishment and not the Sordeath. They needed to think Sinaguard. And the Star Fire would not let me lie.

"Sheriff, the Sinaguard is big, isn't it?"

"Yes."

"To plant there, some of the valleys would need to have good topsoil imported. I have great topsoil on my lands. Someone hiding out—I mean, working hard—could try to please the king and grow as much as possible over a few years, couldn't they?"

Now his eyes shot up, and people were murmuring. His eyes narrowed, and he said, "That is called punishment in my book, boy. What did you do to be assigned such a wonderful position?"

With all this "boy" stuff, I felt like I was ten years old again. "Sheriff sir, private lessons from the king are supposed to be kept private. My mentor told me that many times. Let's just say that big-city people get just a little mad at boys that try and steal a kiss from their daughters." I shrugged and smiled. "Who knew? For some reason, big-city barons do not think a farmer's son is good enough for their little girls." All truth and no lies at all.

There were nods all around and general statements of "That figures" and "Typical big-city folk."

The sheriff asked, "Where you from, boy?"

"Sheriff sir, I would not want to embarrass my father, and I cannot go home. After what happened, I would never claim the capital as my home anymore. I have found that it has evil and rotten people that I just don't understand. How can I say this?" I pretended to think for a couple of seconds. I smiled, stood taller, and proudly said, "I can honestly say my heart is, and has always been, with the Clear Water Valley and my duke. I would give my life for him." He took it the way I had hoped, and again, no lies or misleading. If they took things the wrong way, oh well.

He put a hand on my arm. "Your father will forgive you for leaving and becoming a wizard, boy. He may need help on the farm, but if you're magical, he knows you need proper training. It will take a while and you will need to make a good name for yourself, but all farmers love their wayward sons. Especially after they learn that the big city is no place for a farmer. Hard lesson, boy—hard lesson that some children never learn. Now you're in trouble and being sent away. Baron chasing you, boy? No, don't answer."

"Sir, I …"

"No, boy. I can read between the lines. You went and kissed some baron's daughter, and he has a death wish out on you. Happened before to our sons. Hope she was worth it. To answer your question, we have two inns." He pointed east. "The Silver Cup. Nice quiet place with good food just like your mother makes, or"—he pointed west—"the Night Owl's Laugh. Place where people go for entertainment and to flirt with the girls. They have rooms, but they are rented by the hour."

I knew this was a test of my morals. I said, "The Sliver Cup sounds expensive. Are they good people?"

"Yes they are. They are people you can trust."

I changed my expression to sadly beaten down and lowered my head. "Trust. It would be nice to be able to trust again." I looked up and said, "Thank you, Sheriff."

As I headed east, he smiled and said, "You're welcome, boy. You need something, you just let the owner know. He can set it up."

I stayed magically tuned into their conversation long after my ears could not listen.

"Nice boy, though a little clumsy. See how difficult it was for him to get through traffic?"

"Poor child. He must have had the worst time in that den of iniquity they call a capital city."

"He doesn't seem to have lost much of his innocence. See how embarrassed he was and how much he wants to protect his father's reputation?"

"He's a good child."

"Needs a lot of help. That's a big job planting the Sinaguard."

"Unfortunate he was sent there. Did you notice how wilted he looked when he talked about trust? Darn those big-city fools. They must have chewed him up but good."

"Well, we won't disappoint him. He'll get his seed and all he can transport."

"Michel Tanner, you had better not sell him that trash you save up for the fools in Port Hayden."

"No, Martha, he'll get my best seed if he can afford it. We have children to feed, and I'm not giving it away."

"He's a farmer's boy all right. I wonder if his father taught him how to haggle. If not, he's about to learn."

At that time, a cleric of Solbelli came up to the group with a faraway look in his eyes, and I said to myself, "Darn. I hope he doesn't ruin everything."

The sheriff saw him and said, "Father Bonetie, you look lost. You all right?"

Everyone turned in his direction. The crowd had grown, and there were at least twenty people in the street talking about the new boy. Father Bonetie asked, "Have you seen a young man come by here?"

The sheriff answered, "Yes. Why?"

"I was visited by a Caelum. My wonderful god Solbelli wants me to ensure that this child gets everything he needs. Solbelli has interest in the child and what he is doing."

Now the talk could almost be heard all the way up the street. The sheriff calmed everyone down and asked, "Did this Caelum say anything else about the boy?"

The cleric turned his watering eyes to the crowd and said, "Only one thing. The boy is as honest as a Paladin and not to allow people to take advantage of him."

Just about then, another cleric showed up. This one was from Commeatus, and he happily said, "Hello, everyone. Hi, Father Bonetie. Nice to see you again. Anyone see a young man come by here? Commeatus wants me to help him."

I stopped outside the inn and prayed to Solbelli, saying, "Thank you. I will remember this kindness." To Commeatus, I said, "Thank you. Again you are helping. I will not forget."

I stepped into the inn, and the owner was there behind the counter talking to a young woman. I walked up to him and politely waited until he turned to me. Politeness goes a long way in the farmlands. His smile was friendly and kind. "You need something, young man?"

"Yes, sir. I need a room for a few days, meals, and a bath."

He looked me over and said, "Bath first?"

I took a sniff of myself and said, "Um, yes, sir. That may be best."

His face never changed, but his mind said, *Let's see what this boy is worth.* "The bath is three copper with a copper tip to the maid, the meals are dependent on what you order and how much you eat, and the bed is dependent on several things. Single with privy, single with privy down the hall, double shared with others, the loft, or the barn in the back."

I asked, "How much is the single with privy?"

I cringed when he said, "One gold a night."

In the city, that room would cost twenty gold a night, and people would be happy to get it at that. I asked, "How much for the double?"

He kept his face impassive. "Two copper."

"The single without the privy room?"

"Five copper a night."

I pretended to think on the issue, and he decided he might be losing a customer that was just outside praying for a deal he could afford. "Tell you what, boy. I'll throw in breakfast for free if you take the single without privy for four copper a night."

I smiled and said, "I'll take it. Thank you very much, sir."

"You're welcome, boy. Sign the registry." He turned it around. I could feel the Star Fire preparing to burn me hard.

"Sir?"

He saw my hesitation and wondered, "Something wrong, boy?"

I didn't hear him come in, but the sheriff said, "The boy has had some problems in the big city after leaving home, and just like the rest of us, he doesn't want to embarrass his father by letting people know who he is until he can make a good name for himself. He is too honest to tell you a lie, but maybe he can use a name he likes. How would that be?"

The innkeeper said, "All right by me. Use a good one, boy, as people are going to call you by that name the whole time you're here."

I said, "Thank you, Sheriff sir." He smiled. I pretended to think hard on the subject, and the innkeeper nearly laughed.

He turned to the sheriff and said, "Boy's so honest he hadn't even thought up a different name to use." He turned the register around and wrote, *Charles, single, 4 copper, free B.* "There you are, boy, Named after the hero of Kayland."

I looked at him and said, "I don't think I should do that, sir."

"Nonsense, boy. You'll never match up to Prince Charles. No one will in my mind. But we love that name, and you're just about his age, or what age he would be if he were still alive."

"Prince Charles? He is still alive, sir."

The sheriff and the innkeeper said, "What?"

Oh no. How to get around this without lying! I looked shy and used that to gain time to think. First thing I thought about was to start keeping my mouth shut so I didn't shove my foot in it! "Um, sir, I was watching the court when the queen received a package with a book on castles written by Prince Charles. The queen was overjoyed, but the king was not so happy."

"Boy, listen to me. This is very important. Did you hear where he is?"

"No, sir. The king and queen would have liked to know where he is also. Apparently, he visited all the castles around the continent. They talked long on how he interviewed with other kings and queens."

The sheriff said, "So, our prince is trying to make a living selling books. Most people can't read. Won't get much for a book out here."

"The book is fully illustrated, almost every page. I could get one. I know where they are being sold." I thought, *I should. I set it up with the printer and his line of stores.*

The innkeeper said, "How much are the books going for?"

"Ten gold. I would need to be reimbursed. Ten gold buys a lot of seed."

The sheriff told the innkeeper why I was there and why I needed seeds but left off that the clerics wanted me and that he had sent them in the wrong direction until he could poke around some more.

The innkeeper had to think on this one. "Ten gold. Lot of money for a book. I'd have to send in an order and then wait for months. The book will cost me twice the price by the time it reaches here."

"Um, sir?"

"Yes."

"When I teleport out my first group of seeds, I can bring one back with me. Stopping at the place where they are would not be difficult."

He looked at me hard. "How much you going to charge me for this service?"

I looked down, pretending worry. "You love Prince Charles?"

He looked at me, concerned. Claiming love for an exile could be damaging to the inn and the town, but he was not going to lie. It just wasn't their way. He said proudly, "I love no one better."

I must have beamed with happiness, as he returned the smile very brightly. "I will do this for cost. I will not charge you for travel, and I will try to get the book cheaper." I had just made big points that I did not know I was going to be able to make. They still loved me, and I just let them know I was on their side.

The sheriff said, "That attitude toward our prince would not go over well in the politically filled rooms of the big city. No wonder you were punished so hard. Now things make more sense. There are a couple of priests looking for you. I thought I'd let you know before someone told them where you are."

I pretended a little panic. "Why do they want me? What did I do now?"

The sheriff smiled. "Relax, boy. They say the gods are interested in helping. The gods know, boy. They know you did nothing wrong. Trust in the gods, boy. That's my advice. Always trust in the gods." He turned and left.

The innkeeper said, "Peggy, take Charles to room number two and start a bath."

I followed Peggy, his daughter, to room number two and started unpacking. I left the gold in my haversack where it was protected, but I probably could have left it sitting out on the table. Those people would never have taken anything that did not belong to them.

Before getting undressed, I looked out the window and spotted the two clerics coming toward the inn. I went down to meet them. They were just stepping in when I reached the bottom of the stairs. Father Bonetie held out a hand and said, "Hello, child. I am Father Bonetie of Solbelli, and this is Brother Longstep of Commeatus."

I shook their hands and said, "I am honored to meet you. Are you staying here at the inn? They have nice rooms." The innkeeper smiled.

Brother Longstep said, "I'll probably get a room. I was just passing through until Commeatus told me to stay and help you. Don't know what help you need, but help you'll get. Father Bonetie stays in the back of the small temple of Solbelli at the other end of the town. He was told to help also."

Then it hit me. I didn't need any help with buying seeds. What was going to happen that required the help of two clerics? So I asked, "Did the gods happen to tell you what you are to help me with?"

They looked at each other. "We don't know. What are you doing here?"

"I am buying seeds for planting."

Father Bonetie said, "Then we are here for one reason. To check the seeds for purity and place spells that will preserve them until use and keep bugs out. That would be my guess."

I was about to say that I could do it myself, but then the answer came. A young wizard teleporting large quantities of seed several times a day was going to be difficult enough to explain. Teleporting was a high-level spell, and taking a lot of seed with me made it a very high-level spell. I thought about that and brought some items to explain it away. However, being able to also do clerical spells on top of using the teleporting rods would be unbelievable. These clerics would take care of that issue. I looked at them with a smile and then went to one knee and prayed to both gods in silence, thanking them. The clerics watched me praying and were happy.

Father Bonetie placed a hand on my head and gave me a blessing. So did Brother Longstep. I allowed them both and told my gods that a blessing from good gods is always welcome. I heard a voice from Silvestris.

"Be weary of gifts, boy."

Then I heard Natura say, "Old fool, the other gods only want some temples on his land made permanent and grand, like he made ours."

I said with a hint of possessiveness, "I may grant them temples, and I may make them permanent, but I won't allow them to be as grand as yours."

Natura said, "Oh, he is jealous for his gods. I like that."

"We shall see. He is loyal, and I like that."

That was it. They were gone. I was suddenly tired. That bath was going to feel very good.

I paid for the bath and gave a two-copper tip. I felt cheap giving only two coppers when as prince I would have given two platinum, but being out of character at this point would not be good. The bath was hot, the water clean, and I was refreshed. I thought, while relaxing in the tub, on how I needed to visit people a little more often. I thought the same when I went down to dinner and tasted the wonderful food. The innkeeper's wife could cook well, and it gave me an idea for another good book.

While I was eating, one of the farmers came in and asked for me. He looked shady and acted nearly apologetic while thinking, *Easy prey*. He had a tin with him full of good seed. The innkeeper reluctantly sent him my direction. As he walked up, he tipped his hat. "Good eve, my lord." Others were watching, so I looked at him and then looked around to ensure he was talking to me. I pointed to myself, and he nodded.

I stood up and said, "Sir?"

He smiled inside but not out. "I hear ye are looking for seed for planting, my lord."

I looked at him and noticed the two farmers who were eating in town tonight making quick motions, showing not to trust this one. I answered, "I am looking for good seed. I need strong seed. The best the Clear Water Valley can produce. I am willing to pay a fair price." I looked at his tin and motioned for him to sit.

"I happen to have a lot of great seed. Easily the best available and of many types. What type of seed are you looking for?"

He lied so badly that I did not need the Star Fire screaming at me to know. "I need all kinds of good seeds. I will take all you have if the price is within my budget."

He opened the can and said, "If you know seed, then you will know that this is great seed."

I looked at the contents and picked up a handful. I let it run through my hands, took a seed and tasted it, and said, "Yes, this is very good seed. How much can you provide and at what price?"

Going directly to the point made him think I was a novice at haggling. "I have eighty wagons full of seed, and it's one hundred gold a wagon."

Father would have paid that in a second, but I was supposed to be a farmer's boy, turned wizard, forced into being a farmer. I actually look shocked and nearly choked on my orange juice. "One hundred gold! I am so sorry, sir. I would not pay one hundred gold if you tossed in the wagon and horse to pull it. Even if all the seed is this good, and believe me, I will magically check and have you arrested if not, the entire eighty wagons would not be worth more than one gold each. Especially since I am buying in volume."

It wasn't the ridiculously low counteroffer that caused him to decide to end the conversation. It was the "magically check and have you arrested" that made him change his mind. He closed his tin and said, "I am offended, boy. My seed is worth far more than that." He got up and quickly left.

Once he was out the door, I turned to the two farmers and mouthed a silent, "Thank you." They both nodded slightly.

One asked, "Are you truly going to use magic to check the seed?"

I answered, "It would be very disappointing to a certain king if I failed in my task due to stupidity. I will be magically checking the seed, and I will be using a Circle of Knowing during negotiations. I will be cutting through the haggling, as I am not as good at it as I'd like to be, by asking what is truly a good and fair price for both of us. I know farmers love to haggle. Believe me, I know. But I don't have the choice of failing. I have to succeed in this."

They both nodded. One said, "I have some seed that I can afford to let go. I am replanting this year, but I have enough seed to plant a dozen times. I grow wheat, and I was going to sell the seed for feed, but you seem to need it more. A fair price for both of us would be three gold a barrel." He smiled. "And that includes the barrel. I have approximately six hundred barrels of wheat seed. Can you afford eighteen hundred gold?"

I thought out loud, "Six hundred barrels will be a good start, but I will need a thousand times that. Um, sir?"

His mind was racing. Three gold was good money. Soon it would get out that these farmers could unload all their best seed on a boy who had no idea how much or how far the seed would go. Six hundred barrels of wheat seed would cover several square leagues for goodness sake. And this child wanted seed of every type so he wasn't planting just wheat. "Yes, boy."

"I'll take your seed, please, and do you know anyone else with good seed?"

The other farmer smiled. "I have fifty barrels of apple tree seeds. The best apples in Clear Water Valley. Apple seed is a little more expensive than wheat, but I have three different kinds of apples."

"Just a second please." I did a simple Circle of Knowing spell just to let him know I was actually capable of doing so. He had no idea what spell I did, so I played it up. I turned to the first farmer and asked, "Were you telling me the truth, sir? Is it truly a fair deal for both of us?"

He nearly laughed. "Yes, boy, I was telling the truth."

"Excellent." I took out a pen, ink, and parchment from nowhere that they could see.

One whispered in amusement, "Yep, wizard all right."

I started writing down the wheat transaction. *Six hundred barrels of wheat. Three gold a barrel, including the barrel.* I looked up, "Name, sir?"

"Spike Little."

I wrote down his name and asked, "When can I go to your farm and transfer the wheat?"

"Any time you want, boy. If you had a map, I would mark it down. My farm is not far from here."

I held out a hand, and a parchment map of the Clear Water Valley appeared in it. I unrolled it and asked him where his farm was. He pointed out the exact spot and I placed a "1" on the map and a "1" next to his name. "I can give you half the gold now and the other half after I check and approve the seed. Is that all right with you?"

"Sure."

A bag of gold instantly appeared on the table. I picked it up with a smile and handed it to him saying, "You can keep the bag, sir."

He took it and said, "Hope you don't mind if I count it."

"No, sir. I would expect you to count it. I know I would, and my father would be very upset if I didn't. I remember him saying, 'Fool boy, trust everyone but count every copper.'"

His look said it all. He'd said the same to his son.

I did the same with the other farmer and half a dozen others that night. Bed was late, and morning came before sunrise in the farming district. Stores were open, and breakfast was on the table waiting for me as I came down.

The innkeeper said, "Sleep late in the city, boy? It's almost daybreak. You'll get used to the time again. Breakfast is over, but the wife left you some on that table. Farmers will be here soon to sell you their seed. Eat quick and set your spells. They have heard about your pulling things from thin air and will want to see for themselves. Do some little things if you can, especially in front of the children."

I thanked him and ate quickly. I then set up a nice area. I placed two tables together so I had room for the map and sat down to wait. I didn't have long to wait. Almost as soon as I sat down, the two clerics came in, and one did a Find Magic spell.

Father Bonetie said, "No spells up yet?"

"Oh thanks, I almost forgot." I did a silent, nonmovement, broadened spell of Circle of Knowing. Both their eyes nearly popped out of their heads.

Brother Longstep asked, "What did you just do?"

I had decided that I was going to show just these two that I was somewhat powerful. A simple Circle of Knowing was not difficult, but adding all the specials on it like silent, nonmovement, and broadened made it fairly high. They felt it happen but had no idea what I did.

I looked at Brother Longstep and said as if it were nothing, "I did a broadened Circle of Knowing."

Father Bonetie exclaimed, "Broadened!"

Brother Longstep started doing the math. "Broadened, silent, and nonmovement. Interesting, that was a paladin or clerical spell of seventh circle. What is a wizard doing using a divine spell?"

Father Bonetie answered for me. "Great Solbelli told me he is as honest as a paladin. Now we know why. He has training as a paladin and a wizard. He was trying to become a war wizard."

Brother Longstep asked, "How long have you been in training, child?"

"Fighting from birth, magic since I was fourteen, sir."

Father Bonetie shook his head. "They must have been upset when you were taken away from the Wizard's University for this task, child. Losing someone as fast at learning as you would be felt."

"I never said I went to the university, sir."

They looked at me like I was now a great puzzle to work out. Father Bonetie started to say something, but a farmer came in, and I welcomed him. Talks started and did not stop for six days, except for meals, restroom breaks, and sleep. The clerics watched me constantly and asked questions whenever possible. I did a lot of fun little magical things like causing the ink pen to write by itself, cooling my drink, pulling up chairs for people, grabbing things out of thin air, knowing names and places instantly, and my personal favorite, dimming the light coming through the window so that it did not shine right in my face and increasing the light in the room and on the map with permanent light on the ceiling. I told the innkeeper that I would remove it after the meetings, but he insisted that I leave it. "Save on candles, boy."

There were lots of children, and they were all running around and having fun. I was enjoying myself greatly. Farmers' children are very emotional. Most royalty and high-ranking people teach their children to not show emotion when possible. Not in the farmlands. They encourage it when young and then teach them how to hide it or use it when haggling and other appropriate times.

Farmers have a game called Smack the Emocat. Everyone knows an emocat is blind and hunts by sensing emotion. You have to be completely emotionless to sneak up on an emocat and smack it, and completely emotionless afterward to keep from being eaten by a five-hundred pound, eight-foot long, six-legged, dagger-sharp-clawed, nine-inch-fanged, man-eating terror. Of course, farmers always kill the emocat afterward, as emocats tend to hunt children.

There was one child who came in with an attitude and started messing with everything and everyone. His father told him twice to sit down and stop, and he paid no attention. After he spilled my ink bottle and I magically cleaned it up, I levitated him up sideways and placed him across his mother's lap. She took the hint and did the duty. He behaved after that. I think the most impressive thing for the farmers was having their gold on hand and paying them half in advance.

After six days of constant bargaining, I told the clerics, "Tomorrow we start shipping seed. It's going to be a long day, sirs, so get some sleep and prepare your spells for ensuring my seeds are protected, please." I turned to the innkeeper and said, "Sir, I will be shipping for two days. After that, I will be back to buy more. A lot more. Every little bit helps, so let people know that I will take everything that is the best seed. I also think I may be turning down some of the seed I bought if it doesn't turn out to be as good as they think."

He looked concerned. "I understand, boy. You know, I think you are buying far too much seed."

"I know, sir. Believe me, this seed will stay fresh for as long as I need it. And eventually I will use it all. If you had the chance to obtain all the seed you could at the king's expense and you knew that you might have to try several different things, or plant many times, to get the seed to grow properly, would you not overbuy at first and keep the seed for when it's needed?"

He smiled big, thinking, *So, the boy isn't the fool people think.* He said to me, "Yes, I would. I would buy up everything I could."

"Exactly. Now, I'm not being a thief. I'm not stealing from a king. Goodness knows I would never steal from anyone. However, the king wants this very badly and is willing to pay. I can do this but need all the seed I can get to ensure that every place is planted and grows well. If anyone comes by with good seed to sell, even if it's flowers, woodland trees, or anything else, I want it. Whatever I can get my hands on to make a great place to live and work. It matters not the amount. I will buy a thousand barrels or a single seed if the seed is worth my having. I can never create another Clear Water Valley, but I am going to come as close as I can." I said that last party looking a little homesick.

He smiled. "I think I understand now, son. I think I understand."

"I hope so, sir. In a few short years, I'm going to try to talk you into moving your inn to my home. It's a great inn, and your wife is a wonderful cook."

He laughed. "Don't hold your breath, boy." He put his arm around his wife and said, "My love will never allow me to move." She was smiling approvingly at him and me.

The next day, the clerics showed up a little later than normal. Natura touched my mind, and she was really mad. I went to the window and looked out as instructed. The two clerics were walking across the street, and they were not alone. A cleric from the capital city was with them. A cleric of Natura. A correction was made in my mind, "A false cleric of Natura! An imposter! A fool that you should burn to the ground immediately."

I looked up and said, "And you think I have an evil streak, my goddess? Do not worry. I will take care of this in my own way."

Just before she departed the contact, I heard her say, "Be evil; be as evil as you want with this one. He has destroyed many."

Silvestris said, "We would do this ourselves, Charles, but he is protected by a god that hates nature." That contact dissipated also.

The clerics were talking as they approached. "Brothers, I do not see what help I can be. I mostly stay in the temple, and I am seldom invited into the castle. I don't know everyone."

Brother Longstep said, "But you can ask questions about the city and the castle that someone who has been there and trained there would know, can't you?"

"Well, yes, I can do that much. I know the city very well."

I thought, *Yes, and I know you pretend, Father Spinell. Upsetting my gods is not a good idea. It makes me angry.* I touched the sheriff's mind to make him worried. He had no idea why he was worried, but he stopped rocking and headed toward the inn with hand on sword.

I went downstairs and sat down for breakfast. My staff was by my side. The innkeeper noticed and asked, "Thinking there is going to be trouble, boy?"

"Sir, I can't get the feeling out of my head that evil is coming our way."

He sat breakfast down with a worried look and turned to lock the door. Just then, the clerics arrived. He allowed them in, and then the sheriff squeezed in just before the owner shut and locked the door. As soon as I saw the clerics, I smiled, and then my smile turned to a frown. I grabbed my staff and quickly smacked the fake in the head several times. He collapsed instantly.

The sheriff drew his sword and pointed it at the downed cleric, saying, "You better have a good reason for this, boy. Knocking a cleric of Natura out will not only put you in my jail but will upset a very beloved goddess and all the people in this area. In these parts, she is highly loved."

I said with an anger bordering on hatred, "I know this man. He was on trial in StarHillm-Merge for pretending to be a cleric of Solbelli. He was overcharging the poor and skimming the church's cut. He does not love Natura, who happens to be my goddess. His god hates nature. They wanted to burn him at the stake, but the king, may he live forever, sentenced him to life in the dungeons. That he is out must mean something, but what I do not know. Still, I can detect evil instantly, a gift from the gods, and this one is evil to the core. Natura would never let him serve her."

The sheriff was shocked. "Evil! Can you prove that?"

The two clerics said, "We can." They both did spells, and both agreed that he was evil.

Out in the country, major crimes were not tolerated, and they had a different idea on how to handle them. The bleeding-heart liberals in the city would support a time in jail if one could prove without doubt his crimes. The bleeding-heart liberals in the city. Many in high positions were evil and wanted the laws changed to protect their own hides. The city was trying to push their justice off on the country, but the country had told them to run their own lives and leave them alone. Father agreed as long as taxes were paid and they didn't mess with the army too much. Actually, he had been known to mumble several times that the country had it right.

The sheriff said, "Known evil, wearing our beloved Natura's robes. Carry him outside, gentlemen. I don't want blood on the floor. The good woman of this inn would serve all my meals cold for a moon."

We carried him outside, and a crowd started to gather. The sheriff said, "Gather round, good citizens. I have here a man pretending to be a cleric of Natura while wearing the robes of our beloved goddess. I also have two known good clerics that swear he is evil, and a paladin trainee war wizard wannabe that says he is evil. Cleric of Solbelli, destroy this creature."

Father Bonetie said with anger toward the imposter and sadness that he could not help, "All my charges are for checking and preserving seed. I cannot."

I stepped forward. "I can. Natura is my goddess, and I will do this." I said "my goddess" with a lot of love. The crowd approved. I motioned for everyone to back up. Then I motioned for them to back up farther. They had a circle sixty feet across with the imposter in the center. I did the following in order: a silence spell on him so he could not be heard, a mass cure serious wounds on him so he was in good shape and would get up, and then fly on myself. I raised myself a foot off the ground while bending myself a little backward. I waited while he woke up and stood up. Then I stopped time for him and me. All others were still going at normal speed, so it looked like they weren't moving. I did a fireball, burning him badly, medium heal on him, fireball, medium heal, shaped lightning strike, medium heal, shaped ball of freeze, full healing, shaped fire barrier around him, and paused to let him burn while doing healing spells to keep him alive. I continued this for several hours. He screamed and screamed, but being silenced, he could not be heard. Then I annihilated him just as I changed the speed of time for the two of us to normal. What everyone saw was a flash of fire and then green dust. It looked like a quick and merciful killing. I dropped to my knees and then got up and ran to the side of the inn and threw up.

Everyone was shocked until Brother Longstep said, "Must be his first time taking a life. Did you see how he was bent back? Natura was in him and taking out her anger on the imposter. She how quick she was, how merciful. He went to one knee and started praying. Everyone else did the same, except the sheriff. He came over to me.

"First time, boy? I know. Not easy to kill someone. Having a god work through you has to be a draining experience too. You'll be all right, though you may have some nightmares."

"What did I do?"

"Pardon, boy?"

"What did I do? Is the imposter dead yet?"

Several others heard, and one said, "She blanked his memory. He does not know what she had him do. Praise Natura for her love. No one should have to remember doing that."

"Praise Natura" was said a thousand times before people stood up and started about their business again. I heard in my mind, "I'm not so sure I like fooling them. You know I did not do that. Though I do not fault you for doing so. He was a hateful man."

I thought back at her, "I'm sorry. I lost it just a little."

She answered back, "Be good now, Charles." I felt peace fall over me like a cloak.

The two clerics came over. Brother Longstep said, "Well, that was interesting."

I asked, "What?"

He frowned and shook his head. "You don't want to know. Let's just say the fool is dead and leave it at that."

Father Bonetie said, "I suppose the trip is off for the day? You used a lot of power back there."

I acted like I was checking something in my mind and said, "I didn't use anything important." I hadn't either. I could do little spells like that all day. I was getting better at not lying and yet never telling the truth.

Brother Longstep put an arm on my shoulder and said, "The gods do what they do for a reason. Let's get this trip on the road. I have already said traveling prayers for all of us."

We went back into the inn, and I spread the map. I said, "Everyone, hold on to me." The sheriff was watching as I pointed to number one and the three of us were at the farm and the map was rolled up and in my hand. I put it in my haversack and started walking to the house. We saw the farmer in one field. He waved, and we went over to where he was. His wheat fields looked pristine, no weeds, no unwanted bugs, no birds. Farmers in the Clear Water Valley hired clerics to protect their fields with spells, and I could see the spells with a quick and silent Find Magic.

I said, "Hello, sir, we came for the seed."

"Nice to see you again. It's this way." We headed toward the house.

As we passed the barn, I saw a lot of old barrels with iron fittings that were rusting. They were piled high and appeared heavy, so I thought they were full of seed. "Sir, is that my seed?"

"No, boy. I'd never keep my good seed in the barn. That is seed for city folk. Didn't your father teach you anything?"

We went to the side of his house, and he opened a door that was lying down on the ground. The opening revealed a stair heading into darkness. We descended, and all three of us did illumine spells, and we could see that there were hundreds of new wood barrels with brass fittings, and each barrel was full of seed. I had to smile. I knew this was the good seed, but I stopped and did a spell that checked the quality of every seed instantly. It was perfect. Not a single bug or bug egg, no weed seeds, only perfect, strong wheat seeds. I said, "Thank you, sir, but my spell tells me that there are six hundred twenty barrels."

"Twenty are for my replanting, so leave them here."

"Yes, sir." I turned to the clerics and said, "The protection spells are already in place. Your doing?"

Brother Longstep said, "I travel up and down Clear Water Valley making a living doing these protection spells. Yes, this is my doing. There are many you contracted with that did not require my services. Be careful."

I said, "Thank you. I will." I pulled out a bag of gold and a shining rod. I handed the gold to the farmer, and I took the rod to the center. Then I motioned for the two clerics to join me. I said goodbye to the farmer and teleported all of it, except twenty barrels, to my basement in Sordeath and quickly teleported just the three of us to Lindale in Ginham. I had set it up a few nights back that as soon as seed showed up in the basement, hundreds of creatures would be emptying it out so I could bring in more. The elves set up watches to wait for it. They almost started removing it before I could teleport us out.

Brother Longstep said, "Before we continue, I have two questions, Charles, or whoever you are."

"Go ahead."

"Was that an elf I saw back there in that room you took the seed to?"

"Yes. I have elves helping me. I have a lot of help from a lot of countries."

"Is this Lindale?"

"Yes. You've been here before?"

Brother Longstep said, "I am a priest of Commeatus the traveler." As if that said it all. "What are we doing here?"

Father Bonetie gave a little laugh and said, "That's three questions, Brother. However, I would like to know the answer also."

I said, "I didn't tell you? I need to pick up a book for the innkeeper. I promised."

Father Bonetie said, "Need to keep your promises, child. Any idea where this book is?"

I looked over at Longstep and asked, "Do you know where the Blue Ink Printing office is?"

He looked like he was thinking about it, but he had no clue. "Blue Ink Printing, Blue Ink Printing … no, I don't think I know that one. However, this is easy. We have but to ask." He started off like he was in charge, and I was glad for the help because Father Bonetie had more questions.

"What is that object you teleported all that grain with? Some sort of magic rod? Does it have limitations?"

I said in all honesty, "It has great limitations. First, it can only add to the weight a wizard can take with him. You cannot take other living creatures with you over what a normal teleporting spell allows. Seed and plants do not count as living even though they are technically living. I think the maker was thinking of limiting the user so that he could not teleport an army inside a castle gate." The Star Fire confirmed that I was correct and that the maker was Commeatus. "I can teleport the two of you and another, and if I am touching the rod, I can mentally picture what else I want, and it comes also. Great for building a stone wall. I can move big stones with this rod. It also comes in handy for moving topsoil to valleys."

Longstep said, "It's an artifact of Commeatus and can be used ten times a day. Commeatus will be interested to know you have it. Borrowed some toys to help with this project, did you?"

I thought, *How do I get around this one? I didn't borrow it, and I can't say it belongs to someone else.* To them, I said, "No, sir, this is mine." I said it with as much pride as I could.

Their backs were up again. "And how did you end up with an artifact of Commeatus's?"

"I took it from a shadow demon that attacked me. He lost, and I won. It was a big fight and very painful. I had no idea what the rod was at first. I found magic on the rod. Have you ever fainted from using find magic?"

They relaxed. Father Bonetie said, "Only once when I was younger. I prepare for it now."

I said, "So do I. It's not good to be unconscious when the enemy could be around."

Longstep added, "Not wise at all, boy. You need to be more careful." We came to a town crier yelling out the time. Longstep waited until the crier was finished with his yell and then said, "Good, sir, can you tell us where we can find the Blue Ink Printing office?"

"Sure as can be, Brother. Everyone knows Blue Ink Printing. Famous they is now that they make that book Prince Charles written up and all. Hard to get a copy as it's expensive and takes a long night duplicating each picture. Hired a hundred artists, I hear they did. Good to go check if you can get one. May have to wait and all. Popular book. Seen one, I did. Have a copy down at the Black Tail Pub. Proud of it they are. People like seeing how them rich folk live. Gives 'em something to dream about. You go up that street, go three crosses, and turn left. Up that road for twenty-two crosses, and it be on the left side."

Brother Longstep said, "Thank you. The book sounds interesting. Do your crosses include alleys or single streets that end on the one we are on?"

"Course they do. You have to cross; it's a crossing. I count with walking on the right side. You stay on right, and no go wrong."

"Thank you."

He went back to crying out the time.

Father Bonetie said, "The innkeeper didn't want this book Prince Charles wrote, did he?"

"Yes, sir."

"He may not get one then. Sounds like it's in demand. Price may have gone up too."

I said, "They better have five waiting for me. I saw a painting of the office on the back of a book once, so I teleported directly into their store last week and ordered and paid in advance. They didn't like me teleporting directly in, so I told them I would walk in next time. I forgot we'd have to find it first."

They both laughed. Longstep said, "You get into some problems using teleportation, boy. I'd stop using it so much and walk. You see and experience a lot more walking or riding. Can you ride?"

"Yes, sir."

"Good. After you get the seed home, and when you have the time, walk or ride your land. You don't know what you have until you walk across it."

"Yes, sir."

It was hard not to laugh. Brother Longstep was counting the crossings on his fingers. Father Bonetie noticed and gave me a look of reproach. So I sobered up my face and let the good brother lead us. It didn't take long before we were at the door of the Blue Ink Printing office and waiting in line while people were being turned away.

When we made it to the front, Longstep opened the door and motioned for me to enter. I walked up to the counter. The clerk recognized me and called in the back. "Hey, Clayfoot! You have those five copies for that wizard that likes to teleport into our offices?"

I heard in the back, "He didn't do it again, did he? I'll tan that boy's hide."

"No, no. He walked in this time with two holy men. I hope you did those five copies correctly."

A big man with a voice like thunder came out and said, "Every book that leaves this place is perfect. I'll have it no other way. That's why Prince Charles contracted with us. He doesn't care about the money, just the truth. I put out trash, and he's likely to find out and box my ears." He had a package that looked small in his arm, but it was big and heavy in mine as he placed them into my care. "You're lucky, farmer boy. Since you left, the price has gone up tenfold. We get a hundred gold a copy for these books."

I looked concerned but I felt upset. "Won't that upset Prince Charles? I thought you told me he wanted the middle class and the poor to be able to enjoy them by going to the pubs and such."

"He did, but where is he? Have you seen him to tell him?"

"I don't need to tell him, sir. He will find out. He is everywhere, and he will find out." I took out the books from the wrapping and started to examine each one.

"What you doing, boy? I have other customers. I have no time for you to read them here."

"Not reading as much as checking to ensure I have five good copies. If you are willing to die by cheating Prince Charles, then I am sure you don't mind cheating me."

"Die! Who said anything about dying, boy?"

"The way I hear it, Prince Charles, gods bless him, gets very angry when he finds someone has gone back on a deal. Very angry. They all look correct." I turned to the priests and asked, "Ready to leave?"

Father Bonetie said solemnly, "Let's leave before Charles shows up. I don't want to see what happens."

As we walked out, the look of worry in their faces was classic. People might find the cost dropping quickly. It turns out that the price did not go down. It actually doubled when rumor went around that the office might be shut down if Charles found out, and then the book would be worth much more. Figures!

We went outside and teleported to number two on the map. The farmer was not home, but the son was, and we collected the seed and transferred it to my castle, and then we teleported back to the town. The next day, we did the same five times. I continued to buy and transport seed for an entire moon. Finally, I had enough seed to plant my lands twice. That was my first part of the volunteering.

CHAPTER 9

STARTING RUMORS

Once the seed was planted, we had a lot of changing to do. Irrigation was too much in some areas and not enough in others. The rains came, and two more dams were needed. Before using the staff, I had to remove all creatures that I let in, and some did not want to leave. The gods did help by sending the need to all, and using the Staff of Nature, I made all things grow to firmly established sizes. My forests looked like they had been around for twenty years, while my wheat fields looked new and ready to harvest.

All my orchards were in blossom and set to fruit soon, and I had some of the tastiest carrots ever planted. Shortly after I completed the change, I allowed the helpers back in, and they established themselves properly and as we agreed.

Many were becoming farmers themselves. Fairies loved mushrooms and didn't mind planting enough to trade. Giants were going to help build. Elves were going to build a forest city nearly in the center and had planted grapes for wine and eating, with enough for trade. Even pixies were figuring out what they could trade. I pointed out that a pixie could get nuts and fruit off the top of trees without a ladder. I granted them some of the orchards. But, being small, they asked to work with trusted humans to cart the fruit to market. Shortly after everyone moved in and settled comfortably, I started having a problem with animals.

Now that the planting was completed, and I increased the growth to twenty years, the last item could be added. All the helpers made up so few that you could walk for days and not see anyone or any living thing. I dropped the spells that kept out animals, and we seeded my land with supposedly harmless creatures. In the beginning of the second year, I brought in cattle, sheep, deer, rabbits, chickens, and all kinds of creatures that humans and others considered edible breading animals. They multiplied and multiplied, and only two years into growth, I had far too many. The overabundance of edible farm animals on my land caused others to enter. Where they came from, I was not sure, but I now had predators. I took a tour of my lands to assess the overabundance problem and noticed bears, wolves, foxes, eagles, mountain lions, one dealor, some griffons, several hippogriffs, and numerous other creatures. One creature of note was a small bunch of miniature dragons, about eight in all. I stopped and petted them and gave each a shiny new silver piece. At least the predators were helping cut down the rabbit and chicken problem, but not enough.

Another issue came up. For the last two years, I had paid little attention to the rest of the world, as I was very busy with the plan. Two weeks before, I sent a dream to Annabel about Shadow Mountain and then I took the time to check and see how things were elsewhere. It seemed that there had been a drought for two years and then torrential rains. We did not notice it, as our lakes and dams took care of the water, and we saw nothing unless the lakes in the mountains ran dry or overflowed. I did notice an excess of rain and decided to check out the lakes. They were not full, so I asked the giants why.

"King Charles, you not notice we have very little rain two years. It just catch 'n' up."

"No. I did not notice, my friend. I wonder how others are faring."

I went home to the Dead Lands and checked using the Staff of Maps. I checked Dailith to my west. As I looked in on the queen, she was in a meeting with her barons.

One baron was talking. "We have tried to purchase more food from Kayland, but the weather has limited their output severely. They have given us exactly what we received last year but can give no more. We should be very happy that we received that much with the threat of Shadow Mountain. It is smoking again, and they are worried this time. It seems the gods are not talking, my queen."

Another baron said, "We are running out of food reserves, Majesty. If we don't find food soon, people will die."

Queen Alluvia asked, "Have we looked every place?"

Her duke said, "Every place is having the same problems. We do have rumors about food in the Sordeath. I do not know the truth of such rumors, but we could check. It's that or foraging in the demon realms."

Queen Alluvia looked up with revulsion. "How many would die? The demon realms would love for us to cross the mountains and become snacks for their children. No, I will not send my people against the demons. I have heard many rumors about Sordeath. I am told that there is a new and benevolent king and that the undead are gone. I wish so much to believe; however, I cannot. The letch king has an army undefeated and becoming bigger. I do not want to cross over into his lands and draw his attention. I will go to the king of Kayland and beg if I must."

I cut it off at that point. It was time to finish this, but to do so, I needed to get others on my side. I had the king of the elves and many of nature's kings and queens. Now it was time to gather humans together. Soon Shadow Mountain would put an end to the Clear Water Valley. It had to happen. If I stopped the mountain, the pressure would explode in several smaller places and then across the entire volcano range. That would do far more damage than just Clear Water Valley. This had been my hidden goal. Create another Clear Water Valley, only bigger and more capable. I had done so, and when Clear Water Valley was on fire, I would have a place for the duke to take over. The problem was Kayland could not have anything to do with me until I could get my father to invite me to his castle so that I could talk to him. That was not due to happen for four months.

I checked the other lands, and they were doing much better than my neighbor. You would think I could just teleport into Queen Alluvia's court and let them know I could help them. No way! She would instantly know I was spying on her, and she would be extremely mad and set up protections. However, there was a border town to support the small army the queen had stationed at the pass. I was hungry for a home-cooked meal, and they had a good inn. I teleported to my wall and opened the doors. Then I walked the two leagues into Dailith and their wooden wall and gate.

As I walked up, things started in motion. Nothing comes out of the Undead Lands except undead. For someone from the Sordeath to walk up to the gate meant one of three things: there was an army about to attack, and this was a fear tactic to get the war started; the undead walking up was extremely powerful and couldn't care less about the gate or the army; or it was trying to get through in disguise. Either meant problems for the day captain of the gate. I suppose it didn't help that, since it was raining, I was completely covered, including a hood.

As I walked up to about a hundred feet from the closed gate, I heard a voice. "You, approaching the gate into Dailith, halt and declare yourself and your purpose."

I looked up at the top of the gate, and a hundred archers were just running across. They came to a halt in two nice rows and, standing there, turned as one with bows pulled back to the max. Some were shaky. I put out a hand, and my Staff of Protection was in it instantly. I didn't need a foolish and frightened guard to shoot and everyone else to fire by mistake. That would be painful. With the Staff of Protection in hand, no arrow would touch me.

"You, at the top of the gate. I am the sorcerer Charles, king of the Sordeath and destroyer of undead. I came to have dinner at your inn. I hear the cook is quite good, and I am tired of magical food."

That started a discussion, and finally someone said, "Can you prove your statement?"

I teleported to the top of the gate and said to the man who had asked, "What part do you want me to prove?"

I was dressed in finery fit for a king traveling, and my teleporting to a position that was protected from dimensional travel showed that I was a powerful sorcerer. Bows were dropped, and swords pulled. I looked around and said, "Nice reception. For me? I'm flattered."

I think it was my smile that did it. The captain gave a hand signal to put away swords, but soldiers were still nervous. "Hello, Captain. I know you have made forays to my gate and you've read my laws. You will now find my land open for travel. The eastern side is still closed, as I have a difficult time trusting King Tyler. However, you have a good queen, and I have no problem trusting her. Please abide by all the rules and laws. I do not have jails or dungeons, so punishment is final and fatal. Please. I want to keep good relationships with your queen, so don't allow evil to enter my lands, as they will be destroyed. Other than that, have fun. I assure you this army is no longer necessary." I then teleported to the ground on my side and waited.

The doors opened, and I was let in. A general was waiting. "Hello, Prince Charles."

I knew this general from his visits to my father's castle on behalf of his queen. "Hello, General Armond. How are things on this side of the wall? Oh, I need to point out something before we go any further." I looked directly at him and touched my forehead. The Star Fire flared, and so did his eyes. "What I said was true, as you can see. And I am a king now, however reluctantly."

"Well, well. I see things have changed with you since we last saw each other. You seem to be doing exceptionally well. Things are not so good here. Not good at all, King Charles." There was amusement in his voice. "I thought you said, to nearly everyone, that you did not want power? And here you are, a grand sorcerer and a king."

"Word gets around about a prince who does not want power, doesn't it? Well, General, I do not want power, and I am not particularly trying to hold onto it. I am a sorcerer by no real fault of my own, and a king from necessity. I am sad that your lands are not doing well. What's the issue?"

"We've had drought and them horrible rains. Too many people must have prayed for rains; well, the gods came through. We've been hit by storm upon storm. Two years of drought dried out the land and killed off much of the grass and bushes. Hard rain turned the soil, what little we have in these mountains, into mud. Now the clerics tell us to prepare for several more years of drought."

"Um, General. Tell me, how is this affecting Kayland?"

He could hear the longing in my voice. "They will do fair, not well, but fair if Shadow Mountain doesn't blow. They have reserves of food. They prepared better than we did. They sold us our normal allotted amount but no more. Many will starve without the food we normally produce for ourselves. The queen has left for Kayland to plead with your father. I have been sent here due to the lack of activity coming from the Undead Lands. That normally means a buildup and preparation for attack. You say there is no longer any threat?"

I smiled under my cloak hood. "I and mine will not attack you and yours unless you do something to force us to. I don't see that happening. Your queen and I have always gotten along. We have planted the entire country with forest and seeded fields with grain, and we have orchards and every type of food possible. I have enough food for all of us. So don't worry. Send some people you can trust into my lands, and they can have what they pick. Keep in mind, they need to replant if they take something that requires replanting."

"How is it that your land is not flooded?"

We went into his tent and talked for hours. When I left, it was with full belly from his personal cook and a promise that I could have all I could eat anytime I wanted. He immediately took every wagon and person and part of his army and prepared to enter my lands. It took a while to organize, and he mobilized the town as well. I went with him, he on his big stallion and me on a fire steed I conjured.

"General. You need to ensure the safety of your people. You may want to either cut down on the number of gatherers you are bringing or increase their protection. We have great amounts of food, which caused lots of animals, which causes a lot of predators. I am not taking responsibility for anyone. You have that. I will hold you responsible for your people and their safety."

"Done." He motioned to a sergeant to make it happen.

"In addition, please station a known good paladin at the wall to check for evil on others before they pass into my lands. If my alarms go off, someone dies. You don't want that, and neither do I."

"I understand, and it will happen." Another sergeant left to talk to someone. "I must say, I am surprised that you would allow a foreign army of any size to enter your lands."

I looked thoughtful. "General, I have no problem with your queen, and she has none with me that I know of. I doubt you would start an incident on purpose. Besides, I can easily destroy your entire army if needed."

We rode for a while before he asked, "How did you become so powerful to warrant a curse from the gods like that?" He pointed to my forehead.

I told him about the druid trap and the gods and what I was doing. Why not? I wasn't trying to hide anything except what I was going to do to Duke Edward and the fact that Shadow Mountain was going to blow soon. "And that's it in a nutshell, General. We need the trees and vegetation to help breathe. This is my answer to the childbirth issue, and if it means that you happen to have another food source, then that's all the better."

The general said, "The gods probably knew our plight and set this all up for you to have the power to complete this task."

"My gods, Silvestris and Natura, knew. They wanted to do something, but they are not allowed to directly interfere. No god is." We were riding through my gate, and I pointed to my side of the wall. "You will note the statues to my gods and Potentis on almost every structure. The giants helped with everything. Without them, I would still be building for another ten or so years. As it is, this all took only five years. I am a little late. I told the gods four years to get to this point and five years to finish."

The general said, "I doubt the gods are disappointed, considering how many people will see their statues forever."

"Ah, that would be true, I hope. However, there are many gods interested in this work. Though, I think the part they want completed is in place on time. Now I need to work on the part I need completed. And no, that is not up for discussion. I will say only this much. You will be pleasingly surprised."

We had just reached the top of the last mountain before entering the valleys, and the general was thinking, *This is it. Here is where we see if he has done all he said.*

As we crested the top, the green lush valley spread out before us. He looked long and hard and then turned to his wizard. "Send message to the queen, 'Return to the eastern gate immediately. We have an answer to the food problem. Tell no one.' Then go to our gate and bring her here. We will wait, but the army will continue."

The message was sent and answered, "Thank the gods. Everyone wants to see the king of Kayland. We have a two-day wait. We are on our way."

I looked at the general. "A two-day wait! For Father not to see Queen Alluvia immediately means he is out of the country, sick, or there is a bigger problem than we know. I will be right back." I teleported to my tower in the Dead Lands and used the Staff of Maps. Father was on his throne, so he was not sick or out of the country, but there was a long line of people wanting to see him. There were kings and queens from almost every land and half the barons and dukes of Kayland. I saw my father's posture. He was both upset that he could not help and upset that these people had not prepared for eventualities like this strange weather. If I were there, I could have told him the weather was due to Shadow

Mountain, but I was not there. I dared not touch any minds in my father's own castle. If caught, it would ruin my plans. I teleported back and conjured a new horse. This one was a Caelums steed, and she was beautiful.

The general looked impressed. "What did you find out?"

"There is a long line of royalty trying to see Father, plus most of his own barons and dukes. I think the problem is worse than first thought."

"So, you can spy on your father that easily?"

"Only way I have to see home."

He placed a gauntleted hand on my shoulder but knew better than to say anything. We waited on the mountain top for only minutes before the queen showed up. The general dismounted, and so did I. The general went to one knee.

"Arise, General. Hello, King Charles." It was nearly a laugh.

"Hello, Queen Alluvia. I hope my land can help with the current crises." I motioned with my right arm for her to take a look and stepped out of her way. The seed was now planted, and rumors of food in the Sordeath would spread like wildfire.

There were tears in her eyes as she looked out at the lush garden paradise and saw her army with every wagon the general could confiscate from the town and surrounding areas heading into my apple orchards below. Thought I doubt she could tell what the trees were from there. She turned to me and hugged me long and hard. When she had calmed down, she let go. "How?"

I said, "Some night, around dinner, I will tell the tale properly. For now, just know it is there, and I am allowing you to use it as long as you follow my laws."

She turned to the general. "Laws?"

The general answered, "Kayland's laws except for some very good amendments. All the people that entered read, or were read, the laws and informed that breaking one carries the penalty of death. They will follow these laws, and I will teach any others that you send. We need everyone to start—"

My alarms went off. Evil was entering my lands at the southeastern seaport. Both wizards heard it and asked, "What is that?"

I looked at the general and the queen. "I am sorry. An evil just entered my land from the southeastern seaport. I must go." I touched my horse, and she disappeared. I raised my hand, and my Staff of Extraordinary Power was instantly in it. I twirled it to find the balance and then teleported.

CHAPTER 10

EVIL AND FATHER
ALL IN ONE DAY

I landed on top of the hill overlooking my southeastern seaport.
I had gone to a lot of effort cutting out stone from this section to
build a deep water port for a good city, and just coming into view
was a Kayland warship, the biggest I had ever seen. It looked new,
was easily five hundred feet long and eighty feet wide, and had
four tall masts. There were several lines for rowing on each side,
and they were rowing now. I said to myself, "Nice ship, Father,
but why the pirate flag?" Just then, another ship came into view.
It was an exact copy of the first. I flew up to see better, and there
were five of these ships all flying different types of pirate flags.

I sent an illusion to the lead ship. It looked like I was standing
on the forecastle of the first ship, but I knew I was still flying
above my land. Shouts went up, and people tried to kill my
illusion. The captain came up. "Get off my ship, wizard!"

In an easy, calm voice, I said, "You are entering my land. I
would like to know what you are doing and why."

"That's easy, scum. We are here to take everything we
can, mostly food, but if we find your castle, then we take your

treasure. We know you are by yourself and easy prey. Prepare to be boarded, Prince Charles."

Now how did he find out that? Oh well. "Captain, I appreciate your candor, but I will have to fight. I am very powerful. Do you really want to do this?"

He turned to his men. "What do ya think, ya scurvy rats? Will his father pay more to save him or have us kill him?"

Laughter flooded the ship. That was a mistake, and I was now upset. Something in my mind snapped, and I smiled. "Come to me, fool. Come to me. I could use five nice ships."

They came and docked at the areas I left for building piers. I thought it would be rough tying up without something to cushion from the stone, but they had brought their own cloth-wrapped logs to protect the sides. I stood at the top of the hill overlooking the piers while waiting. I had already completed as many spells as possible to power up and prepare for war. There were at least three hundred men on each ship, and they all piled off.

Most were for gathering food, but several came in my direction. About ten bowmen moved in different directions, spreading out and trying to surround me. Around twenty fighters started to do the same, and several wizards and clerics started in my direction. The captains stood on the bowsprits of their ships and watched with smiles.

I took out the magic users with a few well-placed maximized and shaped acid balls. They were expecting fireballs or lightning. Surprise! The captains were not laughing now. The bowmen and fighters took longer. I took out my bow, an artifact called the Great Bow of Seeking, and fired. I took them out very quickly. Arrows came my direction but stopped and turned back on the ones that fired them. They died from their own arrows.

Now I turned to the ones trying to enter my land without permission and sent fireball after fireball. Hundreds died before the captains called them back. Now the captains were becoming serious. They started organizing their people for a full rush. Typical pirate style. Overwhelm the enemy. Bad tactic to use against a single wizard on open ground. I sent acid fogs out to meet them. Most died in the fog. The ones that made it through died shortly after from wounds, or mercy killings by me. The fog dissipated, and the captains were now organizing another large group and giving new orders.

Someone tried to contact me. I opened the mental channel with a full view portal so I could see them and they me. I thought it was the captains trying to negotiate. I was wrong. It was Father. Dedrick was trying to contact me.

"Hello, Dedrick. HI, Father. I am a little busy right now." I was sending fireballs and lightning strikes one after the other to break the charge up my hill.

Father asked with concern in his voice, "Need help, son?"

I nearly faltered. It had been a long time since Father called me son. "I sent a few more fireballs and some many fingered lightning spells and said, "No thanks, Father. I think I can handle this. It's only fifteen hundred pirates." I moved my body so that the portal would be placed to see the port and the five ships while I sent a ball of freeze toward a group coming up from the back. "Father, did you lose some ships?" A fireball went off directly around me.

"Yes, I did, son. Concentrate on what you're doing and stop talking to me."

"Yes, sir." I flew up and shot several arrows at a wizard that was off to the side. He hit me with lightning and fire that had no effect. He was well protected, so I used the Staff of Extraordinary Power to destroy him. I took him out and two hundred cubic feet of land with him. That's why I didn't use the staff very much. An arrow hit my leg and penetrated to the bone, and another hit my left arm. *Darn that hurts.* I yanked then both out and did a Major Heal spell on myself.

I heard my sister Jennifer gasp; she must have been in the throne room watching also. I turned and ducked as a sword blade whizzed by exactly where my neck had been. I touched the fighter with a Remove Bone spell, and he collapsed and slowly fell to the ground.

"Thanks, Jennifer." I continued to send fireballs and lightning bolts, and then I pretended that my spells were running out. I dropped to lower spells and finally to just my bow. Then I pretended that I ran out of arrows and that I was looking tired. I drew my swords. I took out several more pirates, and then the captains came.

I looked at them while acting out of breath and about dead on my feet. "Out of men to throw at me, Captains? How are you going to sail your ships?"

"Not your worry. Out of spells and arrows? Time to die, boy."

One smiled and said to the portal, "Hello, King Truss. Nice day to watch your son die." The five captains were surrounding me and moving slowly in. "We were going to ransom him. We figure you'll pay nicely to have us kill him. Now it's for free."

Father said, "He dies, and it's war." Again I was shocked. It was the first time Father ever stood up for me.

"He just killed fifteen hundred good men. War or not, he dies."

My brother Richard said, "Don't worry, Father. They're dead. They just don't know it. Charles is the best swordsman in all of Kayland, and I have seen him fake like that before. They have no chance."

The captains heard that and changed their tactics just a little. Things became much more dangerous. I thought to myself, *Thanks a lot, brother. You always give away when I am faking it. Nearly broke my leg once because you said to the cleric, "Watch this. He's faking it and will feint left and strike center."* I dismissed the portal. No need to have my brother giving away everything.

★★★

Father looked at the place where the portal was and said to Dedrick, "Bring that back this instant."

Dedrick blushed. "I cannot. It was his. I cannot do that spell. It is beyond my abilities."

Father looked surprised. "Then do something. I want to know what happened. Where was he? We could send help."

"I am working on it, my king. It will take ten minutes."

Jennifer said, "We would still have contact if brother here would keep his mouth shut. Telling the pirates what was about to happen was not a wise move. Charles had to remove the contact."

Richard looked shocked. "I did not mean to—"

Father cut him off. "You said Charles is better than you. Why? I have seen you defeat him in every battle."

Richard blushed. "Father, I told you before. Charles only lets me defeat him when we are in public. In private, he easily takes me. I have never won when no one is around to see."

Father said, "I hope you're correct. And your sister is correct. You do need to learn to keep your mouth shut. You have so much to learn. You'll get there. Takes time, but you'll get there." Father turned to Eric. "Charles was doing a lot of spells and some I did not recognize. How is this possible in so short a time? Was that really Charles?"

Eric thought for a moment. "That was Charles, sire. The look on his face when Richard gave away what he was doing and his skills were all Charles. Something has happened. Something drastic, and it has made him strong and powerful. More powerful than any wizard I have ever seen. Those spells that you did not recognize were not wizard spells; they were druid. Did you see the plants reach out and tear several pirates apart? Druid spells and very powerful. In addition, he used clerical healing spells on himself and one bard song called Confuse."

Father said, "Then he has learned a little of everything. Probably because we sent him away. Took schooling wherever he could get it. A little here, a little there. No chance to concentrate on any one subject. Not that he would. Always studying that one. Where is that contact!"

★★★

Back on the field, the captains attacked, and two died before they knew what happened. Two others were dead in only seconds. That left me facing only one, and he was good—very good. So I flew up and fire-balled him. Several times actually. I drifted back to the ground and started looting the bodies. I felt Dedrick trying to contact me, so I let the portal open. "Hello, Dedrick. Are you sure you're allowed to contact me? I am still in exile."

He smiled and said, "Glad you're still alive. Your father has something to say."

I looked past Dedrick and said, "Hello, King Truss. To what do I owe this honor?"

"Your mother has asked me to invite you to our thirtieth wedding anniversary. We are having a gala event at the castle. You do still remember our wedding date?"

I looked long and hard at him. "By law, you cannot, even as the king, allow an exile to enter your land for any reason except treaty negotiations. You know this. Are you trying to lure me to my death? You don't look happy about something."

Jennifer started to say something, but Father and I both motioned for her to stay out of it.

"Prince Charles, son, I am not trying to get you killed. The entire kingdom wants you back. We have new evidence, irrefutable evidence that changes a lot of things."

"What evidence?"

"Droland left journals. They were hidden in his room. I have only recently allowed his room to be cleaned out. His journals were found and authenticated. In his own handwriting, he tells how he was planning to destroy us all for some trinket called The Headband of Knowledge."

I shook my head. "The Headband of Knowledge is a minor artifact that is cursed. It seldom gives the truth. Humans have been trying to tame it for hundreds of years, and no one has ever succeeded." It was one of the artifacts I traded to the letches. I tapped my forehead out of thought and heard the intakes of breath as the Fire Star flared.

Father said, "Much has happened to you since I sent you away. I am sorry. Have you been contacting the duke's daughter?"

"I am sorry also, Father." I paid no attention to his question. They had no proof it was me. I thought for a second. I had been waiting for the anniversary invitation that went out to all kings. Father always invited the letch king just for the fun of it. That was going to be my way into Kayland to talk with the king. Now he would be sending it out to me directly. "Father, you cannot invite me to Kayland, as Prince Charles is in exile. It is against the law. However, you can invite the king of the Sordeath and the Dragonback Mountains as long as we talk about a treaty.

Send your invitation to King Charles of the Sordeath, and I will attend your anniversary. Do us both a favor and tell everyone I am coming and that I have permission so they don't try to arrest me. We don't want an incident."

One of Father's eyebrows went up, and the other went down, and that was always bad. "King Charles!"

I closed the portal before he could spin up and chew me out. I thought, *Give him time to get used to the idea and to do some investigation. He'll calm down.*

I had a lot of cleanup to do. I couldn't just leave fifteen hundred bodies lying around, and I needed to finish off the wounded. Like I said, no jails, and punishment was final. Sorry to all the gods, but I was not going to give them a ship to attack someone else.

I reached out with my mind and found who I was looking for. "Orogndormertsus, hear me." I felt the giant kraken stir. "Orogndormertsus, hear me."

"Who calls out to Orogndormertsus?"

"It is I, King Charles of the Undead Lands."

"Why do you call me, tiny king of land? I do not obey humans or any other."

"Great demigod Orogndormertsus, I have a problem I think you will like and may want to be part of."

"Continue, little king."

"I just had a battle with pirates. I have fifteen hundred pirate bodies I need to get rid of. I could stack them in piles and burn them, but I thought you may like a small snack."

"I hear where you are. I am coming."

"Thank you."

Great, now all I had to do was put all the bodies in reach of Orogndormertsus. Not hard to do as he has a very, very long reach. Using transfer portals and Floating Force Wagons,

I transferred the bodies to an area away from my new ships. Orogndormertsus was big, and if a ship was in his way, he would simply crush it and toss it out of his way. It wasn't long before I saw a head and eye emerge from my bay. Not hard to see when the head was bigger than all five ships put together and, when leaving the water, caused a roaring waterfall effect.

"Are these mine?"

"Yes, Great Orogndormertsus. Take all you want."

"Oh nice, some are still squirming."

Tentacles reached out and grabbed bodies, armor, shields, weapons, and all. He murmured when he hit some adamantine armor. "Crunchy, very good."

All fifteen hundred were cleaned out in a matter of an hour. He took his time and played with some of his food. I chased two pirates off one ship that tried to hide and attack me from behind. He grabbed them up quickly. When he was done, I said, "Thank you again, Great Orogndormertsus."

"If you have this problem again, call me. It was a good banquet." Then he disappeared back into the sea.

I teleported back to my tower in the Dead Lands and cleaned up. Then I teleported back to the Sordeath and looked for the queen and general. I found the general down with his men. It was coming on nightfall, and camp was set. Some wagons were heading back into Dailith. The general saw me and asked, "What happened?"

"Pirates." I sat down and told him the entire story, including my father's communication. "Interesting. Seems like my father wants me back."

"Little late for that, *King* Charles."

"Yes. I have plans for that. Now, what's for dinner?"

We talked long and hard that night. I told him that it would be good if my father knew about what was going on over here without it coming from me. He said that he would leak it out and ensure that King Truss knew all the hard work I'd achieved. I thanked him and eventually left to complete some other preparations.

That night, I woke Annabel in her dreams and told her, "Wake everyone and leave. The mountain will erupt in three days. Go! Make them understand."

CHAPTER 11

SHADOW MOUNTAIN

I watched through my map in the tower in the Death Lands as little Annabel awoke screaming. Servants were there in seconds. "The mountain! The mountain! Run. Go get Father. Go!"

I changed over to view Duke Edward. He could not sleep. He stood looking out the shutters toward Shadow Mountain. The rains normally calmed the mountain. This time they seemed to be irritating it. It smoked and sputtered constantly. I could see he had a bad feeling about it, a very bad feeling. A servant ran into the bed chambers, waking the duchess with her noise.

"My duke, Annabel awoke screaming about the mountain. She sends for you."

The duke had been waiting for this. All her life, I had sent Annabel warnings, dreams, informing her when danger was present or coming. She could predict from her dreams, to the second, when someone bad was coming. No one knew how, she just could. The duke had been prepared for the time that Annabel would awake because of the mountain. "Wake everyone. Send messages to all the barons and evacuate the valley!"

The duchess moved quickly. She started organizing everything and getting people moving. The duke ran to his youngest daughter and held her closely. "How long do we have, my child?"

"It was him again, Father. He warned me again. The one at my birth. My protector. He told me to wake everyone and leave. He said the mountain will erupt in three days."

"Then we had better pack. Get dressed and start collecting what you will need. We are leaving this valley."

She let him go and started collecting herself. Two of her older sisters came running in. "What's going on? The servants are insisting we get up and pack. Something about the mountain. Is it that time?"

Their father paused long enough to hug them and say, "Charles contacted Annabel. The mountain blows in three days. I want you out of here tonight, so go pack. Move it." He pushed them away and headed off to the main room, knowing that they were doing as told.

Their mother was already dressed for leaving, and she had several other women in tow. They were organizing the servants. Luckily, there were no visitors at this time. All barons were at home waiting for word to leave. All crops had been harvested as early as possible and stored outside of the danger zone. The cities were on alert, and the army was waiting to help. Sadly, the danger zone included the entire valley. Thank the gods that Duke Edward believed in his daughter. I spent many nights watching and waiting and sending her warnings so that they would learn to believe when this time came.

Nearly half the people had already moved out of the valley, and they set up camps for the rest. The army had spent the last two weeks securing areas for refugees, and they checked out the Sinaguard. For some reason, people thought someone had planted up there. It was empty except two valleys that were covered in wheat and apples. Two weeks before, I had paid a visit to the town and told them the Sinaguard was not fully planted and that the king (me) decided to abandon the project.

The duke continued down into his castle to the wizard section. The wizards were busy sending out messages. Used scrolls of Notify littered the floor, and more were being used each second. The message was simple, "The worst in three days."

Barons and key people all over the valley were receiving the message. People would be mobilizing immediately all the way to the sea. Even the port had to be evacuated. Everything, everything lost except the people and what they could carry or already sent out. Many of the barons had already moved their entire estates. One city—my favorite, Diaden—had already been moved, buildings and all. They tore down the entire city, packed it up, and moved out, heading to Sordeath of all places. They swore to the duke that a wizard had come by a few years back and bought seed to plant the Sinaguard on the king's orders, and then he came by two weeks ago and told them that the king had canceled the order, so the wizard sold the seed to Prince Charles, now King Charles of the Sordeath. So, they figured the king needed some help. He had to order them not to go into the Sordeath until the king could check things out. "And stay away from King Tyler and do not to cross his land."

I watched the duke for several hours as his people moved out. Things were moving fast in the Clear Water Valley. I had to move fast also. My alarms went off. Someone was attacking my eastern border. What was the world coming to?

CHAPTER 12

KING TYLER

I grabbed my battle gear and some rods and wands and teleported to my wall. Sure enough, King Tyler sat on his horse, giving orders to breach the wall. Wizards using Shift magically moved to my side of the wall and were trying to open the gate. Luckily, I had protected against such an easy way in. I drifted down and said, "Leave my land. I will have a talk with your king about this." They attacked. Whatever happened to parley, peace talks, or just asking? I destroyed them all and then sent an illusion to the king. His horse startled and threw him off before bolting.

After getting up, he said, "Prince Charles, King Truss's little brat. So, the rumor is true. You are the idiot that changed the Sordeath into a paradise and then left it unguarded. It will be mine and my sons' by the end of the week. Come to me, and I will end your exile—permanently!"

I teleported to his end of the pass, placed a barrier of stone across the very thin opening, and then flew back to my aqueduct. I used a force barrier to divert the water to fall into the pass, creating a lake where he, his six sons, and his army were camped and waiting to attack. His wizards were dead, so they had no way to magically escape. It took about three hours before they all drowned. I had to constantly dispel or destroy anything that allowed floating or flying. I do not believe any escaped. I then went to their capital city and entered the castle. I reached the queen with very little killing of guards. Most seemed to be out attacking the Sordeath. I found the queen and her daughters and destroyed the evil witch and her brats. Then I did a spell that led me to all that had any claim to the kingship of Ringal through the Tyler family and killed them also. I started on the two cities, the capital and the port. Their walls were quickly down and the cities in ruin. I tried not to harm the citizens. I attacked only the buildings of the government. They were quickly abandoned.

"Charles! That will be enough! Stop this instant!"

I looked up into the heavens and said, "As you wish, my goddess."

I sent a message to Dedrick. "Dedrick, tell Father that King Tyler attacked me. I had to remove his army and his kin. Their border is wide open, and there is no one to guard. His war wizards and clerics are dead. His city walls are down. Now is the time to increase your lands. It is up for grabs, and you need to have this land. It is important to you. Very important."

I then went back to my tower in the Dead Lands and walked into the druid trap. I needed to calm down, and it was going to take a while.

I departed the druid trap shortly after I entered, about a year or so inside. I wasn't keeping track. Outside, only three minutes had passed. As soon as I left, I received two Caelums, and they did not knock.

One announced, "Silvestris and Natura would like to have a word with you, right now!" They took my arm, and I was walking into Natura's temple.

Natura was sitting on her throne and did not look pleased. I went to my knees and then to the floor, prostrating myself. She and Silvestris talked about me without giving me permission to rise, and I was not about to ask. I knew I did wrong; though, if I had not made it into the druid trap and taken the time to calm down, I may have been a little bit obstinate. As it was, I expected to be punished in some way and was prepared to take my medicine.

Silvestris said to Natura, "I know you do not like the manner in which our servant acted, but that fool of a king deserved what he got. Charles did not start this war. With humans, to take over a land, you need to remove people that can rally resistance. After defeating the army, Charles did that by removing the royalty and a few leaders and nothing more."

Natura spoke angrily. "It is not what he did that upsets me. It is what was in his heart. It was cold, evil, and ready to remove the entire land and all its residences. I have worshipers down there. Hidden yes, but they are there."

"He never once thought of touching the Staff of Nature to do what you claim. His heart was cold, true. You know how he is when attacked. Still, his mind kept any thoughts of using that level of power out of the equation. Notice he attacked only governmental buildings. He did not attack the innocent."

"True. There is that, Silvestris. However, he is hard to control."

"I would say impossible, Natura. Yet when he heard your voice, he stopped and left to calm down. He took himself completely out of the picture and took the time to calm himself. Did he fight coming here to see us? He could have, and you know it."

Natura sat in thought about that. "He did stop when I told him to stop. Charles!"

Hard to jump from being startled when lying prone, but I did. In the humblest voice I could manage, I said, "Yes, my goddess."

"Would you have stopped sooner if I told you to?"

"Of course, my goddess."

Eighteen other gods appeared. They had been there all along, but I had no idea. They didn't normally like to get together. One asked Natura in a tone of accusation, "You could have stopped this before he destroyed the country and my followers?"

She looked down at me and asked, "Could I have stopped you, Charles?"

"My goddess, if you told me to allow King Tyler in and to give him the land and kill myself, I would argue the issue, but I would do as told."

Anger erupted in the temple, and I stood up, and power was in my hand. Instantly I stood in front of Natura and Silvestris. "If you want to punish, then punish me, but do not threaten my gods."

Anger was entering into me again until Natura touched me and said, "Calm, Charles." Everyone could easily see the change. I calmed and stood there holding my power in a protective way. Natura said nothing, and neither did Silvestris, but they did not ask me to stand down either.

Gods were backing down and stepping back. A god in the back said, "This is my fault." Nearly every god turned to him. "I saw this coming and did nothing. I knew King Tyler was gathering his forces to attack the Sordeath, and I did not care. I could have warned Natura or Silvestris."

Solbelli walked forward and waved a hand. I was instantly powered down. He said, "From now on, if anyone knows of anything that may attack Charles, please point it out. The pirates would still be alive, though that is no loss, the king and his army would still be alive, and we would not have to change our plans every few of their days."

Natura said sadly, "I will watch closer. I know he has a temper, and I should watch for issues. He does not think of me when he is angry, so I do not know."

Silvestris said, "I will watch closer also. But we need all of you to warn us so we can head this kind of thing off. I thought you talked to your people and told them, 'Hands off.'"

Several said, "They don't listen."

One said, "I told mine about the food so they would know the issue was being addressed, and I warned them, hands off. They immediately boarded ships and came after plunder. Not all of our followers are of goodly nature."

I said, "And a little storm at sea could not have blocked them? Or did that not occur to a god."

Silvestris said, "Shut up, Charles. You think we do not see through his crap as fast as you. Keep your mouth shut. After this conversation, I am taking you out back for a little father-to-son one-way discussion." Thunder rang around the temple with his anger. Several gods nodded their heads, knowing I would be punished, and they left. Others wanted to watch.

Natura said, "When you are finished with him, I want to have a little mother-to-son talk." The way she said it sent shivers of fear down my spine.

I will not create two additional books writing about what they did and how they did it. I will just say. "Ouch!" I went back to my tower, picked up a few necessities, and headed to Ringal to humbly help people rebuild some structures and prepare for Kayland's entrance into their land. I had checked, and Father was absolutely taking advantage of their bad situation. He was sending Richard to take over and setting up another dukedom. Nearly half his army moved into Ringal.

I was there helping people and making friends. It was surprising how many of them hated the prior king. They would have been glad to have me as king, but that was not my plan. It was not my plan to have Duke Edward take over Ringal either, and I was hoping that, in my anger, I did not ruin my plans. I took a chance and touched Father's mind to see. No, Richard was for Ringal. Duke Edward was up in the air still. Richard loved the mountains. He had always been fascinated with them. I had no idea why. Duke Edward was a farmer and needed flat lands—which, by the way, Kayland now had none. Yes, the mountain erupted, and after waiting nine thousand years, I missed it. Natura said, "Part of your punishment."

As soon as Richard moved in with the army, the Kayland flag went up. I immediately left. Ringal was now off limits. Word must have reached Richard that I had been there paving the way with all kinds of help. He had Dedrick send me a mental "Thank you."

Normally, I wouldn't answer, but I sent back, "You're welcome."

CHAPTER 13

THE ANNIVERSARY

Time was coming quickly for Mother and Father's anniversary. I needed something to wear. I took a chance and traveled to Caelum. I was met by two Caelums and several others that were there to watch. "Hi, guys."

"Hello, Charles. I would not expect you back so soon."

I smiled. "Don't tell. Hey, are there any stores up here?"

"Many. Why?"

"I need some clothes fit for my parents' anniversary. Mine are all worn and getting small. The Renew and Fix Broken spells are nice, but they don't replace what is lost due to wear."

They guided me to a long line of shops and took me into one. It was a tailor shop. They left, and I had several sets of clothing made, one set for the anniversary ball and two for wear around places like Caelum and home. I didn't want to look out of place. The one for the ball was sure to blend in. It was the finest cotton weave. A thousand threads to the inch. It looked like wizard robes with gold trim along the edges. The cloak had a hood and lining of some kind of white fur that was so soft and fine it made you want to touch it and rub your hand against it all day. It was very nice but not overstated. If anything, it was a cross between what a grand wizard and a wealthy farmer would wear. The thread was nice but not silk or velvet. The price was a little more than I would normally pay, but I was in a hurry, and they made it to fit right on the spot. The dark pants and light blue shirt were a little tight but moved with me nicely and stretched a little. It showed off my muscles to the max, and the light blue color went nicely against my dark tan and highlighted my eyes.

Now all I had to do was wait for the invitation. I had little to do, so I checked on Queen Alluvia's people, and they were doing fine. They had plenty to eat, and even with as many people as they could afford gathering food, they barely touched my lands. I checked my eastern pass between my lands and Ringal, or should I say Kayland's new western border. The bridge across the river was out due to the war. I didn't even remember doing that. The giants and I made a stone bridge I changed into Laststoneite. That night, I placed it across the river. I stayed on my side when I did it. I watched the reactions, and all the hidden hells broke loose. Richard was still working under the belief that the Undead Lands were full of undead. Darn! I needed to fix that incorrect assumption.

An entire garrison of two hundred men were sent to protect the bridge and ensure no one crossed. I thought, *I can have fun with this.* The next night, I built a wall that rose all the way to the top of the pass, about five hundred feet. In the center was a gate big enough for six wagons to pass side by side. The whole thing was made of Laststoneite, and the gates were shut. I then watched to see my brother's reaction the next morning. It was almost comical how quickly he contacted Father through one of his wizards. Father told him that it was a bad omen and that he should build his own barrier.

The next day, Richard showed up at the bridge and was assessing what would be needed. I opened the gate where all could see, stepped out, put up a sign and a bell with a basket underneath, went back inside, and closed the gate. The bridge had the customary signs about my laws already; you could not miss them. Curiosity got the best of Richard, and he came over to read the new sign. Directly below the bell it said:

Ring once to deliver mail.
Ring twice and wait if you want to talk with the king.
Ring three times in case of emergency.
(And there had better be a life-and-
death emergency or *there will be!*)

I knew he could not resist. He rang twice. *Ding, ding.* The tiniest little sound. I opened the door and asked, "What do you want, brother? Just because we're next-door neighbors doesn't mean you can bug me all the time. I have a kingdom to run, you know."

He grabbed me and hugged me. He let go and held me at arm's length. "What are you doing in the Sordeath?"

"I own the place."

"You? That's not possible."

"You saw me fight the pirates, didn't you? I killed the letch and his undead also. Oh, by the way, you can tell the admiral I said thanks for the ships. Don't know what I'm going to do with them, but thanks anyway." I took a step back and looked at him. "You're getting old. Besides, I told you then that I am king of the Sordeath."

"Old! Why, you little ..." He smiled and messed my hair, saying, "It's nice to see you again." The others were smiling and were very happy that Prince Richard had not summoned the undead with that ring. "Father was very upset that you would lie to him like that. He will be surprised to find you were telling the truth."

I touched my forehead and flared the Star Fire. "I can't help but tell the truth. Like my doorbell?"

Richard said, "Actually, yes. Now Father can send me the invitation, and I can deliver it. Mother was majorly upset with him when you cut the communications. Jennifer still refuses to talk to me. Sorry if I made it harder on you."

"You need to watch what you say during combat, even if you are not participating. Are you trying to get me killed?"

He smiled. "No. I just get overexcited. Say, come on over for dinner. I have a great cook, and there can't be much to eat in the Sordeath."

My turn to smile. I touched his arm and teleported him to my castle where he could get a full view of my lands for a hundred leagues. I waved my hand out and said, "The Sordeath." He was astonished. I teleported us back to the gate. I think I made some of the soldiers upset, but oh well.

I looked at my brother and said, "I have enough food to feed the entire continent. And I can't come over for dinner. I am still in exile. However, if you need food and will comply with my laws, you can come over and harvest anything you want."

He said sadly, "Do you know about Shadow Mountain?"

"How could I not? It has been affecting the weather for years. Finally blew, and now the Clear Water Valley is gone. At least everyone got out in time."

"Thanks to you. We know you've been warning Annabel, and she wants to meet you so badly."

"I would love to see her in person, but I am still in exile, so I cannot visit her. However, there was nothing in the order to keep her, or anyone else, from visiting me."

I could see Richard thinking about that. His face changed a little, and he nearly lit up with joy. "You're right. Father said you can't come into Kayland, and that's why you left Ringal when the flag went up. But that was the only stipulation. May the gods be praised. I can visit you anytime, and so can Mother."

"Not yet. I'm busy. After the anniversary. Father always invites the bordering kings. Until then, things will be dangerous politically with Father."

Richard looked concern. "Father cannot lift the exile. You know this."

"I have a plan. I will see you at the anniversary ball, brother. Be prepared for Father to blow his top. He is going to love this."

Richard frowned in thought. "As long as it's a good kind of blow the top. Don't make him mad."

I smiled. "Don't worry." Then I vanished.

It was only one day before I received one ring. The bell was tied into the towers on the wall and the castle. When someone rang the bell, I would hear it if I was at the castle. Since I was hoping for an invitation, I brought work from the Dead Land Tower to the castle so I could be around if the bell rang. I waited a few hours after it rang, as I was working on a spell that would help me with the Dead Lands. Right now, the only way to fix the Dead Lands was to clear each foot with a high-powered cleansing spell—*each square foot*. I was hoping to widen that spell considerably, or fixing one square mile in the Dead Lands was going to take me over a thousand years. And there were tens of thousands of square miles.

When I was at a good stopping place, I teleported to the wall and checked for any traps on the other side. Then I opened the door. No one was there, but a letter was sitting in the basket. I opened it.

It is with great joy that King David Truss and Queen Susan Truss invite you, King Charles Truss of the Sordeath and Dragonback Mountains, to their third-decade anniversary ball and festivities. To be held starting on the eighth day of the Moon of Chance. The king and queen will receive attendees and presents starting one hour after noon until dusk, at which time the banquet will commence, followed by dancing. On day two, for interested parties, there will be meetings to discuss any issues worldwide.

Presentations: Early Morning: Clear Water Valley by Duke Edward
Late Morning: Sources of food and ways to get more out of the land
by Baron Clemmit
Afternoon: Ringal War by Prince Richard (and a guest speaker)
Late Afternoon and Evening: Open discussion
Days Three and Four: Continued open discussion

I could not help but think, *Not good*. Normally there would be days of celebration. Mother loved to make it the "ball of the decade," and for all the normal five days of festivities to be canceled for meetings to discuss issues, and for Father to expect days of open discussion, meant things were looking bad—really bad. I could go in and give away everything, but that would not work well. There would be fighting and war. I had to stick to the plan, and that meant I had to take my time and do it correctly. It had to be done legally and in a way the other kings and queens would trust. I told myself, "The plan will work. Just take it slow and bide your time." However, if it didn't work, thousands would die.

The day of the anniversary ball, I was sitting in my tower ready to go hours before I had to leave. I was nervous and a little worried. Something didn't feel right. I pulled out the Staff of Maps and took a look at all my lands. No issues I could see. I checked the lands bordering the Sordeath, and everything was fine. I checked the borders surrounding Kayland and found the problem. Or, I should say *problems*. In the south, the mountain elves and druids were massing an army. In the northeastern section, there was an army just massing from Ginham.

I said to myself, "How irritating. King Odoray is massing an army on my father's border." I started to spin up but quickly remembered the fun my gods had with me the last time I lost it. I calmed myself down. *Now, why would anyone want to attack Father at this time? The taking of Ringal was not his fault. King Tyler started that, and I finished it. Ginham should have no problem with that.* The elves and the druids were a big mystery. What did they think they were doing?

Then it hit me. Father was spread thin, very thin. Many of his troops were in Ringal securing the place. King Odoray must have known Father was spread thin and this was a good time to mess with him. The elves and druids knew Father was spread thin. They were going to try to take over the Sordeath. They were there during planting and knew its potential. They had to cross Father's land, but who would be there to stop them?

I prayed to Natura, "Goddess, I have a problem."

Natura said, "I see them, and do not worry, Charles. They have been ordered to stop."

"My goddess, do you want me to give the Northern Druid Suppository to the southern druids?"

"No! You keep that to yourself. You can give them access as long as you are watching what they study, but do not allow them in by themselves!"

"Yes, my goddess. Thank you."

That was the end of the conversation. She seemed heated about letting anyone in the druid trap. There was a lot of information in there that was bad for everyone, and the gods couldn't monitor what people were learning. Must have made them nervous. But she said not to worry, so, just in case, I prayed to Silvestris.

"Silvestris, I just let Natura know we have a problem."

"Hi, kid. What problem?"

"King Odoray of Ginham is amassing an army to the northeast of Kayland, and the southern druids and the Aroan elves are preparing to sneak an army into the Sordeath by crossing Kayland while Father's army is spread thin."

Silvestris said in a very upset tone, "You finish your plan with your father. I know what you're going to do, and I want to see his face. We will take care of these other issues. Not to worry, boy; it's handled." He cut out.

I put the Staff of Maps away and prepared to leave. I put away all my weapons. I didn't really need them anymore anyway, and I could call them if I wanted them. I checked the presents, placed the small crown on my head, and teleported to the circle for teleportation in the StarHillm-Merge castle.

I was received and taken to the line of those waiting to be announced. Several people started screaming, and at least one passed out. I turned down the Star Fire a little more. King Golden Fist of the Mordepths was in front of me. We had talked a lot over the last year. His people were sneaking into my northern lands and stealing food. We made a treaty, and they followed the laws now and could take all the food they wanted.

I was trying to be a little late but not too late. King Golden Fist looked up and back. "You're late, boy."

I had asked him once, "Why is it all the kings and queens, barons, sheriffs, and nearly everyone calls me boy? It makes me feel like a child."

All he said back was, "Exactly."

I said, "I suppose you're not late?"

"I am properly late. Anyone after me is inappropriately late."

They motioned for Golden Fist to come up. He stood taller, about four foot total, and walked in proudly. The announcer struck his staff three times on the floor, making loud bangs. The staff of the announcer strikes once for a normal person, twice for someone important, and three times for royalty. Only once did I ever hear four times. That is reserved for a royal death.

In a very loud and clear voice, he said, "Of the Mordepths, ruler of the Deep Caverns, head of the Iron Clan, benevolent monarch of the Dragons Head, I give you King Golden Fist of the Dwarven Nation."

King Golden Fist walked forward, followed by twenty servants, his general, his wife, I figured, and one little child, couldn't say if male or female. It was a long walk, and knowing Golden Fist, it would be a little while before I was allowed to go. So many people were talking and commenting on his attire it was almost deafening. There were several more screams, and I turned the Star Fire down a lot more so their lies would not kill them.

An announcer came back to me and looked shocked when he recognized me. "How are you to be announced, Prince Charles?"

This was it. Time to start the act. First thing was to let everyone know I am cursed—or the lies told at this ball would kill most of the people present. I looked him right in the eyes and said, "Holder of the Star Fire, divine sorcerer and champion of Natura and Silvestris, grand druid and holder of the Keys of Knowledge, exiled prince of Kayland, sole sovereign of the Dead Lands, monarch of Sordeath and the Undead Lands, King

Charles Truss." I touched my forehead and let the Star Fire flare brightly and then diminish to a light shine. It would stay shining as a warning to all until I wanted otherwise.

The announcer was well trained. His eyes only bulged a little. He looked at the cleric checking people in. The cleric said, "He is not undead." The announcer relaxed a little and then stepped out to wait for Golden Fist to finish with presents and step aside.

There was a baron behind me, and he said, "Charles, did you really mean all that?"

I looked back at him. "Long story, but yes. As you can clearly see, I cannot lie, and those around me cannot lie without great pain and possibly death."

His wife said to him, "Sweetheart, you know that issue with the maid? She looked at my forehead. Were you telling the truth?"

You could see it in his face. For him, this was going to be a long night. "No, dear."

She smiled. "I thought not. King Charles, are you going to be around the whole week? I may need to stand by you while I drill my husband on a few things."

I said, "No need, dear lady. Did you hear the screams? This is a very powerful Star Fire. If you are within sixty feet, he will not lie without extreme pain, and at one hundred feet, it will still be painful. Besides, I do not know how long I will be staying. Father may toss me out shortly."

All she said to that was, "Oh my."

King Golden Fist bowed and stepped to the side. I moved out to the front as the announcer motioned for me to do. The announcer stood tall and stiff and struck his staff three times slowly. I think he wanted everyone's attention.

In a loud, slow voice and emphasizing each section, especially the first, he said, *"Holder of the Star Fire*, divine sorcerer and champion of Natura and Silvestris, grand druid and holder of the Keys of Knowledge, exiled prince of Kayland, sole sovereign of the Dead Lands, monarch of Sordeath and the Undead Lands, I give you King Charles Truss."

I stepped out and walked slowly the entire length of the ballroom. At first, you could have heard a flower grow, and then it started to pick up in background noise, and then it became a roar with several screams of pain intermixed.

I looked a little to the right and left as I walked, giving nods and slight bows to the appropriate people. However, something was wrong. I expected quiet and shunning. Having anything to do with an exile is not good politically. But the girls were peeking out and looking at me like they used to look at Richard. I was almost embarrassed when several gave a low curtsy. They had never done that before. They had always paid no attention to me whatsoever. They had flocked all over Richard. I liked it that way. Now mothers were pushing their daughters to the front. This was not going to help my concentration.

I turned my attention to the throne. Father was not smiling. In fact, he looked like he had just had a fit of pain. Mother was looking like she was going to jump out of her seat and hug me. My brother Richard was looking pleased and had Rebecca on his arm. That's why mothers were presenting their daughters to me! Richard was getting married. The Women's Circle must have announced it earlier. Darn! Richard was not available anymore, Droland was dead, and that left me. It was going to be a long night.

Jennifer looked pleased, but Amanda looked guilty. Grandmother, head of the Women's Circle, had that evil look, the one she used when matchmaking. Duke Edward and his daughters were off to the left, and so was Annabel. To loosen things up, I winked at Annabel where everyone could see me— the same wink I used in all her dreams. She smiled and said out loud while pulling her mother's sleeve, "That's him. That's him, Mother. That's him. He's the one that saved us."

I stepped up to the first step but not on it. In a sincere voice, I said, "Congratulations on staying with the same woman for thirty years, King Truss of Kayland. Most impressive."

He shuffled a little in his seat. Mother's eyes turned a little sour. Father said, "You have a lot of guts, boy, becoming a king so that you could get invited to our anniversary. You know I always invite every king. Interesting way to legally enter lands you are in exile from."

I looked at him hard and asked, "Are you a man of your word, King Truss?"

That surprised him and caused him to become a little angry. To be questioned about his word in front of all these people was a slam against his honor. And to do so with a Star Fire present was the same as demanding the truth. Still, I knew he was a man of his word, so I was not worried about the answer.

He stood up and looked down upon me. "I am."

"Good to know. Did you or did you not swear that anyone who brought your sword back to you, in this castle, would be granted one wish if it was within the king's right to grant? Did you not say the wish could include complete forgiveness for any crime?"

Now he was shocked. He slowly sat back down and answered, "I did."

I continued, "Did not the law givers and legal staff of Kayland make that an overriding law—a law that is to be fulfilled even if it goes against all other laws?"

He looked hard at me and smiled. "If the request is within reason. I cannot give away my kingdom or the treasury."

I held out a hand, and magically a scabbard sword appeared in his lap. "Is this your sword?"

He looked at Dedrick and asked, "How did he do that?"

Protections were in place, and nothing should have been able to magically teleport or shift into the StarHillm-Merge castle's throne room.

He picked up the sword and looked at it closely. He pulled it from the sheath and swung it several times and then showed it to Richard, saying, "You never did remove that kick." He returned his look to me and said, "This is my sword. The Sword of the Kings of Kayland. How did you come by it?"

Under my breath, and so he and several others could hear it, I said, "Long story, Father." Louder I said, "Then I may request one thing?"

Now he looked at me smiling. He knew what I was doing. "One thing. Word it well."

I had thought about this for a long time and knew what I wanted. "I wish complete forgiveness by the crown, the people, the land of Kayland, and my father for any crimes, whether real or perceived, that I may have committed against the crown, people, my family, or the land of Kayland from this moment back through all time, including removal of all punishments, imprisonments, or exiles."

Now it was quiet. Everyone was waiting for the verdict on my wish. Father had to talk with his legal staff, which were always nearby, and get a calling. After only a very short time, all were nodding their heads. Father turned to me and pronounced, "Granted!"

Cheers rose up through the crowd. People were telling people in the back, so cheers continued for some time. Finally, Father held up a hand. "I would offer you a place beside your brother, but you are a king now. So let's keep this formal until the announcements are over."

I nearly laughed I was so happy. Step one down. On to step two. I said, "King Truss, I had a difficult time determining what to give as presents. For Amanda, who I know loves to embroider, I brought Caelum cloth." I held out my hand, and in it was an entire ream of Caelum cloth in purest white. A servant came and took the cloth and brought it to her. I told her, "Caelum cloth is very special. While wearing it, no evil can touch you. It allows no shadow, not even in the folds, and it is very rare."

She checked it out and looked at Mother smiling, then turned to me and said, "I am sorry for treating you so badly, Charles. I did not know the whole story." She gave Father a dirty look. "Thank you for saving my life and thank you for the present. It is wonderful." It was good to see she was still just as spirited.

"For my sister Jennifer, I brought this ring." I held out my hand, and instantly in it was a ring of exquisite beauty. The servant took it and brought it to Jennifer. "That is Solbelli's artifact ring of virtue. It will warn you when evil is around and grant you protections."

Jennifer said, "Thank you, Charles."

"For my brother Richard." I held out my hand, and in it was a rod. The servant came and took it to him. "That is the artifact Rod of Truth. As you can see from the Star Fire and hear from the screaming, I have no need of it. As you hold it, you will know if someone is telling the truth or trying to fool you. It will make it easier judging people in the Ringal. As you know by now, because of King Tyler's reign of terror, lying to royalty has become a survival instinct in most of the commoners."

"Thank you, Charles. I will use it justly."

"For my grandmother." I held up a hand, and in it appeared a water pitcher of such rare beauty that two gods had asked me for it once I made it. I made them duplicates. The servant took it to her. "That is a Picture of Infinite Water. Tell it what temperature you want and pour. Pure spring water will pour at that temperature until you stop it or ask for another temperature. I know how you hate cold water to clear your eyes with in the mornings. Tell it you want warm or hot water, and you shall have it. Fill the tub every night with hot water and relax."

She smiled brightly. She was getting old, and it took little time peeking with the Staff of Maps to find out what she truly needed.

"Thank you, grandson."

"For Mother." I held out my hand, and in it was a brush and mirror. The servant took them to her. "At great pain to myself turning stone to Laststoneite, here are the brush and mirror that match your Laststoneite comb."

She was ecstatic. "Thank you, sweetheart."

"Last but surely not least, Father." I opened my arms, and on the floor was a stone pillar with a lightly glowing ball on top. The pillar stood about three feet tall. "The artifact Telliman."

Father nearly choked. Telliman was a story that fathers loved to tell their children. The story was about a great king who had a stone called Telliman. The stone was sentient and did not permit lies from the one touching it or illusions within one thousand feet. Telliman would make it so that Father knew when he was being lied to and would reduce the risk of assassination by invisible creatures.

Father said, "Thank you, King Truss."

"You are most welcome." I turned to my brother. "Richard."

"Yes, brother."

I looked at Rebecca, and Rebecca showed me her hand with the engagement ring. I shook my head. "Always taking the best for yourself."

His smile increased, and he took Rebecca in his arm and pulled her closer. "Of course."

I raised my hand, and in it was a simple necklace with a blue stone. I handed it to the servant and told him to take it to Rebecca. "Rebecca, I remember how you love to take in strays and tend them to full health. That is a necklace of healing. Once a day, you can touch any creature, including your husband, and he or it will be fully healed of all afflictions. I have set it to work for you, and only you can use it. Welcome to the family."

Rebecca nearly cried—she was always emotional. "Thank you, Charles. Do not fear. I will take good care of your brother."

"I know you will. Ringal needs someone who cares as much as you do. Thank you."

I bowed and stepped to the side with the other kings and waited while the announcer called one group after another. King Golden Fist whispered, "Nice trinkets, boy. Let me know next time so I can bring something better."

Another whispered, "No one can beat those presents. Half of them are priceless."

Another whispered, "Are you going to be spending some time explaining how you came by such trinkets and how you became a king? I have a thousand questions." I just smiled and listened.

Some attendees came late enough that they had no clue that I was forgiven or a king. The looks on their faces were wonderfully funny. Father got tired of it and announced, "Have criers sent throughout the kingdom announcing that Charles is forgiven, starting with one at the entrance hall." Many people laughed.

I watched my family closely. One or another would look at me and smile every now and then. The presents I gave them were taken away to the treasury, reserved for only the most expensive presents. Rebecca and Jennifer were wearing theirs. Father never let go of his sword. Telliman was anchored to the floor and would not be moved. Everything seemed to be going as planned. If step three did not, I would be very upset.

The banquet was wonderful. When you're raised on great food, you tend to take it for granted, but when you've been subsiding on magical food, Protection Banquet, Generate Food and Water or, Brilliant Hideout, which comes with a banquet, you start appreciating real food. Magically created food is real food and nourishing, and to most people, it tastes wonderful. To a magic user, it tastes magical. Still wonderful but magical. It leaves an unsatisfying aftertaste. It's not bad, but it's not very good either. In my studies, I found out why. Apparently, a long time ago, magic users, including gods, were creating all their meals by magic and not relying on the land; therefore, they did not care about the land, as it held nothing they needed. The Over Gods changed several things about magic, and the taste of food was one of the changes. After that, magic users and world gods started caring about where their food came from. Because of this, land and nature became much more important.

I did not have time to eat much. My family was all over me, asking questions and hugging and generally making sure I knew I was loved. Father hugged me for the first time I could ever remember. I lost it and had to go out on the northern balcony to recover. Mother came out, and we talked for a while. She filled in a lot of blanks about what they had found out about Droland, my evil brother, and his contacts. Father, when he found out the truth, cried at the loss of his good son. Droland's journals detailed all the things he had pulled and blamed on me and how easy he found Father to flatter and therefore fool.

I was asked a dozen times how I became a sorcerer and king. So I told them that after the dance, I would grant them a story if they had the time, as it was a long story. Also, so Grandmother would not get any ideas about any particular female, I danced with every female, including young and old. When I danced with Annabel, she hugged me during the entire dance, even though the dance was not slow. I sat down and talked with her for a while. She was so excitable and intelligent and wanted to know more about me. We talked about her blessing, the hunting cats and the dragon I warned her about, and the demons I told her to tell her father about. A little about everything and what she did after the warning. I praised her for heeding my warnings. I asked how things were going now. She cried and tried to tell me but was far too emotional and ran to her mother.

I went back inside and danced a good fast line dance and several others. Grandmother was looking at me strangely. She had an irritated look on her face. Good. I wasn't giving her any ideas.

When the dancing was completed, I sat down on the steps of the throne and had them clear a circle in the center of the floor. I conjured a magical harp and had it play in the background. I summoned the Staff of Maps and created the scene of me leaving the city in exile. The story started, and I must say, I held them spellbound for four hours as I told them about the druid trap, the meeting with the gods, receiving the Star Fire, how I defeated the undead king, the battle for the king's sword, and the changing of the Undead Lands into a paradise.

I finished by saying, "It comes down to this. To get back home and protect Annabel, as I promised, I studied and became a powerful divine sorcerer, a very high-level druid, a demon slayer, an undead slayer, and a king. I didn't want to be a king so much as I wanted to get invited back home so I could return Father's sword and have the exile removed. Yes, I knew about the issue with Shadow Mountain, and I could have stopped it. However, if I did, then this continent would have been destroyed, as that would have caused the entire northern range of volcanoes to go violent. And yes, I found out about the cause for childbirth deaths and developed a paradise to create air to breathe."

Everyone was quiet. I was expecting cheers or questions, but they just stared at me. They were looking at me in a strange way. As everyone watched, Annabel took my hand and led me to a south-facing balcony. Out in the dark, beyond the city gates, were thousands of tiny lights.

Annabel said, "We live in a tent. Father says, and he is right, that as long as our people live in tents, then so do we. King Truss, your father, has offered us beds in the castle, but Father said no."

I looked out on the masses of fires and asked, "How are your people doing?"

"They are starving. We harvested everything, thanks to your warning, and sent it to the cities and castle for keeping. Due to politics, the king gave out the normal amounts to all other lands. We were living off the food we held back, but we ran out of food last week and are trying to obtain more. The pickings are becoming very slim. Someone planted ..." She gave me a suspicious look. "Someone planted a couple of valleys up in the Sinaguard. That has helped a lot, and many moved to the Sinaguard, but that won't last long. It is far too cold to grow much." She was in tears.

I hugged her and said, "I will fix this issue somehow. Be patient."

She said, "I know you will. I have seen it, but I don't know how." She walked back into the ballroom.

Father came out. "It's not just our people that are having a hard time. There are people all over this continent that will starve without that food in the Sordeath. I know you created it for the air, but we need that food."

"I know, Father. It's not a matter of whether or not you and everyone else will get the food; it's how. Though I let Queen Alluvia's people in, I have protections in place that will prevent a foreign army from entering my lands. The amount of people needed to feed Kayland would be considered an army. I need to think, please."

King Golden Fist took Father's arm and pulled him a little ways away. "I know the boy, King Truss. When I stole my way onto his property, my men started to sick up. It was so bad I thought we were all going to die. He came, and the sickness went away. I apologized for trying to steal food, but that darn Star Fire made me eat those words and tell the truth. He told me to wait, and he turned away and started thinking. It took a good long time, but he turned back around, and we created a treaty that allowed us a small amount of people for foraging as long as we keep his laws. Trust him. He will stand there looking out at those lights until he figures out the best way to help us all. Let him alone. Let him think. He's a good boy and will come up with a good solution."

In truth, I had turned around on Golden Fist because I did not want him to see me trying so hard to keep from laughing. I was in tears with suppressed laughter and needed the time to pull myself together. Their hunger was truly not funny. It was the look on his face at being caught stealing food like a child, the only time I had ever seen the old dwarf blush.

Father looked at the dwarven king. "And what if he comes up with the wrong solution?"

King Golden Fist said, "Have an alternative ready. Have several. He will listen. He is probably going through all possible alternatives now. Do not underestimate his intelligence."

Father thought for a minute and ordered, "All interested parties are to move into the war room for immediate emergency discussions. I want a guard on King Charles Truss with every possible protection. Captain, warn us when he stops thinking and tell him where we are."

As he moved off, Grandmother said, "Ladies, come with me. We have a decision to make."

I was fairly sure that Father would not come up with anything, as he had to be politically correct with all the other kings and queens, and that takes a lot of time. But what was Grandmother doing? It could be almost anything. I just hoped it didn't ruin my plans. I stayed there thinking until just before dawn. I knew they had not come to any sort of order. The captain waited for me to turn around.

"King Charles Truss, your father and all other kings and queens are in the war room trying to figure out what they are going to do. I must report to them that you are finished thinking and whether or not you have come to a solution."

He did not look happy about the idea of interfering with the meeting going on in the war room. I could understand why. Every time a servant opened the doors, it was shouting and threats that could be heard. I said, "Don't worry, Captain. I will interrupt their meeting." I walked over to the war room and opened the servant's door and snuck in. I stood there listening for about half an hour before I was noticed.

Duke Reginald of Ginham said, "I will not allow Kayland to have full control of that food source. It is not fair. I cannot allow Kayland to become fat and grow while holding back our lands by half-starving us."

King Odoray added, "I am also wondering about this. You already aggressively and violently took over Ringal and killed their king. What say you, King Truss? How can we trust you?"

That was my cue. Though it was addressed to my father, I took it for being addressed to me on purpose. In a mater-of-fact and quiet tone that I amplified so all would hear, I said, "I don't really care if you trust me or not, King Odoray. I do not trust you."

All eyes instantly turned to me. I added, "I can see that some of you have the mistaken opinion that you have any choice in what I do with my lands. You do not. Also, you should know that Father did not attack Ringal. He sent my brother in to save it from all the turmoil. You see, Ringal made the mistake of attacking me, and I took great offense. I killed the king, his army, the entire royal family, and started killing off all the politicians and high-ranking military. I would probably have gone much further, but my goddess, Natura, told me to stop. I contacted Father and told him it was wide open and he should take advantage. Please"—I touched my Star Fire—"tell me which one of you would not take advantage if you knew Ringal was up for grabs with no army to stop you?"

It was totally quiet until one said, "Why did you not take it?"

"Simple. I don't want to be king over a bunch of people. I am king now over other creatures, but they rule themselves. I jump in only when one breaks my laws. You can stop bickering. I have come to a solution, and it is not political, though it will harm Kayland by removing a great resource. It is by far the best I can think of."

Father took the bait. "What's your solution?"

I looked solemnly at Father. "I have an overabundance of infrastructure except people. You have an overabundance of people without the infrastructure to support them. In the name of the gods, my ward Annabel is living out of a tent! Release Duke Edward and all his people from their oaths. I would have them swear allegiance to Sordeath and the king of Sordeath. Both problems will be fixed, and food can be given out to everyone very quickly. I will make Duke Edward my regent, second only to the king. Duke Edward will run the people so I don't have to. I will want treaties and trade agreements, but Duke Edward will be placed in charge of that. He has a lot of expertise, and most of you already trust him."

This was not difficult for Father. He never got along with the farming land people. He was far too political for them. Richard did, and he was now our neighbor.

Father said, "I think that would be a good solution. Anyone think they have a better one?" It stayed totally quiet. "I did not think so. You all trust Duke Edward. Several times in the past, he has helped you against my orders. You know him to do what is morally correct and to keep politics out of the situation. Duke Edward, come forward." Duke Edward came forward. "Are you willing, my friend, to take on this task? To help run a land of farming with a lot of nature added in and very few politics?" Father gave a great sales pitch, pointing out everything Duke Edward would love. Father must have wanted it badly.

Happily, Duke Edward said, "I am, my king."

Father asked, "Is there any objections that are not political for Duke Edward to be regent and his people running the handout of food?" No one said a word. This would put things back to the way they were, and that had worked for many years. "Then I release you and all yours from their oaths to Kayland and her king."

I stepped up. "Kneel, Duke Edward." A sword was in my hand instantly, and it glowed brightly. He kneeled, and I touched the sword to his left shoulder. "Swear this oath: 'I Edward Scott, former duke of Kayland, do hereby swear to protect the Sordeath, her royal family, and obey her king. I swear to provide food to all without prejudice and in a manner that does not harm the Sordeath. I will treat the Sordeath and her laws, especially the overriding laws set by King Charles Truss, as sacred and will uphold them to my fullest ability. I will ensure that the forests are not molested or cut back and that all sentient beings are equal in the eyes of the law and the king. Though I have loved and will always love Kayland, our big brother, I will be the best I can be for Kayland's little sister, the Sordeath.' Do you so swear?"

"I so swear with all my heart."

I changed the sword to his right shoulder and tapped it before pulling it away. "Then rise, Regent Edward of the Sordeath and Dragonback Mountains."

There were cheers, laughter, toasts, and congratulations for Regent Edward, and generally everyone was very happy. I raised my hands, and it became quiet. "Kneel, Regent Edward." He instantly kneeled, but the look on his face was puzzlement.

I took off my crown and placed it on his head. "I renounce my throne as king of the Sordeath in favor of King Edward Scott."

CHAPTER 14

MAKING PLANS

The shock was wonderful. They were all thinking that maybe they had heard wrong. Father said, "What did you just do?"

I said, "I told you. I don't want power. I renounce my throne as king of the Sordeath in favor of King Edward Scott. Regent Edward is now King Edward. Besides, the laws of the Sordeath are the same as Kayland, and the laws clearly state that no creature with magical power can hold a place within the government of power. That place within the government is further defined as anything over five hundred human people. Before, the position of king was over one person. Now it is tens of thousands, and I no longer qualify. I cannot legally be king of the Sordeath." I smiled.

King Edward stood up. "I am not sure this is legal either, King Charles."

I looked at him and said, "Once a king always a king. I am still king of the Dead Lands. By law, I cannot completely give up being a king, so I am the ex-king of Sordeath. However, the law states that if a king knows that there is someone who would be immensely better at properly running the kingdom, then he can renounce his claim to the throne to that person. It cannot be under duress. It must be an act for placing a better king on the throne. Now, throughout history, brothers have renounced their claim to other brothers that they felt would be better at running the kingdom. If I was the oldest prince in Kayland, and Father died, I would renounce to Richard. However, there is nothing in the law that says it has to be a brother. There is a clause that makes it unlawful for someone not of royalty to take the position. However, King Edward was a duke of Kayland and regent of Sordeath, which are by title royalty. I dislike running people's lives. Our people love you dearly, and who here would deny that you would make a better king than I?"

I waited, but no one said a thing. "I thought not. I do not want the responsibility, and I will be far too busy with my next project to play at being a king over people."

Father said, "Next project?"

"With the help of the gods, I am going to reclaim and repair the Dead Lands. I am king of the Dead Lands until I can trick someone into taking over like I did with King Edward. However, I will need a new name for the land, as I am changing it to forest and grasslands." Another shock. I was waiting for someone to die of shock. I could hear, as he was letting me, Silvestris laughing at their looks, especially Father's.

Father said, "You cannot fix the Dead Lands. It is impossible and suicidal. I just got you back, and I don't want to lose you again."

I said, "Thank you, Father, but I am not back. It's nice that I can now come and go as I please, same with the Sordeath, but I am part of both and not belonging to either. Besides, living in the Dead Lands is possible, Father. I have been living there for years. I am now Ex-Prince Charles of Kayland, ex-king of the Sordeath, and king of the Dead Lands." I added with amusement, "Population one."

King Forsite said, "I knew he was planning something, but I had no idea it was this. I will tell this story of great unselfishness to all my posterity. Correcting the Dead Lands is not thought possible, but living in the Dead Lands was thought to be impossible also."

Father asked, "Why are you doing this? I cannot fault you your choices. Duke Edward will make a wonderful king, and fixing the Dead Lands would be very helpful. But what are you getting out of this?"

I turned a little sad. "Father, I am powerful."

"I noticed, but—"

I placed a hand on his arm, "No, Father. Please listen. I am so powerful that the gods are not sure they should let me live. I am working directly for the gods. I am a god champion for Silvestris and Natura. I love them dearly, and they have helped me greatly. Still, the only reason I am allowed to live is because I am being helpful. The gods wanted the Sordeath repaired, and they want the Dead Lands repaired. After that, there are many other issues created by fools that thought they could mess with the fabric of life and time. I have enough work to keep me busy for a thousand years. I have power, something I never wanted, but since I have it, I am going to use it to help all I can. I gave King Edward the Sordeath for several reasons but mostly because I know he will keep my forests strong and be fair with all of nature's creatures. Another reason is I simply don't have the time to fix the Dead Lands and also run the Sordeath." Cheers rang out again, and we started to move out into the throne room for breakfast. The Women's Circle was there.

When I saw them, I stopped dead in my tracks. We just moved into the main throne room and were heading to the banquet tables. The Women's Circle was standing on the raised throne, looking nearly choreographed and waiting for us. Grandmother had a satisfied look on her face, and that had never been good for me.

Grandmother said, "Charles, a moment of your time please."

Father whispered, "Now what? It's never good when she's being polite."

We changed course and walked up to Grandmother. Nearly everyone that had been at the dance the night before was there now. I said, "Hello, Grandmother. How are you doing today?"

"I am doing fine. The Women's Circle met last night, Charles, and we have decided that you are to marry."

My turn to be shocked. "Marry?"

Grandmother smiled, and so did several others, including Mother. King Edward's wife was not smiling. It was evident that she and half a dozen others from the farmlands were not in agreement with this marriage.

Mother said, "We have decided that you will marry the Lady Margareta of the Barony of Four Forks, which used to be in the Valley of Clear Water and is now under a flow of lava."

Margareta was pushed forward by a woman, not her mother. She had been crying, and her mother was very upset with this decision, but she was keeping quiet and off to the side. I looked long and hard at Margareta and her mother and looked into their minds just a little.

I turned to the assembly and asked, "Is Jeffery Montasmith present? If so, step forward." Jeffery stepped up and was looking at the head of the Women's Circle like someone who would kill Grandmother if he thought he could get away with it.

I said, "Margareta, please don't take this wrong. You would make a wonderful queen, a grand wife and mother, and you are extremely pretty, but aren't you madly in love with Jeffery?"

She choked out, "Yes, I am."

I said, "Jeffery, aren't you insanely in love with Margareta?"

He said in anger, but without turning to me, as clearly his anger was not directed toward me, "Yes, King Charles. I have been, am now, and will always be."

I said, "That's what I thought." I turned to Grandmother and said, "It is very nice of you to suggest this joining, but I must decline."

Grandmother looked upset. "I did not say it was a choice, Charles. The Women's Circle of Kayland has made their decision, and that is final."

"Final, *final!*" My eyes narrowed in distaste, and then the foolishness of it all struck me, and I laughed. I looked over at King Edward's wife, now Queen Rebecca, and said, "Rebecca, please come down from there and bring with you all the members from the former Clear Water Valley."

Rebecca hesitated. King Edward ordered, "Do as you're told, woman."

Rebecca and the others came down and gathered where I motioned. I smiled at her. "Rebecca, note the crown that your husband is wearing. I have made him the king of the Sordeath." A lady's crown instantly appeared in my hand, and I placed it on her head. I let that sink in for a second and to give time for the assemblage to quiet down. "You are queen of the Sordeath. You and these other ladies of the Clear Water Valley have been released from all oaths pertaining to Kayland. You have been sworn to the Sordeath and King Edward." I had to wait for the assemblage to calm. It took a few moments. "As queen, you should be starting your own Women's Circle. Margareta and Jeffery are your subjects. I ask you, as head of your Women's Circle, do you agree to this arrangement?"

It was a lot to take in, but Rebecca was a strong woman, and she took her time to absorb the information. As she did, her smile increased. She said, "I would love to hear how this came about, but I am short on time. As queen, I need to meet with my ladies and work on serious issues like food. However, since I apparently am no longer part of the Kayland Women's Circle and need to start my own, and because Margareta and Jeffery are my subjects and they also would be sworn to the Sordeath and my husband, then no! I do not agree with the Kayland decision. Margareta and Jeffery should be joined together. It has been planned since their births, and they love each other. They will be grand for each other."

Margareta and Jeffery flew into each other's arms. Their mothers had to drag them apart. My father was watching and pretending to be very upset. Inside he was laughing.

I laughed inside also. "That's what I thought." I turned to Grandmother, and the look on her face was of pure astonishment.

She addressed Queen Rebecca. "Well, I, I did not know. Of course Margareta and Jeffery are your subjects and should report to your new circle. We will find another for Charles."

I turned to Father, and he was now pretending a rage, so I gave him more ammunition. "King Truss, please tell me where in our discussions, or the law, it states that a king of a foreign land is subject to Kayland's Women's Circle."

Shock reverberated throughout the assemblage and the Women's Circle. They had forgotten that I was a king of another land.

Through teeth clenched tightly to hold back his laughter, and trying to look upset, Father said, "No king is subject to any Women's Circle. That my Women's Circle decided that they can order a king shows a total lack of leadership and intelligence." He looked hard at Grandmother. "You may not have known that Edward Scott is king, but you did know that Charles is king. You nearly caused an international incident with two lands that have just shown their allegiance toward Kayland. How dare you!"

Mother pleaded, "Sweetheart, we did not think that it would turn out like this. We did not see Charles as anything short of a prince of Kayland."

Father was pretending to be outraged, "Now you are saying a king of another land is less than a prince of Kayland?"

"No, that's not what I meant."

Father yelled, "You did not think! That is the problem! That has been the problem for years now. You make decisions without obtaining all the facts, or you purposefully ignore the facts you don't like."

Grandmother made a bad mistake by saying, "How dare you! This is Women's Circle business. It is none of yours."

Father's eyes went wide, and his entire body screamed, "King!" Even I ducked a little, knowing the rage that Grandmother had just unleashed. Father was angry. All amusement was instantly gone. When he got angry, his tone became deadly quiet, and his words were highly punctuated. "I hereby band all Kayland Women's Circles for the period of six full moons and until the current heads of the Women's Circles step down and others are voted in to take their place, whichever comes later." He turned, saying, "Let's have some breakfast. I need time to calm down. I've wanted to put that woman in her place for years." We headed toward the tables while barons and dukes grabbed their wives off the throne steps and took them into other rooms to have a good long talk. Grandmother just stood there looking totally shocked.

King Edward, arm in arm with Queen Rebecca, said, "Charles, we need to have a meeting to determine the best way to get things started. I know you renounced your Sordeath throne to start with the Dead Lands, but I could use your help. I don't even know what is where in the Sordeath."

I said, "Gather your barons, general, and captains—all you can think of for the planning—and we will start. Father, can we borrow your war room?"

"Of course."

I added, "King Edward, please include the women who have a need to participate. I don't want anything going wrong due to a lack of knowledge they may have that we do not."

Queen Rebecca asked, "Trusting my Women's Circle, Charles?"

"I trust the women of the Sordeath to do what is right for their people and leave politics out of any decisions. They are good women and care enough to listen and give good input. They have always been more down to earth than any other circles I can think of." I went to my knees and nearly blacked out from the Star Fire pain. I choked out, "Except one."

The concern on everyone's face was plain. Father called, "Cleric!"

Eric was at my side quickly, but I motioned him away. "Father, I told a lie, and the Star Fire kicked in. I did not realize I was telling a lie at the time, but the Star Fire does not care if I know I am lying or not. The Star Fire told me what I said wrong. The dwarven Women's Circle is more down to earth." The pain went away, and I got shakily to my feet.

King Edward said, "You may not have noticed, Charles, but many people left very early when they found out you have a Star Fire. Many others have fallen to their knees in pain and quickly told the truth. Many wives and husbands have found out about each other. The smart ones simply did not ask any questions they did not want the answers to."

I looked at him and seriously said, "I noticed the screams early on and turned the Star Fire down considerably; otherwise they would be dead. This is not just a Star Fire. It is *the* Star Fire.

The one all others were created from. It is the original and the most powerful. It took me thousands of years to learn to control it enough to live with it. However, sometimes I make a mistake. It is the main reason I cannot live with others. The Dead Lands will be a good lonely place for me to work."

Mother and Queen Rebecca gasped and exclaimed at the same time, "The Dead Lands!"

Father and King Edward both said, "I'll tell you later."

Mother put her arm around me and said, "You poor child. You should be with others. It must be lonely. You could always live here."

I shook my head. "No, Mother, I cannot control the Star Fire when sleeping, so I've taken to not sleeping much. Still, if I fall asleep and Father tells a joke, or Richard teases Rebecca, they would die from the pain. They would not have a chance. I can control it but not when unconscious. I even have to control it when in Caelum. I would love to stay at home, and Kayland will always be my home, but I need to have another place to stay. I need a place to work magic that could be harmful to other living creatures and to control or not control the Star Fire." I added more cheerfully, "Besides, after thousands of years of studying in the druid trap, I find being alone not so bad anymore." We reached the banquet tables, so I added, "And I wish to have some good food once in a while, so I will be popping in all the time, if you don't mind. I may pop in on the Sordeath a lot at first. They are my kind of people. No offense, but there is too much politics here for a Star Fire to be present."

Mother looked over at Grandmother. "I must agree. There is far too much politics. Banning the Women's Circle for a while may be a good thing."

Father said, "The Telliman will put a stop to a lot of the bad politics. Decisions in a leading position must always take into consideration the emotions of everyone affected. You play politics much better than you think, King Charles."

"I did not say I was not good at politics, only that I don't like it."

We finished breakfast and headed to the war room. Father's war room was the best design in all the castles I had visited. It resembled a small stadium. I made the Sordeath the same way, without some of the little problems this one had. For example, mine had an extra door by the refreshment tables for the servants to use. Mine had one door going out and one for coming in to cut down on servants running into each other with full trays. I added a larger section in the center for maps and planning and many more lights.

When we entered, the war room was full, with people standing in the aisles. I said, "All right, everyone, out of the center and take your stuff with you. I need the center clear. Leave seats for King Edward and his wife, King Truss, and me right there." People scrambled out of those four chairs. "The rest of you, please take seats or stand where you will not be in the way of the view of the center of the room."

While people moved things all around, I changed the lighting. I added fifty permanent flames along the top of the ceiling so that there would be no shadows even if we were standing in the center. "Father, you can have those flames dispelled whenever you wish. They will stay there until you do."

Father was looking up at the lights. "Nice. I think I'll leave them up."

When everyone was settled, I put my hand out, and instantly the Staff of Maps was in it. Father said, "Handy trick." Then he said, "Why, all of a sudden, do I know it's not a trick? You brought that all the way from the Dead Lands."

I smiled. "The Star Fire is tuned down enough to not cause you pain, but it will correct you when it can."

I held out the staff and called forth, "Show me the world of ten years ago." Instantly the world was before us and fixing people's perceptions of it being flat. "Zoom in to show only this continent." Our continent zoomed into view. "Center on the Sordeath." The continent moved just a little left. "Zoom in, showing only the Sordeath, the Dragonback Mountains, and five leagues surrounding both." The entire Sordeath and the Dragonback Mountains were in view, along with the hundreds of passes going into other lands. The Sordeath was so big that it filled the room, and still no details were visible except the fact that it was different shades of brown. "This is the Sordeath of ten years ago. All desert except when flooded, and then all water." I waited for the murmurs to slow down. "Staff, bring this view up to this date." The entire Sordeath turned many shades of green, with shades of brown and tan for the mountains, and blue for lakes and rivers.

King Edward asked, "What are the little blue dots all over? Are those rivers?"

"The blue dots are lakes. See that largest dot with the deep blue color?"

"Yes."

"That lake is twenty leagues long, five wide, and thousands of feet deep."

"But I can hardly see it."

"This is the view you would have if you were floating high above the world. Much higher than the clouds. See that white there on the left? Those are clouds." I stepped down into the map and started pointing out points of interest, zooming in on areas and out to see the entire section of forest and flatlands. I showed them the rivers, bridges, fountains, irrigation methods, the castle, and the two deep ports. I even showed them the five ships that Kayland unwillingly provided. "As you can see, everything is spread out, and not all of it is up for use by humans." I showed them the few places where creatures of all kinds were established and picking fruit or planting grains to barter with. I showed them the giants and told them about the deal I made with them that King Edward would need to honor.

One concerned baron said, "Can you show us the difference between the Clear Water Valley's usable land and the Sordeath's usable land? I understand the forest will be left out, as we cannot touch it. Air for our children, I would have never guessed."

I said, "Staff, remove all forests and sections where creatures have already populated. Remove the rivers and lakes. Remove the mountains that cannot be planted. Good, combine all the rest together and figure out the square leagues. Now make a square out of it." There was a square in the center of the room. "Now, take the Clear Water Valley as it was two moons ago, before the mountain erupted, and do the same removing. Make it into square leagues and superimpose on top of the Sordeath." A tiny square showed up on top of the Sordeath square, about one-tenth the volume. I looked at the baron. "Is that what you wanted to see?"

He said, "Yes, thank you." He turned to King Edward. "Sire, there is no way we can harvest all that land. If we took all of Kayland into the Sordeath, we could not fill it with enough people to harvest all of that."

I smiled. "You are not expected to harvest it all. You have plenty of room to grow. Staff, do the same with the Dead Lands from ten thousand years ago and superimpose it over the Sordeath." They were nearly the same size. "The Dead Lands will provide ranch lands that will be as big as the Sordeath. Oh, speaking of ranch lands. Staff, go back to showing the Sordeath as it truly is today." I walked back across the map to a spot and pointed. "Whoever gets this section of land has a problem. I placed five hundred chickens there, and now I believe there are over ten thousand." I walked to another section close to the first. "Whoever gets this section of land has another problem. I placed five hundred rabbits there." The farmers actually moaned. I had to smile. "Rabbits were not in any part of my training. I have no idea how many there are, but there are far too many, and that's with all the foxes and wolves that have centered on such wonderful feeding grounds." I motioned as if to point out the entire Sordeath. "All over your lands, there are great amounts of food and therefore creatures that eat the food, and therefore dangers—not from the sentient creatures, but nature has bloomed, and with it came predators. While I have been working there, I have had to fight demons, dragons, one devil, and creatures of all kinds, both magical and not. Please keep in mind that all farmers not capable of protecting themselves from predators will need military protection."

King Edward said, "General?"

"Sire, we will figure this out. We have a good military, but they are spread out at this time. As you know, some are in the Ringal, and the rest are spread out along the main road to the coast. We have nearly eliminated the bandits, or they are laying very low. They were surprised to find that farmers know how to use a bow. We have also taken the time to train many in the use of the sword. Most of our people can take care of themselves if they have sons. Others will need help. We will be spread thin if my thinking on the placement of people is anywhere near correct."

King Edward said, "They will be going to the following places. Baron Sonly, please come forward." King Edward walked down to the center and met the baron. "Kneel, Baron Sonly." He knelt. The king had no sword with him, and his hand tried to close on a hilt that would normally be there. I sent a sword with sheath and belt fit for a king to his hand. A minor artifact I did not need. He took it with a smile, then buckled it on, drew the sword, and tapped the baron's head. "You have served me well in the past with orchards in my northern section. Your men are the strongest, and you have the most fighters among our people. You will take charge of the northwestern section, including all the orchards, tree harvesting, and stone for building. Rise, Duke Sonly of the Sordeath." The duke rose and faced his king. His wife nearly fainted; her husband had just become duke of a section of land bigger than the entire Clear Water Valley. "Take with you who you had before."

King Edward said, "Kwedy?"

"Yes, Sire?"

"Get down here." Mark Kwedy tripped down the aisle to the center. The man was clumsy but the best farmer in the land bar none. Even the Star Fire did not dispute it. He and his sons were known for growing anything, anywhere, at any time. King Edward said with a smile, "As much as it pains me to say this, I need your two left feet in the northeastern section. If I am correct, that area could produce the sweetest vegetables possible, and you have worked well with the elves in the past. Kneel." Kwedy knelt. The king used his sword and said, "Rise, Duke Kwedy." Then he turned to the group and wondered, "Now who can I torture with a rabbit and chicken problem. "Green, get down here."

An entire section cheered. Green was made duke over the southwestern section. Then Jack Mores was dubbed duke over the southeastern section. King Edward said, "I have split up the Sordeath into four farming sections, but I need three more areas. We will need a central city and two port cities along with towns and villages. Baron Tailor, if you would join us please."

The old baron came down. King Edward said, "You and your sons have run my central city and my port city for generations. I would have you in charge of all city, town, and village infrastructures. The dukes will supply the people, and the giants will help. The dukes will be in charge of the towns and villages, but you and yours will do the planning, building, and maintenance. The three cities are yours, Duke Tailor. Other lands and people will be jealous of our prosperity. Build the cities and towns strong and capable of defending against anything."

"I will, my king."

King Edward said, "We have much to discuss between who goes with which dukes and how we gather our resources and get them in place. How are we going to pay for this? It's a long way, and we will need supplies." He turned to my father. "Any chance we can get monetary help from Kayland?"

Father said, "I truly wish I could help, my friend, but I need to plan on supplies for Kayland until food starts arriving, and that means funding I don't have."

I interjected, "The Star Fire tells me that, sadly, Father will have expenses that he does not know about. Though I am not sure what they are. There are a few things I need to point out before you go any further. First, traveling will be short and simple. I can create portals that will allow our people to enter the Sordeath immediately. Portals will make it easy and fast to gather your resources and send them to the correct place. There is only a need to travel to the portals. What I am suggesting is costly and requires four constant guards for each portal, and one portal will require a paladin."

Father said, "Expensive, guards, and a paladin?"

"Yes, Father. The portals cost approximately fifty thousand gold pieces in diamond dust, but they last for one moon. I have an artifact that will allow me to make one a day. In addition, portals are thin, so thin that you can cut steel with the edge and not feel any friction. If a child were playing in the area and ran through an edge, gods forbid, he would continue to run for several paces before he fell in two. He would not even know what happened. So, yes, guards. Four guards for each portal, one on each end in both places. The paladin is needed to check for evil. Some people are evil. You know this, and so do they. If evil enters the Sordeath, it will set off alarms, and the alarms will continue to sound until the evil leaves or is dead. The alarms will become very irritating if you let them last too long. The penalty for evil entering the Sordeath is death. Some people will not realize they are evil or will try anyway. Please don't let that happen."

King Edward said, "I have sworn to uphold that law. Evil enters, and it dies. We don't send it back; we kill it. Warn your people. If someone is not sure, then have them checked. However, a paladin at the gate would be a good idea at the start. At least until everyone is used to the law."

I added, "All the new laws need to be gone over so that all understand. You have been keeping these laws anyway. You treat others as equals. Another one that could cause a problem is my unicorn law. Some child chases a unicorn, and the unicorn trips and breaks a leg. That child is in deep trouble. If the unicorn dies, so does the child, whether it was an accident or not. If a farmer is hunting deer and accidently hits a unicorn, it will be the last hunting he ever does, as his life is forfeit. I made a promise to my gods that the unicorns would be protected jealously. King Edward agreed to the law."

King Edward said, "Simple, tell people what you just heard. They will teach their children. Do you really have unicorns?"

I laughed. "I don't. You do. They are the last two pair in existence in the entire plane. If even one dies, the chance of them returning to healthy numbers is ruined. Natura would have a fit and blame all of you. I don't know what she would do in her wrath. For all your sakes, enforce that law. The last thing I want to point out is I will help you out with finances. I have an interest in ensuring that things go well."

King Edward said, "Thank you. The portals, how many do you think we will need?"

I looked at the map. "Staff, show me where the people sworn to the Sordeath are." The map changed to Kayland, and a long line of people spread out from the capital in the north to the southern coast. There also seemed to be a small amount in two valleys up in the Sinaguard and some in Ringal.

King Edward looked closely. "I see Prince Richard has many of my troops in Ringal. They are bunched together, and one portal should bring them all to one place. The Sinaguard will require a portal. If we use our ships stationed in the southern ports, we could take many by sea and pick up our five confiscated ships. We would be able to gather many more and move them by sea. The trick is getting them into position in the Sordeath."

I said, "Not tricky at all. Send the port people by ship, but all others come here. I will make three portals along this line of people that lead to outside Kayland's capital. Father has a huge gathering area for festivals and caravans right about here. Gather your people there. It will take a few days, but that will give the dukes time to work out who goes where. Line them up, and I will create one large portal into the Sordeath. I have a large area set aside in the central Sordeath, beneath the castle, for building a main city. The portal from here will take them to the center of that area. I will create eight other portals to the areas within the Sordeath you suggest. The portals should be open long enough to allow you time to harvest and deliver to Kayland, to your ports for shipment, and to make any changes needed. After that, it's back to long trips by caravans or air ships. King Edward, you do still have your air ships, don't you?"

"Yes, but they cannot take masses of people back and forth. These portals sound like the quickest way, but that's sixteen portals. Do you have eight hundred thousand gold pieces worth of diamond dust?

I thought for a minute on that. "I have the diamonds, but it's not all dust. The larger portal will cost a lot more, so it's about one million gold worth of diamond dust. However, I can turn the diamonds into dust. That's not a problem."

Father said, "On another thought, a portal like that would be priceless in war." Everyone looked at him, and some were thinking, *He's right.*

I said, "I should loan you the book *History of a Foolish King*. That was tried once. The foolish king found his entire army transferred to the 595th Plane of Hell, and several devils transferred to his home. I am sure you've heard of Hollymite and King Oloth the Brave? The correct history shows he was not as brave as he was stupid and lucky."

Someone in the back said, "Hollymite was destroyed, and King Oloth and his vast army disappeared."

I said, "Devils tend to go overboard in their destruction, and King Oloth was given the death of ten thousand screams. Silly name that. No one has lived long enough to reach ten thousand screams. It is said King Oloth died by drowning in his own blood after rupturing his lungs from screaming at only 7,023 screams—which, by the way, was a record. You see, devils have unique ways to keep people alive for decades while they are constantly torturing them."

Someone in the back lost it, and servants were scrambling to clean it up. Mother said, looking a little white herself, "You don't need to be so graphic."

I answered, "Sorry, but I have to tell the whole truth. I said just enough to keep the Star Fire satisfied."

Father said, "With that thing in your head, you are not going to be able to keep many friends."

"It is not in my head, Father. It is in my spirit. I will not be released from it even in death." Father looked shocked, so I returned to the original subject. "The god that controls the Grand Rod of Transportation does not like his artifact being misused and has placed protections on it. I am probably going to have to travel to Caelum and ask for permission in person. I don't want to do that, but it cannot be helped. I have a lot of work to do and cannot afford to waste time."

King Edward said, "How long will it take you to get the rod and permission?"

"About a day. You need to send out wizards with messages to all your people to get ready to move. I will bring your army here first to help with the sorting and to protect the portals, then the Sinaguard and the three Kayland portals. When everything is ready and people are here, I will create the Sordeath portals."

King Edward said, "Please get that permission. We can figure out the rest from here."

I held out my hand, and in front of me was a large chest. I raised my hand, and the top opened. Gold and platinum bricks shined from within the chest. "King Edward, use this to fund your move and building." I turned and hugged Mother. "I will be back." I disappeared.

CHAPTER 15

UNEXPECTED
HELP (I THINK)

I teleported to my home in the Dead Lands and had company. They could not enter my tower but were floating outside waiting. Eight devils, and one was a greater devil, near demigod level. They were looking rather ragged, as even floating in the Dead Lands is a killer. I did a mass heal, and they felt and looked much better. My favorite devil demigoddess was instantly there with them. "Charles!"

She flew into my arms and kissed me passionately, and then she slapped me. "Where have you been? We've been waiting for nearly an entire day!"

"I've been very busy." I opened the door and let them in. I was not worried, as my protections would have stopped them if they were here to do harm. "Refreshments?" Instantly there was a live deer for them to eat. As they dug in, I took her in my arms and kissed her back. "I've missed you."

She put a hand where she shouldn't and said, "I can tell." We disappeared.

When we came down a few hours later, the greater devil said, "Took your bloody time. We have something to discuss."

I looked around at all the blood mess and did a cleaning spell. "What do you want to talk about?"

"Our god would like to speak with you and possibly do you a favor."

I said, "The Great God Malificus is not one for doing favors for free. In return for what?"

He smiled, "Malificus wants …" The Star Fire flared, and pain killed him instantly.

My she-devil demigoddess looked mad. "I told that fool." She looked at the other devils and said, "Did I not tell him about the Star Fire? Fool!" She kicked him hard, and he flew across the room and smashed against the wall, breaking a painting.

"Hey! I liked that painting." I went over to the wall and did an annihilate spell on the devil and then a cleaning spell on the wall and floor. Then I did a repair spell for the painting and hung it back up. "That's better." I turned back to the group. The Star Fire warned me, *Setup.* I said, "So, the Great Malificus did not want anything?" The Star Fire warned that he did want something but not from that greater devil. I said to my devil demigoddess, "Why did you bring that devil here to die? It is one of the reasons you came, isn't it?"

She smiled, and it was a wonderful smile. "That devil was becoming too powerful and too pushy. He wanted my place beside Malificus. I did not have the power to destroy him myself. You did. I knew he could not last long without telling a lie. It's simply not in his blood."

My hand caressed her cheek. "Next time, sweetheart, you don't need to attempt to fool me. Malificus does want something I have, but he has not asked. You probably told that fool you could help him get it. Didn't you?"

She pouted. "Of course I did. I can lie to him all I want. It's you I cannot lie to; however, it is fun trying not to tell the truth while not really lying. Great practice for when I need to talk to Malificus."

I took her arm, and all of the devils disappeared and reappeared in Malificus's temple. Her eyes went wide. "What are we doing here?"

Good question, as this was not the correct place.

"Good question!" The walls reverberated with the voice, and in front of us appeared Malificus.

I went to one knee and said, "Great God Malificus."

He looked at me, and I could feel evil wash over me like a river and try to take me. It did not work, and I felt his disappointment. "So, the little toy of Natura and Silvestris has come calling. You have given me much amusement. I watched as you played with that demon, the cleric fake, and then again as you became evil and half-destroyed Ringal. You are becoming my favorite game."

"Is that why you sent this lovely devil down to try to fool me into giving her the artifact?"

He looked upset. "Saw through that plan, did you? Oh well, it worked enough to bring you here where we can talk."

"I am no match for you, Malificus, not even close. We can talk all you want, but even if I toss out everything you say, I will still probably be fooled into something."

He laughed. "True. I could capture you and keep you here for eternity, and the other gods could do nothing. I could take that ring off you and dominate you if I so desire. But where's the fun in that? I have done it a million times, and it has become boring."

I knew he just lied and did not feel the pain, so something was up. I looked at him closely, smiled, and said, "I could destroy this temple and your illusion instantly." The Fire Star did not stop me from saying it, so now I knew it was true. "This is an old temple that you do not use anymore. You are an illusion and can lie without pain. A very good illusion, but I see through illusions remember. You went to a lot of trouble to create this. Nice job. It nearly fooled me." I teleported to the true temple and right in front of Malificus. He had an orgy going on, and there were all sorts of devils playing with each other and many creatures being used against their will.

Malificus did not like the fact I could find him so easily, and I should not have been able to teleport into his lair. The shock on his face told all. "How?" He stopped his question and regrouped. "I see you've grown in your powers, Charles."

I smiled and asked, "Is this a typical setting or is something special going on? I'm not crashing a party, am I?"

He said, "Actually, it's a party celebrating the return of my artifact. Apparently, it's a little premature."

I still had the demigoddess with me, so I said, "Mind if we join you? It's nice to see how the other side lives."

Malificus waved a hand, and we were in a private room with proper refreshments. "You would not appreciate some of the finer points of that party."

"Probably not. So, which artifact do you want so badly?"

Malificus looked at me in thought. "Do you happen to know where the Expansion Ring is?"

I pretended to think on it for a second. "Expansion Ring … Expansion Ring. I read a passage in a book once that said something about you and the Expansion Ring. Let me think … oh yes, now I recall. The Over Gods took it away from you for misuse. It is one of their artifacts."

He looked upset that I would know this. "So, they aren't looking now."

I shook my head. "No, they are not. But, as you well know, they placed protections on it. If I were to attempt to use it or remove it from its current resting place, they would be watching, and you know it. You don't want that ring. You want your Necklace of Elemental Control back."

His face looked surprised and angry. "Yes, I want that necklace back. I have an uprising on the sixtieth Plane of Hell, and I need that necklace. I was surprised and glad you did not trade it to the leaches."

"The items I took to the leaches were nothing compared to what I kept. The necklace only works in the hidden hells. Why?"

He looked at me as if I were a child. "Creating an artifact that works across another god's territory causes the artifact to lose potency due to the amount of extra energy involved to make it usable against another god's will. I needed something that would be strong enough to keep the Elementals in line."

I changed my look and posture to one of *what's in it for me* and said, "I don't mind trading it if the price is right. I could use it to attack you and use your own Elementals against you, but you have given me no reason to do so. You're not going to, are you?"

"No. I have no plan on attacking you. Nice way to find out if this is a mistake. Let me make it clear. I need it for controlling my own, and I see no reason that you would ever regret letting me have it."

I smiled. "That's clear enough, and the Star Fire did not fry you, so what do you have to trade for such a needed item of great power?"

"He held out a hand, and the devil demigoddess was at his side. I will give you my favorite pet." She smiled radiantly and stepped over to sit on my lap.

"No thank you."

She stopped just before sitting down, looking very upset, and slapped me hard. She said, "Ouch!"

I said, "Break your hand?" I looked around her and said, "If she were always near me, I would never get any work done, and Natura would fry me. I'm walking a thin line with Natura, and that would push me over."

She smiled and ran a talon across my chin. "Am I a distraction?"

"You're far more than a distraction, sweetie." I looked around her again, "Do you have something I could use to help me with my next plan, the Dead Lands?"

She disappeared, and Malificus said, "Not that I know of. I don't see how you're going to do it. I can destroy it, but fixing it is beyond me. I may have something that you would appreciate."

"That would be?"

"I could let all the prisoners go. Many are human. Some are worshipers of nature."

"That would be nice of you, but then you would have a need to go get others to take their place, so no thank you. You do have something I could use. It's not worth as much as the necklace, but it would get you halfway there."

"Go ahead."

I said, "Don't you have the Stone of Carving?"

"Done. We are halfway. I don't understand. What do you need that foolish artifact for? It helps with carving or engraving, but only as good as the carver or engraver using it."

I said, "I make my own wands, rods, and staffs. I am very good after thousands of years of boredom enticed practice. During my time in the druid trap, I took up painting, engraving, and carving. I can make master work items that even you would enjoy, including bows, arrows, and furniture. The stone will make it much quicker."

He said, "The stone would make it instant. What else would you like?"

"I don't know if this is true, but I heard that you have an Over God artifact known as the Chalice of Good. What is that about? I am collecting Over God artifacts. They've messed with me twice now. I have had thoughts of trading their artifacts to the leaches."

He smiled, and his teeth were pointed. "Done. Come with me." We started moving toward another area. "The chalice you are talking about is a pain in the neck. The demigod that brought it to me was a friend of mine, and I had to kill him because the chalice turned him good. He attacked me immediately. Several of my priests have turned disgustingly good, and I had to destroy them also. I tried to destroy the chalice, but I cannot. I cannot come anywhere near it without great pain. Oh, and that ring you wear won't save you from it turning you disgustingly good. Good luck. Here is the stone." He handed me a little stone carving knife, and I took it. "The chalice is in there, no traps, nothing that will harm you, just the stupid chalice. Get rid of it if you can. However, I want the necklace before you walk in."

I held out my hand, and the necklace was in it. "Here it is. Thanks for the stone." I reached for the door.

"Wait!"

I turned to him.

"I need to leave before you open those doors. The protections will be off instantly."

I said, "No need. Goodbye." I teleported past all his protections, grabbed the chalice, and plane shifted directly in front of the druid trap and jumped inside. Hopefully, fast enough that no gods or Over Gods noticed that I had the chalice. Once inside, I said hello to the chalice as I walked toward the building housing my artifacts. "Hello."

"Hello, star and staff vessel."

I felt it try to crawl over my mind to change me to completely good. I let it try. It had no chance. I only wore the ring to make the gods think they could remove it and control me. "Are you finished trying? I know you had to."

"I have tried and failed. You are not far from being very good. Why deny me?"

"I have my reasons. I need to ask you a few things."

"I am willing to answer if the questions will not lead me to do something wrong."

I smiled. "What I want to know is not for something wrong. I want to know I am doing good before I act."

It glowed a little brighter. "That is noble of you."

"Do you know about the Dead Lands?"

"I was thrown in there once a long time ago. Someone trying to destroy me."

"That is sad. The gods, not necessarily the Over Gods, but the gods of my world want me to fix the problem with the Dead Lands and replant so that it is like it was. First question: would that be a good thing to do?"

"I am looking into the future of good. Please wait." I waited about three hours. The chalice glowed bright and then said, "I have checked for ten thousand years into the future, and taking that branch on the tree of life will generate far more good than evil. It would be a good thing to do."

"Thank you. Second question: is there anything that can destroy, reverse, fix, or whatever is needed to repair the Dead Lands?"

"There is an artifact that when paired with the staff and star would give you the ability to repair the land easily."

I thought for a moment. With items like this chalice, I needed to ask the correct questions or I didn't get the correct information.

"If I obtained this artifact and used it, would this be good?"

"No. You cannot control it."

Well, that was a quick answer. I was determined not to use something that would end up being bad. "Is there any other way to repair the land?"

"Yes."

"What?"

"There is an artifact that, if you had it first, would allow you to control the other artifact. Then it would be much better."

"If I had this other artifact and learned to use it, and then used the first artifact, would that be good in the long run? Would I do more good than bad?"

"Yes, very much so."

"What and where are these artifacts?"

The chalice turned light blue and said, "The first artifact is the Eye of Creation. It is on a pedestal in the Temple of Dogma, on the Plane of Diversion. The second artifact is the Hand of Control. You have that in your collection here in the Druid Suppository of Knowledge and Magic. We are heading toward it now."

Well, one of the things would be easy to find. "What does the Hand of Control do? What are its properties? What will it try to do to me? And how do I use it safely?"

The chalice turned a darker blue. "The Hand of Control can use any artifact instantly and control that artifact so that it cannot harm its user. It will grant the wearer immunity to all things, including mind control, but you do not need this, as you already are immune to most everything. The one property that the hand gives that you need is understanding of the gods and why the Over Gods allow them. It will not work for just anyone. The druids tried to use everything in their power to find out what it is and failed, so they tried to destroy it. That created another mess the gods will want you to clean up on a different world. They gave up and placed it here. The hand is not a hand.

It is a necklace that controls your hand and gives it great magical power. It will try to control you and your hand to ensure you do only what the Over Gods want. When it finds out that it cannot, it will obey. When it finds out you are the vessel, it will meld with the star and staff to become one with them. You will become far more powerful. At that point, it will be safe to use, as it will be part of you. At that point, you will not need permission to use that rod of portals. The hand will make it obey."

"I think I will try to get permission anyway. Just to be polite." We were entering the building. It was as big as the library. "Any idea where in here the Hand of Control is?"

"Eighteen floors down and five rooms to your left."

"Thank you." I headed down eighteen floors. There were artifacts coming off the shelves begging me to use them. Some tried to force their way into my pockets, up a sleeve, on my head, or around my neck. I had the same problem each time I went to that place. They all wanted to be needed. I did a couple of spells, and they quickly returned to their racks and stayed there whining. I felt so sorry for them. On the correct floor, I traveled down the hall, counting off five doors on the left. I went in. There were thousands of necklaces in this room, and they all looked the same and gave off artifact-level magic. All but one was faking it. With the Star Fire, I knew exactly which one. I walked over to it and picked it up. "Well, hello, pretty necklace."

"Interesting that you knew. Are you going to try me on? I am tired of sitting on this dusty shelf."

I placed it around my neck and closed the clasp. "How is that?"

"Nice. Hello, Chalice of Good."

"Hello, Hand of Control."

"I suppose you told him about me for a reason?"

I felt his reach slowly and sneakily work its way into my mind. I slapped it down and stopped it completely. It was tough, and I had to fight this one far more than any other. I should have expected that. The Hand of *Control* specialized in controlling.

"You are strong. What are you? You are not mortal. I do not see you aging. You are not human anymore. The vessel! I sense you, Star Fire. I see you, Staff of Nature." The necklace disappeared, and I went to my knees in feelings of power. Waves and waves of magic flowed over me like ripples on a pond flowing over a speck of dust. I felt like I was drowning, and I fought for control and won.

The necklace was gone yet there. It became part of me, and now I had full control over the Star Fire and the staff, and I knew how to use them more than any god had ever known. I knew why the first gods were created and how. The Over Gods had a war with the Ancient Gods. When the Ancient Gods were destroyed by the True Gods, the Over Gods created the Old Gods because they were too busy to handle all the little stuff. The first gods that the Over Gods created did not need followers; that law had been perverted over the millenniums. Now, the new gods were tied down and had to have followers to have power. I did not. I knew the truth as if it were part of me. And I still could not lie. Full control of the Star Fire did not mean power over its properties. I stood up and thought for a minute.

I thought out loud to help me and to let the chalice know what I was thinking, as she was turning red, which, if I recalled correctly, was not a good thing for me. "That was interesting. I can feel the power increase, but that makes no difference. Priority one, correct the Dead Lands. Chalice, please look and tell me. What do I need to do to keep in good with the Over Gods?"

She turned blue, her thinking mode. "You need to fix problems like you planned. The gods cannot, so the Over Gods have allowed you some power with the star and staff. I can see now that they were not expecting you to gain the hand."

Hmm, that's not good. The last thing I want to do is upset the Over Gods. "Tell me, Chalice, will my power increase with the eye?"

"Immensely."

Oh darn. "Chalice, can I remove the eye and give it back after I use it?"

"Not a chance. Even the Over Gods cannot remove what has been joined together as these three have. They fully plan to destroy you when you are no longer useful, even if that means destroying three of their greatest artifacts."

"Very well. Nothing I can do about it now. Tell me, please—if I had this Eye of Creation and learned to use it, what does the Eye of Creation do, what are its properties, what will it try to do to me, and how do I use it safely?"

"The eye destroys and then recreates as the user wants. If you know what you want, the eye can break something down into its original particles and recreate it in the manor of what you want. You need to know exactly what you want. It can do this to an item only a fraction of an atom thin, or to the entire galaxy, or anything in between—your choice. It would have destroyed you and recreated you into what it wanted, but you have the hand, so it could not. The hand will ensure you use it safely and give you all knowledge of its abilities."

"If I had this eye, I could complete my task with the Dead Lands in seconds?"

"Not with the eye alone. With the eye and the staff, yes. The staff is needed to plant and grow things."

"Thank you, Chalice. You have been of great help. Though I will probably be destroyed because of it. I will have completed the two tasks I set out to do."

"You are welcome. Are you not going to ask where I can help?"

"I didn't think you could help any more than you already have. What can you do to help?"

"I would love to be part of the three and possibly part of the four or five. I want to meld with the others. I can give you great foresight. Once melded, I cannot do anything else, but you will have foresight, and that may save you from you."

"How do I let you meld with the others?"

"Hold me to your lips."

I picked her up and held her to my lips. She melded into me, and I felt her power enter me. I now had the power of four artifacts from the Over Gods within me. I plane shifted to the Plane of Diversion. I walked past the ladies, the young men, the gambling, eating, singing, fighting, all the known diversions and many I had never heard of. I walked up to the Temple of Dogma and entered. Illusions flowed over me, and because of the Star Fire, I ignored them. Fire, ice, sound, lightning, acid, and magma shot out at me, and I ignored them. Holy flame and unholy flame engulfed me, and I ignored them. I walked up to the pedestal and was attacked by guardians that looked like balls of energy. I dispersed them. I picked up the eye and plane shifted back to the druid trap. I no longer had to walk in. The hand and eye fought for only a second, and then the hand told me to put the eye in the palm of my hand and squeeze. I did, and it entered me. It became part of me, and I it. I saw creation. The first planes, the gods, the creatures, and I knew how to make a universe out of nothing, how to start time, and how to expand everything, though I did not have that kind of power. Everything I had learned in the druid trap was as nothing compared to the knowledge that poured into me. The chalice was correct. I did not increase in energy, but the knowledge I gained made me immensely more powerful. I was now a god, and I did not need worshipers. I was like the Old Gods.

I stepped out of the druid trap and out of my tower. I opened my mind and destroyed the Dead Lands and recreated them as

Grass Planes and Forests. On the border between the grass fields and forests, I created a circular pillar that rose three thousand feet straight up and anchored to the foundations of the earth. I placed my tower on the top and changed the entire pillar into Laststoneite. Then I put protections on the tower that even the current World Gods could not pass through.

I now knew that the Over Gods were not good or evil. They simply were. They were a form of balance. Nonbiased creatures created out of the dust of stars by the True Gods. Sometimes they fought among themselves, and the devastation destroyed galaxies. Until then, I did not know about galaxies as they truly were, or that the Over Gods had True Gods that ruled them— beings so great that they made the Over Gods look tiny and insignificant. I went to my knees in prayer and asked, "What would you have of me?"

An Over God came to me and said, "You have grown well past the point we wished. We see what you have done, and we know why. Your task here is near complete. You only need to turn it over to your father. It is well. For now, do the bidding of the World Gods. Fix the problems of this world and then on every other world in this galaxy, or as some call it, the Central Hub of the Prime Material Universe. We are an anchor point for this universe, though we are not in the center, and need many things corrected that are below our doing."

"As you wish, my god."

POST LOG

I returned to Kayland and my father's castle. They were still in the war room. Somehow everyone could sense the power in me, which was far too great for me to hide anymore. My voice was strong and my demeanor sure. They all went to one knee.

"Rise, Father. Rise, King Edward. Rise, my friends. I would not have my friends kneel before me." They stood up. We walked into the center, Father and King Edward at my sides, looking worried. "I have corrected the issues with the Dead Lands as I promised. They are now Grass Planes and Forests." I no longer needed the Staff of Maps. Instantly a map of the Dead Lands appeared. "Father, I turn these over to you as the Great Gods have ordered. Do as you wish with them. King Edward, the plan has changed. Look to the south, and you will see three portals. I have placed protections around the edges so no one can harm themselves. There are signs for each stating where they go. Father, one goes to the grasslands, one goes two hundred leagues south of here, that one has another by it that goes another two hundred leagues south, and that one has another that takes you to the sea. Using these portals, any creature or caravan can travel from the southern sea, or the grasslands, to this place in minutes. Station guards as you see fit. King Edward, the large portal leads to the Sordeath, and there are eight portals there, as I promised."

King Edward asked, "How long will these portals stay open?"

I looked at him and smiled. "Forever." Then I disappeared.

I plane traveled to Caelum, and instantly four Caelums surrounded me. They started to ask which god or goddess I wanted to worship first, but before they could, I happily said, "I will attend Natura. Please ask Silvestris to join us. I have finished repairing the Dead Lands and need a new project."

One looked at me and said, "You have changed. Not in attitude but in strength. I feel you, Charles. You are a god. A great god."

I smiled at him. "I know. Natura and Silvestris's plaything is becoming more interesting. Think they still want to play?" I winked at one, and they all laughed. I was instantly taken to her temple. She was just coming around the corner from her apartments with Potentis, the god of strength, in one of his more he-man personas when she saw me. She blushed as if guilty of something.

"Charles, what are you doing here?"

I raised my eyebrows and said, "So, that's why you don't know what's happened. Been a little busy today, Natura? Something you needed from Potentis?"

Potentis took offense and flashed his godly power, saying, "Watch your tongue, child! Or I will teach you a lesson you will never forget."

I flashed my godly powers, and Potentis's eyes opened wide, and he asked, "How did you become a god with power so great?"

"I needed power to fix the Dead Lands for my goddess. So I sought power out and added it to mine. Then I fixed the Dead Lands, and I have come here to ask what my next task is."

Silvestris walked in. "Charles, nice job on the Dead Lands." He looked over at Natura and Potentis. "I see Natura has been too busy to notice." Potentis's eyes rolled up in his sockets in frustration. Silvestris continued, "Come, Natura has a feast set out for Potentis. Let's crash the party. Have any of that Treestorm wine, boy?"

I held out a hand, and one bottle was in it. "It's all yours, my god."

We were walking away from Natura and Potentis toward the smell of food. Silvestris asked, "What did that Over God tell you? My connection blanked out when he showed up."

Natura was doing her best to catch up and regain face. "Wait. That food is for Potentis."

I turned my head back a little and said, "You need to prepare some more, then, Mother Nature. You're going to have a lot of company real soon." I turned back to Silvestris and said in a way that all gods in Caelum would be able to hear it, "The Over God congratulated me on fixing the Dead Lands problem and told me to help fix all the other problems across this world and this galaxy. I need more to do. I will finish up this world first and then start on another. What's next on the agenda?"

We reached the feast and sat down. Gods were pouring into the temple from all sides, talking to everyone. Some talked to me, asking me to do this or that. I stopped everyone and said, "I get my orders from two gods, Mother Nature Natura and Father Nature Silvestris. Tell them, and they will prioritize and tell me what to do next. Please do not expect me to know what is best. I am far too new at this, and I don't want to upset any gods because I mistakenly think another has more important issues. Mother and Father have the ability and can sort this stuff out properly. Tell them, and they will explain it to me, and I will do my best to fix the issue. Consider me the Son of Nature. For me to do any tasks for you, Mom and Dad need to approve it first and let me know."

Natura and Silvestris were just about to chew me out for calling them Mon and Dad, but with all the gods demanding them to order me to do this or that, they never had a chance. Potentis and I ate all we could. Potentis snatched and drank Silvestris's Treestorm wine and smiled at me while he drank it.

I said, "Great God Potentis, aren't you going to ask Mom and Dad to have me fix that issue you have in Qualleter?"

Potentis smiled behind a mouth full of food. "Plenty of time for that, boy. They will make a list of everything and decide what to have you do. It matters not where I am on the list. What matters is how I sell it to them. Meanwhile, this is great wine, and Silvestris is too busy to see I have it. I'm just glad Oprepo is ..."

The wine disappeared. A note floated down and sat on the table with one word. "Thanks."

Potentis stood up, crashing the chair against the wall, and yelled, "Oprepo!"